Praise for Robin Kaye's contemporary romances

Breakfast in Bed

"A fun and spicy story. Robin Kaye is a fresh new voice in romance fiction."
—Susan Donovan, *New York Times* bestselling author of *Ain't Too Proud to Beg*

"Robin Kaye's books are vacations for the soul. Indulge yourself."
—Maureen Child, *USA Today* bestselling author of *The Last Lone Wolf*

"With snappy dialogue, complex characters, and an intricate web of relationships, Kaye has created an extended family that's both honest and enjoyable."
—*RT Book Reviews*

"Readers will be absolutely delighted with the witty dialogue and klutzy scenes that are fast paced and laugh-out-loud funny. Robin Kaye brilliantly uses each of her characters to create a portrait of genuine relationships."
—*Night Owl Romance*

"A fun and sexy romp from beginning to end... Robin Kaye has a knack for reaching right into the reader's heart and giving them a story to match their deepest desires. The chemistry leaps off the page. Bravo, Ms. Kaye!"
—*Affaire de Coeur*

Too Hot to Handle

"Romance readers, prepare to have your every desire attended to... From the brilliant first chapter until the heartwarming finale, I was hooked!"

—*Crave More Romance*

"Robin Kaye hits the perfect balance between an erotic love story and a rollicking good tale. She is definitely an expert in crafting a great love story."

—*Marta's Meanderings*

"A sensational story that sizzles with sex appeal."

—*Passionate Reviews*

"Witty and enchanting."

—*Love Romance Passion*

"An interesting, humorous, emotional story... that will have you laughing and crying."

—*My Two Blessings*

"A solid story line that is intriguing and interesting... the romance is extra steamy with plenty of authentic love scenes to heat up the pages... the characters are heartfelt people who I related to instantly... a fast pace with excellent dialogue and a sassy heroine. I loved everything about *Too Hot to Handle*!"

—*Enchanted by Books*

Romeo, Romeo

"Endlessly entertaining… Kaye's portrayal of modern romance against the background of an old-fashioned, gossipy family rings true."

—*Publishers Weekly*

"Kaye's debut is a delightfully fun, witty romance, making her a writer to watch."

—*Booklist*

"The main characters in this all-around feel-good read have so much personality they almost jump off the page."

—*RT Book Reviews*, 4/5 stars

"Delightfully funny and wonderfully romantic. I stayed up all night to read this book!"

—*Night Owl Romance*

"Skillfully written… The chemistry is flaming-hot and virtually sizzles off the page!"

—*Book Reviews by Bobbi*

"Robin Kaye creates a delightful read that sticks to the reader far past the last page. Completely satisfying, with vivacious characters and a story line that leaves the reader clapping for joy."

—*Coffee Time Romance*

Also by Robin Kaye

Romeo, Romeo

Too Hot to Handle

Breakfast in Bed

Yours for the Taking

Wild Thing

ROBIN KAYE

sourcebooks
casablanca

Published by Sourcebooks Casablanca, an imprint of Sourcebooks, Inc.
P.O. Box 4410, Naperville, Illinois 60567-4410
(630) 961-3900
FAX: (630) 961-2168
www.sourcebooks.com

Printed and bound in the United States of America
QW 10 9 8 7 6 5 4 3 2 1

To my children,
Robert Anthony, Anna Maria, and Isabelle Louise

Chapter 1

TONI RUSSO STOOD ON THE PORCH OF THE SAWTOOTH Inn ignoring the mountains cutting the bright blue sky, concentrating instead on Hunter Kincaid's very confused, very green eyes. She recognized him from the photos on the River Runners's website. They didn't do him justice, probably because there was no way to transmit the pheromones rolling off the man onto an image.

Hunter stared at her the whole way from his old Land Cruiser to the porch. He stopped, tipped his baseball cap back, and then put his hands on his hips. "You're not who I expected to see."

Well, no shit. "Yeah, I guess you'll have to learn to live with the disappointment. I know I have."

"Toni?" A look of relief flashed across his face, then a smile ticked up the right side of his mouth as he made a slow perusal of her from head to feet and back again.

She waited, knowing it would take awhile. Ever since she'd landed in Boise, she'd experienced the same thing. No one quite knew what to make of her. Holding her clipboard to her chest, she wondered if it would have been better to have spent her time in Boise shopping for less interesting clothes. She mentally shook her head and knew it would never have worked. You could put her in a sack, and she'd do something to stand out. She'd long since given up trying to rein herself in. As Catherine Aird said, "If you can't be a good example, then you'll just have to serve as a horrible warning." So far, it had worked for her.

Blowing her bangs out of her eyes, Toni checked her outfit. The short, red plaid kilt wasn't too offensive. She pulled her clipboard away to see she had on her *Stay Away* T-shirt. Maybe he had something against the collage of pistols, brass knuckles, knives, and bullets. But really, he didn't look like a pacifist, not that she wasn't—it was a T-shirt for goodness sake, not a personal manifesto. The kitty-face Mary Janes and red skull-and-crossbones knee-socks were a bit busy. Okay, Hunter's thirty seconds were up. She fingered the D-ring on the studded collar around her neck and cleared her throat. "Do you mind?"

Hunter took a sip of whatever was in the travel cup he held. "Not at all—just wondering if you were going for that naughty-schoolgirl-fantasy look."

"No, I was going for my not-quite-sure-what-to-wear-for-a-meeting-with-Davy-Crockett look. How's it working for you?"

Hunter's mouth worked its way into a full smile. Great teeth. She had a thing for nice teeth, and yeah, his mouth was full of them.

"Really well, thanks. Over the phone, it sounded as if you wouldn't be caught dead out here. When Bianca came to scout for photo shoot locations, she said something about you having a phobia. What changed your mind?"

Toni took in the rustic porch wrapping around the log cabin lodge and decided to sit on a rocking chair. There was nothing else to sit on except the steps, and they needed a good sweeping. "You asked Bianca about me?"

Hunter leaned against the rough-hewn post holding up the corner of the porch. "I didn't know it was a federal offense."

"Bianca was involved in negotiating a big deal so she sent me." Toni placed her clipboard on her lap and clicked her pen a few times in rapid succession. "I had no choice."

Hunter's big hiking boots filled her line of sight. Her gaze wandered up to where neatly rolled, rag-wool socks met hard, tanned calf muscle with just the right splattering of leg hair—not so much you'd be tempted to take a brush to it, and not so little you'd wonder if he routinely waxed. He wore khaki shorts low around the hips, his green River Runners T-shirt pulled tight against his chest and abs. She'd seen him without a shirt thanks to the picture on the website, so she knew if she poked him it would feel like poking a brick wall. She'd bet dollars to doughnuts he didn't get that hard body in a gym.

When her eyes hit his stubbled chin, she encountered another full-toothed grin. Damn, she hadn't meant to be so obvious.

The slap of an old-fashioned screen door broke the tension. "Sorry." James, Bianca's right-hand man, appeared with two cups of coffee. He handed Toni hers. "That's decaf. Maybe you'll be able to sleep tonight."

Not likely. The woods seemed to inch closer and closer to the lodge. God only knew what roamed out there. She took a sip of bad coffee as James, an ex-model and now her partner in managing the series of shoots, shook Hunter's offered hand. James's dark hair glittered with silver at the temples, his bright blue eyes were full of intelligence and humor, and his build was still trim and muscular, but not like Hunter's. Hunter's muscles were brought about by his life's work, James's by a trainer, weight machines, and a strict diet.

"James, this is Hunter Kincaid. Hunter, James Ness."

"Hunter, good to see you again. Do you want coffee?"

"No, thanks, I brought my own." Hunter's handshake turned into a guy hug, which was weird considering James's sexual preference was in direct opposition to the one Hunter oozed.

Toni caught James's eye with a raised brow. A quick shake of his head confirmed Hunter was, in fact, straight. She'd forgotten James had accompanied Bianca on the scouting trip. The guys had obviously bonded.

Hunter set his travel cup on the table and sat. She finally saw what was written on the side of the cup: "The Way to a Fisherman's Heart is Through His Fly," along with a picture of what looked like an insect with a hook up its butt. Nice.

"I was surprised to find Toni here," Hunter said as he eased back on the chair.

James let out a laugh that grated on her nerves. "No more than she, I presume. Bianca didn't give her much notice. Or should I call it warning? Still, Toni can run the show with one hand cuffed behind her back. We won't have a problem."

"I wasn't worried." Hunter watched her over the rim of his cup as he sipped his coffee, no decaf for him. He slept like a baby every night, no matter how late he drank coffee, but he wouldn't mind spending a few sleepless nights with a beautiful woman.

He'd wondered what Toni looked like since the first day she'd called River Runners in January. Her deep, husky, raspingly sexy voice brought to mind an unbidden picture of a young, blonde, long-legged Kathleen Turner. The New York accent was all wrong, but that do-me voice was right on. Man, was he ever way off base. He found himself eye to eye with the polar opposite of the woman he'd pictured. Toni wore her jet black, shoulder-length hair in pigtails. Instead of making her look like a schoolgirl, it made him wonder what kind of underwear she wore, if she was into bondage, or if she just dug the whole collar-and-cuff thing for fashion's sake, and it had him searching all exposed skin for ink. When he didn't see any, he thought about putting himself in the position to do a full body search.

Checking his dive watch, Hunter looked around for the models he'd promised his brothers they'd be working with when they signed on as guides. That was an ingenious idea if he did say so himself. By bringing Trapper and Fisher along, he not only got free guides and someone to distract Bianca, who, on their week-long outing, had been determined to share a sleeping bag with him, but supplied a physician and legal help if necessary. Since his brothers had plenty of vacation time racked up, they jumped at the chance to spend a week escorting ten models through the mountains and down the Middle Fork of the Salmon River in the Sawtooth Recreation Area. Hunter could have gotten his brothers to pay for the privilege, but he hadn't pushed it since Bianca Ferrari, the owner of Action Models, had paid top dollar for his services. "My guides, Trapper and Fisher, will be here any minute for the barbecue and to meet your group."

Toni flipped through the pages stuck in her

skull-and-crossbones stenciled clipboard, which, if he wasn't mistaken, was shaped like a coffin. The clasp was a bat forged from what looked like pewter with onyx stones for eyes. "I've called a 9:00 a.m. meeting tomorrow, and then the models can spend the rest of the day getting acclimated."

Hunter stopped staring at the clipboard and shrugged, trying not to envision what that bat would look like tattooed on Toni's lower back, its wings spanning her small waist. "We can take a short rafting trip and have a picnic down by my cabin. Bianca had planned a shoot there. There's a nice beach with plenty of space for sunbathing and a regulation sand volleyball court. It'll be an easy trip and will give your group a chance to have a lesson on the rafts."

James nodded. "That sounds great. I'll make arrangements to have a lunch packed for everyone. It's gorgeous, Toni. You're going to love it."

Toni paled, which was hard to do since the girl without makeup was pale enough to qualify for a vampire casting call. She was definitely a candidate for skin cancer. Hunter made a mental note to make sure she wore plenty of sunscreen—he'd be happy to help with the hard to reach spots.

She shook her twin ponytails as her lips drew into a deep frown. "I'm sure you'll have fun. I'm going to stick close to my cabin. I brought plenty of reading material."

Hunter crossed his arms. "You really need the lesson on the raft, and the only way to do that is to get you on the river."

Still shaking her head, Toni backed away. Not a good sign.

"If you want to get out of the sun and hang out in my cabin and read, you're more than welcome to. Put your book in a Ziploc, and bring it along."

Toni held her clipboard tight against her chest. "I won't be joining you."

Hunter moved toward her like he would a spooked horse. "You're not going to supervise the photo shoots?"

"Of course I will. That's my job."

It took him a moment to compute what she'd said since she'd spoken so fast. He tried his most encouraging smile. "Then you'll want to come tomorrow. If not, you're not going to be able to do at least two of the shoots Bianca planned."

Toni stared at James as if she expected him to jump in and save her.

Hunter watched the silent argument going on between them. When no words were spoken, he cleared his throat. "It's perfectly safe. Everyone wears PFDs and even lightweight helmets. We teach you everything you need to know in case you fall in. We show you how to get back into the raft, how to paddle, and what to do if we get stuck. We'll be running down a lazy part of the river tomorrow. I promise there will be no class-five rapids."

When James did nothing more than shrug, she tossed her clipboard on the table and turned on Hunter with both hands on her hips. "What the hell is a PFD?"

"A personal flotation device."

"And why would I need a helmet?"

"The helmet protects you in the rare instance you should fall and hit your head on a rock in the river."

Toni blinked twice and looked as if she needed to sit down and put her head between her legs.

"Are you okay?"

She didn't answer. She just stood there, wide-eyed, looking as if she wasn't breathing. Really not good.

The purr of Trapper's Sequoia broke the silence. The engine died as doors opened and shut.

Hunter looked for help from James who suddenly found his shoes very interesting. Great.

When boots hit the steps, Hunter turned. "Trapper and Fisher, this is James Ness. He's working with Toni Russo, the manager of Action Models in New York." Hunter turned back toward Toni only to find she'd disappeared, coffin clipboard and all.

—∿∿—

Trapper watched Toni slip around the corner of the inn and then run down the path toward the cabins. He whispered to Fisher, "Did you remember to wear deodorant today? I know it wasn't something I said since I didn't say a thing."

Fisher did a sniff test. "Deodorant, check. I even brushed my teeth before we left, but I didn't get close enough to breathe on her, which, when you think about it, is a real shame."

Hunter said something to James then chased after the hot, Goth chick.

Trapper leaned closer to Fisher. "Looks like Hunter has dibs on Toni. That means you owe me a twenty. Didn't I bet you that he'd go after the first model he set eyes on?"

Fisher opened his wallet and pulled out a Jackson. "I'm not sure I actually owe you this since Toni isn't a model. Hunter said she was the manager of the modeling agency—if the manager is that hot, just imagine what the models look like."

"Stop being cheap, and hand over the money."

Fisher did, and Trapper stuffed it in his pocket before his baby brother changed his mind. "You know what this means, right?"

Fisher smiled wide. "We get first dibs on the rest?"

"Exactly."

James seemed awfully interested in Hunter and Toni. When they were out of sight, James whistled. "Brave brother you have there."

Trapper leaned against the porch rail. "Toni doesn't look that scary to me."

James sat and curled his hand around a steaming mug of coffee. "Oh she's not. She's all bark and no bite, but that doesn't mean she's not a handful. Hunter has an uphill climb, that is, if he can talk her into ever coming out of her cabin."

"Agoraphobic?"

James shook his head. "Nah, just not a fan of the great outdoors. Well, the great outdoors without paved streets, high rises, and a Starbucks on every corner."

Trapper tipped his straw cowboy hat back. "At least it wasn't personal. Fisher and I were wondering." He sat beside James, who stared at the cabin Hunter had followed Toni into. "You don't have anything to worry about."

James pulled his gaze away from the cabin. "I'm not worried."

"Yeah, I can see that." Trapper sat back and made himself comfortable. It could be awhile. "Hunter is great with anyone skittish, be it people or horses."

Fisher dragged a rocking chair over and took a seat.

"Oh yeah, Hunter's used to it in his field of work. Hell, he specializes in it. He spends a few weeks a couple of times a year running a camp for abused kids."

Taking off his hat, Trapper twirled it on his finger. "It's amazing how he can reach out to kids who are afraid of their own shadows and have enough baggage to fill a freight train. After a week with Hunter, you wouldn't recognize them."

Fisher nodded. "He's a real miracle worker, my brother."

Trapper couldn't agree more. "Toni should be a walk in the park compared to some of the kids he's worked with."

James nodded but didn't look convinced.

"You'll see. I'll bet you the twenty I just won from Fisher that Hunter has her out of that cabin inside a half hour."

James smiled. "You're on."

—◦◦◦—

Toni knew running away in the middle of introductions was rude. Still, it was less embarrassing than hyperventilating and passing out in front of three completely gorgeous strangers.

She'd fought to keep the panic at bay ever since she'd climbed out of the van that had taken her and the Action Models crew through vast mountain wilderness for the three-hour trek from Boise. With each mile they'd driven deeper into the wilderness, the panic increased exponentially.

She ran into her cabin, throwing herself on the bed before the door slammed shut behind her. Toni buried her face in a feather pillow, concentrating on taking deep, slow breaths.

The door to her cabin opened and closed quietly. She didn't raise her head. She thanked God James was there and that he understood. He was the closest thing to a father she had. Not that her father was dead or anything—he'd just never been interested in the job.

"I know. I made a complete fool of myself. But believe me it was better than what would have happened if I'd stuck around. At least I didn't pass out."

She focused on her breathing. Nothing was said, but nothing needed to be. It was just nice to have James close by. The creak of the cane chair next to her bedside table told her he'd sat. When she finally had her breathing under control, she rolled over and shot up in bed. "Hunter?"

Hunter sat perusing the book she'd set on her bedside table—*He Comes First: How to Find Your Perfect Man and Marry Him*.

She didn't know which was more mortifying, her behavior, or the fact that he knew she was reading that book. "It's not mine."

Hunter peered over the top of the book and raised an eyebrow. He must have practiced that look since he was a kid. It bothered her that it worked.

"Okay, it's mine, but I didn't buy it. My mother sent it to me. She believes in marriage—she must since she keeps trying it, over and over and over. After number five I thought she'd give up, but apparently she hasn't."

The man said nothing.

"Some girls might find the strong, silent type attractive. I don't."

He turned the page and kept reading.

"Just so you know, I'm not looking for a husband, but I would like to have a healthy, long-term relationship. So I thought, what could it hurt? You know? It stands to reason you'd look for the same thing in a long-term relationship as you would in a spouse. I mean, really, marriage is nothing more than a long-term relationship with a license attached and a divorce in the making. Since I'm not into doing paperwork or being legally bound to anyone, I plan to forgo the whole wedding thing."

When he didn't comment, she blew her hair off her face and crossed her arms. "Are you always so talkative?"

"With you it's hard to get a word in edgewise." Hunter closed the book and held his finger in it as if not wanting to lose his place. He'd gotten farther into it than she had. "I thought I'd let you finish."

"I'm done."

He set the book on the table and slid the chair around to face her. The tall bed put them eye-to-eye. "No, you're not."

Toni took a deep breath. She wasn't known for her patience, but dug for it, since pissing him off on their first day was probably not a good idea—especially considering she'd have to work with him for the next week. God help her. "I think I would know when I'm finished babbling. I usually don't babble. I may talk to myself or mumble on occasion, but I never babble. You caught me off guard. I thought you were James. He's the only one brave enough to come into my cabin without an invitation. This begs the question, what made you think it's okay to waltz in uninvited?"

Hunter threw his ankle over his knee as if he didn't have a care in the world. "I'm not much of a waltzer. Walking usually works for me." He cocked his head and grinned. "Though there have been times I've found running effective. I told James I was going after you, and he didn't try to stop me."

"The charm is so not working on me. I deal with beautiful men on a daily basis. I'm immune. So since James didn't stop you, you assumed you had permission to invade my personal space? Why?"

The corner of his mouth quirked up. "It wasn't as if you stopped me either."

"I would have had I known it was you."

"But you didn't, and I'm here. Why don't you tell me what you're so afraid of?"

Toni shook her head. "That's personal."

"And your mother's five marriages aren't? Not to mention your low opinion of the institution of marriage and your interest in hooking up with someone."

"I'm not interested in hooking up."

His eyebrow rose again.

"Not hooking up the way most people think of hooking up. I'd just like to have a normal, stable relationship with a normal, stable man."

She snapped her mouth shut, not sure why she was even talking to him about this, especially since it didn't look as if he was buying it. Since it was the God's honest truth, his cynicism ticked her off. She pulled her pillow onto her lap, hugging it to her chest. "What?"

"Maybe our definition of normal is different. I can't see you going out with anyone boring enough to be defined as normal."

She sat up a little straighter. The guy certainly knew how to get under her skin, and not in a good way. "You don't know anything about me."

His low, sexy chuckle grated on her nerves. "Toni, I've learned more about you in the last half hour than I know about most of my best friends."

"You don't know much about your friends then, do you?"

"I know how long their skis are, how much they weigh, their favorite beer, what kind of flies they tie, and who they're married to or dating—all the important stuff. Now why don't you tell me what's got you so spooked you almost passed out at the thought of taking a raft down a lazy river?"

"No."

"Afraid of the water?"

Damn, the man could have been a cop. All he was missing was the bare lightbulb. "Not particularly."

"Then what is it?"

"None of your business."

"That's where you're wrong. I own River Runners, which makes you one of my guests. Everything about you that affects the quality of your experience is my business."

"Nice try, but no cigar. The only thing you're responsible for is following the schedule I emailed you last week and keeping my models safe. The rest is my business and mine alone."

He stood and inspected the living area of the small cabin as if he expected to see something more than the rustic couch, coffee table, chair, TV, desk, and a few lamps. He returned to the bedroom section against the far wall, peeked into the bathroom, and then opened the closet, which served as a partition separating the two spaces. "Did you get everything on the packing list?"

"Yeah, why?"

"Because you can't wear a getup like that on the raft tomorrow." He reached into her closet and pulled out her checkerboard, slip-on, canvas Vans.

He was going through her closet? She got off the bed and pulled her sneakers from his huge hands. "Do you always invade everyone's personal space and property, or am I just special?"

"These will work fine. You might want to put on a bathing suit or at least swap that skirt for a pair of shorts. Oh, and don't forget your sunscreen, sunglasses, and a hat tomorrow. I'll be here at 9:00 a.m. sharp." He grabbed a hoodie out of her closet. "Everyone's meeting up by the lodge for the barbecue. You might think about changing into a pair of jeans. And I'm sure you'll need this." He tossed the hoodie to her; she caught it with one hand. "Once the sun ducks behind the mountains, the temperature drops. I'll wait outside for you to change."

"You ignored my question."

Hunter turned and looked her up and down again. "I didn't ignore it. I don't know the answer yet."

"You don't know if you invade everyone's personal space?"

"No, I don't know if you're special, but I'm looking forward to finding out."

Hunter stepped outside. He leaned against the closest tree, pulled his sat-phone off his belt, and dialed his sister. God, this was going to kill him.

"Speak."

"Great phone manners, Karma."

"Ha, you're just jealous you can't answer the same way, Mr. Businessman."

"Yeah, you're probably right. I need a favor." He could almost hear her deciding how to make him pay. "I need you to buy me a book and bring it up here tomorrow."

"Oooh, this is gonna cost you. What book and where?"

"You have a pen handy?"

"Do I need one? It's not one of those boring treatises on history or literature you're so fond of, is it? If it is, I'm going to charge you twenty bucks a pound to lug it all the way up there. And why the urgency?"

"It's a paperback, and no, it's nothing like my usual reading material. You have to promise you'll keep this a secret." Man, he was going to be paying for this forever.

"This is just getting better and better. What is it? *The Joy of Sex* or something?"

"Worse. It's called *He Comes First: How to Find Your Perfect Man and Marry Him*."

"You're kidding, right?"

He pulled off his hat and wiped his brow on his forearm. "Unfortunately, no."

"Spill."

"That's not part of the deal."

"It is if you want to get your hands on a copy in the near future."

"Fine." He held back a groan. "A woman I know is reading it. I just thought it was something I could use—"

"To become her perfect man?"

"No… well, maybe for a little while. I thought it could be fun to screw with her."

"Literally, figuratively, or both?"

"Not your business."

"And what about that whole 'men come first' thing? I thought the woman was always supposed to come first, sexually speaking, of course. But maybe that's just wishful thinking."

"I'm not talking to you about this. Are you going to bring me the book or not?"

"Okay, I'll bring it, but you owe me big. What's her name?"

"Why do you want to know?"

"The usual reasons. I'm a nosy little sister, and I want to meet the woman who would incite you to call me and ask me for something you know you'll never live down."

"Karma, how about this? If you don't bring me the book, I'll tell Trapper who backed into his brand-new Sequoia."

"You wouldn't dare."

"Wanna bet?"

"Fine. I'll bring you the damn book, and I'll find out on my own who the lucky lady is. Heck, I'll probably know more about her than you do before I'm halfway to wherever it is you expect me to deliver your package."

"Doubtful."

"Which reminds me, where are you?"

"I'm up at the Sawtooth Inn now. Tomorrow morning we're taking a raft trip to my place. When can you come?"

"Lucky for you, tomorrow's my day off. I guess I can meet you at the cabin. Want me to bring anything else since I'm making the trip?"

"Has Mom made any cookies lately?"

"I'm sure she will if she knows you want some. I'll

see you tomorrow afternoon. Call me if there's a change of plans."

"Will do… and Karma? Mum's the word, okay?"

"Sure, but it'll cost you."

"Believe me, I know." He ended the call and waited. He'd give Toni another three minutes, and then he was going in after her.

Hunter checked his watch and called Emilio, one of the campers he'd worked with and wished he could have kept longer. Emilio had begun to show progress just in time to go back to the streets. "Emilio, it's Hunter."

"Hey."

Street sounds came blaring through the phone. "What's up?"

"Just hangin'."

"Pat said you missed curfew last night. What's up with that?"

"Dude, I had my girl with me. I wasn't thinkin' 'bout no curfew."

"You should be thinking about your curfew, but more importantly—be safe. Real men protect themselves and their girls."

"I hear ya. Hey, I gotta go. Later."

"Emilio, I'll talk to you tomorrow."

"Yeah, sure. Whatever." The phone went dead.

Hunter cursed under his breath. Emilio didn't believe him, and why should he? He had absolutely no reason to think Hunter would follow through on his promises. No one else in his life ever had.

Hunter slammed the phone back onto his belt and felt like punching the tree he leaned against. Emilio was slipping away, and there wasn't a damn thing he could do about it. It was a good thing he had another problem to concentrate on.

Just as he turned toward the cabin, Toni stepped out wearing skintight black pants with what looked like black leather suspenders hanging from the waistband. The pants were tucked into tall, high-heeled black boots that laced up the front and had four black straps hanging from hooks and draping around the calf. Hunter swallowed hard as his gaze moved up to the black-and-white-striped top that fit her like a second skin. She wore the same wrist cuffs she'd worn earlier, but she'd changed collars; this one sported studs and rings with silver chains draped between them. Her hair was down and so straight and shiny, it looked fake. She caught her bright red bottom lip between her teeth and watched him with wide eyes. She looked like something out of a steaming hot sexual fantasy. He'd never had a sexual fantasy of the Goth variety before. He was pretty sure that was about to change.

The shadows lengthened, and although it didn't get dark until after ten at night in high summer, the first hint of the evening chill had settled. Hunter cleared his suddenly dry throat. "You forgot a jacket."

"Oh." She wrapped her arms around herself. "I'm not going to stay long." Her gaze skittered to the edge of the clearing and back to him.

"We're having a bonfire after the barbecue. Come on, it'll be fun." He took her arm and walked her toward the barbecue.

"Yeah. Fun is subjective... obviously."

He wasn't sure why she was so nervous, but whatever it was, it had her wound tighter than a duck's ass. The farther they got from her cabin, the slower she walked, and the more often she glanced back.

Maybe she was reconsidering going back for her jacket or possibly rethinking the outfit choice. She looked fine to him. Mouthwateringly so. But he figured Karma would probably think Toni was over-dressed. He didn't know what they wore at barbecues in New York, though if the few episodes of *Sex and the City* he was forced by assorted girlfriends to watch were accurate, they dressed a whole lot different for just about everything. In Idaho, shorts or jeans and T-shirts were good for every occasion except weddings and funerals.

She stopped dead in her tracks, and Hunter almost stumbled over his own feet.

"You know, I'm really tired. It's been a long day, and I'm still on Eastern time." She backed away. "I think I'll just go back to my cabin and crash."

"You're not even going to eat?"

She shook her head and bolted.

Since Toni looked more terrified than tired or angry, Hunter didn't take it personally. He just wanted to know what had her so upset.

When he arrived at the barbecue, James was deep in conversation with Trapper.

Trapper shook his head, dug a twenty-dollar bill out of his pocket, and handed it to James. "Little brother, I'm disappointed in you."

"Yeah, and why is that?"

"I just lost a bet to James that you'd have Toni out of her cabin in under a half hour."

"I had her out of the cabin and halfway to the

barbecue before she made up some excuse about being tired and bolted. What's going on with her?"

James let out a sigh. "That, my friend, is Toni's story to tell. If she chooses to share it with you, she will. I'll fix her a plate and make sure she's okay."

Shit. Hunter had wanted to do the same thing, but then barging into Toni's cabin uninvited twice in one day might not be the best idea. "I need to know what's going on, James. I can't do my job if I have to be afraid of Toni freaking out and disappearing. This isn't New York."

"I believe Toni is painfully aware of that. I'll talk to her, and we'll see you all in the morning."

James made his way to the buffet that had been set up and piled two plates with food before moseying off in the direction of Toni's cabin.

Trapper handed Hunter a cold one. "James said she's not into the great outdoors."

"Yeah, that much is obvious, not to mention an understatement. She's terrified. Why is a mystery—she's told me everything but."

"Everything?" Trapper speared Hunter with the look he had that makes everyone spill his guts. Everyone but Hunter, that is.

"Nice try, Trap, but that hasn't worked on me since I got caught under the bleachers with Jeannie Coleman in the sixth grade." Hunter took a draw off his beer before going to get some grub, leaving Trapper to give up on the idea of an inquisition. Hunter wasn't about to say anything that might incriminate himself. He knew better.

James knocked on the screen door to Toni's cabin with his foot. "Toni, it's James."

"Come on in. Everyone else does."

His girl sounded disappointed. She must have expected Hunter. "I can't get the door. My hands are full."

The door opened a crack, and Toni looked out before opening it fully.

"Did you think I'd bring the paparazzi?"

"As if, I was just making sure Hunter wasn't lurking." She moved aside to let James in. "Hunter just walked right in here earlier as if he owned the place. I thought he was you. I was shocked when I found out who it was."

James handed her a plate. "Oh, so I was right. You are disappointed."

Poor Toni was completely flummoxed. "Now or then?"

"Both." But she was definitely disappointed now.

Toni gave him a confused look, and avoiding both the table and the subject, took her meal to her bed and crawled up, sitting cross-legged in her vintage cabbage rose, blue, and white cotton pajamas. She'd taken off the collar and wristbands. With her hair down, she looked like every other pretty twenty-six-year-old woman. Unfortunately, he was the only one who ever saw the softer side of Toni. She wore her Goth clothes like armor. James understood why. He just wished *she* did.

Toni took a bite of a barbecued chicken leg. "Thanks for bringing me dinner. I was getting hungry. I tried to go…" She licked her finger and then waved her hand. "I just couldn't."

"You're welcome." James sat at the end of the bed and leaned against the footboard facing her. "I'm sure if I hadn't thought of it first, Hunter would have brought you something. He's a good guy, not to mention single and gorgeous."

"He makes me nervous. He looks at me as if he's trying to read my mind."

"Maybe he can. I hear he's great with troubled youths—he has a way with them."

"I'm hardly a troubled kid."

James gave her his "get real" look. "You used to be. Hunter's observant—maybe too observant." He held a chicken leg and pointed it at her. "You're going to be working closely together. He's smart. He's going to figure you out on his own, so you might as well just tell him why you're afraid and get it out in the open. It'll save us all time and trouble."

The expression on Toni's face said she wasn't buying it—her and her damn walls.

"I spent a week with him, Toni. Believe me, he'll understand and help you out."

"James." She nudged him with her foot. "You swore you wouldn't say anything."

"And I won't, but that doesn't mean I don't think you should. You should give him a chance."

"Why?"

"Because for some reason, he seems to have taken a shine to you." James ignored Toni's eye roll, moved over to sit beside her, and smiled when she leaned back against him. "He went after you, didn't he?"

"To my eternal embarrassment. He found me with my face buried in a pillow trying not to hyperventilate. I'm sure I made a real strong impression—just not the kind that makes a man want to peel my clothes off."

"I guess that depends upon just how much of your

butt was showing when your head was buried in that pillow. You were wearing a really short skirt."

Toni laughed and elbowed him in the ribs. "Thanks so much for pointing that out. As if I didn't have enough to be embarrassed about."

James threw his arm around her and gave her a squeeze. "I live to serve."

"Even if Hunter is understanding, how am I supposed to get the models' respect if I'm falling apart?"

"Exactly. The only way they're going to respect you is if you do your job, and you can't do your job if you don't figure out a way to deal with your phobia. All I'm asking is to let me and Hunter help you."

"I'll try, but you're the only one I've ever talked to about it, I would never have bored you with my own personal nightmare if you hadn't been with me when I found out about this trip."

"Yes, but I was, and there's no way you're going to pull the wool over Hunter's eyes. You don't have much choice but to accept his help. Everything he gives you beyond that will be a bonus."

"James, having one mother giving me dating books is bad enough. I don't need two. Sheesh, you're turning into a regular yenta."

James watched Toni toy with her food.

"He found the dating book my mother sent me." She nodded toward her bedside table. "He was reading it and probably thinks I'm out to hook up with the first man I set eyes on. I was so mortified I babbled like a lunatic."

"No, he probably thinks you're quirky. Guys like quirky."

"Somehow I doubt that—especially when the quirky

girl is surrounded by beautiful models. Not that I'm even interested. Could you see me and Survivor Man? I don't think so."

—•—

Hunter didn't have much of an appetite but took his plate and sat with his brothers.

Trapper moved over to make space at the picnic table. "Thanks for striking out again. You cost me twenty bucks."

Hunter decided to ignore him. It was Trapper's own fault for betting. He never seemed to learn. "Have either of you talked to Ben and Gina lately?"

Trapper's gaze wandered from one beautiful model to the next. "We're surrounded by gorgeous women, and you want to talk about family?"

Hunter shook his head and picked up a barbecued rib. "I was just wondering if that private detective found out anything more. I've been working twenty-four-seven all summer and haven't had a chance to talk to the newlyweds."

Their cousin, Ben, his wife, Gina, and the whole family had been searching for Gina's brother Rafael who'd been put up for private adoption when Gina was six years old. The only thing they had to go on were the memories of a terrified child, which wasn't much.

Fisher stopped gnawing on his corn-on-the-cob. "I think they've found seven possibilities. Dick Sommers is following up on them."

A red-headed model wearing goose bumps and an oversized bandana disguised as a dress sat next to Hunter. "Hi, I'm Yvette. You must be our fearless leader."

He wiped his hand on a napkin before shaking hers. "Your fearless leader is Toni. I'm just the guide— Hunter Kincaid."

"Nice to meet you." Yvette didn't let go of his hand. "I thought I'd come over and break the ice."

Fisher leaned in, practically knocking over Hunter's beer to shake the woman's hand. "I'm Fisher. I'm a guide and a doctor."

Hunter rolled his eyes. "We couldn't get him to stop watching *ER* when he was a kid."

Fisher took an awful long time to let go of Yvette's hand. "Yeah, like you weren't glued to *Grizzly Adams*."

"It was better than those stupid law shows Trapper always watched. Remember the Susan Day poster he hung over his bed?"

Trapper set his beer down with a thunk. "Hey, watch it. She was hot."

Yvette scooted closer to Hunter. "Who's Susan Day?"

"Never mind." Hunter shook his head wondering what planet she was from. "You're probably too young to remember."

Trapper kicked him under the table. "I'm Trapper. There's a bonfire after the barbecue. Are you going?"

"Of course, James said it was a meet and greet." Yvette touched the inside of Hunter's leg, and he jumped. "I can't wait to get better acquainted with you."

Hunter removed her hand and set it on top of the table as he rose. "I can use another cold one."

Grinning from ear to ear, Trapper slid into Hunter's spot. "A beer or a shower?"

When Hunter returned with three more bottles, he made sure to sit next to Fisher. As soon as he settled, a set of twins straddled the bench, sandwiching him between them.

"Hi." The pair said in stereo.

"I'm Candace, but you can call me Candy."

Fisher leaned forward and caught Hunter's eye. "Sweet."

"And I'm Randy."

Trapper took a swig of his beer and grinned. "Even better."

Hunter cleared his throat as he looked from Candy to Randy, feeling like a piece of meat slapped between two slices of Wonder Bread—bleached with no nutritional value. Not that he had a problem with that, but at the moment, all he wanted was to have a private conversation with his brothers. "If you ladies have finished eating, you should go put on some layers. It gets really cold up here at night."

One of the male models strolled over, sat beside Trapper, and gave him the once-over. "Looks like the party's here. I'm Ari." He scooted closer to Trapper. "And who might you be?"

Hunter enjoyed watching Trapper squirm. He wondered how PC his big brother would be if Ari ended up on his lap, which seemed to be the model's objective.

Trapper stood. "Trapper Kincaid, Judge Trapper Kincaid." Taking advantage of his full six-foot-four height, he looked down at Ari. "Hate to break it to you, Ari, but we don't bat for the same team, and I'm not a pinch hitter either."

"A judge, huh? I always wondered what they wore under their robes."

Trapper sat his hat on his head and adjusted the angle. "Clothes."

Fisher snorted beer out of his nose, and Hunter tossed him a napkin. "Don't mind Fisher. He's just learning to eat in public."

Yvette laughed. "I gathered that." She gestured at Fisher. "You uh… have a little corn stuck in your teeth."

Ari stood locking in on his second target. "I have dental floss back in my cabin if you need some. It's Oral-B."

Fisher laughed. "Thanks for the offer, but I've got some fishing line back in the truck."

Hunter stood and collected the plates. "It's getting cold. I'm going to get my jacket. You might want to do the same."

He moseyed toward the trucks with his brothers. "Finally, before we get interrupted again, tell me what Dick Sommers found out. You said he had seven possibilities?"

Fisher took out his Swiss Army knife, pulled the toothpick from its sheath, and poked it between his teeth.

Trapper took the last swig of his beer and tossed it in a waste barrel. "He's checking them out."

"Which sucks." Fisher ran his tongue over his teeth.

Trapper stopped and looked over. "Why? At least we have something to go on."

"Sure, but what are we doing? Nothing. I thought this was a family thing."

Hunter nodded. "Fisher's right. We should all be more involved. After I finish up the season, I'll fly to New York and see what I can hunt down. We can't let Dick Sommers have all the fun."

Trapper raised an eyebrow to that. "And I don't suppose this has anything to do with Toni Russo or the models who were just plastered to you, does it?"

Hunter just smiled at Trapper. "Jealous, older brother?"

"Hardly."

"Trapper, get real. I'm free from September through mid-November, and I want to help Ben and Gina find Rafael."

Fisher laughed. "Sure, okay. But let me just say, if I were going back to New York anytime soon, I'd sure as hell look up any number of the models at this shindig. Look at them all."

Trapper chucked him on the arm. "Ari would love that. I'll make sure he gets your number."

"No thanks. He went after you first. I don't like playing second fiddle."

"But Hunter's throwbacks are okay?"

"Damn straight—the operative word being *straight*, which, unfortunately for Ari, we both are. Right?"

Trapper laughed. "I know I am, little brother. Is there something you want to tell us?"

Hunter opened the back of his Land Cruiser. "Are you two done yet, and do I have to remind you that these people are our clients? You can explore your sexuality later. We've got work to do."

Trapper rocked on his heels. "Lord knows we're going to have our hands full just keeping them out of the bonfire tonight."

Fisher reached into the truck and pulled out a fire extinguisher. "Don't worry. I've got it covered."

The next morning Hunter was up with the birds. At a quarter to nine, after a nice breakfast at the lodge, he knocked on Toni's cabin door. She answered wearing a big, black straw sun hat, its brim almost concealing her face, a black fishnet, see-through cover-up over a bathing suit that was… something completely unexpected.

The black one-piece suit was right out of a 1940s pinup calendar—plain, save for a little ruffle on the sweetheart neckline, held up by wide straps, and a small ruffle at the leg where it ended like those boy shorts his old girlfriend wore all the time. He suddenly knew why those photos stayed on the walls for years and years. Her suit barely hinted at cleavage, but was so damn sexy he had to shake his head to clear it.

"What is it now?" She stuck her hands on her hips and spread her legs as if she was getting ready to fight. She had long, powerful legs, not the sticks some girls walk around on. Toni's were cut without being bulky. Damn, even in those checkerboard Vans, she looked hot. It probably wasn't a good idea to mention that seeing her in an old-fashioned bathing suit scrambled his brain.

"One good breeze, and your hat will be history. Do you have a baseball cap?"

"I thought we had to wear helmets." She was cute when she was exasperated.

"We do when we're on the raft, but this is for the hike to the river and the time we're off the raft. Believe me, as pale as you are, you'll need a hat. I have one you can wear if you want."

She took a step back. "Hike?"

Damn. In a tenth of a second she went from mad to scared. He preferred mad—it was kind of a turn-on. He imagined she was always sexy, but anger made her go from hot to scorching. When she was scared though—shit, he had no defenses. "We're about a quarter of a mile from the river. It's an easy hike."

"Nothing about this trip is easy."

"Why is that?"

Toni shook her head and mumbled something that sounded like, "I can't do this."

James, Trapper, Fisher, and a pack of models chose that particular moment to join them. No matter how many beautiful women surrounded him, Hunter couldn't take his eyes off Toni. She had all the signs of being terrified of something; he just didn't know what. On that subject, her mouth was shut, which seemed out of character.

James slid beside her, threw his arm over her shoulder, and pulled her close. "How you holding up?"

"Just peachy, thanks. I have to get my other hat." She took off her floppy hat and gave it a wave. "Survivor Man said this one won't cut it. Everyone go on ahead. I'll catch up."

Hunter didn't move. "I don't mind waiting."

She stepped into his personal space. A tough New Yorker replaced the terrified woman. "I don't need an escort. I'm a grown woman. I think I can find the river on my own." Not that it looked as if she was planning to. He had a feeling if she went back inside that cabin she'd shut the door, slide the bolt home, and shove a chair under the doorknob just for good measure.

Hunter didn't need reminding that she was a woman grown. He knew it with every fiber of his being. He had a sudden urge to make use of the collar she wore around her throat, whether to pull her closer or make her stay, he was unsure. He didn't have to be Einstein to know she was past ready to bolt. He wanted to know why. "I'm sure you can. I'm just not sure you will."

With a toss of her head, she had James clapping his hands. "Okay, let's get down to the rafts everyone. Toni and Hunter, play nice, and don't be too long."

Chapter 2

TOO BAD HUNTER WOULDN'T LEAVE WITH JAMES AND the models. Toni needed a moment. Okay, she needed a millennium. She waited until everyone was out of earshot of her cabin, which was a while because it was eerily quiet in the middle of nowhere. There was an occasional bird caw, a breeze rustling the pine boughs, and then nothing but clean air and the scent of pine—so not the thing she ever wanted to smell again. At least it was dry there, unlike her first and last experience in the New Jersey Pine Barrens, which were swampy, boggy, and above all else, buggy. The memory had her rubbing her arms trying to brush off the feeling of ants crawling all over her. She gave Hunter her best New York glare. "Do you want to tell me why you feel the need to be my bodyguard?"

"I think of myself as more of an escort than a guard—unless you need one of those too."

"I don't need or want either."

"You tell me why you're ready to hyperventilate at the thought of a quarter-mile hike, and I'll leave you alone... if that's what you want."

"I'm afraid of the woods."

"Why?"

"I got lost."

"When?"

"I was six."

"Where?"

"The New Jersey Pine Barrens."

"For how long?"

"Three days."

"Alone?"

"Yeah, just me and my vivid imagination."

He took a step closer and touched her arm. "Is it always this bad?"

She shrugged and looked away. She'd expected to be teased, but he didn't. She feared he'd try to placate her, but no. Nor did he try to make light of it. He listened to the facts. "I'm from New York. As long as I stay out of Central Park, I'm fine. But then Bianca got involved with a big hush-hush deal and couldn't leave the negotiations, so she sent me. It's not going well."

"You never tried to go back before?"

"Why would I? I'm not a masochist."

His winged brow had her fingering her collar. She suddenly felt very exposed and found herself tugging the hem of her fishnet cover-up. It didn't help.

"If it makes you feel any better, I haven't lost a guest yet."

"It doesn't. It's not rational. I know that. I can't control it so I deal with it."

"Stay close to me."

She tamped down the urge to roll her eyes. "Is that supposed to make me feel better?"

"No, it's supposed to make *me* feel better. I'm not sure there's anything that will help you."

"A plane ticket to New York would do the trick." She did her best to smile. He didn't bother smiling back. No, he was all business.

"I'm working under the theory the human body can't survive in a constant state of panic for long, so after an extended period—"

"I'll die?"

"No, you'll stop having panic attacks."

"What's your definition of an extended period?"

"Probably longer than yours. I guess we'll find out."

Toni went into her cabin and looked longingly at the pillow. Maybe she could put that in a Ziploc bag and take it with her. On second thought... she'd have to settle for a brown paper bag. With her luck, she'd wear the sucker out before she even saw the river. The door opened and shut. She didn't need to look to see who it was. She felt him behind her and wasn't at all happy about it. The last man she needed was a modern Davy Crockett wannabe.

Toni turned and shot him a glare. "What? You think I'm incapable of finding a better hat and meeting you outside?"

"Not incapable, but you're doing a great job of avoidance. What's the bag for?"

"I don't have a Ziploc big enough for my pillow, although I know they make one. It wasn't on your required packing list. A paper bag is more portable, and I just never know when I'll feel the need to hyperventilate or make one of those cute hand puppets." She shut her mouth and put her hand over it to make sure she didn't start babbling again.

Hunter awarded her a full smile. "Don't stop talking for my benefit. I like listening to you. So tell me... would your puppet have one of those cute collars you like to wear?"

"I guess I can draw one on if you'd like."

"Yeah, I think I would."

She grabbed her white cap with rivet holes and a black bird stenciled on the side. When it wouldn't fit over her pigtails she took them out, tied a ponytail, and pulled it through the back of the hat. Hunter took her arm and steered her out of her cabin. Great.

He looked around as he led her to a trail through tall pines.

"There sure is a lot of wildlife out here."

"Don't worry. They're just as afraid of you as you are of them. As long as you make a little noise, you probably won't see them. In bear country, people walk with bells on their walking sticks or backpacks so the bears hear them before they see them."

"I take it bears don't like bells."

"That's the idea."

Toni wished she could erase the smell of pine and replace it with the scent of exhaust, while pretending she walked down Broadway instead of a dirt trail. She should have recorded all the lovely city noises and put them on her iPod. What she would do to hear the familiar honking of irate cabbies and the occasional comment foisted upon the poor driver who offended them, buses' air brakes, tires squealing, and the inevitable sirens adding to the heavenly cacophony.

Hunter nudged her shoulder, breaking her concentration. "Did you bring sunscreen?"

"I'm working on my visualization technique here. Do you mind? I'm pretending I'm on Broadway, and you're not helping. No one has ever asked me if I had sunscreen while walking down Broadway."

"Sorry. I'm just afraid you'll end up with a nasty burn. But a sunburn through that cover-up you're wearing will make a real interesting pattern on your skin—like a red and white fishnet stocking. You can start a new fashion trend."

The sound of rushing water had Toni's throat going dry. She pulled a bottle of the wet stuff out of her bleeding heart backpack and took a sip. Why didn't she fill her prescription for Xanax? She could use one... or a dozen right about now. The cabin she'd all but hidden in since her arrival was no longer in sight.

"You okay?"

"Just skippy. Why?"

"You're turning even whiter than usual again."

"What do you expect? I can no longer see civilization."

He took her hand. His was cool and dry. Hers was not. "What's the worst thing that can happen?"

"I can get lost and never be found."

"I won't let you get lost. It's bad for business."

"No one would notice. They didn't the last time."

Hunter stopped, which stopped her, since he was holding her clammy hand. "I'd notice. So would everyone else."

"You're nice to say so, but no. Most wouldn't, and I'm fine with that. I don't like to stand out too much."

Hunter raised his brow again. It was getting annoying.

"I might dress a little loudly—"

"A little?"

"Fine. I dress like a freak, but I still blend into the wallpaper, especially around a bunch of models in New York."

"Is that why you do it?"

"Do what?"

"Work with models so no one will notice you. Although I noticed you, and I'd bet a year's salary that Trapper and Fisher noticed you too."

"You have to notice me. I'm the boss."

Hunter shook his head. "No, I'm the boss. You work for the client. There's a difference. I own River Runners for a reason."

"You don't play well with others?"

"I play with others just fine."

The look in his eye and the gravelly quality of his voice made her think of the kind of play involving plastic sheets and wessonality. Not that she ever partook. But the man did have expressive eyes, or possibly the altitude was getting to her, turning her into a delusional sex kitten.

"I don't like working for them. I want to run things my way."

Toni did her best to rip her mind out of the gutter. Heck, they didn't even have gutters here. Where did mountain peoples' minds go to play without a gutter?

"I make the rules."

That set off a few alarm bells. He might as well have hit his chest with his fist. Maybe he was the mountain version of Tarzan. Her pointer finger twitched to poke him. "Oh, so you're a control freak."

Hunter shrugged and looked as if he considered it. After a moment, he shook his head. "I like to say I'm commanding."

"Semantics." Before Toni realized it, Hunter had dragged her to the river. She removed her hand from his as soon as she saw the rest of the crew. Two orange rafts lay onshore, and a bevy of models surrounded the two men she'd run from earlier.

Hunter pointed. "That's Trapper and Fisher."

Fisher looked like a blond version of Hunter with a twist of California surfer dude thrown into the mix, and Trapper, well, he looked like a more attractive version of the Marlboro Man, with collar-length blond curly hair, chiseled features, and rugged exterior. "Hunter, Trapper, and Fisher. You three aren't brothers are you?"

Hunter smiled. "What tipped you off?"

"The family resemblance. Your parents have a hell of a sense of humor."

"Yeah, well. My dad was trapping when Trapper was born, hunting and fishing when Fisher and I were born. When he wasn't there for our baby sister's birth, Mom finally divorced him."

"What's your sister's name?"

"Karma."

"Like I said, your mom has a hell of a sense of humor."

Trapper walked up to her and held out his hand. "I'm Trapper, the older, wiser, and better-looking brother. You must be Toni."

Toni wiped her hand on her cover-up and shook his. "Guilty as charged."

Fisher dragged himself away from his adoring fans and joined the three of them. "Hi Toni. I'm Fisher, the smart one."

"Nice to meet you. All of you. I'm sorry about yesterday. I didn't mean to be rude." She pulled her clipboard out of her bag. "I want to take a head count before we start with... whatever it is you've dragged me out here to do."

Hunter cleared his throat. "Just give you a nice, easy lesson on rafting and then a picnic. Smile, Toni. This is supposed to be fun."

"Yeah, whatever you say." She turned to face the group of seven women and four men including James. She went down her list. "Aristotle, Becky, Candice, Chad, Harrison, Jordan, Layla, Roxanne, Randy, Yvette, and James. Good. Everyone is accounted for. Hunter, the show is all yours."

—◆—

Hunter wasn't sure which of the models were giving his brothers more attention, Ari or the twins. Ari looked like he had a definite thing for Fisher, but Fisher didn't seem to notice—he was too busy paying attention to the women. Hunter decided to take pity on his twin and put Ari in Trapper's boat.

Toni had backed away from the group after she'd done roll call. She had a way of hiding in plain sight. The models had all donned their bathing suits. The tans looked store-bought and so did most of the breasts. "Okay, everyone have their gear? Let's put it on. Trapper and Fisher, give everyone's gear a once-over, would you?"

Hunter brought Toni her PFD and helmet. "Let's get this on you and cinched up tight."

She looked a little shocked. "You're really going to make me do this, aren't you?"

"Damn straight." He helped her into the PFD.

"This doesn't look like any life preserver I've ever seen, not that I've ever really looked at them. I guess I should be thankful it isn't DayGlo orange. Red would have been nice, but the robin's egg blue isn't too offensive."

The vest zipped up the front and a whistle hung from a D-ring next to a zippered pocket built into a padded section cupping her breasts. The back was padded as well.

"This is really unattractive."

When Hunter tried to zip it for her she stopped him. "I think I can handle zipping. I learned that in preschool." He waited until she zipped, and then he cinched the sides tighter.

"Am I supposed to be able to breathe?"

"Yeah, but it has to be snug." He gave it a tug to check the fit and then set the helmet on her head and adjusted the chin strap. "There you go. You're all set."

"For what?"

"Fun, Toni. We're going to have fun."

"Right. In your world maybe. In mine, it's called torture."

"Great attitude you have there. Come on. Let's put that clipboard and the rest of your gear in a dry bag."

"You're going to separate me from my clipboard?"

"If I don't, you'll drop it in the river. Which do you prefer?"

"I prefer to go back to my cabin where I belong."

"Not if you want to hit all the photo shoots, you don't."

"Fine. Take it, but if you lose it—"

"I won't. Relax and try to enjoy the experience. This is recreation."

"Right."

Hunter took her bag and stowed it on his raft with his most important gear—the first aid kit. He sealed the bag and tied it down. Toni watched, leaning in to inspect his work. "Don't worry. It's not going anywhere without me."

"What if you lose the boat?"

"Like I said before, I haven't lost a client or a raft yet."

"Yeah, that's what my brownie troop leader said too. I feel so much better now. Why is it I'm always the worst-case-scenario girl?"

"Maybe it's the positive attitude."

Hunter ignored Toni's eye roll and took everyone through the basics of rafting by rote. "Okay everyone, let's make sure your helmet is on nice and snug. A finger or two under your chin is fine. More than that, you could lose it, thus canceling the effectiveness of wearing a helmet, and we all know we're not wearing it for fashion's sake. Same with your PFD. Make sure it's on tight so you'll be able to self-rescue. If it's loose, you'll sink down, and it will float over your face. This makes it hard for us to see who you are and decide whether or not we want to pull you back into the boat."

Ari and Chad laughed. Toni didn't. She was getting paler by the moment. Going for the short version, he held up the paddle. "Your paddle is the most important part of your gear. It determines if you're able to keep yourself in the raft."

Hunter turned the paddle to demonstrate. "Put your hand on top of the T-grip, tuck your thumb under, and wrap your fingers around it. Your other hand wraps around the shaft about six inches above the top of the paddle. This will give you nice, long forward strokes—"

He waited for Yvette and the male models to stop laughing about stroking and shafts—they were worse than the kids from his camp. Hell, they were worse than his brothers. Hunter had a boat full of adults with the emotional maturity of teenagers.

"As I said, this will give you long forward and strong backstrokes, so you'll be able to help the guide get the raft where it needs to go and keep yourself balanced in the boat."

Toni moved slowly toward the back of the group. He probably should have made everyone get in the rafts before the lesson. Too late now.

"The raft is made of an oval tube that forms the perimeter and cross tubes. Sit on the outside tube, and tuck your feet under the cross tube in front of you. This way you're supported with your feet, your butt, and your paddle.

"Every time you take a forward stroke you're pushing the raft in the direction you want to go and keeping yourself balanced.

"Every time you wave the paddle in the air and scream, you have a tendency to fall into or out of the raft. Falling into the raft isn't a big deal. Just grab your paddle, sit back on the outer tube, tuck your feet under the cross tube, and continue. If you fall out of the raft, I want you to lie on your back, point your feet downstream, and float. Look for a raft, and be prepared to get hauled in."

James sidled up to Toni and put his arm around her. Hunter took a relieved breath before he continued.

"Do not, I repeat, do not stand in the river. If you do, you can get your foot or feet trapped between rocks. The water pushes against your back, bottom, and head, then pushes you head first into the river, and there you stay. It's not a good time. It's a great way to ruin an otherwise perfect day, or at least complicate it. When your head is underwater, it's difficult for us to see you and harder still to pull you out."

If he wasn't mistaken, he heard someone whimper. Probably Toni. Damn.

"So, on your back, feet pointed downstream, and look for help. You may be asked to swim toward the raft. If you are, flip onto your front, and swim like hell. Got it?" He looked around and saw everyone nodding but Toni.

"To save someone, you reach down, grab onto the swimmer's PFD by the straps, say, 'I'm going to rescue you,' straighten your legs, and stand, pulling the swimmer into the raft on top of you. After that, you can bump fists, friend each other on Facebook, sit back on the tube, and we can continue with our day."

Yvette raised her hand.

"Yes?"

"Are you looking for a volunteer? I like being on top."

Hunter shook his head. "Thanks. Fisher's going to demonstrate later."

Ari waved his hand. "Can I haul him in?"

"Not this time." He took a quick glance at Toni. James was still with her, but she had backed away and was practically standing in the trees.

"The only time you can let go of the T-grip on your paddle is if a swimmer is out of reach. You offer them the T-grip, pull them toward the raft, then grab them, and pull them in. Any questions?" No one raised a hand. "Are we ready to go?"

Everyone answered in the affirmative, and Toni paled even more.

Hunter waded through the models, making it a point

to avoid Yvette, and found Toni. "You'll be fine. You're going to be in Trapper's raft—"

Toni's eyes were the size of saucers. "I thought I was going with you."

"I'll be right behind you, and if you get into any trouble, I'll be there to help you out of it. Trust me."

She nodded and stepped away. He could almost hear her shutting down.

"You'll sit right in front of Trapper and next to Fisher before he demonstrates falling in and getting rescued. You're going to do fine. If you should fall in, I'll be there to get you. Remember what I said. On your back, feet pointed downstream, and keep your eyes open. I'll pull you in. Understand?"

"Perfectly."

She turned and walked away, standing close to the tree line. Shit. He felt as if he just kicked a puppy.

Toni stared at the orange blowup raft she was supposed to go down the river on and wondered if she ignored it, and Hunter for that matter, if they would both go away—preferably without her. She could still find her way back to the cabin, but if she got on that raft, she wasn't so sure.

"You're not thinking of running back to your cabin, are you?" Hunter had snuck up on her while she was busy planning her escape.

"I sat through your little rafting class. Since I'm an auditory learner, I don't see why I have to go."

"I won't force you. But for your own safety, I can't allow you to go on any other rafting trips until after you have a lesson on the raft. The decision is yours."

"The word *decision* connotes a choice. You're giving me no choice."

"I'm sorry." He shrugged but didn't look the least bit contrite. "I'm just doing my job to ensure your safety. Now let's get you in the raft. It's easy. You'll see."

Hunter took her arm and pulled her toward the first raft. She stopped at the river's edge and twisted out of his grasp.

Hunter gave her arm another tug and looked as if he were counting to ten to keep his temper. "What is it now?"

She wiggled her ankle out in front of her, admiring her brand new Vans. "I'm going to get my shoes wet."

"Yeah, so?"

"They're brand new."

"Did you bring water shoes or sandals?"

"No. The list said those were optional."

"Okay." He bent over and picked her up. By the time she stopped screaming and flailing, he was up to his knees in the river and was near the rear of the boat. She had a death grip on his neck and thought about climbing him, but he held her legs in one arm so tightly, she didn't think she'd be able to manage it. He wore a smile on his face, which was so close to hers she noticed the dark green ring circling the lighter green iris of his eyes. The scent of his fresh-laundered shirt along with a combination of Ivory soap, deodorant, mountain air, and Hunter himself was oddly arousing. The altitude was making her crazier than usual. "Put me down."

"Gladly." He set her on one of the big tubes running across the raft. "You need to sit here on the outside tube so you can paddle. Just remember to tuck your feet under the cross tube. That'll help anchor you."

"I'm not deaf. I watched and heard your presentation." Still, she stayed on the middle tube holding on for dear life until everyone had piled into the raft. James sat in front of her and gave her a smile before Hunter handed out the paddles, keeping the biggest, prettiest ones for himself and Trapper.

"I want a big one." Better to hit him with as soon as he got within range.

He shook his head. "Sorry. These are guide paddles. They're longer and help us steer. Maybe once you're ready, I'll give you a chance to guide the raft."

Fat chance—like that's ever going to happen. "Thanks, but no."

He patted the outside tube. "It's time to move over here now, Toni. You'll do fine. Pay attention to Fisher when he takes a dunk and shows everyone what to do if you fall out."

Toni remembered her brown paper sack was in the dry bag—on the other raft no less. A whole lot of good it was to do her there. Hunter patted her back and gave the raft a shove before getting into his own and sitting on the back. She almost dropped the paddle when she grabbed the tube.

Fisher sat directly across from her. He looked over and bit his lip, probably silencing a laugh. "The only time you let go of your paddle is to pull someone in. It's easy. Watch and learn." He held his paddle in one hand and fell backward into the river, then floated with his feet pointing downstream as everyone in Hunter's boat paddled toward him.

"Remember to stay on your side of the raft." Hunter's voice cut through the terror clouding her mind. "If everyone moves over to one side to save the swimmer, the raft will capsize. When you're close by, you can hold onto the business end of your paddle and offer the T-grip to the person you're rescuing." He held onto the paddle, and Fisher grabbed the T-grip. Hunter pulled Fisher toward the raft and grabbed hold of the straps on Fisher's PFD. "I'm gonna save you now—" With his knees bent and feet anchored under the outside tube, Hunter stood, pulling Fisher out of the river and onto him as they fell into the raft. When Hunter and Fisher were settled again, Hunter steered his raft up beside her. "See, it's easy. Remember. Always go for the person first, gear later. Any questions?"

Toni caught his eye and realized she wasn't paddling. "Are we there yet?"

Chapter 3

TONI TRIED TO PADDLE WHEN TRAPPER TOLD HER TO. At least she wasn't hyperventilating—well, not enough for anyone to notice anyway. The river moved so fast, she couldn't imagine what the other parts were like if this was considered lazy.

They paddled, avoiding rocks poking up out of the river.

She stopped obsessing about falling in and concentrated on matching James's strokes. *Lazy river my ass*. As long as she stared at James's back, she wasn't focusing on the trees and rocks flying by at ungodly speeds.

Rafting was much louder than she'd expected. Not that she'd ever spent time wondering how loud rivers were, but still, the sound of water rushing all around was a constant roar.

They'd been at it about twenty minutes when Trapper had them paddle to the far bank. A rocky beach came into view.

"Everyone paddle. Let's hit the beach up there."

Toni paddled as if her life depended on it. She'd much rather be on dry land than on a blowup raft in the middle of a raging river.

Trapper slid off the boat, grabbed the rope in front, and tugged it to shore. Since her feet were already wet, thanks to her lack of paddling ability, Toni jumped out and ran toward the riverbank. God only knew what lived in the water. When she looked at her checkerboard Vans. It was hard to believe there was a foot and a half of water between them and the air. The water was amazingly clear and really, really cold.

Hunter slipped off of his boat and pulled it behind him as he grabbed her arm. "Be careful. The river rock can be slippery when you're not wearing proper footgear."

She wanted to shake him off, but the thought of falling in the frigid water stopped her.

"I watched you. You did just fine. Good job."

"Why didn't you tell me I was going to get all wet in the boat? If I had known, I'd have walked out on my own and gotten into the raft." Toni rolled her eyes when she saw Hunter's expression. She'd have better luck trying to sell him the Brooklyn Bridge. "I would have."

"Yeah, okay, if you say so, but what would have been the fun in that? The look on your face when I picked you up was worth the price of admission. And after you finished flailing around, it was almost enjoyable. By the way, you're heavier than you look."

She hit him. She didn't realize she had until her fist came in contact with his midsection. Shocked, Toni waited for retaliation. There was none. His only reaction was a low grunt.

"I meant that as a compliment. You're more muscular than I expected. You must work out." He rubbed his abs. "You're also stronger than I'd imagined."

"Thanks, I think. Though, just a hint, it's never a good idea to tell any woman she weighs more than you thought she would. Most don't think it's a compliment—especially not models."

"Point taken. So... what do you do?"

"When?"

"To work out?"

"Oh." She stepped out of the river and across the beach not knowing where to go next. She had no idea where she was. "I kickbox, run, and take stick fighting classes."

"I should have known you wouldn't be into something as mundane as yoga and Pilates."

James trudged up to them. "Everyone's out. Are we heading up to the other beach?"

Hunter looked shocked to discover there were other people around. "Yeah, we are. You know the way, right? Why don't you go on ahead with the others? I'm going to make sure the rafts are secure and get Toni's bag."

James waggled his eyebrows at Toni, but was smart enough not to say anything. When Hunter walked away, James let out the laugh he'd been holding back. "I'm surprised you haven't progressed past the point of slugging the men you like. I thought girls outgrew that by the time they're in their early teens."

"What?"

"You heard me."

Toni turned to tell him he was barking up the wrong tree, but James had already started downstream, and all the models followed. Trapper and Fisher carried coolers up the rocky path away from the river. Hunter carried her backpack.

"Here you go, all safe and sound. It's still dry too."

"Thanks." She tossed it over her shoulder.

He took her arm and steered her toward the path.

"I think I'll stay here and make sure nothing happens to the boats."

Hunter blew out a breath of undisguised frustration. Toni had that effect on people. "They're tied up. They're not going anywhere."

"Yeah, well, neither am I."

"I can't leave you here. There's a buddy system. No one goes off on their own."

"Yeah, and whose my buddy?"

Hunter smiled. "I am. You can hang out in my cabin if you want, but then you'll miss out on the beach. Do you play volleyball?"

"Why do you want to know?"

"I was just thinking, with your reflexes and strength, I'd pick you for my team."

Toni didn't realize he'd led her up the rocky path until she looked to her left and saw the sheer drop to the river. "That's so not fair."

His superior smile told her he knew exactly what she was talking about. "Whatever works, right?"

"Wrong."

Hunter stopped and turned around. He was on the uphill slope, so she had to crank her neck to see his face.

"Are you going to make me carry you again? Because I can. It's not a problem."

"It would be for me. I'm fine walking on my own. I just don't want to be here. I would have been happy staying by the rafts."

"Yeah, but then I'd have had to stay too. Them's the rules. Since the food is up there…" He pointed over his left shoulder. "That's where I want to be."

She'd skipped breakfast, so yeah, by lunchtime she would be kind of hungry, unless he devised some other trip to scare the daylights out of her.

"What's it gonna be? Are you walking? Or do you want a piggyback ride?"

"Funny. Are you going to stand there all day, or are you gonna lead the way?"

He took her hand in his and pulled her around him. "After you. Go straight up the path."

From the cliff top, Toni gazed down at the river and had the urge to step back. She saw the rafts tied on the beach. Beside her, a meadow teeming with wildflowers bordered dense forest.

Hunter watched her every move. It was uncomfortable feeling like the subject of a science experiment.

"Isn't it beautiful up here?"

She looked around again and nodded. The mountains in the background were some of the biggest she'd ever seen, dark gray peaks with a spattering of snow cut across the bright blue sky.

Pointing up the path, Hunter made his way into the meadow. "The cabin is right over there."

Toni followed. "You live here?" His cabin was a log home that looked like it belonged on the cover of *Country Living*. It seemed to fit with the strange landscape in a way an apartment building or a brick row home never would. More's the pity.

"This is my base of operations in the summer. In the winter, I have a place right outside of Boise on Castle Rock."

"Castle Rock?" Toni picked a wildflower. She would have liked to know what kind it was, but didn't ask.

"A ski resort. I run the ski school, restaurant, and the ski shop on the mountain."

She stopped and held the flower behind her back. "Do you ever see civilization?"

Hunter looked at her as if she were nuts. It wasn't too much of a stretch to see that in his estimation, she wasn't the picture of mental health. "Every day. The Rock is a half hour drive from Boise. There's a gorgeous view of the Boise Valley."

"Yeah, but you live on the mountain."

"Uh huh. I have a car."

"You drive in all that snow?"

"They keep Castle Rock Road clear so people can come up to ski."

Of course they did. "You really are a regular mountain man, aren't you? Have you ever lived anywhere but on a mountain?"

"I grew up in Boise. I went to the College of Idaho in Caldwell. That's not technically the mountains, but I've always been able to see them from wherever I've lived. I spent some time in New York last year. It was fun, but I can't imagine living so close to eight million other people. I need my space."

"I can't imagine living up here all alone. Just me and my TV."

Hunter pulled a blade of tall grass and stuck it between his lips. "I don't have a TV—not here at least."

Toni stopped and stared. He had to be pulling her leg. Who didn't have a TV? "You're kidding, right?"

"I guess I could get a dish or something, but why bother?" He looked out over the mountains as if he'd never seen them before. "I'm only inside to sleep, and half the time I'm on a guide trip living in a tent." He studied her again. "You don't look like you watch a lot of TV either."

How did he know that? The guy seemed to see

so much more than she ever thought she let on. Toni couldn't help but stare at him. "I spend most of my free time at a rec center. I work with the kids on their reading or help them with their homework. In the summer we usually have things going on. You know, arts and crafts, summer reading programs, field trips—that kind of thing."

Hunter seemed like a pretty stoic guy. The most expressive she'd seen him was a smile. That last little tidbit brought out a full smile and raised both his eyebrows. "Really? That sounds like fun."

Toni toyed with the flower she'd picked, pulling off the petals. "I grew up spending a lot of time at the rec center, so I thought it was a good way to give back. The kids need to know there's someone out there who cares about them. They often don't get that at home."

"Did you?"

"Did I what?"

"Know that someone cared about you?"

No, she hadn't. And damn him, he somehow knew that. Great. How did she end up back on the specimen table? "Look, Hunter. You're a nice guy, and you're fun to look at and everything, but I'm not interested."

"In what?"

Wow, okay, she felt like a fool. "Nothing. Forget I said anything. I just thought… well, you saw that book I was reading."

"Yeah, you're looking to hook up. I remember."

"Not just hook up, but even if I were, I'm not interested in hooking up with a mountain man."

"Gee, Toni. I don't remember making an offer."

"Yes, well. Don't. You're not my type."

"Then it's a good thing I'm not interested in interviewing for the position." He took a step toward her and crossed his arms. "I was just thinking back to that book of yours I was reading while you had your little meltdown yesterday—"

"It wasn't a meltdown."

"The book talks a lot about figuring out what you want in a man. I think it requires more specificity than a quote normal man unquote. You sound as if you have a pretty good idea of what you don't want. Maybe you should start thinking about what you *do* want."

He didn't wait for a response before he turned and walked away. Toni gave him some space, but not too much. She followed him over a slope toward his cabin. It had a lot of windows and was topped with a green metal, high-pitched roof, probably to keep the snow from gathering. And it wasn't alone. There were other buildings too.

"That's the cabin. If you want to hole up inside, you're more than welcome. Make yourself at home. There are plenty of pillows if you need one. If you're interested in going to the beach, it's up the path a few hundred yards. The food is in the cooler. I think they labeled everyone's lunches. There's a john in the cabin, and then there's always the outhouse over there. I'll see you later, Toni."

Hunter took off up the hill toward where he said the beach was and left her standing alone in the tall grass. Mountains surrounded her. Everyone must have gone on to the beach because there wasn't a soul around the cabin. Toni got that panicky feeling again and tried to keep her cool. She wanted to kick herself for opening her big mouth. She should never have said he wasn't her type. If she didn't know better, she'd think she hurt his feelings, which was ridiculous, since every one of those models would do him in a minute. Well, the single women and Ari, at least. She'd stuck her foot in her mouth. She was as far from his type as she could get. She'd known that the moment they'd met. "Way to go, Russo. You idiot."

"You really shouldn't talk to yourself like that. You'll start believing it."

Toni spun around and almost ran into James who had come out of nowhere.

"I saw Hunter headed toward the beach. It's not like him to leave you all alone. Lovers' quarrel?"

"Cut it out, James. Hunter's not interested. He made that clear. I'm not interested in him either. I even told him he wasn't my type."

"Darlin', I don't think you have any clue what your type is."

"Yeah, that's pretty much what he said. Look, I guess I'll go into the cabin and make decisions about the schedule. I have the map with me. I figure we can do the easier shoots first and then take on the more challenging ones."

"What makes you think Hunter's not your type?"

"Oh, I don't know, James. Maybe because he's as outdoorsy as you can get, and I hyperventilate at the thought of standing in the middle of a freakin' meadow. Speaking of which, if you'd like to continue the armchair analysis, would you mind moving it into Hunter's cabin? I'm sure he has a couch in there somewhere."

James put his arm around her and steered her toward

the cabin. "I thought you were doing better today. Sure, you looked like you were going to lose it when Hunter picked you up and put you in the raft, but you were a trooper. You did great."

"Oh yeah, I'm just ducky. Thanks, but I'm on the verge of a meltdown and have been ever since we started up the mountain. Honestly, James, I don't know how much more of this I can take."

James gave her a squeeze and rubbed her shoulder as they trudged through the meadow. "Don't forget what a great opportunity this series of photo shoots is. If Bianca hadn't been in the middle of deal negotiations, she'd never have given you the chance to show her all you're capable of. This is your chance to turn a job into a career. It's all up to you. Don't let a few trees get in the way of your whole future."

"Great. All I need is a little more pressure. Thanks—like trying to keep from completely losing it is not enough."

James dropped his comforting hand and bumped shoulders with her. "Don't get all dramatic on me too. You missed Yvette. She threw a fit when I told her she'd have to keep her bathing suit on when she sunbathed. It wasn't pretty."

Toni opened the door to the cabin and walked into a bright kitchen and great room. A huge stone fireplace was the focal point and went from floor to ceiling. In this part of the house it had a really tall vaulted ceiling and windows everywhere. "I can imagine. Yvette hates tan lines. I think if it were up to her, she'd never wear anything. The way she walks around the dressing rooms, you'd think she wasn't interested in modeling clothes— just her body."

"There is that, but I think she was trying to impress the boys. Fisher was all for it, but I put my foot down. This is work, after all."

"If it wasn't, I wouldn't be here." She stopped in the center of the entry and stared. The logs didn't stop on the outside of the house. They formed the inside walls, the exposed trusses, the floor. It seemed as if everything in the house was made of wood save the huge fireplace, the leather furniture, and antler chandeliers, which looked weird to her but fit. Toni walked past the cozy leather couch and chairs and dropped her backpack and her hat on the dining room table.

The house was über clean—immaculate. Who knew Merry Maids came out this far? "I'll do some work. Just promise me you'll come back to get me before you leave? Okay?"

James patted her back. "As if Hunter would leave without you. You might have hurt his feelings, but I don't think he's going to give up that easily."

"On what?"

"Wow, you really don't see it, do you?"

"James, I love you, but I hate it when you speak in riddles. I'm so not good at figuring them out."

James walked over to the door and opened it. "Tell me about it."

⚬⚬⚬

Hunter stalked over to the beach. Man, he'd never been shot down before he'd even made an advance. It wasn't as if the thought hadn't occurred to him, but shit. He didn't hit on just anyone and never on clients. She wasn't interested, and it was fine with him. After all, he wasn't that hard up, which is why he'd been relieved when he saw Toni had replaced Bianca. He'd spent a week avoiding Bianca's come-ons when she was there on her scouting trip, and he wasn't looking forward to doing it for another week. One of the reasons he'd invited his brothers was that he'd hoped Bianca would take one look at Trapper or Fisher and go after one of them.

Toni made him rethink his entire policy on clients. But then, when he thought about it, Toni really wasn't the client—she just worked for the client. A technicality, but when it came down to it, he made the rules. It was a damn shame she wasn't even interested.

He hiked to the boulder they used as a clothing rack and pulled off his shirt. He had seven models to entertain. The last thing he needed to do was coddle a spoiled Goth girl with a smart mouth and sexy voice. Okay, so she was cute and smart and funny—especially when she started babbling—but she also had some serious baggage. The only baggage he was interested in was a lightweight backpack. All he wanted was a good time. When a man lives four months in the mountains and six months on the slopes, he doesn't have time for a relationship—especially with a city girl who has a fear of the wilderness. No sir. Toni might be cute as hell, but she definitely wasn't the woman for him.

"Hey, what'd you do with the Goth chick?"

Hunter threw his shirt on the rock and found Trapper walking toward him. "I didn't do anything with her. I think she's hiding in the cabin. Why?"

"Just curious. What's her deal?"

Hunter didn't like his brother asking questions about

Toni. He wasn't interested in her, but the thought that one of his brothers might be did strange things to his gut. "I'm not sure. She got lost in the woods when she was a little kid, and she's never gotten past it."

Trapper leaned against the boulder and crossed his arms. "That must be rough."

"I guess." Okay, so he felt bad for her. He had no clue what she'd gone through since she definitely wasn't into sharing that... everything else, sure, but not the root of the problem. Women. He found himself shaking his head.

"What?"

He'd forgotten Trapper was even there. Shit. His brother had a lot of experience putting the screws to people. The last thing Hunter wanted was to be on the witness stand with his big brother doing the questioning. "Nothing."

"If you're so concerned about her, what the hell are you doing up here?"

"I'm not concerned. Well, okay, she's a guest, and it's my job to see she enjoys herself, but that's it. I'm not interested in anything else. We both know I'm not relationship material."

"Why do you say that?" The curiosity that glowed in Trapper's eyes made Hunter nervous.

"I'm just like dear old dad, remember? We all know how he handled his relationships. He left. With my work, could I do any better? Between the camp and River Runners I'm working all summer, and you know how crazy things get on the mountain during ski season. I'd be leaving all the time. What woman in her right mind would put up with me?"

"Anyone with a brain. Besides, it's not as if you're gonna do this for the rest of your life. It's a job.

Priorities change when you meet the right woman. They did for Ben."

"It doesn't matter. Toni's miserable anyplace she can't find a latte on every street corner. She has a panic attack anytime she's more than ten feet away from a building. I can't solve her problems for her."

"Did she ask you to?"

"No."

"But you'd like to…"

"What?"

"Solve her problems. It's a thing men do. We can't help ourselves. It's that damn Y chromosome, or that's what Karma says."

Shit, he'd forgotten all about Karma. Hunter checked his watch. If she met Toni, God only knew what would happen. Karma would figure it out, because that's what little sisters did, and then she'd make his life more miserable than usual. "Look. I better get down there. I called Karma last night and asked her to bring something to the cabin for me. If she meets Toni it won't be good."

"Why?"

"What if Karma starts dressing like Toni?"

"Good point. Go on. I'll stay here and keep an eye on Fisher. I tell you, that boy thinks he's died and gone to heaven."

Hunter put his shirt back on and laughed. "Yeah, like you're not interested in one of your seventy-two-hour flings."

Trapper ran his hands through his too-long hair. "We have a seven-day contract. That's a hell of a lot longer than seventy-two hours. We'll see what happens on day three or four."

"I should have known." Hunter shook his head and turned toward the cabin, almost running into James.

"Where are you off to?"

"The cabin."

James blocked the way. "Maybe you should give Toni some space."

What the hell was it with everyone? You'd think he couldn't do anything unless it involved Toni. When he thought about it, going to head off Karma did have something to do with Toni, but not in the way they thought. "Toni can have all the space she wants. I'm going down to meet my sister. She's dropping some stuff off for me."

"You have a sister too?"

Hunter narrowed his eyes. "Yeah, why?"

"I'm always looking for new models. After seeing you and your brothers, I figure since your sister went swimming in the same gene pool, she must be spectacular, and maybe she wouldn't have a problem being photographed."

It was bad enough Hunter would spend all eternity owing the little brat, and now James wanted to check Karma out to see if he could make her the next Kate Moss. "I'm sure she'll end up at the beach later. She won't leave before seeing Fisher and Trapper and sticking her nose in where it doesn't belong. There's no need to wait for her with me."

James held up his hands. "Okay, I get the point. I know you don't want me hanging around."

"That's not what I said. I just need to talk to Karma. It's private, and she's not much for privacy to begin with. So now, not only is she going to be pissed at me for not inviting her to be a guide, she's gonna want to stick her nose into my business."

"She's a guide?"

"Yeah." Hunter wasn't happy about it either. "She's as good as they get."

"Then why isn't she here?"

It was one thing to invite his brothers for a week of playing with models and a whole other thing to invite his little sister. "I figured you'd come out here with at least a few male models. If you had a little sister, would you want her hanging with men who look like Bruce and Chad? Nope. Call me a chauvinist, but there are some things that will never be equal. Karma is the last person I'd invite to work this job."

"Yet you invited your brothers."

"They're my brothers, not my little sister." Hunter had spent a week with James and Bianca, so it wasn't as if they didn't know each other. But now James was giving him the third degree. It didn't make sense. "James, all I want is to see Karma come and go without meeting any of you. Since I know my sister, in order to do that I'd have to best her in a wrestling match—which is not a given—duct tape her mouth shut, tie her up, and drive her smart little ass back to Boise. In other words, I don't stand a chance in hell."

James didn't bother hiding his grin. "I for one look forward to meeting her. She must be a hell of a woman to be able to keep up with you and your brothers."

Chapter 4

KARMA KINCAID PARKED IN FRONT OF HUNTER'S PLACE, climbed out of her Jeep Rubicon, and stretched to relieve the stress only a three-hour drive through the mountains could produce. She grabbed the book and a tin of oatmeal cinnamon chip cookies, hoping Hunter didn't catch on that she'd eaten about a dozen on her trip from Boise to Stanley.

The front door opened before she had a chance to juggle her packages to free her hand. She looked at the woman sizing her up and smiled. Ah, the object of Hunter's infatuation.

Karma knew the woman who'd catch Hunter's eye would not be the plain vanilla type. Oh no, she'd have to be an extreme flavor, Cherry Garcia or at least Chunky Monkey. This one looked more like a Dublin Mudslide with a scoop of the others added for shits and giggles. Hunter never did anything halfway—not in his work or his women, but for the first time Karma wondered if he'd be able to handle this one.

"Can I help you?" The stranger asked, guarding the door like a Rottweiler.

"I came to drop something off for Hunter. Who might you be?"

"Oh." The stranger stepped back and fingered the D-ring on the collar she wore. "Come on in. Hunter is up at the... um... beach."

Karma nodded and slid past, setting the cookies atop the refrigerator before heading toward the master bedroom. He'd requested the cookies from Mom, and Karma had spent all night baking them. If Hunter or any of her brothers knew she was the creator of all "Mom's" cookies, she'd never live it down. It took a long time to get them to think of her as anything but a girl. She wasn't about to blow it now. "Hunter called me yesterday and said he'd be here this afternoon." She stepped into his bedroom and placed the bag containing the book in the top drawer of his desk, but not before checking to see if Hunter's mystery woman had followed. She hadn't.

Karma tossed her backpack on his neatly made bed, sat beside it, and bounced around a few times to get his goat. She'd never seen the point in making a bed since you ended up making a mess of it the next time you climbed in. It was a huge waste of time. Obviously, Hunter didn't think so. She was cursed with neatniks for brothers. Fortunately, she hadn't inherited that gene.

Karma peeked in the drawer of his bedside table to make sure he had a stash of condoms. After reading the back cover of the book Hunter requested, she'd stopped and picked up a box just in case. Up here, taking a midnight run to the nearest drugstore could take hours. He only had a few, and from what she knew of Hunter's sex life, they were probably expired. If Hunter succeeded in his quest with the nameless wonder, he would definitely need more. She slid the box into the drawer because no matter how much she'd love to have a little niece or nephew, she didn't want an accidental one.

The bedroom door opened wider right after she'd closed the drawer. Getting caught restocking Hunter's stash of condoms was not something she'd enjoy. Karma considered asking Miss Nosy Pants if she was the flavor of the month, but from the look on the stranger's face, she was probably wondering the same thing about her.

The girl blushed. "I'm sorry. I was looking for the restroom."

Karma wasn't going to invite her into Hunter's personal bathroom. She'd let him do that himself. "It's the next door down on the right." Karma was busy deciding if she should have a little fun with cuff-and-collar girl, or if she should take pity on her big brother and introduce herself. As usual, fun won out. "So, how do you know Hunter?" Karma slid off the bed and walked toward Nosy Nelly.

The girl fingered the collar around her throat. "I don't. I mean, we just met. Hunter is the guide for my company's photo shoot. I'm the manager of Action Models. Toni Russo."

Karma ran her fingers through her windblown hair. It was a rat's nest—an open window and curls didn't mix. "It's nice to meet you, Toni."

"Nice to meet you too." Toni was obviously waiting for Karma to introduce herself, but what would be the fun in that?

Karma picked up her backpack and stepped toward Toni. "I guess you should get to the bathroom then, huh?"

"Oh. Right." Toni turned toward the kitchen.

"Wrong way." Karma opened the door to the bathroom and flipped on the light. She didn't bother looking in; she knew it was immaculate. Someday Hunter would make some lucky lady an excellent wife. Karma on the other hand, not so much.

She smiled, knowing Toni had no choice but to go in and pretend to pee. When Toni shut the door behind her, Karma went back to the kitchen to see what Hunter had cooked for her to reheat—the only thing she'd allow her brothers to see her accomplish in the kitchen. The fact that she could hold her own, sometimes even excel at cooking and baking, was a secret she'd take to the grave. As usual, his refrigerator was stocked. She zeroed in on the leftover roast. It was a little early for lunch, but for Karma, it was either that or cereal, and never having been a cereal girl, she fixed herself a sandwich.

Toni reappeared and sat at the table, pouring over a bunch of notes clipped onto the wickedest clipboard Karma had ever seen.

"Hey, Toni, where'd you get that clipboard?" Karma snagged a Coke out of the fridge and grabbed her sandwich before heading over to check out the clipboard. "Oooh, that's nice. I want one bad. I use a clipboard every day and hang it on the wall in my office. I've never seen one that was a work of art."

"Oh thanks." Toni lifted it and showed her the back.

"Even cooler."

"I bought it at a little shop in SoHo. Do you ever get to New York?"

"Not often, but I have. My cousin lives there... in Brooklyn actually. Maybe I can have him or his wife pick it up for me. Would you write down the name of the shop?"

"Sure, I'd be happy to." Toni tore off a blank sheet of paper and jotted it down.

Karma sat opposite Toni. "Oh, I'm sorry. I didn't ask if you wanted a sandwich. I'd be happy to fix you one. Between the homemade bread and the roast beef, Hunter's got the makings of a dreamwich."

"He made the bread?"

Karma took a bite and chewed. Heaven. After a sip of Coke to wash it all down, she nodded. "He has a bread machine. It's not like there's a market down the street. There is one in Stanley, but it's definitely not close. When you live up this far, making everything is par for the course. Lucky for him and me, he's an amazing cook. Me—I'd starve without takeout."

Toni nodded. "Yeah, me too."

"So, do you want a sandwich?"

"Oh—thanks, but no. The Sawtooth Inn provided lunch for everyone. I guess I could grab it and eat with you." Toni stood there waiting until Karma realized she was looking for permission.

"Sure. If you don't mind eating early, that would be great."

"I skipped breakfast so an early lunch sounds good. I'll be right back."

Karma took another bite of the sandwich and watched Toni scoot out the door. Oh yeah, Hunter would definitely need those extra condoms. He was really lucky his little sister thought ahead.

When Toni returned, she opened a brown paper sack and pulled out her sandwich. "How long have you known Hunter?"

Karma took a sip of her drink and licked the mayo off the side of her finger. Toni passed her a napkin. "Thanks. I've known Hunter all my life. We grew up together."

"That must be nice. Do you see him often?"

Karma couldn't help but snort. "Not as often as I'd

like. It's hard to have any kind of relationship with Hunter; he works up here all summer, and in the winter he's always busy on the Rock."

"That must be difficult for you."

"You get used to it."

"I guess. Still, don't you worry about him around so many other women? I don't know how you do it. This week he's guiding ten models, seven of whom are female."

"Eight. You didn't count yourself, did you?"

"No, but I'm hardly a threat."

"I wouldn't say that."

Toni rolled her eyes, obviously unaware of her own appeal. Odd, since Karma and anyone who wasn't legally blind would take one look at her and think Toni was gorgeous in that no-nonsense, naturally beautiful way. She didn't look the type to care enough to spend hours putting goop all over her face before she'd be seen in public, not that she needed it. Karma laughed. "Am I worried?" If she were worried about anything, it would be Hunter getting in way over his head with this chick. She shook her head. "No, not especially." Damn, this was easier than third-grade math and a lot more fun.

The door swung open and hit the wall. Aw hell, Hunter had caught her, and just when things were beginning to get interesting.

"Damnit, Karma. When did you get here?"

Hunter saw she'd been there long enough to make a sandwich and wolf down more than half of it. Not to mention drink his last Coke. He grabbed the can off the table and finished it. "Did Mom make me cookies?"

"Yeah, they're on the refrigerator. I put the book in

your desk and stashed the other things I thought you might need in your bedside table."

Karma smiled that wicked smile of hers, and he knew exactly what she'd stuck in his drawer—damn, the girl was embarrassing, not to mention perceptive.

"You're welcome, by the way."

Toni's eyes went wide when he tugged on Karma's hair. "Toni, I see you've met my little sister, Karma. I'm sorry."

Karma looked up at him with that same grin she always wore when she was getting him in trouble.

What the hell was she up to? God, the possibilities were endless. "I trust you're not behaving." He grabbed the tin off the top of the fridge. "And you helped yourself to my cookies too."

"You're just lucky there's any left after the trip. I left before I could eat breakfast, and I missed dinner last night since I was driving all over Boise running your little errands. I had to go to two stores." She turned to Toni. "I do him a huge favor, and this is the thanks I get."

Hunter shoved a cookie in his mouth and offered the tin to Toni. She shook her head and slid the tin away. "Thanks, but no. She's your sister?"

Hunter nodded. "Yeah, why? Who did you think she was?" Damn Karma and her games.

Toni shrugged. "I don't know… a girlfriend maybe?"

Hunter closed his eyes and rubbed his forehead where a headache was settling. "Karma? Why would Toni think that?"

Karma threw out her arms. "I haven't the foggiest."

"You could have introduced yourself."

Karma's Cheshire grin peeked out again. "Well, what would be the fun in that?"

Toni pushed away her lunch before crossing her arms. "Where have I heard that before?"

Hunter couldn't help but notice Toni had hardly eaten a thing. "If you don't like the sandwich, I could fix you something else. I have plenty of food."

"No thanks, I'm not very hungry. Besides, you're the one who said I'm heavier than I look, remember?"

"That's not what I meant, and you know it."

Karma laughed. "I'm sorry, Toni. You'll have to excuse my brother. He can't help himself. I'm told he takes after our father—a sweet-talker he is not. His mouth sees more feet than a treadmill at a crowded gym. I know him. Any comment he made about your weight was meant as a compliment. It's his way of saying you're in great shape, which, by the way, you are."

Hunter couldn't wait to get rid of his sister. He'd thought once she grew up, Karma wouldn't be such a pest. He'd been wrong.

Karma's hand slid toward the open tin. Hunter slapped the top on. Craning her neck back, Karma looked up at him. "Do you really want to go there?"

"Fine. You can have one more, but that's it."

Shaking her head, Karma looked back at Toni. "Brothers."

Hunter secured his stash of cookies and grinned. "Oh, look, you've finished your lunch. Thanks for stopping by." He pulled the little brat right out of her seat and walked her toward the door. "It's a long drive back. You better get on it."

"Oh, no rush. I'm not working tonight, and lucky you, I have a few days off. I was thinking of hanging out here. You don't mind, do you?"

"As a matter of fact—"

She cut him off. "Where are Fisher and Trapper? I have tins for them too."

Hunter crossed his arms to keep from strangling her. "And you ate all mine?"

"Yours were on top. Sorry." She looked anything but. "I'm sure Trapper and Fisher will share. Not."

Hunter scrubbed his face with his hand. "They're at the beach. Did you bring a suit?"

Karma pulled off her T-shirt and tossed it at him revealing her turquoise bikini top. "I never leave home without it. And if I do, it's on purpose." She grinned again and waved to Toni before sashaying out the door.

~~~

Toni stood beside Hunter at the window watching Karma as she headed toward the beach. Her cutoff jeans had holes in all the right places. "Just wait till Bruce and Chad get a load of her."

When she looked up at him, she figured he was mad about the models who were probably going to go after his little sister.

"You thought I had a girlfriend and was coming on to you at the same time?"

Then again, maybe not. She wondered if it was a rhetorical question, but he waited too long for the lack of conversation to be considered a pregnant pause, not filling the silence like she'd hoped he would. She really didn't want to answer him, especially since they were alone in his house, and he seemed so affronted. She crossed her arms, mimicking his pose. "You said you weren't coming on to me, remember? Subtle you are not. You might as well have used a bullhorn."

He didn't say anything. He stared at her like a guy stares at an engine when the car won't run. As if he were expecting Manny, Moe, and Jack to show up and say, "It's the carburetor." Unfortunately for him, no one had figured her out yet, not even her. If she understood half the things she did or felt, she'd be tempted to hand out CliffsNotes to anyone interested. Hell, the wave of jealousy that had hit her when Karma walked in and made herself at home was a real shocker. Toni still couldn't figure out what was up with that. "You wouldn't be the first guy to have a girl in every port, or campground, or whatever."

Hunter tilted his head toward one shoulder and then the other, all the while staring at her, as if looking from another angle would change his view. Then he squinted like she did when she looked at her Victoria Frances poster of a girl in a graveyard.

Hunter cleared his throat. "Where did you just go?"

"To a graveyard."

"Do I want to know how that happened?"

Toni put some space between them and stood on the other side of the table. "It's the way you look at me, like you'd look at an optical illusion. Like, if you just stared long enough or caught me at a certain angle, I'd make sense."

"And where does the graveyard fit in?"

"Oh yeah. I have this poster that uses lenticular imaging to create the illusion of depth. It refracts light in different directions so the image moves and changes depending on the angle from which it's viewed. It's of a beautiful woman in a graveyard. I like graveyards."

"I like beautiful women."

Of course he would. "Last I counted there were seven of them at the beach. You might want to run back up there to get your pick before your brothers take the best ones. I'd keep away from Yvette though unless you like exhibitionists. Then go for it. She's your girl."

"Not interested. I need to get my mail. I'm still managing a business, you know. Are you up for a hike? It might help you with that little problem of yours."

"It's only a problem when I'm here."

"And you're here for the next week, so what do you say? Step out of your comfort zone. Take a chance. I won't let anything happen to you." He held out his hand, and for some reason she took it. He graced her with a smile. "First things first." He walked her toward his bedroom—she hadn't gotten to see much of it when Karma had been there. Toni stepped in, and the first thing she saw was a window that took up most of the wall opposite the bed. What a view. River, meadow, mountains—stunning. "It must be a bitch trying to sleep in."

"I'm an early riser. But the real show is at night."

Oh yeah, she could just imagine. The way he said it made her think all sorts of naughty thoughts. She tried to shut down that side of her brain. Being in the bedroom of a gorgeous man who not only held her hand—his thumb tracing circles on her palm—but stood very close to her, made it difficult. The room smelled like him, which unfortunately for her, was not a turnoff. Lodge pole furniture with deep colored Navajo rugs and wall hangings gave the room a masculine look without being off-putting, though it looked as if a woman had designed the bed—high and covered with pillows. The sheets had a sheen to them and looked soft and made to lounge on. Pictures of Hunter on the bed wearing nothing but the corner of a dark sheet floated in her mind.

"Take off your top."

"Excuse me?" She could swear he just told her to undress. She wasn't sure if it was real or imagined.

"We need to get you slathered with sunscreen. I'd really hate for all that creamy white skin of yours to burn." He pulled her into the bathroom. A tub big enough to hold four adults comfortably sat directly under the skylight. A steam shower with multiple heads took up the far wall. He stopped next to the double vanity and pulled a tube of sunscreen out of the medicine cabinet. He squeezed SPF 50 into his hand and then rubbed them together.

"Turn around."

She did, only to find herself facing the mirror. She put her hands on the cool granite countertop.

"Oh—and you might want to take off your collar too."

Instead of looking at him through the mirror, she turned her head to look at him directly. "Why?"

"Ever heard of tan lines?"

"Fine." She unhooked her collar and laid it on the counter before slipping off her cover-up. His big hands went to her shoulders, massaging as he spread the warm sunscreen over her skin. Hands worked their way up her neck and down her back, skimming the bathing suit straps off her shoulders. Letting her head drop forward, she stretched tense muscles as his fingertips slid beneath the back of her suit with a gentleness that surprised her.

The man had amazing hands. Unbidden visions of

what she'd like him to do with those hands had blood pounding through her head as Hunter massaged her neck and back, leaving trails of heat wherever he touched. When his fingers slid past her neck to the sensitive flesh behind her ears, it was all she could do not to moan. It had been ages since a man had touched her and even longer since she'd wanted one to. She closed her eyes and didn't open them until he turned her around. His big hands cupped the back of her neck, tilting her face toward his.

"I did your back. You better handle the front." His voice sounded rough as his gaze flew from her lips to her chest and back again. When their eyes met, his pupils were dilated, leaving only a ring of green around the circle of darkness. She swallowed. His thumbs traced her throat to the base of her neck as his breath fanned her face. She reached out to steady herself, her hands at his waist. Ridges of muscles tensed beneath her fingers, and for the life of her she couldn't stop staring, just like she couldn't stop herself from going up on her toes until she was nose to nose with him. Hunter didn't move forward like she wanted him to. He didn't kiss her. He just stood there watching and waiting.

The front door slammed breaking the spell. He handed her the sunscreen. "I'll meet you in the kitchen."

"Thanks," she croaked.

"My pleasure."

Toni blew out a breath. Well, almost anyway. Talk about perfect timing. On the other hand, maybe she'd misread him. He hadn't moved to kiss her, even though she'd given him ample opportunity. She slathered her arms and chest with sunscreen before resting her foot on the edge of the tub to get her legs. Hunter neither agreed nor disagreed with her when she told him he wasn't subtle with his come-ons—he simply changed the subject. The man was irritating, kinda like a rash. Scratching it always felt good while you were doing it, but in the end, it only ended up spreading the rash around and making it worse.

"Toni, are you coming?" Hunter hollered.

Maybe it would be better for her to keep her distance. She was never one to make the first move—ever, and going up on her toes was as close to a first move as she planned to make. He let that one slip away. She wished she could thank him for it.

———————

Hunter waited by the door, thankful his twin had interrupted them in time to keep him from doing something stupid, like kissing Toni.

It had taken him a full five minutes to get the damn problem in his pants under control. Yeah, as much as he hated to admit it, he was lucky Fisher had slammed his way into the cabin looking for the key to the outbuildings, so he could get the volleyball net and show off his form. Fisher loved the ladies. Hell, Hunter did too—he just didn't go sniffin' around every female within a thirty-mile radius. No, he chose Toni, the one who didn't seem to like him. He only wished he could decide if the feeling was mutual. The episode in the bathroom told him that although she may not like him much, she was attracted to him, and as much as he would prefer not to be, he was attracted to her like a rainbow trout to his Pheasant Tail Nymph fly.

Unfortunately, in this case he was the trout, and if given the choice, he'd rather not end up in a hot frying pan. When Toni looked at him, he saw what he saw in so many of his camp kids. Something lost. Sometimes it was the loss of innocence. Sometimes it was the lack of love or trust in their lives that grabbed him by the throat. Whatever it was with Toni, it called to him the first moment his gaze met hers. It drew him, and although he wasn't sure he wanted to explore it, he didn't feel as if he had much choice. There were some things you just had to do. Getting to know Toni, really know her, was one of them.

"You bellowed?" Toni strode from his bedroom as if she owned the place and had the balls to look pissy.

He'd seen that look on numerous other women—the one that said he was going to have to pay dearly for whatever he did to drive her to such a state. He couldn't think of what he'd done in the last few minutes except behave like a perfect gentleman. But looking back, it could be any number of things, which didn't bode well for him or their strange relationship. Still, he was in his element, and Toni wasn't. He had the advantage. He hoped. "Are you ready to go?"

Hand on hip, Toni tilted her head just so. Hunter had the urge to nibble her long, bare neck, even though he knew it would taste like sunscreen since he'd put it there himself. The woman had the most amazing skin. It felt like velvet under his calloused hands. She hadn't put the collar back on, and he wasn't sure if he missed it or not.

"To me, a trip to the mailbox entails going down to the lobby by way of the elevator and then crossing to it. I suspect here, like everything else, mail collection and delivery is different. Where exactly is your mailbox?"

Hunter smiled. "About a mile and a half down the hill." He snagged her hand, tossed a backpack over his shoulder, and drew her out the door and to the path. The driveway went there too, but it was a longer walk and not as pretty. Though right now, he couldn't take his eyes off Toni long enough to enjoy the view of anything but her.

"That's crazy. You actually think I'd choose to hike three miles, in the wilderness no less? Well buddy, let me clue you in, I wouldn't by choice walk three miles through the wilderness with you or anyone else…"

And she was off. It was amazing how she could babble on without noticing she was doing the very thing she was arguing against. And when she argued, her color rose, her eyes brightened, and she spoke with her hands, which made him smile. It was as if she thought her face wasn't expressive enough. She had to add the hands for punctuation.

"…even if there were a million-dollar gold Starbucks card at the end of that rainbow."

Ah, so he was right. He'd pegged her for a Starbucks girl. Before he'd met his cousin-in-law Gina and her friends, he'd thought Seattle girls held the record for caffeine addiction, but after being up at Ben and Gina's cabin in Three Whores Bend with a bunch of New Yorkers, he knew different. Seattle girls couldn't hold a coffee cup to New Yorkers. Hunter stepped off a small rock ledge and held Toni's hand to help her. "I have Starbucks coffee, and I'm a hell of a barista if I do say so myself." They were almost eye to eye. "I even grind my own beans."

"You do?"

Her eyes widened in what looked like a combination of awe and surprise, so he pushed his advantage and slid his arm around her. He couldn't stand not touching her. She leaned into him, her soft curves molded to him as if they were custom fit. He swallowed hard and nodded. If he moved his head to the left a few centimeters, their noses would touch.

She licked her lips, and he held back a groan.

"Espresso?" Her nose brushed his as her hands slid up his arms to his shoulders.

"Oh yeah." Shit. Toni worked for a client, and he made it a point never to fool around with clients. Long before he and his brothers started River Runners, Hunter learned it was bad for repeat business—especially if said client wanted to return to vacation with her new significant other. The one time that happened, it hadn't bothered Hunter. Unfortunately, the same could not be said for the lady. He'd learned a valuable and rather expensive lesson. He lost a week's work when he was replaced with a guide who hadn't shared her sleeping bag. But this was completely different. For one thing, Toni would never return unless forced. For another, if Toni did show up expecting to share anyone's sleeping bag but his, it would bother him a whole lot. He'd want to rip the guy's arm off and beat him with it. And since Hunter hadn't so much as kissed Toni yet, it made the decision whether to kiss her a foregone conclusion.

Chapter 5

THE BRUSH OF HUNTER'S LIPS WAS SO LIGHT, TONI couldn't be sure it really happened. She was more aware of the sweet scent of cinnamon on his breath, until he angled his head and increased the pressure, sending a rush of warmth from her mouth to parts of her body she'd forgotten existed. His fingers grazed her jaw, barely touching her, in direct opposition to the arm wrapped around her waist, holding her fast, chest to chest, thigh to thigh.

She breathed him in, sliding her hands across his shoulders, her fingers tunneling through the soft hair at the nape of his neck, drawing him deeper into the kiss. His tongue traced the seam of her lips, circling, teasing, before spearing into her mouth, shooting more heat through her already overloaded system.

A moan resonated through her mouth and chest. She wasn't sure if it was hers, or his, maybe both, but the vibration sent a twisting ache of need straight to her belly. Her heart slammed against her ribs as his tongue wrestled with hers for control, shattering her thoughts into a billion pieces, forcing her to do nothing but feel. The sharpness of his teeth, the slide of his tongue, and the hardness of his body against hers played havoc on her senses.

He ended the kiss, and when she opened her eyes, she found him watching her.

"I'm sorry."

Her heart took a tumble. "You're sorry?"

He pulled her close, tilting her chin to look at him. "I'm sorry we're doing this here. I'm not sorry I kissed you. If Karma knew, I'm sure she'd tell me, you, and everyone else that I'm not the most romantic guy in the world, but even *I* can do better than this."

"Oh." He wasn't sorry. That was good at least—or maybe not. She wasn't sure, nor could she figure out if her inability to think clearly was because of Hunter's proximity or the altitude. She hoped it was the altitude.

A smile spread across his face. "I know a beautiful little place we can go."

"Does it involve mail?"

"No, it involves you, me, and water."

"What kind of water?"

"Warm, secluded water. Interested?"

Toni looked around. Crap. She was in the middle of the damn forest, and somehow he'd gotten her out there with the promise of coffee.

"Toni?"

"You cheated. You brought me out here under false pretenses."

"No, I just let you walk while you argued. Whatever works, right?"

"You and your family say that an awful lot, you know."

Hunter tightened his hold on her like he didn't want to let her go just yet. She never would have imagined feeling as comfortable in the middle of nowhere as she did right now. He kissed her ear. "Are you going to stay mad at me?" His breath against her ear and the rumble of his voice through her chest had her rethinking the idea of moving. All of a sudden, right there, in-the-middle-of-the-woods didn't seem all that bad. "Or are you going to let me show you one of the most beautiful and best kept secrets in the area?"

She shrugged, and he kissed the tip of her nose. "Good girl." Grasping her hand, he pulled her off the beaten path toward the sound of rushing water. "I found this place a few years back when I was kayaking."

"Kayaking?"

"Nothing wrong with your hearing. If you don't like it, we can leave, and I promise to take you back to the cabin and make you as much espresso as you can drink."

Hunter had a way of making her do things she didn't want to do without her even realizing she was doing them. So far, he was batting a thousand. Facts were facts. She didn't have to like them. At least if she admitted it, she might get something out of the deal. "Bribery will get you everywhere."

Hunter stopped and stole a kiss before he winked. "That's good to know." As he led her toward the river, the trail narrowed and changed to rock. Hunter scampered up a huge boulder and pulled her after him. "You really need to get some decent hiking boots."

"Why?"

"So we can come back here without worrying you're going to break an ankle."

"Oh, that's such incentive."

"It is. You'll see." He jumped off the boulder, and grabbing her by the waist, helped her down, letting her slide along the length of his body, reigniting all the flames that were doused when he dragged her through the forest. The man had incredible upper body strength—he lifted her like she weighed nothing, without even a telltale grunt of strain. After eating her weight in chocolate for the last week angsting over this trip, she knew she'd put on more than a few pounds.

"We're almost there." He followed the path, pulling her along behind him and then stopped. "Come, stand in front, and look at this."

She shimmied around him, and her breath caught in her throat. If the panorama of snow-covered mountains wasn't amazing enough, the crystal clear river under an endless blue sky, cut only by green pine forest, made it spectacular.

Hunter wrapped his arm around her middle and pointed over her shoulder to a huge bird with the largest wingspan she'd ever seen.

"That's a bald eagle, see it? He's catching a thermal and heading to the ridge lift. Watch him."

The eagle soared like a glider, gaining altitude on invisible waves of air, his white head bright against the blue sky.

"See that spot in the water?" Hunter pointed down to the river. "There, right below that boulder. That's called an eddy. I was playing in it one day—"

"Playing?" She saw what looked like a whirlpool in the middle of the raging river, below a boulder big enough to picnic on. What some people thought of as fun truly eluded her.

"Yeah, playing. You see, the water runs around the boulder, and then back upstream toward it. If you get right behind the boulder, in the heart of the eddy, you can float around, resting, relaxing. It's almost like surfing and going nowhere. I was in my kayak playing in the eddy when I looked over here and saw this." He pointed to a spot at the edge of the river with big rocks in a semicircle. "It's a natural hot spring. Really hot, so I put the rocks around and let in just enough of the cold river water to make it the perfect temperature. Come on. It's big enough for two."

She turned around to question him, only to see him reaching behind and pulling his T-shirt off like guys do in the movies. She figured they did it that way to show the hem of the T-shirt slip over the actor's washboard abs. Normal people crossed their arms in front and pulled their shirt over their guts, and well... whatever else, before pulling it over their heads. Her way certainly wasn't as sexy as his.

Toni thought she was prepared to see Hunter shirtless. After all, she'd seen him on the website and worked around models all day long. It wasn't as if she was lacking in beefcake.

The only word that came to mind after seeing Hunter Kincaid shirtless was magnificent. The man was perfection personified, except for that little flaw he had that enabled him to get her to do things she wasn't interested in doing.

Toni wasn't sure who kissed whom. All she knew was that she'd lost control of everything the second Hunter's lips met hers. She knew from the first kiss he was potent, but she'd never guessed anything could be like this. One second he was pulling off his shirt, and the next he slid his mouth over hers. Hunter might be a slow starter, but he definitely knew what he was doing and exactly what he wanted. He controlled the kiss, teasing her with his lips, varying pressure. His hand cupped to the back of her head, changing the angle, before tracing his tongue across the seam of her lips. His tongue slipped in, penetrating, searing, and she reveled in it. His body surrounded her. His tongue, hot and wet, invaded. One hand massaged her scalp as the other traveled down her spine to her ass and pulled her hips against his, lifting her leg. His erection hit that perfect spot, and this time she was sure the groan was hers. Beyond the Niagara Falls roar of blood pounding through her ears, she heard applause. Her eyes shot open as two orange rafts flew past down the river. "Oh God." She felt faint. She couldn't breathe. It was happening again.

"What's the matter?"

Her leaden leg slid down his, and if he hadn't been holding her so tight, she was sure she'd have hit the ground.

"Toni, what's wrong?"

"They're gone. They took the rafts. They left us here."

"Who?"

She pointed as the big orange rafts got smaller the farther downstream they traveled.

"Son of a bitch."

Hunter was going to kill Trapper. He'd expect Fisher and Karma to pull a stunt like that, but Trapper knew better. "It's okay. Karma's with them, which means she left her Jeep at the cabin. We're not stranded. We'll take off early in the morning and get to the Inn before we need to leave for the first shoot. I've got you, Toni. You're fine." He sat her down on a rock. "Breathe. Nice and slow." When she dragged in a few breaths, his were easier. "Good girl."

She stared down river and then looked around as if she'd never seen the area before. Trying to figure out what went through a woman's head was difficult enough, but trying to figure out a terrified woman was impossible. "James promised he wouldn't leave me here."

Hunter didn't know what shocked him more, the fierce protectiveness he felt for Toni, or the jealousy that washed over him at the mention of James. The man was old enough to be her father, and he was gay for cryin' out loud. "They probably thought they were doing us a favor, giving us time alone together."

God, she looked as if she was about to cry. He hated when women cried. He squatted so they were face-to-face. "It's fine. You're not alone, and you're not lost. I've spent almost every summer of my life up here. I know this place like the back of my hand. I won't let anything happen to you. And you know what?"

"What?"

The color was slowly returning to her face. "I've got great coffee, and they don't." There... he coaxed a hint of a smile out of her. Crisis averted. "Now, where were we?" He leaned forward and kissed her, just a light kiss, nothing more than that. It was that moment he realized his mistake. Being with Toni was like skydiving. It was great, the best thing ever until you remember you're gonna have to hit ground eventually and realize you've forgotten your damn parachute. He figured he might as well enjoy the trip down, since it would undoubtedly be a rough landing.

He looked into her eyes and couldn't decide if they

were the lightest of blues or if they were gray. Right
now, they were gray and unshuttered, eyes that could
decimate him with a look. He did the only thing he
could do to remedy the problem. Avoiding her eyes, he
reached over and slipped her shoes off before pulling
her to her feet. He made sure she was steady before he
let go. "You, me, and nice, warm water. Come on."
He kicked off his shoes, tossed his pack beside them,
and led her down the path to the heart of the spring.
Together they eased in. Hunter's hands ran over her
wet skin. The soft spring water made her skin slick
and slippery.

She floated out of his arms, just far enough away to
make him wish he hadn't let her go.

Pulling the band from her hair, Toni slipped it around
her wrist before dipping under and resurfacing, her black
hair a stark contrast to her pale skin.

"You are so beautiful."

She looked shocked, as if no one had ever told her
that before, which was ridiculous. Despite the Goth
clothes, she was one of the most beautiful women he'd
ever met. Hell, she was every bit as gorgeous as the
models working with her. But then his whole take on
Goth had changed in the last twelve hours. Who said
Goth couldn't be sexy?

Their legs tangled as they floated together and apart,
the slide of skin on skin erotic. She floated around the
small pool, while he willed her to come back to him,
wanting to peel her bathing suit off her body and explore
every inch. If she didn't do something soon, he'd have
to take a dip in the river to cool off; he wasn't sure even
that would help.

She slipped beneath the water, arching her back, heading toward him, her bottom the last thing to disappear below the surface before her head popped up. Her momentum brought them together. He caught her in his arms. Her thick black eyelashes sparkled with unshed water, and her eyes widened when she came in contact with his erection. "I like this."

He pulled her tighter against him. "Are you talking about the spring... or this?" He rocked his pelvis against hers.

"Both."

"Good answer."

Toni's arms and legs wrapped around his neck and waist. Nose to nose she stared into his eyes as if she were waiting for something.

"What color are your eyes?" She obviously hadn't expected that.

"Gray, but sometimes they look blue or green depending upon what I wear. The official color is gray though. Do you know what they say about women with gray eyes?"

He shook his head, his nose bumping hers, drawing her closer. Still they had their eyes locked. "No idea."

"We're unpredictable. That's not always a good attribute."

In the hours since they'd met, he figured out the unpredictability thing was kind of a given. He could say one thing for her—she wouldn't bore him in the next week—which was more than he could say for any other woman he'd ever hope to know intimately. "I guess I have to take my chances then."

"It's not a good bet."

"Probably not, but the cards are dealt. I'm not about to fold just when the game's getting interesting."

"Okay, then. I'm all in. I like games."

———

It's a game. Nothing more. Right now, wrapped around his firm body, Toni could think of nothing but the feel of him between her legs, her chest against his, his breath on her face, and the darkening of his gorgeous green eyes. Being with Hunter kept her from thinking about where she was. It was as if she walked a tightrope, and Hunter was her safety net. A temporary one, but as long as that was understood, she wasn't about to fold either. Nope, she was all in.

Toni intentionally kept her eyes open as her mouth slid over his, nipping his lips, trying to torment him with the rasp of her tongue. His hands slid from her waist to cup her breasts, which seemed hardwired right to her core. As if her legs had a mind of their own, they tightened around him until she felt his hardness against her. Hunter sucked her bottom lip into his mouth and nibbled as her bathing suit straps slipped off her shoulders. She floated back, pushing off the rock he leaned against. He held her suit as she floated out of it and away from him.

Her eyes closed against the bright sunlight, cut only by shadows of the tall trees on the riverbank. The warm water, the sun on her skin, and the feeling of Hunter's eyes on her was intoxicating. She'd never skinny-dipped before. When she opened her eyes, all she saw was Hunter with the sun at his back, water sluicing from his body as he rose above her. She'd seen her share of beautiful men, but Hunter brought beauty to a whole new level. He'd lost his shorts on his way across the pool. He was all muscle, ripped but not bulky, and his tan told her that, unlike her, skinny-dipping was a way of life for him.

———

Hunter wanted to explore every inch of Toni's body. He just wished they were in his bed instead of in the water. The water seemed like a good idea at the time. Now though, seeing her floating around, if he spent as much time exploring her the way he wanted, they'd both be pruney before he finished. As much as he wanted to make love to her, he didn't want their first time to be here. Besides, he'd come unprepared. He tried to remember if he had a condom in his wallet, but since he hadn't needed one in the past six months, he didn't think so.

She floated in front of him, her breasts peeking through the clear water as if standing at attention. He pulled her onto his lap, his hands cupping her breasts. He slid his cheek against one tight nipple, eliciting a sigh from her. Toni's body slipped around him as if it were made to do just that, her skin so pale it was almost translucent. He wrapped one arm around her small waist, his hand coming to rest on her flat, muscular stomach.

Toni stared at him, those light eyes taking everything in. He held her gaze as his lips slid over her breast, sucking the nipple deep into his mouth. Her fingers buried themselves in his hair, holding him fast. With every suck, her hips rocked. His erection slid between her folds, brushing against her. Toni's head rolled back, her hair floating around her like a black drape in the water. She held herself in that position, back arched, eyes closed. One move was all it would take to bury himself deep within her. He switched breasts and did his best to hold his control.

"Oh, Hunter…"

He smiled as her fingers raked his scalp to his shoulders, anchoring herself to him. His dick twitched as she slid down the length of him, hot and slick with more than just water. God help him. He reached between them, his thumb circling the swollen bundle of nerves as he pinched her nipple between his teeth and slid a finger deep inside her. Slick and tight, her inner muscles vibrated around him as he slid a second finger in and curled it to press against her center while his thumb rubbed harder.

Toni went off like a Roman candle in his arms. He watched her come. He couldn't say he'd ever watched anyone else come. If he had, he certainly didn't remember it. The way Toni looked, he was equally certain he'd never forget. All he could think of was how beautiful she looked, flushed pink from the sun and enjoyment, her eyes wide open as if in shock. His name flying like a mantra from her lips in a breathless whisper, as if it was ripped from somewhere deep within her soul… over and over… his name.

Toni felt herself sinking. She thrashed in the water until she got her feet back on the bottom of the spring, only to see Hunter jump from the edge. One minute she was in Hunter's arms, and the next he was literally jumping into the raging river. "Hunter!"

She stood naked and climbed onto a rock in time to see the top of his head disappear under the white water and then reappear much farther downstream than she thought possible. "Hunter!" Toni lost sight of him and stepped out of the spring into the river, trying to get a fix on him, but he was gone. The ice cold water numbed her feet in seconds. Hunter was swimming in this? He'd die of hypothermia or drown. She ran down the riverbank searching for him.

"Hunter!" All she could do was scream his name, over and over, while she ran barefoot across the river rock until a huge fallen tree stopped her.

She was alone.

All the air left her lungs as reality hit. Hunter said he wouldn't leave, and he had. She bit back the scream that bubbled in her throat and reverberated in her mind. She had to think, but the image of Hunter being washed downriver, mangled by rocks, probably dragged to his death, was unstoppable.

She was alone.

Shaking from fear and the cold cutting like knives into her feet and shins, she hugged herself and squatted, afraid she'd fall. The trees seemed to draw nearer, overshadowing her. Panic ebbed closer and bubbled like the river, numbing her. Her vision grayed, and she did her best to breathe without hyperventilating.

She had to get out of there. She wasn't that same six-year-old who had cried for three days straight in the Pine Barrens, and she wasn't lost—or at least she hoped she wasn't. She had the ability to traverse the New York subway system blindfolded. She should be able to find her way back to the cabin. She was a grown woman. A naked grown woman. Toni took a deep breath and stood. The shock of blood rushing from her head made her wish she'd taken it a bit slower. Shivering, she eyed the river, trying to retrace her steps to the hot spring.

Hunter wasn't coming back. He'd left her. He was probably dead. She wiped away the tears streaming down her face, trying to clear her vision enough to find her bathing suit.

"I'm okay. I'm okay. I'm okay." But a vision of Hunter's battered body kept intruding on her mantra.

She had to get back to the cabin and call 9-1-1 to report Hunter missing. She grabbed her suit and tugged it up her legs. Did they even have 9-1-1 here in the middle of nowhere? She wasn't sure. No one told her what to do in the event a man you were making out with suddenly took off and dove into the river. Tugging on a wet bathing suit was not an easy thing to do, especially with hands that shook like wind chimes in a tornado.

Toni tried to remember where Hunter had left her shoes. She had to get to the cabin. Get a phone. Call for help.

Pain, deep and heavy, crushed like an anvil sitting on her chest. Shallow breathing made her light-headed. Through tears she found her shoes, stabbed her feet into them, and took off at a dead run in the direction of the cabin—or at least she hoped it was the direction of the cabin.

All the rocks looked the same. Where had they turned toward the river? She climbed over a boulder, jumped down, and ran, praying she'd find the trail.

Toni scraped past branches cutting her arms and legs. She tripped and fell. Her knee ached, but she didn't waste time brushing it off. She just ran. The trail opened in front of her, and she turned to her right, sprinting, jumping over the step where Hunter had first kissed her. *Dead*. Dear God, he was in her arms one minute and dead the next. She wiped the tears from her eyes and saw the cabin in the distance. She had to find a phone. Call for help. But what did it matter? Hunter was gone, and she was alone.

~~~

Right after Toni came apart in Hunter's arms, something tan flew past the edge of his peripheral vision. He turned his head just in time to see his shorts float out of the spring and into the river. His shorts with his wallet, containing all of his ID and the keys to his truck. "Fuck!"

He flew from beneath her and jumped over the rock into the river. By the time cold water hit him, expelling all the air from his lungs, his shorts floated downriver on the current.

Hunter swam past his eddy hoping his shorts would get caught in it, but no such luck. The white water enveloped him as he swam hard. His shorts bobbed a body-length ahead, drifting toward the center of the river he knew as well as his own limits.

Shit. If he didn't catch them in the next few seconds, they were gone for good. He kicked hard and ignored the cold as he slid around a rock and grabbed for his shorts, wrapping the fabric around his hand before turning to swim for shore. The river had taken him downstream faster than he'd hoped. This was not good.

He swam as if his life depended upon it, and knowing the river like he did, it might. Things started getting really hairy a little farther downstream. He probably should have let the damn shorts go. By the time he pulled himself from the river, he was a hairsbreadth away from some seriously scary shit. Not smart. If anyone else on his team had pulled a stunt like that, he'd fire his ass.

He sat on a rock catching his breath while chastising himself and pulling his shorts on. Toni. Shit, shit, shit. He'd left her there all by herself and jumped into the river. She was probably having a panic attack. Could he be any more of an insensitive asshole? Probably not. A guy didn't get a girl off and then jump into the damn river.

What the hell had he been thinking? Okay, he knew what he'd been thinking—he'd thought of all the shit he'd have to deal with if he lost his wallet and keys. The hours he'd have to spend in Boise replacing everything and making endless phone calls to credit card companies, equaled time he'd have to spend away from Toni. He only had seven days with her. Seven days suddenly seemed way too few.

"Toni!" He screamed her name as he ran barefoot upstream, cursing himself and every rock, stone, and branch he trod upon. By the time he got back to the spring, the river's chill had left him and was replaced with the cold sweat of dread.

"Toni?" She was gone. So were her suit and shoes. Thank God she'd left his. His feet were raw from running over rocks to get back to her. Jumping into the river had been a spectacularly stupid move on his part, especially considering what Toni must have thought.

It didn't take Hunter long to find her trail. He would have had a harder time following a herd of elk. She'd been running, and from the look of it, she'd fallen. Was that blood he saw on the rock? She was probably panicked because of his stupidity. Who could blame her? He called himself every name in the book as he followed her path through dense pine. When he hit the trail, he saw she'd gone the right way. Pride filled him. At least she was keeping her wits about her, though no one would blame her if she hadn't. He picked up speed and ran flat out, all the way calling her name. When he saw the cabin, he knew she'd made it that far. The door was left wide open. He ran in. "Toni?"

He heard crying. Shit. When he stepped into the bedroom, she was searching his desk. "Toni?"

She stopped and looked at him, the leftover terror clear in her eyes. There was a flash of relief just before a swirl of emotions coalesced into what looked an awful lot like anger.

"I'm sorry, Toni. I should never have left you."

"You're sorry?" She hiccuped through tears. "You left me, and I thought… I thought you were dead!" She hugged herself, her fingers digging into her own arms. "I ran down the river after you. I saw your head go under, and I didn't see it come back up. I thought you'd drowned!" She took a stuttering breath. "I pictured you trapped under the water, your head smashed against a boulder. You left me. You promised you wouldn't. I was trying to find a phone to call 9-1-1 and have the river dragged. And I don't even know if they have 9-1-1 here." She threw her arms out wide. "No one told me what to do if the man you're making out with takes a flying leap into a raging river. I thought you were dead, Hunter. Dead. You left me just like everyone else."

Her knee was bleeding, her arms were scratched, and she was shaking. "Shhh… it's okay." He pulled her into his arms, and she pounded on his chest a few times before she wrapped her arms around him and cried.

"You could have been killed. Was I so awful in the spring that you risked your life to get away from me? You could have stopped or said, 'Hey, Toni, I'm just not that into you' or something."

"God, no, it wasn't you. My shorts with my keys and my ID floated into the river. I didn't think. I just reacted. I'm sorry I scared you. I was stupid. I'm so sorry."

"You could have been killed. Dead, like… I don't know… dead. Were you trying to kill yourself?"

"No." He didn't bother telling her she was right, but he knew the river. He was a strong swimmer. He knew he'd be fine, well, mostly. He just hadn't considered her. And that made him feel like the world's biggest asshole. "I'm fine. I'm sorry. I'm sorry I frightened you. But I'm proud of you too. You did exactly the right thing. But it would have been nice if you weren't quite so fast."

"Where is your phone?"

He walked her backward into the bathroom. "It's in my backpack, why?"

"Where was your backpack?"

He lifted her to sit on the counter, making a space for him between her legs, and reached to get a washcloth out of the cabinet. He turned on the tap and ran the hot water. "My pack was by my shoes."

"I ran all the way up here and left your phone by the water?"

He stopped and looked into her now bloodshot and swollen eyes. She had dirt streaked across her face. "I should have told you where the phone was. And I should never have left you like that. Can you forgive me?"

She nodded but didn't say the words. He was a selfish bastard; he wanted to hear them.

Hunter soaped the cloth and wrung out the excess water before bending down to wash the cut on her knee. Once he was sure it was clean, he worked his way up and washed the scratches on her arms. She said nothing, though he could tell by the look on her face, there were a thousand and one things running through that quick mind of hers. He'd never experienced a quiet Toni Russo before. He much preferred it when she babbled. He finished washing her injuries, took her hand, and helped her off the counter. "Come on. Let's get you into a warm shower." He turned the water on and adjusted the temperature.

When he reached for the straps to her suit, she pushed him away. "I can do it myself."

"Okay." He knew when he was being dismissed. "I'll be in the kitchen if you need anything." He pulled a towel down for her and left her to it, closing the door behind him.

Hunter stepped out of the bathroom and wanted to kick himself for the hell he'd put Toni through. She'd need something to wear so he pulled a clean T-shirt from his drawer and rummaged around until he found the pair of silk boxers his sister had bought him for his birthday. He'd never worn them, never planned to, but the thought of Toni wearing them made him smile. He was just glad she wasn't in any position to refuse. He was also thanking his lucky stars he had the rest of the night to try to make amends for the huge blunder he'd made.

Chapter 6

WHEN HUNTER WAS STRESSED, HE COOKED. IT CALMED him, and since he'd made that crack about Toni's weight, he knew she hadn't eaten much for lunch. Maybe a nice meal and a couple bottles of wine would help her to forgive him.

He'd bet his bottom dollar Toni was a woman who enjoyed food. He'd never known a passionate woman who didn't, and on the passion scale, Toni was off the charts. The memory of how she looked when she came apart in his arms made his dick twitch. He took a big gulp of wine, which didn't help the fit of his shorts any, but it made him care less about his discomfort.

While the tuna thawed, he grabbed his favorite knife and a cutting board and chopped the vegetables. Once he had them roasting, he took out a loaf of challah he'd made the day before and cut it up for a quick bread pudding. He tossed in a handful of raisins and dark chocolate chips before pouring the bread and custard mixture into a loaf pan and placing it in the water bath waiting in his second oven. Then he started the apple and port wine compote.

By the time the shower shut off, the vegetables were roasting, the compote simmering, the bread pudding baking, and he was well on his way to finishing the salad. He tossed what was left of the fennel into the salad bowl and turned the roasting vegetables—red pepper, eggplant, cherry tomatoes, onions, fennel, zucchini, and garlic. Perfect. He threw in a handful of kalamata olives and added a few sloshes of a very nice white wine—a 2009 DAOU Chemin de Fleurs Paso Robles he'd been saving for a special occasion. He couldn't imagine a better woman to try to woo with it. He was just lucky he had two chilled bottles—the way Toni had looked when he'd left her, he wished he had ordered a case.

Hunter poured Toni a glass and refilled his own before starting on the salad dressing. Grabbing a bowl, he whisked together a nice Italian and sprinkled it with a few fennel leaves. There. It was simple meal, yet a feast for the eyes and soul, or so he hoped.

Hunter tossed the tuna steaks on a hot grill. While they seared, he turned on dinner music, wishing he knew what Toni liked to listen to. Since he was in the mood for some bluesy jazz, he clicked on his favorite playlist and set the table for two while humming along to Corinne Bailey Rae.

Hunter felt Toni's presence before he heard her. She stood in the living room wearing the clothes he'd set out and looked uncertain. "Feeling better?"

"Yeah, thanks for the clothes."

"You're welcome." He'd decided against candles, because it was still bright out. In the past, he'd always appreciated the long summer days when it stayed light past ten in the evening. For now, he'd have to just imagine her washed in flickering candlelight with his T-shirt slipping over her bare shoulder. She'd tied the T-shirt at the waist, probably because it would look like a dress if she hadn't. The effect was anything but functional.

Her wet hair hung straight, her lips were bright pink, probably from biting them, although it could be from the sun. He wanted to kiss her, but then he remembered the steaks. He ran back to the kitchen to turn them, hoping they weren't overdone. "I poured wine."

Toni watched him move toward her and hugged herself before he got too close.

"Are you cold?"

She shook her head and took the wineglass he offered.

"I hope you like tuna. While you showered I threw dinner together."

He went back to the kitchen and pulled out the vegetables. He plated them, took the tuna steaks off the grill, and sliced and arranged them on each plate.

A silent Toni was unnerving. She eyed him like she would a hairy spider.

"The salad's in the refrigerator if you want to grab it."

She did, but he couldn't help but notice she was sure to keep her distance. Great. He took another swig of wine and whisked the dressing a few more times before pouring it over the salad. "The salad tongs are in the drawer directly in front of you."

"I didn't expect you to cook." Toni found the tongs, tossed the salad, and then brought it to the table.

So she does speak. He picked up the plates and set them on the table before taking a chance and wrapping his arms around her, pulling her close. "I really am sorry."

She looked at him with guileless eyes. He liked that about her. When Toni looked him in the eye, Hunter saw the truth. If she didn't want to talk about something, she told him point-blank. There was no beating around the bush, no lies he could see, and he saw more lies than anyone, but maybe Trapper.

He realized a little too late he couldn't stop at holding

her. No, he pretty much had to kiss her. She tasted like the wine she'd just sipped, cool and tart. He took it as a challenge, but then everything with Toni had been somewhat challenging. "So, are you going to forgive me?"

"It's not that big a deal."

"Yes it is. It was a major screwup, and it was all my fault. I didn't think about you. I'm not used to having anyone…" he stumbled. What the hell was he supposed to say? He wasn't used to having anyone who cared about him? That was kind of presumptuous. Anyone to care about… which, when he thought about it, fit the bill. But she didn't look at all ready to hear that. He couldn't say he wasn't used to anyone counting on him. That wasn't true. Everyone he guided counted on him, just not the way he hoped Toni would. Damn. "I promise not to let you down again."

He kissed the skeptical look right off her face, and this time she kissed him back. Oh, she was still mad, but as long she took it out on him with kisses, he could definitely get behind that.

He slid his hand under the back of her T-shirt, traced her spine, learned every bump and curve of her, and loved the feel of her body against his. She ended the kiss before he was ready, but since dinner was cooling, it was probably for the best.

Her cheeks were pink, her eyes dark and bright, and her lips swollen. She stole his breath.

He held her chair only to be met by a look of surprise. She surveyed the meal, and her eyes widened. "I can't believe you did all this." She sat, and he took his seat, scooting a little closer to her.

"Why? I cook every night I'm home. It's about an

hour and a half to Ketchum and the closest restaurant."
He reached over to serve her salad.

"If it were up to me, I'd starve."

"No, you wouldn't. You'd learn to cook after a month
of eating frozen dinners."

She gave him another incredulous look.

"What?"

She placed her napkin in her lap. "How do you know
so much about me?"

He sipped his wine and thought about it. "I spent the
entire day watching and listening to you. I think it would
take a lifetime to figure you out, but I have to hand it to
you, you fascinate me. I want to know everything about
you, and since you're tight-lipped about certain things, I
find it necessary to make deductions. It's good to know
I'm right."

Toni almost choked. She fascinated him? "What is
this, figure out the weird girl?" Suddenly it didn't feel
like the compliment it had a second ago.

Anger flashed in Hunter's eyes. "I don't think you're
weird. I think you're beautiful, passionate, and smart.
Fascinating. I say what I mean, Toni. I don't give back-
handed compliments. Why is it that's all you hear?"

"I don't know." She'd never thought about it. She'd
also never confronted anyone like she had Hunter. She
wasn't sure what it was about him that made her blurt
out the first thing that came to mind. She had no filter
where he was concerned. "I'm sorry."

He shot her the same look she'd seen when she told him
she wasn't interested, and at the time, she really hadn't
thought she had been. Sometime through the day that had
changed; now she just *wished* she wasn't interested.

Hunter was a complication she didn't need, but one she didn't want to give up either. When she'd thought he was dead, she'd been upset—like anyone would be, but it went deeper than that. She felt a profound sense of loss of something beautiful, something she might never find again. And that something covered a lot more feeling than a few kisses and a mind-blowing orgasm should instill. She'd known him only hours, but that wasn't the way it felt.

Toni took a bite of tuna with a piece of roasted red pepper and tomato on it. The flavors exploded in her mouth, and her eyes nearly rolled back in her head. Hunter was a seriously awesome cook. She'd be stunned to have a meal this wonderful at a five-star restaurant in Manhattan; to think he threw it together while she showered was unbelievable.

When she opened her eyes, Hunter watched and wore what could only be described as a shit-eating grin.

"This is so… incredible. I'm not sure I'm going to be able to carry on a conversation. I'm sorry, but this is…" She shook her head trying to come up with a proper label but failed. She needed a thesaurus. "Stunning, amazing, magnificent, luscious, delectable… they all pale in comparison."

Hunter took a bite and chewed. He looked like one of those über-sophisticated wine tasters, which was funny considering his attire—a T-shirt and shorts he'd risked his life to save. "I would have liked the tuna to be a tad more rare, but you distracted me."

Toni rolled her eyes. "It's perfect. Where did you learn to cook like this?"

"My mom is a great cook, so she started me off." He

sipped his wine and then holding it by the stem, rolled it around in the glass, watching it slide back into the bowl.

Toni stared at his hands, strong, scarred, and beautiful—hands that looked as if they should belong to a concert pianist, but full of character too.

"All the Kincaid men are good cooks, but Karma…" He shook his head, but the side of his mouth tipped up. "Mom was never able to get Karma to fall in line. I started as a short-order cook on the weekends during high school. I worked as a guide in the summers, which meant outdoor cooking, and then as a cook off season all through college, moving up through the restaurants my grandfather owned. Well, Grampa Joe really isn't related, but he's like a grandfather to me. I made it to the big time before I quit."

"You just quit?"

"Yeah, I did. I wasn't happy. I love to cook, but I don't like being indoors all the time, not to mention the hours. No, I like my life just fine the way it is." He took another sip of his wine.

Toni thought she saw a flash of something other than contentment. But then, what did she know?

"When I get a wild hair, I go to the restaurant on Castle Rock and give the chef a day off with pay. It's great to cook and know I can spend the next day skiing, teaching, or doing whatever else I want to do."

"It must be good to be king. Me, I pretty much have to do what I'm told." Toni looked down at her plate and found it was almost empty. She wanted to cry. She felt this way whenever she read a really great book too. She'd curse the dwindling pages.

"What's the matter?"

Hunter was watching her again.

"Dinner's almost gone. I hate when perfect things end—the perfect meal, a great book, a wonderful movie, a play. The entire second half, I know it's dying in a way. And no matter how wonderful it is, I'll never see it, taste it, read it, or hear it for the first time ever again."

He pushed his plate toward hers. "You're welcome to eat off my plate, but that won't help with the first time conundrum." He took a bite of tuna and looked deep in thought. "I guess it's a good thing we'll have a week of firsts, though I'd really hate to see you sad every time you experience one."

In one sentence he took the conversation from polite dinner chat deep into sexual territory. Judging from the heat she felt in her cheeks, she'd turned bright red. Damn her and her Irish skin. God forbid she should get her father's Italian olive complexion. No, she was paler than pale. Toni finished her wine only to have Hunter refill her glass the second it hit the table.

Hunter apparently wasn't waiting for a response, which was probably a good thing. It wasn't often she was left speechless.

He picked up her empty plate, and when she rose to help, he waved her back. "I promised you coffee. Do you want regular or decaf?"

She sank into her seat and picked up her wineglass. "What's the point of drinking decaf?"

"Ah, a woman after my own heart. I keep it in the freezer for my Mom when she visits. Caffeine keeps her up all night. Though, to be perfectly honest, if the same happened to you, you wouldn't hear me complaining. Dessert should be about done. I just need to finish the sauce. I hope you have room."

"Dessert?"

Hunter pulled a pan from the oven, flipped it onto a cutting board, and lifted the inverted pan off a weird looking loaf. Whatever it was smelled positively heavenly. He placed slices on two plates, arranging them so one slice leaned on the other. It drove her nuts that from where she sat, she couldn't tell what it was. After he had the servings on the plates to his satisfaction, he took a saucepan from the back of the stove and spooned something chunky over the top and then drizzled sauce over each portion like they did in restaurants. Then he took something small and red out of the refrigerator and placed it on one plate beside the tilted masterpiece. Weird, since there was only one something. He looked it over and cleaned the edge of the plate with a towel. Amazing.

He brewed the espresso, cut a sliver of lemon peel for each cup, and then set the coffee and dessert on a tray along with a sugar bowl and utensils. By the time he was done, she'd finished her wine.

Hunter carried the tray from the kitchen. "It's getting a little cold. Do you want me to light a fire? We can have our dessert in the living room."

"You don't have to go to any more trouble."

"It's no trouble. I have a gas starter, but even if I didn't, I wouldn't mind. Besides, it gets pretty cold at this elevation once the sun goes down."

She followed him to the living room. She hadn't noticed the cold until she stood, probably an effect of drinking too much wine. Hunter set the tray down, and she could only stare. "What is that?"

"Bread pudding with raisins and chocolate chips and an apple port wine compote." He set the plate with a rosette made out of what looked like the peel of the apple on the coffee table and sat beside her.

"Wow, Hunter, you can cook for me anytime. I wish I could reciprocate, but the best I can do is Toaster Strudel, and that's only if my toaster doesn't burn it. I feel as if I should take a picture of everything you serve."

"I'm told it's better if you just eat it." He put his arm around her and sipped his coffee, but made no move to sample his own portion.

"Okay." She cut off a piece, a little hesitant because she'd never been a pudding lover, but this stuff didn't look like any pudding she'd ever eaten. She scooped up some of the apple compote and tried to get the whole thing into her mouth without dripping it on Hunter's T-shirt. Sweet wine, apple, chocolate, and raisins flirted on her taste buds along with warm bread pudding. "Oh my God." She couldn't help but moan. "This is better than sex."

Reclining in a deep slouch, Hunter pulled her closer to his side, balancing the plate on his flat stomach before tasting his rose-less pudding. "No. Not better than sex, but I'll admit it's close."

"Yeah, well, speak for yourself. For me, this is definitely better than sex."

Hunter's nose brushed her temple. "That may be your experience so far; but then you've never made love with me."

———

Hunter sipped his coffee and watched Toni demolish the dessert while he wondered what kind of idiots she'd slept with if she considered his bread pudding better than sex. He knew it was good, but damn, he couldn't think of any food he'd eaten that could compare to great sex.

Toni ran her finger through the remnants of the port wine reduction. When she caught him watching, she reached over and slid her finger into his mouth. He really liked her. She was surprising and so refreshing compared to other women he'd dated. Her eyes widened before they darkened as he sucked her finger in, licking off the port and then nibbling the tip. When she tried to take her hand back, he caught her wrist and tugged her over, settling her on top of him. "There. That's much better."

"I'm crushing you."

"No, you're not." He kissed her before she could say whatever she was revving up to. Catching her just as she opened her mouth, he took full advantage of her surprise. She straddled him, pressing her chest to his as he slid his fingers through her thick, still damp hair.

She'd used his shampoo, and the scent on her drove him wild. Their tongues tangled, vying for control. Her mouth waged war as her body relaxed and molded to his. He could kiss her forever. She wrapped her arms around his neck, settling on his lap, coming in full contact with his erection. All the air escaped his lungs, and she moaned before rocking against him.

Damn. He'd planned a nice slow seduction—a good dinner, conversation, a couple bottles of wine, dessert and coffee, sipping port, necking on the couch... but once she came in contact with his dick, she went from zero to sixty in under three seconds. Not that he wasn't right there with her. He took her mouth the way he'd take her body if they both weren't fully clothed.

She pulled away. "Hunter?"

"Yeah?" His hands went to her hips, holding her still because if she did any more rocking and rolling on his lap, he just might embarrass himself.

"I guess it's time for sex."

"What do you mean… time for sex?"

"We've done the wining and dining, dessert in front of the fire, nice music. Sex comes next, right?"

Warning bells went off in Hunter's mind, and not just because she was straddling him and felt too good for words. "I cook for a lot of people. I don't sleep with all of them. Sex wasn't the reason I cooked."

"Sure, whatever. But if you don't want to have sex here on your couch, I think we should move. Not that I have a problem with having sex on the couch, if that's cool with you. I mean the fire's nice. I just don't want to wait, and you seem up for it. So—"

Ignoring the niggling feeling that something wasn't right, Hunter lifted her as he rose. He was probably making too much of it. Maybe it was a sign of inexperience or nerves. He swallowed her scream and tried to turn off those damn alarm bells as Toni wrapped her arms around his neck and her long legs around his hips. He didn't think he'd make it all the way to the bed, not for the first time, at least, but the rug in front of the fire was nice. He filled his hands with her ass, cushioning her as he knelt and came down on top of her.

"Here?" She reached for the hem of his shirt and pulled it over his head.

"Now." He grabbed the waistband of her shorts, since that's where his hands were, and thanked God she wasn't wearing underwear. She was already going to work on his shorts when he pulled her T-shirt up. She let out a laugh when her arms got stuck between them.

"I'll get my shirt. You lose your shorts."

"Deal." Seconds later, he had the condoms out of his pocket and his shorts off. He threw his clothes over his shoulder and took a second just to stare. Toni was spread out in front of him, the firelight dancing on her pale skin. "You are a vision. I don't know what part of you to kiss first."

A blush spread from her neck and moved to her face, which surprised him considering her frank discussion about where and when they'd have sex. He decided to start where her blush had. Toni had a long, graceful neck, and when his lips touched the pulse point on the side of it, she blew out a breath and ran her hands down his back.

"Hunter?"

"Toni?" He nibbled on her earlobe.

"Do you think I could get on top?"

He stopped what he was doing and rolled over. "Sure."

She lay on her side and did her own visual examination of his body. "It's not that I didn't like what you were doing. It's just that you've already seen me, but I didn't have time to explore you before you went and jumped into the river."

He cringed. "I'm sorry."

Toni ran her hand over him, her fingers tangling in his chest hair. "I didn't say that to get another apology. I just"—she slid her leg over his as her hand moved south—"want to explore you too."

His stomach muscles tensed as her fingers roamed over them. Hunter blew out a breath and sucked air back in when she reached for his erection, wrapping her fingers around it. She kissed a trail from one hard nipple to the other, her hand sliding down the length of him and back. He did his best to keep his hips on the floor when every instinct he had was to raise them. Her hair slid over his chest, tormenting him almost as much as her lips and busy tongue were. He gathered her hair, holding it, giving him a clear view.

The visual was one he was sure he'd see again and again in his dreams. Her breath on the sensitive head had him swallowing hard. He closed his eyes. So much for the lack of experience—Toni definitely knew what she was doing, and he wasn't sure how much more he could take. "Toni?" He hardly recognized his own voice.

"Problem?" She slid her mouth over him, wet, hot, and damn… her tongue traced the ridge around the head before sucking him in deep, her lips meeting her hand.

He thought he may have said no, but he was groaning too. It felt so amazing…

When Toni stopped, he wasn't sure if he was thankful or not. He took a deep breath as she kissed her way back up his chest. "So, how do you want to do this? Do you want me on top or what?"

She wasn't looking at him. Not his face anyway, and the alarm bells he'd been trying to ignore were louder now. He'd never choreographed making love before, never discussed it so technically. He pulled her on top of him, face to face, but she avoided his eyes. "Toni, what's going on?"

"Nothing… other than the obvious. I guess if I have to tell you, I'm doing something wrong."

"That's not what I'm talking about. What's going on with you?"

"I'm trying to have sex. I mean, you set the stage, sex comes next, and well, I'm here…"

"Shit." He rolled her off him. "I don't expect you to have sex with me because I made dinner."

"Do you just want me to finish what I started? I can do that." She stroked what was left of his erection, and he pulled her hands away.

"No." Damn. "I can't do this." He reached for his shorts, thankful he hadn't thrown them far, and stepped into them, zipping the fly. He tossed her the shirt and went looking for the boxers he'd pulled off her earlier. "We need to talk, and when we do, I'd appreciate it if you would look me in the eye."

Chapter 7

TONI SAT ON THE FLOOR BUTT NAKED AND TRIED TO figure out what the hell was going on. She'd thought things had been going fine until Hunter pulled a Dr. Jekyll on her. She slid the T-shirt over her head and caught the boxers he tossed her way before standing and anchoring her hands on her hips. "What is your problem? I thought you wanted to have sex. Don't tell me it wasn't part of the plan. I'm not an idiot."

Hunter walked shirtless to the kitchen and got himself a glass of water. "Do you want something to drink?" He drank a full glass and poured more.

"No. I want to know what I did to piss you off. I held up my end of the bargain. I was just trying to make sure you got what you wanted. I don't understand you. What did you want me to do?"

He came back to the living room and sat on the couch, shaking his head at her like you would at a dog that messed on the carpet and should know better. She pulled on the boxers and tried to control the urge to run. This was just great. She didn't know where the hell she was or how to get back to the inn. She was trapped. With him.

He patted the couch beside him. At least now he didn't look that angry. "Come here, and let's talk."

"You know, Hunter, I think we've talked enough. I guess I read you wrong. If you don't want to have sex, that's fine by me."

He placed his water on a coaster on the coffee table and stood, coming toward her. "I don't want to just have sex. I want to make love to you."

She rolled her eyes.

He put one hand on her waist and one finger under her chin, lifting it so she had to look at him.

"What do you want from me?"

"I've wanted to make love to you since the moment I met you. I want to learn all about you. I want to know what you taste like, how it will feel when I'm inside you and you're coming. I want to be able to look into your eyes and share that with you. That's not having sex. That's making love. Sex is the physical act. Making love is so much more."

Toni thought it was bad facing a mad Hunter, but this version was downright scary. She stepped away and looked him square in the chest. "I... I... I don't know if I'm..." Capable? Why did that sound so pathetic? And worse, why did it scare her so badly? She blinked away unshed tears. God, she was turning into a head case.

He moved closer and pulled her into his arms. "It's okay. We don't have to do anything until you're ready."

Jeez, what the hell was she in—a freakin' Lifetime Movie of the Week? "Are you for real? Guys don't turn down sex. What's wrong with you?"

She took a chance and looked him in the eye. He smiled at her—that toe-curling crooked smile she was learning to like a bit too much.

"Nothing is wrong with me. You've just been sleeping with the wrong men."

"Oh, and you're the right man?"

"I guess you'll find out when you're ready. Just say when."

"Yeah, *when* hell freezes over."

———⁓———

As if Hunter didn't feel like a total asshole already, that's what his sister and Gina would call him to his face if they knew what a mess he'd made of the whole situation. Still, there was a big difference between making love and sex, and he couldn't imagine a man not wanting to make love to Toni. She was beautiful, intelligent, and from what he could see, extremely passionate about everything but sex. To her, sex was something you did by rote, like brushing your teeth. He walked backward with her to the couch and pulled her down along with him. She tried to scoot out of his arms, but he had one wrapped around her waist. She couldn't go far. "Tell me about your last relationship."

"Relationship? I'd hardly call it a relationship—it was more like a series of dates. I've never had a let's-go-steady-talk-everyday-and-see-each-other-every-weekend kind of relationship, if that's what you're asking. Hence the book my mother gave me. See? There's nothing to talk about."

"Did you break if off, or did he?"

"Do you have a hearing problem?" Toni stared him down, but he wasn't about to give up. "I don't know. I guess it was just a case of a mutual lack of interest."

"The man must have been brain-dead."

She ignored his comment and continued. "I hadn't realized I hadn't seen him in a while until I ran into him at the gym." She took a deep breath and looked at him through the corner of her eye. "We exchanged nods."

"You exchanged nods?" What the hell did that mean?

"Yeah, pretty much."

"And you'd slept with him?"

Toni turned so her back was practically to him. He pulled her closer so she leaned against his side.

"I didn't sleep with him. I had sex with him."

He tucked her shoulder under his chin. "You had sex with someone who didn't rate more than a nod?"

With an exasperated sigh, she turned to face him. "Now that I think about it, I guess I wasn't interested in a repeat performance. If I had been, I would have talked to him. But..." She shrugged and shook her head. "No, it was definitely a case of a mutual lack of interest."

Toni stared into the fire, her mind probably going a mile a minute. Was she examining her life? Her relationships or lack thereof? He wasn't sure, but the expressions crossing her face told their own story. Her body tensed visibly as if she'd figured something out or maybe saw something in herself she wasn't happy with.

"You know, just because I had sex with Mark doesn't mean I sleep around a lot."

Hunter reached over, squeezed her thigh, and wished she hadn't given the creep a name. "If you're dating men like that Mark guy, it's no wonder you don't make a habit of it." He was thankful she laughed.

"So, Dr. Phil, what broke up your last relationship?"

"I work a lot, and I'm gone for extended periods. She wanted a nine-to-fiver. She's a nice woman, but I wasn't who she needed me to be."

Toni stared at him. "And you made love to her?"

He stared right back. "Yes."

"Does that mean you loved her?"

"No, it means I cared about her."

"Can you make love to someone you don't care about?"

"No. And in case you're wondering, I care about you, Toni."

She wrapped her arms around herself. "I guess I care about you too. I was really upset when I thought you were dead."

Hunter couldn't help but laugh. "I'm glad."

"You're glad I was upset?" She moved away from him. "You think that was funny?"

He leaned over, gave her a quick kiss, and slid closer. "No, I'm glad you care about me."

She broke eye contact. "Yeah well, this caring thing is new to me. I'm not sure I like it."

He kissed her again, and this time she held on for the ride. She was sweet and innocent for a woman who purported not to be. He slid his lips from hers and toward her ear. "Ah, another first. The first time is always scary."

He pulled her back onto his lap, sucked her earlobe into his mouth, and nibbled as she tilted her head, giving him more room. He wanted to explore her, inside and out.

He gave her ass a pat and wished he hadn't tossed her the boxers earlier. "We better get to bed. We're going to have to leave here by 8:00 a.m. to get to the inn in time for work tomorrow."

She didn't move off his lap. She turned her face so they were nose to nose. "What are we going to do in bed?" She was clearly uncomfortable, yet still direct.

Hunter held back a chuckle. He didn't want to get

slugged by her twice in one day. God she was sweet when she was completely out of her element. Her eyes got all wide. "We'll probably lie down, talk for a while, watch the stars come out, cuddle up together, and sleep."

"Oh." She slid off his lap and stood. If he wasn't mistaken, she looked a little disappointed.

"Something wrong?" He went to stir the fire, making sure it would be banked for the night before closing the screen. When he turned she was studying him so intently, she practically squinted.

"Are we going to make love?"

"I guess that's up to you." He hit the lights, put his hand on her lower back, and gave her a little push. "Come on."

~~~

Toni was more confused now than she'd been at any other time today, and that was saying a lot. Hunter slipped his arm around her and led her to his room. What the heck was he up to? She'd never met a guy who after a few false starts didn't just want to get off. He wanted to talk and cuddle? What was up with that? Not to mention all this talk of making love. She'd never known a guy to say the *L* word unless he was after something.

"I'll find you a new toothbrush." He switched on the lights in the bathroom, handed her one fresh from the dentist's goody bag, and turned to leave.

"You don't want to brush your teeth too?"

He shot a surprised look over his shoulder, and she took a second to drink him in. He was really beautiful for a guy. "I thought you'd want some space."

"You do have two sinks. I'm not afraid of spitting in front of you if that's what you're worried about."

"I'm not worried." He started brushing before passing her the toothpaste. He was the neat, squeeze-the-tube-from-the-bottom type guy. She squeezed from the middle. That was the way she'd always done it before, and she didn't think now would be a good time to change. He'd have plenty of time to squeeze the toothpaste back into place after she left, but for now, she wanted to shake things up, as least as much as he'd shaken things up in her world.

Toni didn't remember ever brushing her teeth in front of anyone—not a boyfriend or even a parent. She'd always been alone, though she chose to think of herself as the independent type. Even when she was little, she remembered coming home to an empty apartment, climbing up onto the counter of the bathroom to clean out her own cuts and scrapes from the playground. It was a far cry from the way Hunter cleaned her scrapes earlier. She couldn't remember another time anyone had taken care of her.

"What are you thinking about?"

She spit and rinsed, cleaning out the sink while she did. There was nothing worse than spit stains in a sink. He rinsed his too and even wiped down the countertop. "Nothing earth-shattering. I was trying to remember if I'd ever brushed my teeth with anyone before or shared a bathroom."

"No brothers or sisters?"

She shook her head, avoiding his eyes, and dried her hands on the towel. "Nope. I'm an only child."

"What about your parents?"

She put her toothbrush in the holder next to his for the morning. "They divorced when I was a baby. I guess one of them must have taught me to brush. I don't remember."

Hunter threw his arm over her shoulder and led her to bed, pulling down the covers. "I used to dream of having a bathroom to myself. I had to share with my sister and two brothers. The place was as busy as a one-hole outhouse at a keg party."

The big bed faced a wall of windows. She climbed in and scooted over. "Don't tell me you had an outhouse."

He slid in beside her and pulled her into his arms. "No, we had indoor plumbing and everything." He hit the lights, and the room went dark.

Toni didn't know what to do with her hands or how to lie there, especially since Hunter lost his shorts before joining her in bed.

Once her eyes adjusted to the darkness, he'd scooted down to her level with his head close to hers and pointed to something in the sky. "That, right there, is Pluto."

"Ah, an amateur astronomer." His naked body pressed against hers, his heat radiated through the T-shirt and boxers she wore, and he was discussing a planet? Or was it a star? She didn't know if Pluto was the planet that had recently lost its planet status, or maybe it was Uranus. She swallowed the laugh that always followed the word Uranus and did her best to stay very still.

He slid closer, and her hand hit something. She didn't need to be Einstein to figure out what that something was, especially since her hands were at her side. God save her from gorgeous, naked men who didn't want to have sex.

"I bought this place for the windows. I can look at the stars all night and not feel closed in. Look—the moon is a waxing gibbous."

She was still picturing what was lying against the back of her hand. "Huh?" She totally missed that last part.

"The moon. It's almost full."

His upper body was plastered to hers, and his erection twitched against her hand as his foot slid up the inside of her calf. They were still cheek to cheek and would be nose to nose if she turned her head toward him to speak. She tried to control her breathing. "You're a show-off." Controlling her breathing wasn't working very well. She sounded breathless. God, this talking crap was better than foreplay, or maybe it was foreplay.

"And I thought you'd be impressed." The rumble of his words traveled through her body. She was impressed all right—impressed, horny, scared, but mostly horny. Hunter was the most beautiful man she'd ever seen up close and personal, and if he was for real, he was nice, and in his own way, sweet and considerate. He also smelled amazing, like pine, fresh water, and a scent that was all his own. He lay naked against her with his erection rubbing her hip. How the hell was she supposed to carry on a conversation? He thought they'd talk and then to go to sleep? Sleep was *sooo* not happening. "When."

Hunter turned to look into her eyes. "When what?"

"You told me to just say *when*. I said it."

"You want to make love?"

More talk? She wanted to roll over on top and have her wicked way with him, but that's kind of what she'd done before, and he'd shot her down. She didn't think she could deal with that twice in a lifetime, no less on the same night. Taking a deep breath, she tried not to sound as nervous as she felt.

"I'm not sure I know how to make love. I'm guessing it has something to do with eye contact. Since you say there's a difference between making love and sex, I gotta wonder if it's like the difference between fresh-squeezed orange juice and frozen. Fresh is preferable, but frozen isn't half bad, and it lasts longer, which is a plus in the sack. So—"

Hunter kissed her. He didn't tell her what the difference was. He just rolled on top of her and silenced her with his mouth. She couldn't complain though; the man was a hell of a kisser. He wasn't a wet, sloppy kisser like most guys she'd tongue wrestled with. No, his kisses were full frontal assaults in the best possible way. He didn't just kiss with his mouth; he used his whole body. His hands roamed her breasts, her sides, the tender flesh of the inside of her elbows, behind her knees, all the while tongues tangled, parried, played. For other guys, kissing seemed to be something they did because they had to—like tagging first base on their run toward second. But not Hunter, he wasn't going anywhere fast. He paid more attention to kissing than most guys did to the ninth inning of the seventh game of the World Series.

With the score tied and bases loaded.

She finally stopped timing the kiss and laid back and enjoyed the feeling of his body on hers, the soft hair on the nape of his neck, the scratch of his beard against her chin, and the way his lips were soft and firm at the same time. Kissing Hunter wasn't a fight for control; it was more of a dance—slow, easy, and exciting.

Her hands explored his sides, his muscles rippling under her touch as wetness and heat pooled deep in her belly. He'd hardly touched her, and she was well past ready. Not to mention impatient. Damn, she'd spent the day on a sex roller coaster. There were so many ups and downs, she didn't know if it would ever pay off.

Hunter pulled his mouth from hers and put his upper body weight on his forearms, increasing the pressure on her pelvis, sending a mini-earthquake through her. A little more pressure would be all it would take.

"Toni?"

"Hunter? Does making love always involve talking? Because right now, I'm more interested in *doing*. I'm sure there will be plenty of time to talk about this later, okay?"

She pulled the T-shirt over her head then tossed it around his neck like a scarf, drawing him close. This time she was the one to silence him with a kiss. God it felt good. She sucked his tongue into her mouth and rolled her hips.

She kind of failed at the whole silencing thing since he groaned, but at least he wasn't talking.

When his body slid off hers, fear spiked through the haze of passion. A tug at the waistband of the boxers set her mind at ease and had her eyes blinking open only to be captured by his with some kind of magnetic force. She was incapable of looking away, not that she'd want to. He looked wild kneeling over her as he slid on a condom. His breathing was labored and his every muscle so pronounced, she wished she could trace them all with her tongue. His hair was mussed, his cheeks were high with color, and his eyes were dark and bright at the same time. All he was missing was a loincloth, and he could be the next Tarzan.

She reached for him, wishing she hadn't hurried him along quite so much. She would have liked to pick up where she'd left off earlier. Just the thought of it had her squirming. She imagined he'd go right for intercourse since he'd taken the time to don a condom, so she was surprised when he slid between her legs, held her hips in his big, rough hands, and didn't stop at kissing his way up her inner thigh.

In Toni's experience, oral sex was rarely done well, which, when she thought about it, was kind of like kissing. She shouldn't have been surprised that, like with kissing, when it came to oral sex Hunter clearly excelled. She was knotting the sheets in her fists within a minute. He took her through the paces with his mouth on her, teasing, tempting, torturing, and always controlling how close she got. She'd almost reach the point, and he'd pull her back before sending her right up to the brink. Her breath caught, and her back arched as his body rose over hers. There was a smile on his face, and those eyes held hers as his erection slid deep just as an orgasm crashed over her. Every move he made intensified the orgasm, swamping her, bombarding her with feelings so intense they drowned her, leaving her nothing to hold on to but him. She'd never experienced anything like it, and his eyes held hers captive, stripping her of all defenses. Leaving her exposed. Vulnerable. Scared.

"Hunter?"

"Stay with me Toni." With every thrust of his hips, she felt more and more out of control. They were connected in every way, their eyes, their hands, their bodies. He touched her mind, her soul. His body shook as another orgasm crashed through her. She thought she heard him call her name, but then she might have screamed his too. Her last coherent thought before her mind completely shut down was that this making love thing could not be good for her—nothing that amazing could be, or everyone would be doing it all the time. It was probably addictive.

Hunter had been blindsided. He'd heard rumors about things like this, but he hadn't believed them. Making love was great, even when it was bad. But damn, nothing had prepared him for making love with Toni. It was like they had some kind of cosmic connection that intensified everything a billion times. He was lucky he survived.

And he couldn't wait to try it again.

He slid his arm under her and rolled, pulling her along with him, and settling her on top. She fit like she was made for him. It felt incredibly right, just like making love had.

She remained quiet. When it came to making love, she definitely wasn't interested in conversation. He wasn't much for talking either, though something did need to be said. He wasn't sure what exactly that was. "You rocked my world" seemed a bit clichéd. But then the reason clichés became clichés were because at the heart of every good cliché was the truth.

"Toni?"

"Hmm?"

"Are you okay?"

"A huh." She shifted, using his chest as a pillow, and

then stilled. He wasn't sure how long they rested like
that. He enjoyed her weight on him as her breathing
evened out and felt her relax totally. When his lids grew
heavy, he rolled her off him before kissing her and getting up to rid himself of the condom. When he returned
to bed, she was snoring. It was a soft, quiet snore, but a
snore all the same. He slipped back in beside her, pulled
her into his arms, and spooned, feeling as if all was right
in his world.

———∿∿∿———

Toni woke with a start as the morning light shone on
her face. She blinked and tried to move, only to be held
in check by an arm wrapped around her waist. She'd
fallen asleep with Hunter. She'd never slept with anyone before and couldn't remember a time she'd slept so
well—which was weird considering she was in a strange
bed. Sleeping with a strange person. Not that Hunter was
strange exactly. Toni's thoughts evaporated when a kiss
landed on the crease of her neck where it met her shoulder. Hunter's arm moved, his hand caressing her from
breast to stomach. His body spooning hers slid into a
more assertive position—his leg slipped between hers.
His erection slid against her sex.

Another kiss, another slide, and the hand that had
been on her stomach moved south and hit the bull's-eye.

Her hips jerked against him as he slid back and forth.
If she arched her back just a little, he'd be buried deep
inside her. She wanted it with every fiber of her being.
Another first. And as Hunter would say, firsts were always scary.

"Hunter, please." Toni arched her back, the head

of his erection tight against her opening. She pressed her advantage.

"God, don't move, Toni. I'm not ready."

"Could have fooled me." She stilled, holding her breath. "I need…"

"I know, babe." He reached over her and pulled open the drawer to his bedside table. "Protection."

Protection. She closed her eyes and cursed herself for not considering that. Her only thought had been that she wanted him. Before she stopped chastising herself, he'd flipped her onto her back, spread her legs, and had his mouth on her. His tongue speared into her, and she teetered on the brink of orgasm.

Toni'd had a few orgasms in her day, but never so quick, never so strong, and never more than one. Each orgasm she'd ever achieved had been hard-won until Hunter.

The two of them together caused an explosive chemical reaction. It was hot, intense, and uncontrollable. She'd never had reason to hold back before. But with Hunter everything was different. She wanted to make this last. She might as well have tried to hold back the river.

Hunter slid up her body, holding her hands, and entwining their fingers before he entered her in one quick thrust, knocking the wind out of her. He filled her completely as pleasure mingled with pain. He stilled, and she wasn't sure if it was for her benefit or his. When her eyes locked on his, the possession she saw in them was her undoing.

Hunter might as well have put the word *mine* on the billboard in Times Square.

Worse, she liked what she saw. She'd never forget the thrill that rippled through her—that alone was enough to make her want to run for the hills even considering where she was.

Mine. Every thrust of his hips punctuated it. Mine. Every second of their connection magnified it. Mine. The sound of her name on his lips right before his soul-stealing kiss confirmed it.

Fear shot through her like a pinball—hitting one thought only to smack hard against another. Her breath caught in her throat just before the mother of all orgasms drowned everything out but his words.

"Stay with me, Toni. Stay with me."

No. She couldn't. Hunter was too much of everything. Too nice, too perfect, and too good at getting under her skin. Her first impression had been correct. Being with Hunter was more addictive than any narcotic with twice the buzz. He was in a word—dangerous.

She was done playing with fire. Well, just as soon as she could get away from him. But until then, she might as well enjoy the heat because she had a feeling it would be a cold day in hell before she'd experience anyone like Hunter again.

Toni came apart, and Hunter tried to hold on through the exquisite torture. It would be hours before they'd have the opportunity to be together again, and he wasn't ready to let this round end. He held on by a thread, but when she opened her eyes, their connection pulled him into a vortex of sensation leaving him completely defenseless. It was like going down a class six, rapid blind. He had no idea what lay ahead. The adrenaline rush was amazing, but the risk of uncharted waters had the hair on the back of his neck standing straight up. It was way too late to get back to shore, and he was already too far downstream to take a less dangerous course. He had no choice but to ride the rapids and hope for the best.

Hunter collapsed on top of her, and it was several minutes until he was able to move. She buried her face in his neck, her breathing almost as erratic as his, and her body tensed. He ran his hand down her back meaning to soothe, but doing just the opposite. She moved, her inner muscles tightening around him, and to his amazement his body responded in kind.

"Toni, if we're going for round two, I've got to take care of the condom."

"No time." She gave him a quick kiss and lifted herself off him. "I'm just going to jump in the shower. Can I borrow a pair of sweats or something until I get back to my cabin?"

"Sure." Hunter rolled onto his side and watched her walk naked to the bathroom. There, across her lower back, was a tattoo very much like the one he'd pictured when he met her. Shit. He could kick himself for not taking the time to examine it. A mistake he wouldn't make twice. He waited for the shower to start and then went to join her. He saw no reason to waste water.

Chapter 8

TONI SET THE WATER TEMPERATURE IN THE SHOWER, and before she could even close the glass door, Hunter stepped in behind her. That was so not a good thing.

He wore a shit-eating grin, as if he'd just hit the jackpot. His eyes sparkled as he backed her up against the very cold wall and kissed her senseless.

It took a moment, but she finally remembered she was supposed to be staying away from him. He was dangerous after all. She ended the kiss. "What was that about?"

"When I met you I wondered if you had any ink and pictured a bat on your lower back. When you got out of bed, I finally noticed your tatt. It's almost exactly like I imagined, but yours is nicer."

"You imagined me naked?"

"No, I just wanted to put myself in the position to do a full-body search. I didn't imagine you naked until later."

"You're such a dog." She stepped under the showerhead and, eyes closed, turned to wet her hair.

"If you think I imagine every woman I meet naked, you're wrong. I told you. I've wanted you since the moment I first met you. Maybe before that. I've been curious about you since we spoke on the phone in January. That's not something that happens often."

"Thanks. I feel so special."

He poured shampoo into his palm and ran his hand over her head before lathering her hair and massaging her scalp. "You are. And unlike you, I'm not being face-tious. Have I ever told you that I love your hair?"

"No. You haven't." She really sucked at staying away from dangerous men. Toni held back a groan as Hunter massaged her head, neck, and shoulders. Especially dangerous men with talented hands.

"Well, I do, and I love your tattoo."

"Thanks."

He turned her around to rinse her hair.

She visualized putting up defense shields like they did in *Star Wars*, but he wasn't letting her. It would probably be easier if he wasn't running his hands up and down her body. Darn him.

When he took the only bar of soap, she wrestled him for it. There was no way she'd survive a body massage—not without jumping him.

She watched him as she lathered up. Why did he have to look so good? The water sluiced over his body, his muscles making little ripples as it traversed the hills and valleys of his abdomen—until it reached his... Her eyes darted from his growing erection to his face just in time to catch the lopsided grin she was beginning to recognize.

"Don't even think about it. We don't have time." She turned to lower the water temperature. They both needed to cool off.

Hunter wrapped his hands around her waist and drew her back to him. She glanced at him over her shoulder.

"We have plenty of time if we grab breakfast to go."

Oh no. "I doubt there's a Mickey D's around the corner."

His erection nestled in the crevice of her bottom. "The coffee's on a timer. It will be waiting for us when

we get out, and I have a lot of quick breakfast fixings."
His hands were already tormenting her, and once his
mouth joined in, she was a goner. She had absolutely no
willpower where Hunter was concerned. Her defensive
shields couldn't stand up to an all out assault by Hunter
Kincaid. She was totally outgunned.

———

Hunter wiped the steam off the bathroom mirror as Toni
slipped out. He spread a handful of shaving cream over
his face, wet the blade, and took the first swipe, only
to discover it wasn't the sharpest blade in the box. He
usually shaved once every three days when he was in the
mountains. Shaving on the trail was way overrated. He
wasn't due for another couple days, but he'd rather have
some good face time with Toni without worrying about
giving her beard burn.

Pulling a fresh razor out of the cabinet, Hunter tossed
the old one and made a two-pointer into the trash can.
Instead of hearing a satisfying ping of an empty can,
he heard more of a muffled thud. Ah, the box Toni's
toothbrush came in.

Checking his reflection in the steamy mirror, Hunter
saw the telltale grin of a guy who'd had the best sex
of his life three times in the last twelve hours—a man
who liked knowing there was another toothbrush in the
holder next to his. It had been awhile.

He glanced at the toothbrush holder, and his smile
died. His was the only one there. He looked around expecting to see Toni's on the counter, but it wasn't. It
wasn't in the drawer where he kept the now squished
tube of toothpaste. Where else would she have put it?

The niggling feeling that something was wrong returned with a vengeance. She didn't seem the type to
take a toothbrush with her. It wasn't as if she didn't have
one at the inn—he'd seen it standing in the cup beside
the sink when he checked out her cabin. He peered into
the trash can.

"What the hell?"

Toni might not have said much after making love, but
tossing the toothbrush in the trash made a commanding
statement.

He should finish shaving before going to talk to her
since he didn't want to walk around all day with one
clean-shaven stripe down the side of his face. Nor did
he want to stalk through the house naked, wearing only
shaving cream and a towel. Besides, he had no idea what
to say to her without sounding like an idiot. Why did
you throw out your toothbrush? Not planning on using
it or me again?

He took a swipe and removed a sliver of his chin.
"Shit." Shaving while angry wasn't a great idea. He
stuck a piece of toilet paper on the cut and continued,
feeling like a first-class fool.

He rinsed his face, wrapped a towel around his waist,
and stomped out of the bathroom. The T-shirt and boxers
she'd worn the night before were tossed on the unmade
bed, and the sweats he'd set out for her along with her
bathing suit and cover-up were gone. The last thing he
needed was a reminder of her when he returned home,
so he ripped the sheets off the bed, rolling them and her
clothes into a ball before tossing it in the hamper.

It was 7:30 a.m.; he still had a half hour before
they had to leave. He heard her rummaging around his

kitchen, helping herself to breakfast. It was just as well. He'd lost his appetite.

Hunter grabbed a set of sheets from the linen closet. Better to spend the time making his bed and getting a better handle on his temper than saying something he'd probably regret later. Hell, he couldn't think of one thing to say that wouldn't make him sound like a freakin' pansy. And he most certainly wasn't a pansy.

His phone rang, and he picked it up. "River Runners."

"It's Trap. I thought you'd sound more cheerful this morning."

He held the phone on his shoulder and tossed the open fitted sheet over the bed. "Oh yeah. Why's that?"

"If I need to explain, you've got even bigger problems than a nonexistent love life."

Hunter pulled the sheet around the corner of the mattress. "Wanna tell me what the hell were you thinking leaving me and Toni here like that? She practically had a meltdown when she saw you heading downriver without us."

"Damn. Karma and James thought you two would like the time alone. I was outvoted."

He tossed the flat sheet over the bed with a snap. "Trap, you're in charge when I'm not around. It's impossible for you to be outvoted."

"I thought I was doing you a favor. Sorry. From the sound of it, you must have struck out."

"No comment." He adjusted the length of the top sheet and then started the hospital corners. "Was there a reason you called?"

"Yeah. James wanted to know what the plan is for the day. Toni has the schedule."

Hunter stuffed a pillow in the case and tossed it on the bed before reaching for another. "Mountain biking on Galena Summit."

"You want us to meet you at the lodge?"

He drew the blanket over the sheets and smoothed them down. "No, we're leaving for the inn in a few minutes. Toni needs to change clothes." Hunter pulled up the comforter and tossed the throw pillows up against the headboard. "We'll be at the meeting at 9:00 a.m. as scheduled. Just get the equipment together— and Trap?"

"Yeah?"

"Stay the hell out of my business and my love life."

Hunter rolled his eyes at his brother's laughter.

"So, you do have a love life, huh? I was beginning to wonder. You and Toni looked hot and heavy by the river."

"Yeah, well, looks can be deceiving." Hunter ended the call and dropped his towel in the hamper before rummaging through his drawers for clothes.

"Are you about ready to go?"

He looked over his shoulder to find Toni holding two travel mugs, staring at his bare ass through the doorway. Great. "I'll be ready in a minute." Since they wouldn't be on the river, he stepped into boxer briefs and then shorts.

She strolled into the bedroom, sipping her coffee like nothing was wrong. Like he hadn't just found her toothbrush in the damn trash can.

"Who was on the phone?"

He turned, shaking out a fresh T-shirt then slipping his arms into it. "Trapper." Hunter pulled it over his head and ran his hands through his almost dry hair. "He wanted to know what the plan was. James told him you had the schedule."

The sweats she wore hung off her hips. She handed him a mug and hiked them up. "If he and James were so interested in finding out about the schedule, they shouldn't have stranded us here. I had planned to go over it with everyone after we got back."

"I already gave Trapper an earful, but I can't say I'm sorry it happened." He tried to figure out if she regretted making love last night. And this morning. Twice.

"Hey, you don't hear me complaining about last night, but I reserve the right to be royally pissed at anyone who thought it was a good idea to take off without us. I'm managing this trip. That's kinda hard to do when I'm miles away with no way to communicate with the people I'm supposed to be managing. Believe me, James will hear about it when we return."

He watched her over the rim of his mug. She might not be complaining, but the toothbrush told him she wasn't looking forward to a repeat performance—at least not here. Maybe she was one of those women who liked staying in her own place. He just hoped he'd be welcome too. He'd planned to stay at the inn for the duration of the contract anyway. He even had his duffel bag packed and sitting in his truck.

Hunter didn't know which end was up. He took two steps toward her to see how she'd react, and when she didn't move, leaned in for a kiss. He saw her smile when she realized what he was about. Just a quick friendly kiss and he felt a lot better. "Thanks for the coffee. I needed that."

"You're welcome. I hope you like bagels and cream cheese. I packed a couple for us to eat on the way."

"Sounds good." He decided not to take the whole toothbrush thing personally. After all, she hadn't said anything to make him think there was a problem. But then she hadn't said much of anything to make him think there wasn't a problem either. He tossed his daypack on the bed. "I need to get some things together in here. I think your bag is out on the couch."

"Oh right."

He watched her go, and when she was out of sight he took a deep breath, reached into the bedside table, and put his condom stash in the inside pocket, all the while thanking Karma for her forethought, even though the idea that his little sister bought him condoms weirded him out considerably. He just wished he knew whether or not Toni was interested in using any more of them. He zipped up his pack and on his way past his desk remembered the book he'd asked Karma to bring. Maybe it would help him to figure out what was going through Toni's mind. He didn't hold out much hope, but it couldn't hurt.

Toni sat in the Jeep, sipped her coffee, and watched the way the mountains continuously changed color. She stretched out in her seat, little twinges reminding her of what she'd spent the night and all morning doing with Hunter. A woman could go a lifetime without having sex that good. She should know—she had.

"What are you thinking?" Hunter took her hand in his and brought it to his lips for a kiss.

There was absolutely no way she was going to tell him. "The coffee definitely makes up for the bagel."

"Not to mention the sex."

"You don't hear me complaining about the sex, do you?"

Hunter still hadn't released her hand. He kept busy tracing little circles on the inside of her wrist. It was distracting as hell.

Hunter shot her a sideways glance along with a cocky grin, and then returned his eyes to the road. "No, but then you haven't said a word about making love."

"What's to say?"

"Way to kill a man's ego, Toni. Do you do this to all the guys you date?"

"We're not dating."

"No? Then what are we doing?"

"We're having a fling. Dating insinuates the possibility of a future. You and I both know there's no future."

"We do?"

She turned and really looked at him for the first time since they got out of the shower. "You can't be serious. Hunter. I live in New York. You live here. What are we going to do? Fly cross-country for a booty call a few times a month?"

"Is that the only problem?"

"There is no problem. You've known me what—less than two days?"

He shot her one of his crooked smiles that curled her toes. "Calm down, Toni. I'm not proposing. I'm merely keeping an open mind. That's all."

"An open mind?" She looked toward the heavens. "He's keeping an open mind." Relieved when he turned into the inn's driveway, Toni tossed open the door as Hunter rolled the Jeep to a stop in front of the lodge, her gaze zeroing in on James. She slid across the seat to step out and realized Hunter still held her hand. Toni looked down at their joined hands, and then at Hunter. "Don't do this now."

"Do what? I was only going to tell you that it looks as if Trapper and James have the equipment ready to go." He pointed over at a trailer hooked up to a big SUV.

"Thanks." Okay, so she got to wear the dunce cap for the day. She'd been afraid he'd pull one of those he-man overtures like kissing her in front of God—or in this case, James—and everyone. Then she remembered the entire crew had witnessed her kissing Hunter during their desertion, while floating away in those damned orange boats.

She took a deep breath and stepped out of the Jeep, heading straight for her cabin. First things first—she had to change—she didn't look very professional wearing her bathing suit under a huge pair of Hunter's sweatpants—then she'd have a little chat with James, the deserter.

Of all people, Toni thought she could trust James. He knew how freaked out she was to be there. He was her best friend—her *only* friend really—and understood how she felt about being left behind. The fact that he'd left her with Hunter didn't matter. He'd left.

She unlocked her cabin and tossed her bag on the couch on the way to the bedroom. Thinking about the stunt James had pulled had her spitting mad, not to mention embarrassed. Did he think she needed his machinations to get a date? If she had wanted to sleep with Hunter, she could have jumped him in her cabin as easily as his. That way, she wouldn't have to be trapped with him, she wouldn't have had to sleep with him, and she wouldn't have woken up with him either. Of course, she had to admit spending the night at Hunter's was no hardship. She surely ate better at Hunter's than she would have at the inn. It was nice to have the privacy, and it wasn't as if anyone cared who she chose to sleep with.

Toni stripped before rummaging through her drawers, wondering what one wore on a photo shoot not involving water in the middle of the wilderness at the summit of a mountain almost nine thousand feet above sea level. She dragged on a thong—always a safe choice considering she had no idea what she'd be wearing over it, pulled on her black poison skull, button-up sleeveless top with a cute little ruffle around the hem, and searched for something that would work. She held up a red, stretchy, short skirt with rivets along the bottom. Cute, sexy, and still comfortable. Good. Now for the shoes. She took out her favorite ankle boots with bat buckles, and after pulling on a pair of black thigh-high stockings and her skirt she stepped into them and smiled. Toni looked like herself again. Better to handle whatever came her way.

As if on cue, there was a knock on the door. She answered it and found James wearing a sheepish grin.

"You're on my shit list."

He pulled her into a hug before holding her at arms-length and looking her up and down. "Don't tell me you didn't get lucky with our mountain hottie."

"That's completely beside the point. You promised you wouldn't leave without me, and you did anyway.

Some friend you are. You know how I feel about being out here. You practically threw me into a full-blown panic attack."

"Oh, come now. Hunter was there to comfort you. I'm sorry you were upset, but I can't say I was disappointed to see you and Hunter practicing your full-frontal snogging."

"I'm here to do a job, and I don't need Hunter complicating it."

James followed her to her bedroom and sat on the bed while she brushed out her hair. "A little complication never hurt anyone, especially when a man looks as good as Hunter. I think you'd want to see him complicate the hell out of your time here. He's just what the doctor ordered. A woman like you needs to learn to live a little."

"This from the man who only yesterday lectured me about the difference this trip could make to my career. Now I'm supposed to learn to live a little?" Toni parted her hair in the back and smoothed one side, tilting her head before tying off a pigtail. "I live just fine on my own."

When Toni tied black skull-and-crossbones ribbons on the pigtails, James shook his head.

She looked at his reflection in the mirror. "But they match my blouse."

He got up and let out a long-suffering sigh. "Yes they do, but Toni, sometimes less is more. Unless more is an improvement, it's best to leave well enough alone."

She untied the bow and tossed the ribbons onto the dresser. "The same can be said about men."

James turned and looked as if he couldn't believe what he'd just heard. "Are you telling me that more time with Hunter would just be more?"

"That's exactly what I'm saying."

"You know, it's bad enough you're lying to me. I just hope you're not lying to yourself." Shaking his head, James headed toward the door. "Toni, there's a whole lot you've yet to learn about relationships."

Before she could ask what exactly he was talking about, he walked out and shut the door behind him. She threw herself on her bed and hugged the pillow to her chest. If James didn't buy it, she doubted Hunter would. Still, what choice did she have?

———ᴖᴖ———

Hunter leaned against Galena Lodge, reading his copy of Toni's book with the cover rolled back so no one could see the title. With a pen in his hand he made notes in the margins and kept one eye on Toni while she worked. He couldn't believe he'd been reduced to reading self-help dating books.

He felt more than heard Trapper come up to him. His brother was as quiet as a mountain lion when approaching its prey. Hunter slipped the book into his backpack and straightened.

"Wanna tell me why you're not wearing the satisfied grin of a man who spent a sex-filled night with a beautiful woman who seems to have a penchant for handcuffs?"

Hunter didn't shift his gaze from Toni and Yvette's conversation. He didn't need to see the look on Trapper's face. He could hear it in his voice. "Something's going on with Toni, and I can't figure out what. For someone who fades into the woodwork, she's spent the last six hours surrounded by people."

"She's doing her job."

"Yeah, and avoiding me." Hunter took the cold bottle of water Trapper offered him. Too bad Trapper didn't come just bearing water—no, it was liberally sprinkled with advice and lectures. Hunter really hated lectures, and for a guy who never had a relationship last more than seventy-two hours, Trapper gave more relationship advice than Dear Abby and Dr. Ruth put together.

"What do you want her to do? Just stop the photo shoot and come over here where you're pouting so she can ease your worried mind?"

"I'm not worried, and I'm sure as hell not pouting." Not exactly. He was confused—not something that happened often—and confusion didn't sit well with him. He wasn't the type to play games. He cared about Toni and told her so. As of last night, she said she'd cared about him too. So what the hell was going on now?

Hunter finally caught Toni's eye. She looked up from her conversation with Yvette and gave him a nod before turning away.

"Son of a bitch. She did not just give me the nod."

Trapper grabbed his arm. "The nod?"

Hunter shook off his brother and anything he might have said.

Toni closed her eyes and tried not to snap at the Lycra-clad redhead who'd been the fourth person to ask about her and Hunter. Fifth, if you counted James, who was still on Toni's shit list. She was doing her best not to lose her patience. "Yvette, do you have something you need to ask me about the shoot?"

"No. I just wanted to find out Hunter's status."

"Don't you think he would be a better judge of that than I would?"

"I don't know. I've watched the way he looks at you, and I can't figure out if he's undressing you with his eyes, or if he's going all caveman."

Visions of Hunter kneeling naked beside her, doing the best caveman impression she'd ever seen, swam through Toni's mind. Yeah, he could play one hell of a caveman all right. She blinked and tried to focus on Yvette.

"Still, what Hunter thinks isn't the issue. It's whether or not you're receptive to him that matters."

"Excuse me?" Could Yvette be for real?

Yvette looked at Toni as if she had the IQ of a gnat. "If you're not interested, Hunter's ripe for the pickin', and I do love pickin' up men like him. Very hot caveman types."

Toni swallowed the urge to claw the shrew's eyes out just before Yvette pasted on her most beatific smile — the one reserved for the cameras. "Oh, oh, oh. Look out. Caveman at three o'clock." She sucked in her flat stomach making it look concave and pushed out her surgically enhanced breasts, displaying them to great advantage, before flipping her hair. Toni wondered if Yvette had any idea of how bad a cliché she'd become. Probably not.

Closing her eyes, Toni rubbed her forehead to ease the tension headache taking hold, wondering what in the world she'd done to deserve this. She'd had about all the crap she was going to take.

As if the sun slid behind a cloud, Toni and Yvette were suddenly standing in a shadow. Since the last she looked there wasn't a cloud in the sky, chances were good the shadow was man-made, so to speak. She took a deep, calming breath only to catch a whiff of Hunter.

The guy always smelled really good but was definitely not at all calming.

"Yvette, would you give me a moment with Toni?"

Yep, definitely man-made. Definitely Hunter.

"Sure. I'll just be in the lodge if you need anything. Anything at all, Hunter."

It was all Toni could do not to stick her booted foot out to trip the Lycra'd bimbo. If the shoot had been over, Toni would have. She'd have enjoyed the hell out of it too. After getting a glimpse of Hunter's angry face, she was tempted to turn tail and follow Yvette. "Are you going to speak, or are you just gonna stand there snarling?"

"I'm not snarling."

"Fine, whatever." Toni tried on her best smile for size. She still had to work with him after all. "I have two photographers, models, and the rest of the staff waiting for me. So if there's something you need to say, now would be a good time to do it."

"You want to discuss it here?"

"No, I don't want to discuss it at all, but since you're fired up about something and stomped all the way over here, I don't seem to have much of a choice in the matter."

Hunter looked at the proximity of the others and took her arm. "Come over here." He tugged her to the trees.

Great. She pulled her arm out of his grasp, not wanting to go any farther. "What is the problem?"

"I was wondering the same thing—you're the one who just gave me the nod."

"You want to know what my problem is? Fine. I'm up on the top of a freakin' mountain at nine thousand feet in The-Middle-of-Nowhere, Idaho, and every female and a good portion of the males have a thing for the man they know I spent the night with. And if that's not bad enough, every one of them expects me to give them a report on my relationship status, instead of doing my job. They should be thinking about the damn photo shoot and not my sex life or theirs. But no, they're more interested in who gets you next."

"What?" If the shocked look on Hunter's face was an act, he missed his calling.

"You heard me. So forgive me if I'm just a tad put off by the situation."

"You're jealous."

"You wish." Ooh, that arrow looked like it hit home. Shit. She could really be a bitch sometimes; it just popped out when she least expected it. She took another Hunter-scented, not-so-calming breath, and lightened her tone. "I'm just—" Frustrated, horny, and okay, she'd admit she didn't like the way everyone stared at him as if he was a slab of meat in the prime aged beef section of the Fairway Market. She definitely didn't want to go there. "Look Hunter, this thing—you and me, last night—is a complication I don't need."

He stepped closer, just a hairsbreadth away—so close, so tempting, so damn sexy. "There's nothing complicated about it."

He had that bedroom voice going, all low and gravelly, and her body reacted like Pavlov's dogs to a ringing bell. Shit.

"All you have to do is kiss me and then get back to work."

"Kiss you? Are you dense? Hearing impaired? Delusional?"

He smiled that crooked smile that made her want to fan herself. "No, but I know people. One kiss is all it'll take to keep everyone from wondering what's going on with us. You've been avoiding me like the plague. Just give me a kiss, make it a good one, and everyone will know we're together. Their questions will be answered, and we can go about our day."

"But we're not together. We're not anything."

"What?" He took a step closer and bent down a little so they were face to face. "We were something several times last night, not to mention this morning. What happened between then and now?"

"This." She threw her hands up to encompass the mess of a shoot. "This is what I was afraid of. Everyone's more interested in watching us than getting their work done."

Hunter set his hands on his hips. "And you're doing nothing but giving them more fodder for the gossip mill."

"Me? I'm not the one who stormed over and took me away from my work. I'm not the one who spent the entire shoot glaring at me from the lodge. No, that was all you. I'm putting my foot down. I can't do this and do my job effectively. I'm sorry."

"So that's it? You're sorry?"

She looked him in the eye and nodded. "That's all I'm capable of."

"That's bullshit, and you know it. You're not incapable. You're scared. You're using this as an excuse to avoid me just like you've spent your life avoiding all the other things that scare you."

"Am not."

"Are too. That's why you avoid Central Park, and that's why you threw away your toothbrush this morning."

"How do you know about that?"

"I saw it in the trash, and I certainly didn't put it there."

"You know what, Hunter? You can tell yourself whatever you want. If that story makes you feel better—have at it."

"Toni, it's normal to be scared. It's to be expected even. But the toothbrush thing surprised me. I've watched you fight your demons since you got here. Until this morning, I never took you for a coward."

She turned and stalked across the grass toward the lodge. "Yeah, well cowards live to tell the tale. Right now, I'd be happy to survive this trip."

Chapter 9

TRAPPER STEPPED OUT OF THE SHADOWS. "THAT DIDN'T go well."

Hunter stuffed his hands in his pockets to keep from punching something or someone, namely his big brother. "Thanks for the recap. I'd never have figured that out on my own." He kicked a nearby fallen limb and turned back to Trapper. "What the hell were you doing? Spying on me?"

Trapper took off his hat and inspected the hatband. "Believe me. Your love life isn't all that interesting. Especially now. I just came to make sure you were wearing flame retardant boxers—I haven't seen a crash and burn like that in a while." He spun his hat around on his finger and flinched. "She threw away the toothbrush you gave her? Man, that's harsh."

"It wasn't an engagement ring for God's sake. It was just a damn toothbrush. Don't you have some model to chat up, or God forbid, some work to do? I'm not paying you to hide in the woods and spy on me."

"You, little Brother, are not paying me at all. So don't even go there."

Hunter stared down Trapper for a few beats until he realized how stupid it was to be pissed off at his brother. He broke eye contact, took off his baseball cap, and beat it against his thigh. He still wanted to punch something—a tree would hurt too damn much,

and Trapper didn't look like he was going to do his
buddy a favor and give him an excuse to let off some
steam. No. He looked like he was going into lecture
mode, which was all fine and good, when Trapper was
wearing his judge's robe and had a captive audience
as he lorded over everyone in his courtroom. But they
weren't in court, and Hunter wasn't in the mood for
another lecture.

"What are you gonna do to change her mind?"

Hunter hadn't expected that. "How does anyone
change a woman's mind—especially a woman as difficult as Toni?"

Trapper set his hat back on his head and adjusted the
brim to its usual cocky angle. "I guess all you really
have to do is give her a reason to question her decision. Since Momma didn't raise no fools, it shouldn't
be all that hard to figure out, even for a simple mind like
yours." A slow smile spread across Trapper's face. "I
don't know about you, but I've got a job to do. I have
two other siblings and a bunch of models to keep a close
eye on." He turned on the heel of his scuffed cowboy
boot and ambled back to the lodge.

Hunter pulled his phone off his belt and called Emilio
again. He hadn't been able to reach him the day before
and felt the kid slipping away. "Emilio, it's Hunter
again. Give me a call, and tell me how things are going.
I always have my phone on me. Call me anytime. I'd
like to see you come out here again. Let's make a plan
next time we talk." He repeated his number twice then
hit the end button. "Damn."

By the time Hunter looked back at Toni, she was
walking toward him. He thought she might be coming

back to talk. His mood lifted until he saw the trail map she studied and the group that followed.

Toni stopped at the trail marker and nervously fingered her collar before squaring her shoulders and stepping onto the trail. He couldn't believe it. In order to avoid him, Toni was going to start the next part of the shoot without him. He was the guide for cryin' out loud. If she didn't want to go with him, she could have requested Fisher, Trapper, or Karma. But since she didn't, Hunter really had no choice but to make sure she and the crew got to where they were going safely.

He pulled the water bottle from his pack, took a long drink, wiped his mouth on the back of his hand, and headed toward the trail. He stayed behind her, not wanting to give Toni an excuse to send him packing. He'd let her go on thinking she was without a guide, but he'd do his job and keep her and everyone else safe.

Hunter followed and worked on a game plan to show Toni she was all wrong about them. The only strategy he came up with was to do his job and make sure Toni could do hers. Close proximity wouldn't hurt either. He just had to show her he was more of an asset than a complication.

~

Toni looked from the little blue line representing a stream on the map to the roaring torrent of water before her and couldn't believe her luck. The line sure didn't look like an accurate representation of that raging waterway. How was she supposed to get her crew and all the equipment across that?

The rest of the group formed a semicircle, all probably

thinking the same thing—she should have asked Hunter or one of the River Runners to guide them. This was definitely not her brightest move. She could practically read their minds. She sucked, and Hunter would know what to do, or better yet, would have known the creek was too big to cross.

They all stared at the water with such intensity it was as if they believed if they concentrated hard enough, a bridge would suddenly appear. She wished.

Toni looked from the stream to the map and back again, hoping there was another trail coming from somewhere accessible which would give them a less arduous path to their destination. She didn't see one. The only thing she was sure of was she had to find a way to cross it to get to the spot on the map Bianca had marked with an *X*—the place Bianca described in her extensive notes as the perfect site for the rest of the photo shoot.

A hand came out of nowhere, reaching across her right shoulder from behind. She screamed, jumped, and spun around, losing her balance just as she recognized Hunter. He grabbed her arm, keeping her from tumbling into the raging creek.

"What are you trying to do, give me a freakin' heart attack?" She took a swing at him. Unfortunately, Hunter reacted like he'd been a prizefighter in a past life, easily avoiding contact. When she didn't connect, Toni found herself spinning again. Arms flailing, she flew backward toward the water. She was going in. She was going to be swept downstream like those people on the news who do stupid things like playing in storm drains during a Nor'easter.

Hunter grabbed her around the waist, pulling her

against his chest, and trapped her arms at her sides. "Calm down, will ya?" He held her fast, whispering in her ear.

"You just scared me into next week, and you're telling me to calm down? What do you do, spend all your time thinking up ways to torture me?" She struggled against Hunter's hold.

He didn't release her until he had dragged her well away from the creek, which was just fine by her. He seemed to swallow back a few responses. One look in his eyes, and she knew he was thinking of all the ways he'd tortured her just that morning and left her wanting more. Damn him. She tried to regret their recent sexual acrobatics. It was an epic failure. Still, he didn't need to know that.

"I didn't mean to scare you. I was just trying to show you there might be a place we could cross the creek about a hundred yards up." He took the crumbled map from her shaking hands and pointed it out. "Here, where this other trail crosses the stream. If that's the trail I remember, there's a fallen tree just beyond it that's large enough to walk over, even carrying bikes and equipment. Do you want to wait here while I go and check it out?"

Stay here and face the humiliation of having been saved twice by a river jockey? Not happening. Toni shook her head. "No, I want to see it for myself. Everyone else, wait here. I'll be right back." She turned without waiting for a response and followed the stream.

Hunter cleared his throat.

Toni wanted to hit him again, and Lord knew, except for Hunter, she'd never hit anyone in her life. She wasn't a violent person. What was it about him that brought out the worst in her? "What is it now?"

"Come and look at the map."

He was so damn cool and collected. He spoke to her like someone might to an unruly kindergartner, and it didn't set well. She blew the bangs out of her eyes and stomped back to him, her arms wrapped around herself to keep from hitting him again and losing what was left of her temper.

He stood beside her. "The lodge is here." He pointed to a spot on the map. "We're on this trail." He followed the dashed, black line to the blasted blue line. "This is the stream." His finger stopped its movement. "The place I mentioned is up here." He ran his finger along the stream to another trail.

"Oh." She'd been going in the wrong direction. He could have easily taken the opportunity to make an even bigger fool of her than she had herself, which was saying something. She calmly took the map, and avoiding everyone's eyes, walked toward the possible fallen tree. When she didn't hear Hunter, she turned and caught him staring at her with a weird look on his face. She didn't even want to guess what he was thinking. "Are you coming?"

"I'm right behind you." He shouldered his pack and followed her.

When they were out of sight of the rest of the group, Toni turned to face him, careful to anchor her hands on her hips to keep them from shaking. He walked so silently through the woods, he was like a ghost—she'd had to look back for him a few times to assure herself he hadn't vanished into thin air.

She'd been terrified when she took the group away from the lodge and led them into the wilderness. She repeated the mantra, "I'm not alone. I have a map. I'm not lost." She also replayed the conversation she'd had with James again and again about how important this opportunity was for her. Still, all of that hadn't stopped the tentacles of terror from creeping over her. By the time she'd hit the stream, she'd been about a minute from panicking—her control had been slipping. Then Hunter had to go and scare the crap out of her.

Sure, she'd overreacted, but ever since she'd realized he was beside her, the terror vanished. Okay, well, maybe not when she thought she was going to be swept away by the rushing stream, but even then she'd had a feeling Hunter would have saved her. He was always telling her he hadn't lost a client yet—but he hadn't mentioned how many he'd bedded.

Wow, that thought came out of nowhere.

Hunter closed the distance between them slowly, looking as if he were studying her again. "Do you need to rest? I brought water. You need to keep hydrated." He crouched down and dug through his ever-present backpack.

Who was she kidding? He probably "made love" to plenty of desperate, willing women. After all, what else was there to do here at night? She wasn't stupid. She'd seen Yvette and the rest of the models throwing themselves at him.

"Do you want me to take the lead?"

She blinked, wondering what he was talking about. Visions of last night and the way he took the lead in bed sent a tremor through her.

"You should really bring along a sweatshirt. It can get cool in the shade."

"What?"

"You look cold."

"Oh no, I'm fine." She wasn't cold—she was hot. "I just…" Why had she stopped? She looked down at herself, her hands anchored to her hips, her stockings covered with runs. Her favorite boots were a mess, dusty, with streaks of caked on dirt thanks to almost falling into the stream—twice.

Hunter opened a bottle of water and handed it to her. "Truce?"

"I'm not fighting with you."

The crooked smile formed on his mouth. "Well, you haven't taken a swing at me for about five minutes. I guess that's a good sign, huh?"

"If you hadn't snuck up from behind me like a ghost and scared the life out of me, I wouldn't have felt the need to protect myself."

"First of all, you never need protection from me, Toni. I'd never hurt you."

He looked so sincere. But then people always judged themselves by their intentions; they judged others by their actions. Unfortunately, that thought did nothing but call into question her actions, something she didn't want to think about at the moment.

"How much farther do we need to go?"

"You need to drink about half that water, and I'll tell you."

She rolled her eyes and took a drink—not because he told her to, just because she was thirsty.

"With the elevation and the dry climate, you have

to drink a lot more than you do at home. We only have about fifteen percent humidity here. What's the average in New York?"

"In the summer? About ninety percent. Sometimes ninety-nine."

He shook his head. "It's a wonder you have to drink at all. Here, you don't feel as if you even sweat, it evaporates so fast. You really need to pound the water, babe. Dehydration can lead to some serious shit. And the last thing I want is my brother examining you."

"Don't call me *babe*. I'm not your girlfriend."

"Yeah, I got that loud and clear."

"Then why did you follow me?"

"Well, there's certainly nothing wrong with your self-esteem, is there? I'm not following you. I'm doing my job. If you hadn't left for the second part of the shoot without a River Runners employee, I, or one of the others, wouldn't have had to follow you. We would have been guiding you."

She blew out a breath and looked up at him. "Okay, I admit that wasn't my brightest move."

"It also goes against our contract. Bianca hired River Runners for a reason—to keep you safe and on schedule. Whatever happens between you and me is a completely separate issue. It has absolutely nothing to do with our work here. Like it or not, we'd both be a lot more successful if we figure out a way to work together."

"I don't have a problem working with you."

"Good. Because if this job goes well, Bianca might use River Runners again. And with what she pays, it puts me just that much closer to my goal."

Hunter took the half-empty water bottle from her,

twisted the cap on, and stuffed it into a mesh pocket before taking the lead.

He mentions a mysterious goal and then walks away. What was up with that? "Goal?" Toni followed trying not to notice how great his butt and legs looked in those khaki shorts. "You want more than this?" She held out her arms, taking in the whole forest. "Guiding city slickers through the woods and down rivers." Probably all the while sharing his sleeping bag with willing females—a dream come true for guys like Hunter. "I guess it feeds your need to control everyone and everything."

Hunter stopped midstride, and the look he gave her made her wonder if she'd finally pushed the man too far.

"I don't control people. I only control myself. Even when gorgeous Goth women and young gang members do everything within their power to make me lose it."

Toni threw her head back and laughed. She didn't bother trying to stifle it since there was absolutely no way she could. She didn't get the whole gang member thing, but the gorgeous Goth women—that was laughable. She figured she might as well enjoy it. She took great pleasure laughing right in Hunter's face.

"What's so funny?"

"You are either the world's best liar, or you're seriously delusional. You've been trying to control me ever since I met you."

"I wasn't controlling you. I was helping you—there's a difference. Someone had to push you out of that cabin."

"I would have done it on my own."

The look Hunter shot her made her want to slug him again. "Get over yourself, Hunter. You have faults just like the rest of us. Superman you ain't." She looked him

up and down and tried to imagine Pee-wee Herman.
After all, she had to do something to keep the hormones
in check. "If that was the only example of your controlling personality, I'd agree, but you have to control
everything—even sex." Not that she was complaining
about the sex—at all. But with him looking at her like
she was a big scoop of Chubby Hubby ice cream and
he'd been on a fast in the Sahara for ten days, she was
likely to do something stupid—like strip in the middle of
the woods and have an earth-shattering orgasm just before he jumped into a raging river, or they got a round of
applause from the people she was supposed to supervise.

"I did not control the way we made love. All I did
was refuse to have sex by the numbers. When we finally did make love, believe me babe, there was no
control involved."

The whole Pee-wee Herman thing was so not working. Nope, all she could see was Hunter looking every
bit as mad as he did turned on. Damn. She needed to re-
erect those defense shields she'd put in place earlier—
the ones that allowed her to tell him a little white lie
about there being nothing between them. And it was
a hell of a lie. The one thing between them was some
strong chemistry and an unbelievable magnetic attraction. But chemistry always fizzled out. Too bad she
didn't know the cure for magnetic attraction.

When he pulled her close and kissed her, the shield
shattered along with any recollection of the half-dozen
people waiting downstream and the fact that she had a
shoot to finish before they lost the light—not that the
light was a concern since it stayed light so freakin' late
it was absurd.

The defensive shield was obviously defective—she'd just take a moment and enjoy the way his tongue stroked hers, the feel of his arms holding her close, his chest pressing against hers, and the five o'clock shadow that tickled her cheek.

―—―∿∿∿—―—

Toni got that same wide-eyed look she did whenever she was shocked. Her breath hitched, her lips parted, and he knew in his heart that she felt it. Whatever this connection was, whatever was going on between them—it wasn't one-sided. He definitely didn't need to read the section of the book about sexual compatibility. They had that in spades.

Some control he had. He couldn't help himself, and when she kissed him back, a rush of relief swept through him right before that need for more, which always followed whenever he so much as touched her. If the others hadn't been waiting for them, he'd toss his control right in the creek. But he still had a job to do so he ended the kiss and took her hand. "We need to get back to the group." The dazed look on her face disappeared when he gave her hand a tug. "Come on. That tree should be right around the bend."

"Why did you do that?"

"Do what? Kiss you? I guess my control isn't all it's cracked up to be, huh?" Thank God for the tree. It was there just as he'd remembered. He dropped his pack to the ground and climbed up, jumping on it a few times to check the stability. It was fine. Needing to put some distance between them, Hunter walked across the fallen tree and used his boot to break off the branches poking up.

When he jumped down, Toni had her head buried in the map.

"Come on. Let's go get the others."

"There has to be another way to get there from here." That wide-eyed look of terror he'd seen before covered her face. "One that doesn't involve climbing across a tree over raging water."

"Not unless you don't mind a little rock climbing. It looks worse than it is. I'll be with you every step of the way."

"Oh, and that makes me feel so much better." She turned white again and leaned against the tree.

"You might want to stick your head between your legs, babe. You look about ready to keel over."

Her eyes snapped back to his, and she gathered her strength, straightening her spine and tilting her chin in that cocky way she had that made him want to walk right up to her and suck on the section of neck it exposed.

"Do you want to wait here while I get the others?"

Fear flashed in her eyes.

"I'll leave the map with you. You know exactly where we are. I promise. I'll be right back."

She shook her head, and Hunter saw her exhaustion. He'd kept her up most of the night—they'd both had a damn good workout. Then they were up at the crack of dawn, and she'd spent most of the afternoon under a lot of stress, working directly under the hot sun. He pulled the water bottle from his pack and gave it to her.

"I'm fine. I'll come with you."

"No, this is a great time for you to take ten and rest. Just sit here. I'll be back with the crew in two shakes."

"Two shakes? What does that mean?"

Hunter kissed her and pulled her into his arms, and she let him. She must have been more scared than she was letting on. "It means I'll be back in less time than it takes for a lamb to shake his tail twice."

"I didn't even know lambs had tails. What do they look like, cotton balls?"

"That's a rabbit's tail. A lamb's tail looks like a dog's, only it's covered with wool. And they're usually docked."

"Get a clue, Hunter—that was a rhetorical question."

"Right." He took one more look at her. She wasn't hyperventilating, but she still looked pale. "I'm going to get the others. Don't move, okay?"

"Oh and I was so looking forward to a game of hide-and-go-seek. Not. I'll be fine. I'll try to figure out how we're going to get everyone, two bikes, and all the equipment across there." She pointed to the tree and then swallowed hard.

"Nothing to figure out. I can pack it across. No big deal."

Hunter ran all the way back to the others, not wanting to leave Toni for a second longer than he had to. She didn't like to be left alone anywhere—especially not in the woods. Still he couldn't see dragging her back and forth for no good reason.

By the time they made it back, Toni was pacing. She looked about ready to pass out. So much for her resting. She'd crushed the plastic water bottle—he just hoped that she drank the water first.

Hunter quickly got all the gear packed across the tree. The models and photographers scampered across as if it was something they did on a daily basis. Toni was the only one left on the other side, and she did not look happy about it. He returned and held his hand out to help her up.

Toni crossed her arms. "Hunter, I can't."

"Sure you can." Everyone watched them from across the creek. "I'll help you. All you have to do is trust me. I've crossed this tree at least a dozen times—it's plenty safe. It's as wide as most of the trails you've walked to get here. Just don't look down, and you'll be fine."

"Yeah, don't look down."

He held out his hand again. "We're a team, remember? James made this trip sound as if it's a big break for your career. I can't do this without you, and we both need a win here."

"Fine." She reached for his hand, put her booted foot on the fallen tree, and he hauled her up. Her foot slipped. He caught her about the waist and pulled her to him.

"You really need to get some decent hiking boots, babe. These things might be great in the city, but they have no tread. Up here, tread equals safety."

"Thanks for the tip. A lot of good it does me in the middle of nowhere. I don't suppose there's a mall close by? I can just run out and meet you back here in what? Fifteen years? Maybe by then you'll have built a real bridge, not some unfortunate accident of nature."

"Come on. Time to practice some teamwork." He turned her around and held her close, her back to his front. "Step back on my boots and feel free to close your eyes. I'm just going to walk us across."

Toni looked over her shoulder at him. "If we were alone, I'd probably take you up on that, but we're not, and I don't want to become the running joke of the group I'm supposed to lead."

"Understandable."

"I can walk by myself… just, you know, hold onto me in case I slip again."

"You're sure?"

"No. The only thing I'm sure of is I don't want to do this."

"Let's just put one foot in front of the other and pretend we're walking down Broadway. Okay? You're safe. I've got you, and there's no way I'm ever gonna let you go."

Toni did a double take. Hunter didn't just say what she thought he said, did he? As if she wasn't already scared to death, that statement brought her fear to new heights. She pictured a caricature of herself, looking way too much like an overweight Olive Oil with pigtails instead of a bun and her heart pounding so hard it showed. By the time she could speak, she and Hunter had somehow crossed the creek, and she hadn't even noticed.

"Just stand here, and I'll help you down."

He jumped and plucked her right off the log so fast, she wrapped her arms around his head and held on tight, smashing his face between her breasts. So much for not making a fool of herself. As soon as she knew she wouldn't end up on her ass, she released his head. "Sorry."

He slid her down his body wearing his trademark grin. "Anytime."

She gritted her teeth. "Not another word, Hunter."

He gave her a final squeeze before letting her go. "I was just going to say we make a great team."

"Yeah, like the Cubs. Just great."

Chapter 10

TONI SAT BY THE FIRE IN THE INN'S DINING ROOM. THE log walls and pinewood tables, each set with a votive candle and Mason jar filled with wildflowers, gave the place a certain unsophisticated charm. If she hadn't been starving, she would have just gone back to her cabin to figure out a plan for the next day's shoot. Since she'd skipped lunch she was famished and knew when she got to her cabin, it would take an act of God, or Hunter, to get her out of there.

Speak of the devil. Hunter walked in, spotted her, and without even asking for permission, sat his nearly perfect butt down on the opposite chair.

Toni quickly doused her smile. Yeah, for some reason she still couldn't figure out, every time Hunter came to mind or into view, she found herself smiling—even when she was aggravated with him, which was her dominant mood most of the time. Okay, since she was not one to lie to herself, she admitted that aggravation was tied with attraction. Acknowledging the problem was the first step to solving it. She just wished she knew how.

"I thought I'd find you here." He took off his hat and ran his hand through his hair. The man was so perfect; he didn't even suffer from hat head. Sometimes life just wasn't fair.

"Oh yeah, finding me in the dining room during the

dinner hour was a real stretch. You're a regular Einstein."
She knew she sounded bitchy, but she couldn't help it.
"Sorry. I'm starving and tired—it's so not a good com-
bination for me."

"I'll take at least partial responsibility for the exhaustion"—he smiled that crooked smile that always made
her toes curl—"but the starvation is all on you."

Work. She had to work with him, nothing else. She
pulled her eyes away from his smiling face and focused
on her notes. "I've rented a jet boat on Redfish Lake
for tomorrow. Are you or one of the other guides able
to captain it, or do I need to call them back and hire
someone to drive the boat?"

"I can handle it."

"Good. I love crossing things off my list." Which she
did with a flourish. "So I guess I'll see you tomorrow
morning at nine." She set her clipboard aside and picked
up the menu.

"That's it?"

She went back to her list. "I had James go over the
supply list with your people. He said they had everything
ready to go. I rented the boat. I briefed everyone but you
just before I got here, so we're all on the same page."

"I wasn't aware there was a meeting scheduled."

"There wasn't. Everyone was in one place… well,
everyone but you. I figured I'd see you before I went
back to my cabin. All the information on tomorrow's
shoot was sent to you. There were no material changes.
Do you have any questions?"

"About the shoot? No."

"Good. Then I'll see you in the morning. Have a
good night."

Hunter stood and stared at her for a moment. "You know, Toni. It doesn't have to be this way."

"And this is why what happened last night was an epic mistake. We need to work together. At least *work* is something I understand—*people* are a mystery. Especially people like you."

Hunter sat back down. "What do you mean—people like me?"

"Look at yourself. You seem so comfortable in social situations, but you chose to live in the middle of nowhere without even a TV for company. You don't make sense—but then people would probably say the same about me. I guess we're both a little weird."

"I didn't realize my having a home in the mountains was weird. Maybe it's just strange to a person living on an island with ten million other people." He shrugged and leaned back. "Why do people think you're weird? That seems to be a bit of a sore spot for you."

"They think I'm high maintenance, which is ridiculous. I admit I have high expectations, but I don't expect anyone else to hand me what I want. I've worked hard to get good grades. I was accepted into a decent college, and I found a job that allows me to do what I want to do. I've done it all on my own."

Hunter raised an eyebrow. "So much for the team spirit we talked about today."

"Fine. You win. I've done it all on my own except for this. You were right. Without you, I'd have given up after the first night here and hightailed it back to New York. Are you happy now?"

"I'm not gloating. You have a team for a reason, Toni. You're not expected to do the whole thing yourself."

"Right, but just because we're working together doesn't mean there needs to be anything more between us."

Hunter leaned over the table. She reached for her collar and then stopped herself. He saw that and smiled. "Just because there doesn't need to be more between us doesn't mean that there isn't." He stood again and shouldered his pack. "I'll see you in the morning. Sweet dreams."

After he left, she felt very alone, which when she thought about it, was exactly what she'd wanted. Well, that and to be fed. She checked her watch. She'd been sitting there for a few minutes and had yet to see a server. If she'd been in New York, she would have gone to another restaurant. Obviously, that was not an option. The inn was the only game in town—if this was even a town.

A harried looking server bustled into the dining room, tying her apron as she approached. "Hunter came by and said you were here. I'm sorry. We usually don't serve this early."

Toni picked up her paperwork. "Oh, okay. Is there any way I could get a sandwich to take back to my room?"

"Oh no. It's fine. I just didn't know you were here. I'm sorry you had to wait. What can I get you?"

"Is the trout fresh?"

The girl grinned. "It doesn't get much fresher. We have our own trout stream out back."

Toni didn't know if the server was kidding or not. She was too tired to even think about it. "That sounds good then."

"What will you have to drink?"

She craved caffeine and for an instant wished she

was still at Hunter's place where he made coffee that would rival that of the most talented barista. The thought of drinking the swill the inn called coffee was just too awful to contemplate. "Can I have a Coke?"

"Coming right up."

"Thanks." Toni was tempted to move her bread plate and lay her head on the table.

"Hey, Toni. Mind if I join you?"

Karma—oh, this day was just getting better and better. "No, not at all." Toni lied. She should have asked if she could have had dinner sent to her cabin.

Karma tossed her backpack on the floor beside the chair Hunter had just deserted and grabbed a menu. "Do you know what the special is?"

Toni studied Karma, wondering how she missed the family resemblance when they'd first met. "No clue."

"I heard you gave Hunter what-for today. What did he do to piss you off this time?" Karma put her menu down, giving Toni her undivided attention.

"Nothing. We were just... ironing out some work-related problems."

"Wow, that's a good one. And you know, if you hadn't looked down and to the left like that, I might have believed you. I spend too much time watching *NCIS* and reruns of *Law and Order* to fall for it. You've got to work on your lying skills." She leaned toward Toni, like her brother had moments ago. "Just so you know, Trapper told me he overheard the fight you had with Hunter."

For the first time in her life, Toni was happy to be an only child. "I don't know what Trapper told you, but I didn't lie, and Hunter and I did not fight. If Trapper misinterpreted our discussion, that's his problem. Serves him right for spying on us."

"Oh, he wasn't spying. Trapper's nothing like me." She shot Toni a wicked smile she'd seen Karma use before. "He was just doing what men do in the woods—taking a leak. Me—I definitely would have spied. Face it, you and my brother have something hot and heavy going on, and I'm interested in the outcome. You see, with one more female in the family, we'll be tied with the guys... well, if we count Jasmine."

"Who's Jasmine?"

"My cousin Ben and his wife Gina's dog."

"You better hope Jasmine has puppies or your cousin has twin girls, because there's absolutely no way Hunter and I will... you know..."

"Hook up?"

"Exactly. Sorry to disappoint you. But I'm definitely not the woman for him."

"Hmmm."

All Karma said was hmmm, but that one word spoke volumes. "You don't understand. We both have jobs to do, and we don't need complications."

Karma sat back in her chair and reminded Toni of a female version of Hunter. "I see."

"Do you? Hunter and I work together. This trip means a lot to me professionally, and Hunter too. If Bianca uses River Runners again, it would bring him that much closer to his goal."

"Oh my God. Hunter told you about the kids? Wow. He almost never talks about River Runners Camp. I think the only reason he told me, Fisher, and Trapper was because he wanted our help. The more help he has, the more kids he can bring up. And really, how could we refuse to help those poor kids?"

Kids? What kids? She wanted to interrupt, but Karma was on a roll.

"They come here so closed and scared or loud and looking for a fight, and after a week or two out here with Hunter, they grow so much. Hunter's like a kid whisperer. Who wouldn't want to be a part of that?"

Toni held up her hands. "Wait. Back up. How did Hunter get into this?"

The server came back around, dropped off Toni's soda, and took Karma's order. A house salad, cheeseburger, and fries with ranch dressing for both her salad and her fries. Toni almost laughed. If the models ever saw Karma eat like that and stay as thin as she did, they'd freak.

Karma put her napkin in her lap, rearranged the silverware, and sipped her water before starting up again. "A friend of his from college worked in a shelter for disadvantaged and abused kids in East LA—now he runs the place. A few years ago, Hunter went down to visit Pat and came home with this great idea to bring a few of the kids from the shelter here to get them away for a little while. You know, show them there's more to life then just gangs and drugs. He started small, and now every summer River Runners brings a group up here for a week or two."

His goal was to have a camp for disadvantaged kids? "Hunter does all this on his own?"

Karma laughed. "No, we all pitch in, but Hunter does most of it. Several of the River Runners staff and a few psychologists from Boise volunteer, and Hunter picks up the transportation cost, food, and equipment. We teach the kids to raft, fish, camp, and do some rudimentary orienteering. We have campfires, cookouts, and a whole lot of fun. After a couple of weeks out here, the kids learn to trust themselves. They gain some much-needed self-esteem and even learn to trust each other and the staff. They blossom. When Hunter can work it out, he brings them back out to Castle Rock on their winter break and teaches them to ski. It gets them off the streets, shows them there's a whole big world out there, and people they can count on."

Toni took a sip of her Coke, trying to process all of this. She was stunned, so much so she found Karma staring. She set her glass down and shook her head to clear it. She'd had no idea. "Well, that's some goal. But it sounds as if he's already achieved it."

"No way. Hunter's been working himself half to death trying to fund it so he can pay a full staff and have River Runner's Camp up and running all summer and then follow up with them over winter and spring breaks. But that takes a lot of money. Especially since he wants to build cabins on his property so he can start taking on a few kids with physical disabilities."

"Doesn't he have help?"

"Like I said, a lot of the guides volunteer. Trapper, Fisher, and I do too. Hunter does most of the cooking. The kids have to help some, but that just teaches them their way around the kitchen or campfire and what foods are healthy and taste good. Fisher does his doctor thing when we need it. Trapper gives everyone scared-straight talks whenever he gets the chance, and I'm like the camp mom in kind of a weird way."

"I know Hunter can't handle the kids all by himself.

I'm talking about the funding. Has he started a charitable foundation? A 503c?"

"No."

"Why not?"

Karma shrugged. "Whenever we talk about it, all he says is he wants to do it himself. I don't know how well you know my big brother, but the man can be a little stubborn and controlling."

"Really, I would never have guessed."

After Toni's kiss-off, Hunter really wished he could go into the inn's kitchen and cook. But it wasn't his kitchen, and chefs had a real problem with other chefs horning in on their turf. It was one thing if he owned the place—like he did the Grille at Castle Rock—but it was another if he was a disgruntled guest who'd just been dismissed by the same woman who left claw marks on his back less than twelve hours before.

He let the screen door slam behind him, and after grabbing his duffel from his truck, he stalked off toward his cabin to read the damn book and figure out how to get a better handle on Toni.

When he saw his mother's familiar car, he almost headed in the opposite direction. "Son of a bitch." Like he needed more family here.

When Grampa Joe walked around the back of the Range Rover, Hunter regretted not running for cover. Gramps was an eighty-two-year-old force of nature— nothing stopped him, which was why Hunter tried to keep his distance, especially since Gramps had recently made it his business to get his eldest grandson, Ben, married. Ben and Gina were happy now, but that didn't make up for the underhanded way Gramps went about getting them together. The last thing Hunter wanted was to be the next grandson in his sights.

"Hunter! I'm so glad I found you." His mom quickened her pace and gave him the usual hug and kiss. Her hands went to his face, holding it for inspection. "You look angry."

"Not angry. Just frustrated. It's work."

Kate Kincaid had a notoriously sensitive bullshit meter—she'd picked up on his fib as evidenced by the purse of her lips and the furrowing of her brow.

"Mom, what are you and Gramps doing here?"

Grampa Joe slapped Hunter on the back. "Karma called and asked Kate to bring some clothes up for her." He shot Hunter a knowing smile. "I offered to drive."

Hunter rubbed his eyes. Mom wasn't the only one with a bullshit meter. He knew Gramps had better things to do than to take a day off and drive to Stanley. The old man usually had companies to run and small countries to take over. But maybe Gramps was listening to his doctors since he'd had a double bypass and had given up vying for world domination. His version of slowing down meant he had more time to mess with his family's love life.

"Well, boy, I guess when Karma dropped off that book on dating you asked her to bring, she hadn't expected to stay for a week."

"If I'd known she'd be coming to stay, I never would have asked her to bring the damn book to me in the first place." Hell, he'd known he was asking for trouble. He just didn't know how much. "I was hoping she'd go home the same day. When that didn't pan out, I figured she'd only stay for a day or two. Thanks to you and Mom, I'm suck with her for the duration."

Gramps's eyes twinkled. God only knew what Karma had said when she called home. She must have mentioned Toni, or Gramps would never have made the trip. She was dead meat.

Hunter's mother pulled a bag from the back of her Range Rover. "Karma and the boys are meeting us for dinner in the inn." She handed the bag to him. "You take this and join us."

His mom wore that take-no-prisoner's look, which meant he didn't have a choice. He'd freely admit he wasn't man enough to take on his mother when she looked like that. But that didn't bother him. Gramps wasn't either, and he was technically her boss. That too was up for debate, since when it came right down to it, Mom had bossed Gramps around for as long as Hunter could remember. Sure, Gramps groused about it an awful lot, but when push came to shove, Kate Kincaid always came out on top.

Hunter nodded his acquiescence and took the rear, hoping to pull a Toni and fade into the woodwork. When he stepped in behind his mother and grandfather, he cringed. There was Karma, taking a big bite of a salad, sitting next to Toni, who had a deer-in-the-headlights look. "Son of a bitch." His mother pulled Toni out of her chair for a hug.

Trapper appeared next to him. "I see Karma's been up to no good."

Fisher took the other side. "We certainly had nothing to do with it. But damn, I'm glad it's you and not me."

Hunter turned to Fisher. "What in the hell is that supposed to mean?"

"It means Gramps is back on the marriage bandwagon, and tag, you're it."

Chapter 11

ONE MINUTE TONI WAS EATING HER SALAD AND listening to Karma tell embarrassing stories about Hunter, and the next she was being introduced to Hunter's grandfather and mother. Oh my God, not only introduced, but hugged.

Kate Kincaid, Hunter's mom, pulled Toni right out of her seat and hugged her like she was some long-lost relative. Toni looked over her shoulder and saw Hunter wincing. Trapper, Fisher, and Karma were all smiling and enjoying themselves far too much. So was the old man.

"Mrs. Kincaid, it's um… great to meet you." Toni wanted to run and hide. Unfortunately, she was stuck between Hunter's mother and grandfather. Trapper and Fisher blocked the only exit.

"Just look at you." Kate held Toni at arm's length, giving her a once-over.

Toni hadn't even been back to her cabin to change after the photo shoot. Her stockings had more runners than the New York City Marathon, her boots were ruined, and her pigtails were probably crooked.

"Karma told me you were beautiful, but she didn't do you justice. It's no wonder Hunter is so taken with you."

Toni shook her head and reached for her collar. "Um… I don't think… I mean, Hunter and I aren't—"

Hunter's grandfather wore a Wile E. Coyote smile.

He looked like a nice old man at first glance, but she saw something more—he had that man-on-a-mission look. Unfortunately, that look was directed at her.

"Mom, Gramps, leave Toni alone." Hunter must have come up behind her to save her again. Thank God.

"Oh come now, boy." Hunter's grandfather stepped closer to Toni and threw his arm around her, pulling her close to his side. "We're just introducing ourselves. You don't mind us joining you? Do you, Toni?"

"I... um—"

"Good." Hunter's mom smiled and finally let Toni go. "Trapper, Fisher, pull a few tables together."

Karma stood and helped the guys, while Toni tried to come up with an excuse to get the hell out of there.

She glared at Hunter as he pulled out her chair then whispered in her ear as she sat. "I'm really sorry about this."

She was relieved when he took the chair beside hers. Unfortunately, Hunter's grandfather sandwiched her between them, and his mother faced her. Fisher and Trapper flanked their mother, and Karma sat at the end of the table. She was surrounded.

Toni covered her mouth with her hand. "How can I get out of here?" she whispered in Hunter's direction.

He placed his napkin on his lap and leaned toward her. "If you figure it out, let me know, and we'll both make a break for it."

Toni toyed with her salad. She'd lost her appetite.

"So Toni," Kate said. "Karma tells us you're from New York and work with children."

Toni looked over at Karma who slouched in her seat.

"No, it only feels like I do. I manage Action Models."

Fisher and Trapper were all smiles. If she didn't know better, she would swear they were enjoying this.

"Karma, I thought you said Toni worked at a rec center."

Trapper raised his eyebrow. "Figures. Karma's the stoolie."

Toni took a bite of her salad before looking at Kate. "I do volunteer at a rec center a few blocks from my apartment. I'd love to work there, but the rec center can't take on any more employees. We have a hard enough time keeping the doors open as it is."

Kate sat back in her chair and folded her hands serenely on the paper place mat. "You and Hunter have so much in common. You're involved with the rec center, and Hunter has his River Runners Camp."

Hunter seemed to be looking everywhere but at Toni. "Yes. Karma just told me about the camp. It sounds like a wonderful program. I had no idea Hunter was involved with anything like that."

There now, maybe his family would lay off when it came to matchmaking. She smiled and gave herself a mental pat on the back. When she looked up, everyone at the table glared at Hunter, who, if she wasn't mistaken, had blanched.

Hunter cleared his throat and slid his chair back before taking her hand and standing. "Excuse us. Toni, could I have a word?"

"Now?" Everyone's attention went from Hunter to her. Great. Of course Hunter would stand there brooding silently. The whole man-of-few-words thing was really beginning to get irritating. "Fine." She took her napkin from her lap, laid it next to her barely touched salad, and removed her hand from his. "Excuse us," she said as she rose without meeting anyone's eyes.

With his big hand on the small of her back, Hunter steered her out of the dining room, into the next room, and around the corner.

"Way to screw up all the progress I made, Hunter. I had them believing there was nothing between us until you pulled your little stunt."

"While I'm not happy with my family's involvement in my love life, that doesn't mean I'm going to lie about it."

Toni crossed her arms. "What lie? Everything I said was the God's honest truth. Karma told me about your camp, and you didn't."

"I'm sorry." He looked just as contrite as he had after he'd jumped in the river.

"You're sorry? Why? Are you sorry for not telling me about the camp or for the Kincaid family fiasco going on in the dining room?"

Hunter couldn't keep from touching Toni, so he stepped a little closer and rested his hands on her waist. She didn't look angry—just confused. For a very bright woman, she had no clue what was expected in a relationship. "People who care about each other share things like their goals in life and their work."

"Okay. So?"

"I care about you, and I didn't tell you about River Runners camp. I was going to after you mentioned the rec center, but then you gave me the brush-off."

"I wasn't interested in you then."

"But you changed your mind. You do that a lot when it comes to me."

Toni shrugged. "Hunter, you're like exceptionally good dark chocolate. What's not to love, right? So I get a huge box of Belgian dark chocolate." She stuck her hands out to show him the size, which would weigh in at twenty-five pounds easy—obviously an exaggeration.

"Okay. I'm the chocolate?" He was confused. Since all the women he knew couldn't resist anything chocolate, that couldn't be a bad thing. But with Toni, one never knew.

"You're the chocolate, but not just any chocolate. You're Belgian chocolate. It's the best chocolate on earth."

"So that's a good thing?"

"Yes, I just love Belgian chocolate. So much so, I unwrap the huge box, and I eat and eat. It's so good I can't stop. I make a total pig of myself. The next thing I know, I feel sick, I've gained ten pounds, and I have a zit the size of Manhattan on my forehead."

This was a ridiculous comparison, but she obviously didn't think so. She was serious.

"Don't you see? Nothing that decadent can be good for me. You're my Belgian dark chocolate, and I suck at resisting you. I have no willpower."

"Thank God." He kissed the crease above her nose that showed up every time she was confused then kissed the tip of her nose. "Chocolate has been proven to be very good for you."

Her lips parted, and her eyes darkened.

"High in antioxidants."

She looked more stunned and turned on than confused now.

He leaned in and teased her lips. "It stimulates

endorphins." His nose rubbed hers before he kissed the corner of her mouth. "It gives you a feeling of pleasure." He nibbled her bottom lip. "It's a natural antidepressant."

Her fingers tunneled into his hair and gripped his head as she kissed him with promise and desperation.

Hunter groaned, leaning into her, pinning her against the wall. Need like none he'd felt before grabbed him in a stranglehold. If she kept kissing him like that, they'd get enough exercise to keep from gaining weight for sure. Hell, they'd have to guard against withering away to nothing.

Someone cleared his throat. Toni stilled, and her eyes shot wide open.

"Sorry to interrupt, but Toni's dinner is on the table."

"Fisher." Hunter didn't turn around. "She'll be there in a minute."

He closed his eyes and rested his forehead against hers until his brother's footsteps faded. "Resistance is futile. Let's just give up trying to avoid this and enjoy our time together."

"Okay. But not at work. Work is work, and this is... well, whatever it is."

"Agreed." He gave her a quick kiss and stepped back, fighting the urge to pick her up and get the hell out of there.

Hunter took Toni's hand and returned to his family. He held her chair while Trapper and Fisher exchanged money. God only knows what they'd bet on. Karma teased Gramps around a mouthful of cheeseburger about his low sodium and low cholesterol diet while he snuck fries from her plate.

His mother shifted her glare from Gramps to him and

back again. When he sat beside Toni and put his arm around her, the glare disappeared. Thank God, because nothing was worse than being on his mother's bad side. Toni stared at her dinner.

He leaned toward her. "Something wrong?"

"No one but Karma has food. It would be bad manners to eat in front of everyone."

"Not when they hijacked your dinner it's not. Go ahead. Eat before it gets cold. Besides, I have a feeling you're gonna need your strength. Just leave a lot of room for dessert."

"Leave Karma's fries alone, you ornery old goat," his mother said.

Gramps was caught with a mouthful of fries. He swallowed. "Maybe if you didn't feed me so much damn rabbit food, I wouldn't have to steal French fries from my granddaughter, you smart-aleck woman."

Toni toyed with her food and watched wide-eyed as his family did their usual sparring.

"This is normal, nothing to worry about."

Someone must have ordered for him because a thick rib eye was served a moment later. He bit into the rare meat and smiled. It was almost perfect. He could have done better, but then that was the problem with eating out. It was almost never as good as his own cooking.

Gramps looked over at Toni's plate and thankfully kept his utensils on his own food. Toni's plate didn't have anything his grandfather would see fit to steal. Hunter was grateful. "Toni, tell me about this rec center where you volunteer. Do you handle the fund-raising?"

She took a sip of her soda. "I help out with it whenever I can. I'm able to use some of the resources of the modeling firm, and I've met a lot of photographers who are willing to donate their time and photos for our news-letters and fund-raising campaigns. Every little bit helps, but it's a constant battle."

Gramps pulled out his wallet and removed a business card. "You should give Tom Delany a call. He handles my charitable trust. I'm sure he can find some money to help out your rec center."

"Thanks, but what about Hunter's camp?"

Gramps smiled that smarmy smile of his, and Hunter felt his back going up.

"The boy won't take any help. It's not as if I haven't tried. But even I have to follow IRS rules; unless he starts a charitable foundation, my hands are tied."

She turned to Hunter. "If you're trying to fund this camp, why haven't you started a 503c?"

Hunter had the attention of the table. Fabulous. "When I want something, I earn it. I don't expect handouts. I want to work for it, achieve it myself." He had to admit it sounded pretty lame when he said it out loud. From the looks coming from Toni and the family, they agreed.

Toni laughed. "You're such a guy. You doing every-thing yourself is helping a handful of kids. Don't you think it would be better to start a charitable foundation, do some fund-raising, get a little help from Grand Daddy Warbucks over here—" She turned to Gramps and flashed him a smile. "No offense, Mr. Walsh."

"None taken, Toni. But please, call me Joe, Gramps, or Grampa Warbucks is fine too." He laughed and slapped his hand on the table. "I've never met anyone with the gumption to call me that to my face." He leaned back in his chair and turned toward Hunter. "I like your girl, Hunter. She's got moxie."

Hunter rolled his eyes. Gramps didn't know the half of it. The old man could really shovel on the charm, and Toni ate it up.

Toni shook her head at him. "Don't you see? With a little help and a 503c, you could afford to help hundreds of kids lead productive lives in the future."

He liked her a lot better when her mouth was on him. He swallowed hard, and he thought of all the places her mouth had been and hopefully would be again in the near future. He checked his watch. "Thanks. I'll take it under advisement."

"I do fund-raising for the rec center. I donate money as well as time, but I'm not stupid enough to think I can do it all myself."

Stupid? What he did was not stupid. He had his reasons. "You don't understand. This is my family. Sure, Gramps gives millions to charity every year. But I want the River Runners Camp to succeed because I made it happen, not because Gramps wrote a check." He looked over to the man who was like a father to him. "I appreciate your willingness to help, Gramps, but I want to succeed because I made it on my own."

Toni elbowed him. "And your freakish need for control is more important than those kids?"

He took her hand and put it on his lap to keep her from elbowing him again, or worse, slugging him. "It's not freakish."

"That's still up for debate, but that wasn't the question. Is your stubbornness more important then helping those kids?"

She had her face in his, so close he smelled his shampoo on her hair. He held her hand and felt the passion flow through her—not sexual passion, which was a real shame, but probably a good thing since they were sitting there in front of his entire family, and her hand was disturbingly close to his dick. A passion for kids he'd rarely seen in anyone. She was right. Maybe if he'd gotten some help, Emilio wouldn't be MIA right now. "No. Nothing is more important than the kids."

Toni smiled her thousand-watt smile. "Good. It's settled then. All you have to do is get your brother the judge to help you put together a 503c." She turned to Trapper. "I assume you're a lawyer too. Am I right?"

Trapper smiled right back. "Yes ma'am, you are."

"So you'd have no problem helping Hunter with the paperwork?"

"None at all."

"Great. See how easy this is?" Toni cut a bite of her now cold fish with the side of her fork, raked her nails farther up his thigh before squeezing it, and popped the fish into her mouth—all innocent like.

"Thanks." Hunter brought her hand back to the table and released it. The last thing he and his dick needed was any more encouragement in front of his family. It was bad enough he'd been at least half hard since he first set eyes on her. He shifted in his seat and sawed a piece of meat off his steak.

"Oh come on." Toni replaced her hand on his leg, rubbing his thigh. Her thumb brushed his dick, and he almost shot out of his seat. "It's not as if you're asking for help for yourself. You're just giving Grampa

Warbucks over here and everyone else involved a way to help all those deserving kids. You're doing them a favor."

Hunter chewed his steak, and ignoring the loud buzz of sexual awareness, he thought about what she'd said. As much as he hated to admit it, she did have a point. "Okay."

Silence fell over the table except for the clink of Karma's dropped utensils. She quickly picked them up. "Did you say okay? Just like that?"

Another twenty changed hands, this time from Fisher to Trapper.

Hunter felt like grabbing the money and stuffing it in his own pocket, since it was obviously him they'd been betting on. "Yes." When it came to stubbornness, Hunter freely admitted he suffered from his fair share, but he wasn't obstinate. He was also no idiot. He'd been reading the book Karma brought up every chance he got. In chapter eight it talked about how highly evolved men had no problem admitting when they were wrong. He was a big enough man to admit he was wrong—he just wished he didn't have to do it in front of his whole family. "Toni's right. In the end, all that matters is what's best for the kids."

Karma put her hand out, and both Fisher and Trapper passed a twenty over. She winked at Hunter, mouthing the words *Chapter Eight*, and stuffed the loot in her bra.

Hunter choked on his beer. Son of a bitch, she had her own copy.

Toni smacked him on the back while he tried to catch his breath.

Gramps looked past Toni to Hunter. "Well, boy, I'm awful glad Karma brought what you needed to get the job done. I think it'll come in handy with this little filly."

Karma slurped her water and grinned.

"As nice as this dysfunctional family reunion has been, Toni and I have a lot to do before tomorrow's photo shoot." Hunter didn't mention getting naked was his top priority, followed closely by making love to Toni repeatedly. His mother didn't look happy. She'd just have to get over it.

Kate dabbed her mouth with her napkin. "Can't we talk you two into at least staying for dessert?"

Hunter stood and shook his head as he shouldered his duffel bag and backpack. "Sorry Mom. What we need to do really can't wait."

Toni looked relieved as he helped her out of her seat. "Hunter's right. We have a lot to go over, and I'm about dead on my feet. It's been really nice meeting you Mrs. Kincaid, Grampa Warbucks."

Gramps let out a laugh and slapped Hunter on the back again. "She's a real spitfire."

"You don't know the half of it."

Before Toni could get around him, Gramps grabbed her and pulled her into a hug. "You be sure to call Tom Delany as soon as you get home. And if you ever need anything else, my number's on the front of the card."

"Thanks, Gramps. I'll be sure to do that."

Kate waited for them as they rounded the table. She pulled Toni into another hug. "I'm so glad I got to meet you, Toni. Now don't be a stranger. We'll expect to see you in Boise often."

"Mom, let go of her, will ya?"

Kate released Toni. "Only so that I can get a hug and a kiss from you too."

He leaned down and pulled her into a hug.

"I like her, Hunter." She whispered in his ear. "Now don't do something stupid and screw it up."

"I love you too, Mom."

She gave him a kiss on the cheek and then wiped her ever-present lipstick off it with her thumb. "You could remember to use that phone you always wear around. You know how it works. You press the buttons, and you can talk to people on it. It's not supposed to be just for show."

"Yes, ma'am."

"And take good care of Toni. Make sure she wears sunscreen. She's very fair."

"I will." He turned and waved, "See ya," grabbed Toni's hand, and made a break for it.

Hunter walked with Toni toward her cabin, holding her hand, and wondering what was going through her mind.

"So that's your family, huh?"

"Pretty much." Hunter still stung from the embarrassment that was his family. He couldn't believe Karma had ratted him out, and his mom and Grampa Joe had come all this way just to meet his new girlfriend. You'd think he was sixteen.

"What about your dad? What's he like?"

"We were close when I was a little kid. He took me out fishing and hunting. You know, all the guy stuff dads and boys do."

"Out here maybe, definitely not in New York."

"Dad and Mom split the sheets when Karma was a

baby. He had visitation rights for a while, but then one weekend Trapper, Fisher, and I were waiting for him to pick us up, and he didn't come."

"How old were you?"

"I don't know, seven or eight. I haven't seen him since." He looked over at her and shrugged. "We were lucky though. We had Grampa Joe. Gramps was always there for us, and my mom is great."

"I'd say you're pretty lucky in the family department."

Hunter threw his arm around her and pulled her close. "Yes, I am. And you haven't even met Ben and Gina yet. You're gonna love them. Ben's like another brother, and his wife Gina is a real hoot."

"Karma mentioned them. They live in New York, right?"

"Park Slope. We've been seeing a lot more of each other lately. The whole family is on a mission to find Gina's brother, Rafael."

"What, no cell phone?"

Hunter shook his head. "It's a long story, but Rafael was given up for adoption when Gina was six. She's been looking for him ever since."

"How does a six-year-old look for anyone? She was practically a baby."

"At six, she'd been taking care of Rafael and her little sister, Tina. She's an amazing woman despite having a nightmare childhood. When she married Ben, Gina, her sister Tina, and her brother-in-law Sam ended up with a whole new family. The Walshes and Kincaids take care of our own. Now we're trying to find Rafael. I'll introduce you to the rest of the gang when I come out to visit you."

Toni stopped dead in her tracks. "What are you talking about?"

Hunter stopped and looked around. They were alone, so he pulled her closer and kissed her. "I'm talking about coming out to New York to visit you just as soon as I can. Maybe you can fly back for Labor Day weekend."

"Why?"

"Because it's pretty hard to carry on a relationship if we don't see each other."

"A relationship?"

"Yeah, you know, the thing where you talk to each other on the phone all the time. Miss the other person like crazy when you're not with them. Spend as much time as possible together and rack up frequent flier miles like mad. And when you are together, you have nonstop earth-shattering sex?"

She looked at him as if he was nuts.

"What did you think? That we'd just part ways after the shoot is done and never see or talk to each other again?"

"I don't know. I hadn't really thought about it."

Hunter tried to put aside the slam to his ego and reminded himself that the idea of a relationship was all new to Toni. "I'll try not to take that personally."

"I didn't mean it as a cut, Hunter. It just never occurred to me. I don't think that way."

"I guess I shouldn't be surprised—it doesn't sound as if you've ever seen a real relationship that works."

"And you have?"

"Yes, I have. I've just never found someone I cared enough about to change my life and career to make room for a relationship—until I met you. So I guess you better put your thinking cap on then."

Chapter 12

TONI DRAGGED HER FEET AND WALKED BESIDE HUNTER toward her cabin, holding hands and sneaking glances at him. He hadn't said anything after dropping the relationship bombshell. For that, she was grateful. She didn't want to think about the future. All she wanted to think about was the way she'd spent the whole dinner on a slow burn. Damn Hunter and all his talk of how good chocolate was for her. When she'd revealed her weakness, he'd taken full advantage of it.

Toni stopped at her door and pulled out her key. Her hands shook. She wasn't sure if it was nervousness or excitement. She swallowed hard and looked up at him. The porch light highlighted the sharp angles of his face. God, he was beautiful. Their eyes met, and she melted just a little more.

Hunter had a way of turning her to jelly with just the slide of his hand or the look he gave her now. He'd spent most of the meal touching her. Sure, she'd retaliated, and although no one else seemed to notice him jump when her hand brushed his fly, she definitely did, which just made her squirm. He stepped forward and took the key card. Of course he had no problem figuring out which way to slide it into the slot. He pushed open the door and held it for her to precede him.

He stepped in behind her and started talking before she could even put her clipboard down.

"Toni, I just want—"

"Stop." The last thing she wanted to do was talk. "We'll talk later. I promise, but right now—" She slammed him back against the door and almost laughed at the shocked look on his face. She pulled his head down to hers and kissed him. Hunter groaned just before he dropped his bags and wrapped his arms around her, crushing her against him with brute strength. She pushed back enough so she could shove his shirt up, her hands running over his chest as she sucked his tongue into her mouth and then raked her teeth over it.

Pulling his shirt over his head, Hunter dragged in a breath when her mouth closed around his flat nipple. She kissed her way to the other, tasting the hint of salt on his skin and the flavor that was all his own. She tried to unhook his belt but fumbled—he finished the job.

Toni was thankful he took over and did her best to catch up with him. He watched as she unbuttoned her blouse and pulled her hair out of the pigtails. After shaking it out, she reached for her collar.

"Leave that on. You never know when I might need to use it."

Toni's hands stilled, and his words sent a shot of heat right to her core.

He slid his finger through the D-ring and tugged her toward the bed. His mouth met hers in a bruising kiss—hard, hot, and drugging. He explored her mouth, nipped her bottom lip, and soothed the spot his teeth had raked as his fingers tangled in her hair, massaging her scalp and keeping her from escaping—as if she would. Toni would gladly kiss him for however long he wanted. But that didn't keep her from wrapping a leg around his hip and sinking her hand into his shorts.

Toni stilled as Hunter's rough hands slid up her sides to cup her breasts. He snapped the front clasp, pulling off her bra with her blouse, turning her, his front to her back, facing the mirror. The searing intensity in his eyes held her captive.

"Look at you." His eyes followed the reflection of his dark hands sliding over her white stomach to her breasts. "So beautiful."

Toni tried to see herself as he would. Her lips were red and swollen. Her hair looked wild. The heat in his eyes sent her girl parts screaming for more. "Thanks, but there's no need for seduction, Hunter. I brought you here, remember?"

"Babe, you're the one doing the seducing. Not me. You've been seducing me from the moment I first laid eyes on you."

He must have lost his shorts because when he slid her tight skirt up, his erection was hot and hard and nestled against her lower back. She took his hand in hers and brought it down between her legs. She watched his reaction in the mirror, having never before asked for what she wanted even wordlessly, and was thankful the man could take a hint. He slid the fabric of her thong to the side, and she watched as his fingers disappeared inside her.

"Yes." She reached across the dresser to anchor herself and spread her legs as he pressed his thumb against the bundle of nerves, and his fingers slid in and out sending her world spinning toward bliss. One hand on her breast pinched the hard nipple, while his other tormented and teased her below. Within a minute she was caught up in the sights, sounds, and feelings of his hands on her. Still, she wanted more.

She reached back and took hold of his erection. "Hunter. I want you. Inside me. Now."

His fingers stilled and retreated as she held his gaze through the mirror. Rising to her toes, she slid the hard length of him between her legs and rocked, his erection slipping against her wet folds.

Toni leaned forward and pressed back against the hard tip as he glided home, filling her in one swift thrust. His hands held her hips, stilling her as he pulled out slow and steady. She was on fire, and slow was not what she wanted—what she needed. She needed Hunter. She needed his wild side, the one that broke through the tight control he held.

Taking the hand that had brought her so much pleasure, Toni drew it to her mouth and slipped his fingers between her lips, sucking them in deep, tasting herself, all the while staring straight into his eyes.

Hunter went wild, bucking against her. He took her hard and fast, sending her into a climax the likes of which she'd never known. He pulled her up against him as she came and bit down on her shoulder, sending her even higher. His name flew from her lips as he hand-grazed the length of her body, his wet fingers stroking the tight bundle of nerves and dragging her screaming into another realm. She gasped as his face contorted, body shaking, and he thrust twice more before she felt his release flooding her. They collapsed on the dresser, the surface smooth and cool against her heated chest and face.

"I hurt you."

"No." She couldn't say more, but she felt him stiffen against her.

"Babe. I'm sorry. I…" He lifted himself off her and slid out, leaving her chilled and feeling suddenly empty. "I didn't mean to…"

"I did." Toni gathered the last of her strength and reached for him. The poor guy looked horrified. She wrapped her limp arms around him and smiled as she kissed his lips. He held her like she was made of china, and the thought of it had her fighting back a fit of giggles.

Her legs felt as if they were made of rubber bands. Needing to lie down, she pushed him back against the bed and fell on top of him so they were nose to nose. "That was amazing. Hunter, you can take me on the wild side whenever you want." She had to laugh then; the shocked look on his face was priceless.

He rolled them over, pulling her up farther onto the bed before kissing her and slid her leg over his hip. Her eyes shot open when she felt him hard against her.

"Maybe the next time we'll try it without clothes on. What do you think?"

"Probably not a bad idea."

Hunter pulled off Toni's boots before sliding her skirt, thong, and stockings down her long legs. She lay there on the bed boneless, her pale skin tinged with pink except for the red spots on her hips from when he pounded her into the dresser. He cursed under his breath.

They needed to have a conversation. For the first

time in his life he'd completely lost control and had unprotected sex.

He pulled the white comforter down and lifted her, placing her back against the pillows. After toeing off his boots and socks, he lay beside her and dragged her back against him. He cringed when he saw the red spot on her bare shoulder where he'd nipped her. Damn, he took her like a rutting boar. "Toni?"

"Hmm?"

He slid his arm around her waist and pulled her closer, spooning around her. "I fucked up... royally."

"Hunter," she said on a sigh. "I already told you. I liked it. I've never felt anything so... intense and exciting." She tried to turn, but he held her tight against him. He really didn't want to see the look on her face when she found out the truth.

"But the thing is... Toni, I wasn't wearing a condom. I'm sorry. I wasn't thinking straight. I've never had unprotected sex before so I'm clean. It's just—"

She did roll over then. "It's okay. I've always been very careful about that too. It's not as if I've had much of a sex life, but I've never messed up before. So stop blaming yourself. It was just as much my fault as it was yours—probably more, and I'm on the pill so there's nothing to worry about. It's fine."

He brushed the hair off her cheek and tucked it behind her ear. "Why are you on the pill? Not that I'm complaining, mind you. Just curious."

She laughed. "Because without it, I have mood swings that give PMS a bad name followed closely by the cramps from hell. Now with the new pill, I only have four periods a year, and it helps with the PMS."

"Is that healthy?"

"I've never had a problem, and I don't smoke. I'm young, so for now… it's fine." She moved up his chest and kissed his neck. "Hunter?"

Damn, one kiss, and he was tenting the sheet. "Toni?"

"Were you serious before?"

"Before what?" She'd stiffened in his arms. All thoughts of his hard-on disappeared.

"Before… you know… when we were walking over here."

"When we talked about our relationship?"

Her fingers tangled with his chest hair. "What does that entail?"

He lifted her chin and looked straight into the eyes of a very nervous woman. God, she slayed him. "It means we'll see each other, we'll burn up the phone lines, we'll get together as often as humanly possible, and we'll see where it leads."

"That's what I don't get. Where can it lead? I mean, look at your life and look at mine. We live in two different worlds."

"Not that different."

"You're here, and I'm in New York. It doesn't get much more different than that."

"I live in Boise. We have modeling firms, ad agencies, and rec centers—all the conveniences of home."

"Do you have any good delis?"

"No, but we do have access to a corporate jet, and Ben would be happy to deliver anything you want from New York whenever he's coming out."

"But what if it doesn't work?"

"Toni, the way I look at it, we have two choices. We

can give it a try and see how it goes, or we can just end it. If we did that, we'd definitely lose." Hunter pulled her closer. His hard-on slipped between them as she settled on top of him. He kissed her, tasting her fear and uncertainty. "I don't want to lose this." He rocked his pelvis against hers and pulled her legs forward to straddle him. "I don't want to lose you."

She sat up, shaking her head, her black hair flying about her shoulders. "I'm not talking about sex."

"I'm not either." He sat too, and when she leaned away from him, he gave her collar a tug, pulling her close. He really liked that collar. "I'm talking about you." He kissed the shocked look off her face and wrapped his arm around her waist, dragging her closer still. "I don't want to lose you, Toni. I don't want to ever stop feeling the way I feel when I'm with you."

"It's only been a few days. You hardly know me."

"I guess you don't believe in love at first sight then."

"I'm not sure I believe in love at all. As far as I can see it's lust at first sight—so okay, we have that in spades. You and me, we're like some kind of chemical reaction now, but that will fizzle out soon enough, believe me. I've seen it happen time and time again."

The thought of Toni having any kind of reaction to another man did nasty things to his gut. "Are you talking about personal experience?"

"Yes... no. My mother's been married five times. My father's on wife number three and kid number four. That's personal enough for me."

"Oh babe." He held her close and rubbed her back, trying to forget the fact she was naked and sitting on

him. "I know it's hard to believe, but people have long
and loving relationships all the time."

She rested her head against his shoulder. "You don't.
I don't. What makes you think that two people like us
can make it work?"

Hunter tipped her chin up so she had to look at him.
"Because I've never met a woman I've cared about as
much as I do you, and it's only been three days."

She rolled her eyes. "Two and a half."

"Can you imagine what it'll be like after a week? If
this keeps up, I'm never gonna want to let you go."

Toni'd fallen asleep in Hunter's embrace and had awo-
ken to kisses on her shoulder and sleepy, arousing ca-
resses. He kissed her between yawns and teased her with
gentleness. She'd never had lazy morning sex before.
Hell, she'd never had lazy sex ever.

Hunter seemed content to just be together, touching
and tasting in groggy exploration. There was no urgency, no desperate frenzied need for completion, just
a slow build of quiet intensity where every kiss was af-
fecting, every touch powerful, every look heartrending
in its tenderness. The combination, the gentle assault on
all fronts, seduced and unnerved her.

The way he made love filled her with indescribable
emotion so strong, so beautiful, and so overwhelming it
was impossible to ignore.

Hunter's eyes locked on hers, and she was incapable
of looking away, incapable of protecting herself from
the current arcing between them. The physical and spiri-
tual connections were tangible. He touched her body,

her mind, her soul. He filled her with longing and sated her with—whatever this was. She understood lust, and that was definitely part of it. There was need, there was desire, but the three of them together didn't hold a candle to this connection they'd built.

Tears rolled down the sides of her face, but she didn't know why. She was not a crier. She had nothing to cry about. Fear, bright and sharp, pierced her consciousness.

"Hunter?" Her breath caught in a whirlwind of sensation, escalating the fear, the excitement, and the hold he had on her.

Hunter fought against his own need. Toni was all that mattered, and she was seconds away from shattering. Her inner muscles hummed, clenching him, pulling him deeper. In her eyes he saw fear warring with longing. Tears rolled down the sides of her face. She knew. He was sure of it. His love was what she both feared and wanted.

His name flew from her lips in a strangled cry as her orgasm rolled through her, pulling him in. He thrust hard, deep, gritting his teeth against the onslaught of heat, wetness, and her inner muscles convulsing around him like a thousand fingers. He let go, flooding her with his essence, with his love, and then unable to hold himself above her he collapsed, spent and exhausted. With his last ounce of energy, he rolled them over onto their sides and pulled her close, kissing away her tears. He didn't let them bother him. They were just a release. Hell, he'd been so caught up he almost cried too. "I love you, Toni."

The words flew through his head, and when she stiffened in his arms and gasped, he knew he'd said them out loud. He nuzzled her neck and kissed her trembling lips. "It's all right, babe. Just relax." He stroked her side and felt the tension running through her. "It's still early. We can catch a few more hours of sleep if you want."

She pushed him over onto his back and then climbed on top of him, straddling his legs—oblivious to the picture she made. "You tell me that, and you expect me to go to sleep?"

Hunter pushed pillows against the headboard and sat, leaning back against it. "I guess not. If you want to talk about it, go ahead."

"I don't want to talk about it." She pounded on his chest, and he caught her hand. "I want you to take it back."

"Why?"

"'Cause it's not true. It can't be true. People don't fall in love in three days."

"Really, how long does it take? A week? Three weeks? A year?"

"I don't know. I've never been in love."

"Yeah, well, it took me less than three days. Maybe less than one, I'm not really sure when it happened. It kind up snuck up on me."

"What do you want from me? Why would you lie about this of all things?"

"Now hold on a minute. I just told you how I feel. I don't expect you to feel the same, and I'm certainly not asking anything of you. But you need to understand that I don't lie. I love you, Toni, and I'll be damned if I'm going to take it back, so you might as well get used to it." He tugged on that collar of hers and gave her a hard kiss. Too bad it didn't erase the look of doubt mixed with despair on her face.

Chapter 13

WHEN HUNTER STEPPED OUT OF THE CABIN, TRAPPER was waiting for him.

"You're up early."

"Yeah. I need to get something from my truck."

Hunter didn't bother to stop to talk. He figured if Trapper really wanted to say something, he'd get off his ass and follow.

"I was thinking—"

"Always a dangerous thing." Reaching into his pocket, Hunter pulled out his keys. He unlatched the swing-out tire carrier on his Land Cruiser, opened the back doors, and reached into the cargo area, pushing around duffel bags until he found the right one. Bingo. When he straightened, Trapper was leaning against the side. "You better not scratch my paint job."

"With what? My ass? Besides, what's it matter? This damn thing is older than I am."

"It's a classic." A classic Hunter had spent a few years, and he didn't even want to know how many thousands of dollars, heavily customizing. Trapper knew it. Hell, he'd helped him install the V-8 engine where a V-6 used to be. Hunter closed the back doors and swung and latched the tire back into place before locking it. Nothing was gonna get him down today, not even his big brother. "What do you need, Trap? Because I'm going back in, and believe me when I say I don't want company."

"I was wondering, since you and Toni seem to be shackin' up, if Fisher could use your cabin so I don't have to share with him? You ever hear that boy snore? He sounds like a moose with a sinus infection. No wonder he can't keep a girlfriend."

Hunter pulled the key card for his cabin out of his shirt pocket and handed it to Trapper. "Have at it. I sure as hell won't be needing it. But why don't you take the cabin?"

"Because that would leave Fisher in-between the Candy and Randy's cabins, and that spells danger. Your cabin is secluded. That's a much better way to keep him out of trouble."

"And you surrounded by women."

Trapper smiled. "Precisely. Do you have a problem with that?"

"Hell no, just as long as it's not Toni you're after."

"Toni's taken. Fisher and I figured that out when you went running after her that first day. Though it looks as if she's gonna be the last one to grasp the concept. She might need a little nudge in the right direction."

Hunter rubbed the back of his neck. "I'm nudging, but she's as stubborn as a mule. Every time I push, her first instinct is to kick. I gotta tell you, she packs a pretty mean wallop."

"I didn't know you were such a pansy. Maybe Gramps is right. Women are like horses. You gotta break them gently. It's like blanket training. You just don't toss the blanket on its back. You have the blanket lying around for a while. You let the horse smell and nuzzle it, and before she knows it the blanket is on her back, and it's not a big deal."

"I'll keep that in mind."

Trapper tipped his hat. "It's nice to see a smile on that ugly face of yours. Just, you know, remember what I said. Toni's like a skittish mare. You have to keep one side of her mind occupied while you lay the groundwork for the other. You know how to do that, don't you?"

"Don't worry. I've got it covered. It's all good." Okay, now he was lying. Toni was having kittens over the love thing. Damn. He'd never thought when he finally did fall in love, the woman he fell for would tell him to take it back and accuse him of lying. Though, with Toni he really wasn't all that surprised. Disappointed maybe, but not surprised.

Hunter checked his watch. It was still early—way too early to call Pat in LA. He hadn't heard from Emilio in three days and was really worried about the kid. Damn, he made a mental note to call Pat later to see what the hell was going on and returned to the cabin. When he opened the door, Toni sat naked on the bed doing cell phone surgery. She'd pulled the battery and SIM card out and was putting them back in wrong.

"Problem?"

"Yes. My phone isn't working, and I need to call Bianca today. I thought it was just the charge, but it's been plugged in since I got here."

"There's no cell service out this far. You can use the landline, but they're gonna rape you with the charges." He pulled his satellite phone off his belt. "You're welcome to use mine if you want."

"I need to call my mother too. God, this is so embarrassing."

"Why?"

"You don't know my mother."

"She can't be any worse than mine. Mine kisses me and brands me with her lipstick. She drives three hours to meet my girlfriend, and then tells me not to screw it up. Surely yours can't be any worse."

"Wanna bet? You can't imagine—and I spend my life trying not to do just that."

"Do what?"

"Not imagine my mother."

Hunter set the duffel on the floor and sat beside her on the bed. Damn she looked good. He'd never slept with a woman who looked as good first thing in the morning as she did when she was pulling his shorts off the night before. His dick perked up, and he swallowed hard trying to remember what they'd been talking about. It was difficult, since the only thing she wore was that collar. Her mother. He reached around her to pick up his sat phone. "I'm sure she's not that bad. After all, she raised you." He handed her the phone, and she dropped it on her lap. Damn, he'd never been jealous of a phone before.

Toni shook her head. "No, even my mother admits I raised myself while she was doing whatever she was doing at the time."

"Where is she, New York?"

"No, she's in Florida. She bought a place down there."

"Your mother stays in Florida in the summer?"

"She likes the heat."

"She must. Go ahead and give her a call. Do you want me to leave you alone?"

"Why?"

"Privacy." He smiled. "I thought you might want to tell her about me."

Toni rolled her eyes. "Please. The woman doesn't need any encouragement. Believe me, the last thing I'm going to do is mention you."

That's all it took for his dick to wilt. He slapped his hands on his jean-clad knees and rose from the bed.

"Hunter, I'm sorry. I didn't mean that the way it came out." She set his phone down and slid off the bed, wrapping her arms around his waist and resting her head against his chest.

His arms went around her, his fingers raking through her hair at the base of her neck. Her scent drove him wild. He tried to ignore it, but it was like a siren's call.

"It's just that my mom and I are... we're not like your family."

"I gathered." He held her shoulders and stepped back. If he hadn't, he'd have picked her up, thrown her on the bed, and they'd have ended up being late as hell for work. "Look, don't mind me. I'm just gonna make some coffee. The crap they serve at the inn is enough to make me give up caffeine. You go ahead and call whoever you want."

Toni smiled at the thought of coffee. Maybe this relationship thing wasn't so bad after all. She picked up Hunter's phone and dialed her office. She might as well get the bad stuff over with first thing. "Bianca, please. It's Toni Russo." She waited and listened to the Muzak version of "The Girl from Ipanema" and watched Hunter putter around.

"Toni? Is there a problem?" Bianca's voice came through in a rush.

"No, why would you think that? Everything is fine, we're on schedule, and we're all doing well."

"Good. How is Hunter? Was he very upset that I didn't make the trip?"

Toni's eyes flew to Hunter. "He didn't seem to be." She didn't think she should mention the relief she'd seen on Hunter's face when he found out Bianca wasn't with them. Which made her wonder what that was all about.

"Tell him for me I'm sorry I'm not there. Tell him we can finish what we started if I'm able to come out in the next few days or the next time he comes to New York."

"Bianca, that's something you should discuss with him on your own."

"You're probably right. I mean, why would I send a message with you, of all people? Things like this need a personal touch. Have him call me."

And just what the hell was that supposed to mean? "He's right here if you want to talk to him."

"Oh, that would be lovely." Yeah, she'd just bet.

"Before I do that, I called to make sure you haven't made any changes to the schedule."

"No. No changes."

"Okay. I hope the negotiations are going well."

"They are. We're just tying up loose ends today, you know, dotting the i's and crossing the t's."

"Glad to hear it. I'll get Hunter for you. Hold on a minute."

Hunter looked over when he heard his name and shook his head as he held up his hands and backed away. Interesting. Toni slipped off the bed, covering the mouthpiece. "I told her you were here."

"Why did you do that?" He took the phone. "Hi, Bianca. How goes the war?"

For the first time all morning, Toni realized she was

butt naked. She grabbed Hunter's T-shirt he'd tossed on the dresser and put it on.

"That's good. I'm sorry you couldn't make it, but things are going well in your absence. There's nothing to worry about. Toni has everything well in hand. She and James are doing a great job."

Hunter came up behind her and slid his hand under her shirt, trailing his fingers over her stomach. "No. We're getting along just fine without you. It's not a problem. Okay, thanks, Bianca. I'll put Toni back on. Oh, all right, I'll be sure to tell her. Bye."

He hit the end button on the phone before kissing Toni's neck. "Bianca said good-bye."

"That's not all she said."

Hunter nibbled that spot just above her collar. "Babe, the last thing I want to do right now is talk about your boss."

"And why is that?" Toni pulled away and went to pour herself a cup of coffee. She needed to put some distance between them, and caffeine was a great excuse. She'd been told she had a personality problem before she had a cup, and right now, she was more than a little ticked off.

Toni took her first sip and then turned to find Hunter looking at her strangely. She went to the dresser to figure out what to wear. "Bianca told me she was sorry she couldn't come out and finish what the two of you started." She pulled out a pair of jeans and a T-shirt before glaring back at him. "What exactly was she talking about?"

Hunter poured himself a cup and watched her over the rim of his travel mug before he answered. "I don't know. I guess it was something about the shoot."

"That's odd since she told me to tell you that you can finish it when you visit her in New York—and that it required 'a personal touch.' What kind of personal touching was she referring to? Why don't you tell me exactly what went on between you and Bianca?"

"I don't think I like where this is going."

"Join the club. It's not often I'm asked to tell the man I'm sleeping with that my boss can't wait to get together with him again. God, Hunter. What do you do? Have relationships with all the women you guide?"

Toni stomped into the bathroom and shut the door before ripping the T-shirt off and starting the shower. She felt dirty.

The door swung open. "Toni, you don't ask a question like that and then slam out of the room."

"I didn't slam." She turned to him. "Do you mind? I'm taking a shower."

"Not at all." He pulled off his shirt and unbuttoned his jeans. "I'll join you."

"You're not invited."

"Tough."

She stepped into the shower and tried to close the door on him, but he was too fast for her. Fine. Showing him her back, she hogged the water.

"I don't have anything but a business relationship with Bianca."

Turning, she wiped the water from her eyes. "Like the one you have with me?"

"Hardly. I don't sleep with clients—ever. It's bad for repeat business."

Toni grabbed the shampoo and squeezed way too much into her hand. Damn. "I'm a client, and you didn't know me for twenty-four hours before you slept with me."

He tried to help her lather her hair, and she slapped his hands away.

"You're not a client, babe. You work for one."

"That's a good one, Hunter. Nothing like splitting hairs." She stuck her head back under the showerhead. He still wasn't all that wet, and it looked like he was cold too. Good.

When she was all rinsed, he moved her out of the way and stood under the shower. "Don't get mad at me because Bianca wouldn't take no for an answer. Why do you think I was so damn relieved she didn't come?" He looked over his shoulder as he reached for the soap. "Hell, I brought Trapper and Fisher to protect me, or at least distract her. The woman was relentless. Besides, she's not my type."

"Oh, and what's your type?"

"You are. By now, that should be obvious to you. I've never told anyone outside the family that I love her. You're the first, Toni. There's nothing between me and Bianca—no matter what she says or wants."

"She obviously didn't get the memo."

"That's not my problem."

"Maybe not, but it's certainly mine. What do you think Bianca's going to say when I get back to New York, and she hears about us? And don't think for a minute she won't get a full report from Yvette and the others."

He didn't have an answer for that.

"Great, this is just what I need. I came here to make a name for myself—not to land the man my boss struck out with. If I had known—"

"If you had known, you would have done what?"

"I would have stayed the hell away from you, that's what."

"So your job is more important than what we have together?"

She didn't know what to say. She liked what she did. She also liked getting a paycheck. She had a life in New York, and as much as she cared for Hunter, she wasn't sold on the whole relationship thing. Sure, they were all hot and heavy now, but the old saying "out-of-sight and out-of-mind" was a truism for a reason. And to be honest, she had a bit of a problem believing Bianca threw herself at him, and he didn't take the bait. What man in his right mind would turn down a supermodel for God's sake?

"Never mind. Your silence speaks volumes." Hunter opened the door and stepped out of the shower.

Great. "Hunter. Wait."

He stopped and looked at her.

She quickly rinsed off and stepped out, grabbing a towel and wrapping it around her. "I... I don't know what to say. I mean, sure I care about my job. Who wouldn't? I need the paycheck, and I like what I do. Is that so wrong?"

Hunter shook his head. "No, I just thought... You know what? Never mind."

He pulled his shaving stuff out of his ditty bag and sprayed shaving cream into his palm.

"What did you think?"

"Nothing, Toni. Let's just drop it."

"Drop what? You may not believe me, but this is the first fight I've ever had with a boyfriend. I don't know how this works."

He ran his razor down the side of his face and looked at her in the mirror. "It's not a fight. It's a disagreement."

She rolled her eyes. "I don't know what you were doing, but I was fighting."

He turned and lifted her off her feet and sat her on the counter, making a place for himself between her legs. "I understand we're in different places. I'm a patient man. I can wait for you to catch up. But babe, I've never lied to you, and I never will. When I tell you something, you should at least give me the benefit of the doubt."

"Okay. But Bianca is so beautiful, why wouldn't you—"

"Bianca's beauty is only skin deep. You're beautiful inside and out. It's just hard to get through that wall you've built around yourself."

"I don't have a wall."

He leaned over her so they were face to face. "Babe, you not only have a wall, you have a damn alligator-infested moat to boot."

"Right. And you had such a hard time getting past it."

"I just learned your weakness and took full advantage."

"What's my weakness?"

"Coffee, dark Belgian chocolate, and me."

Okay, so he had her there. Speaking of coffee, she took a sip of hers. "When you're right, you're right." She tugged on the edge of his towel, and it fell to the floor. "You should really shave naked."

She spread her legs more, grabbed his butt, and pulled him closer.

"Babe, you're playing with fire."

She leaned back with her hands behind her and took a deep breath; the towel she had wrapped around her fell away.

"Are you trying to kill me? If I finish shaving now, I'm gonna end up slitting my throat."

"Then you'd better shave later."

———

Hunter captained the jet boat across Redfish Lake and then led the party to the base of the large peak Bianca had chosen for the mountain climbing shoot.

Toni was more confident when it came to this shoot. She'd done plenty of climbs—of course, those were in the middle of Manhattan and not the mountains of Idaho. Still, she felt at home with the harnesses and even climbed the face just for shits and giggles. As long as she pretended she was in the city, she didn't have a problem; and she had to admit, reaching the top was a hell of a lot more fulfilling when she looked at the view spread out before her. It sure beat looking out a window at the cityscape of downtown Manhattan or Brooklyn.

When her feet hit the ground after rappelling down, Hunter gave her a high-five. She could tell he wanted to give her a kiss—heck, it was all she could do not to plant one on him, but when they were working, he was all business, which was the way it should be.

The morning session went well. Toni worked closely with the photographers to get the shots she needed. How they angled each shot changed the look of the degree of difficulty, and since she needed a good mix for the project, she took great pains to make sure she got them.

During the lunch break Hunter, Fisher, and Karma took off on a climb. Hunter told her they were going, but he failed to mention it was the expert climb. She'd never have known if she hadn't had the map in her bag.

Toni ate her lunch and watched the three of them. The higher Hunter went, the more nervous she became. They were all good climbers, but they weren't using any equipment—just their hands and feet.

James joined her on the rock and shaded his eyes to watch the trio. "We really should get a few shots of them. They're amazing—especially since the guys have taken off their shirts. Damn, they sure know how to grow 'em here."

Hunter jumped from one point to another through the air without so much as a hand on the mountain. Toni's heart raced and then stopped. She closed her eyes tight and waited for the scream. When she heard none, she opened her eyes just in time to see Karma make the same jump, only she looked more like a ballet dancer. "How the hell are we going to get through this shoot if the three of them break their damn necks?"

"Are you worried about Hunter or the shoot?"

"Both. Look at those idiots. Hunter and Fisher look like Tom Cruise in that *Mission Impossible* movie, and Karma—I don't even know what she looks like."

"Darlin', Hunter and Fisher look far better than Tom Cruise could ever hope to. Besides, Tom's short. I like my men tall and strapping."

"I wish you luck with Fisher or Trapper. Hunter's mine."

James just raised an eyebrow. "I was wondering how long it would take you to figure that out."

"Yeah, I'm really slow. It's only been three days for God's sake. Give me a break, will you?"

"I don't know if you were watching, girlfriend, but that man's been head over heels since the first moment he set eyes on you."

Toni shook her head. "James, do you really believe in love at first sight?"

"I do as of three days ago—at least on his part. I'm still up in the air when it comes to you though. You're a tough nut."

"I'm a nut all right. Oh, and thanks for the heads up about Bianca and Hunter. You should have heard the way she talked about him when I called her this morning. It was as if they'd had a hot affair, and she's expecting to take up where they left off the next time he's in town."

"Bianca certainly wasn't subtle about what she wanted from Hunter last month, that's for damn sure. You know Bianca." James slid his arm around her and gave her a hug. "Hunter pretended to be oblivious. I did my best to run interference, but I could only do so much. Bianca can get downright pissy when she doesn't get what she wants. Believe me, Hunter is a hunter. He doesn't like being the prey—especially to a woman like Bianca. He didn't catch any of her passes if that's what you're worried about."

"I'm not worried, but you should have told me. What do you think she's going to do when she finds out about me and Hunter? I could lose my job over this."

"I like Hunter, Toni. He's a good man. And to tell you the truth, I didn't even think about Bianca. But does it really matter?"

"My job? Hell yes, it matters."

"Don't borrow trouble. I don't think your job is in jeopardy, but even if it were, I wouldn't complain if I were you. You and Hunter seem to have something special."

"How? He's here." She pointed up at the side of the mountain, wishing he would just come down from there already. "And I'm all the way out there." She pointed her other arm toward the east—at least she thought that was east. "How can this work?"

"So, you'll move. Just because you've never thought of leaving the city doesn't mean you can't."

"Look at me, James." She plucked her baby doll T-shirt off her chest. It was white with red Gothic print that said, "I'm Disinclined to Acquiesce to Your Request." "Do I look like I'd fit in here? And Hunter can't leave. He has his whole family, his businesses—a real life."

"But he doesn't have you."

Toni looked to see where Hunter was—way too high up for her peace of mind. She swallowed hard.

"Honey, you don't need to be in New York. You can make a statement anywhere. And it's true Hunter isn't likely to move to the Big Apple. But there's nothing keeping you there. You don't have much of a life to leave. I love you, sweetheart, but you have to admit your social life is a bit anemic."

"Anemic?"

"I was trying to be nice."

"If anemic is nice, I'd hate to think what you'd say if you weren't."

She and Hunter hadn't talked any more about the whole relationship thing since she interrupted his shave, and that was just fine with her.

"Well, as much as I love talking to you about my anemic life, I have to call my mother."

Thinking of her future with or without Hunter and having to call her mother was enough to give her indigestion. The potential damage to her career was already done. She wouldn't be able to hide their affair from Bianca even if she stopped seeing Hunter now, so what would be the point? The only certainty in Toni's life at the moment was this seven-day period—anything other than that was the unknown. She'd jump off that bridge when she came to it. What other choice did she have?

James shook his head. "I swear you're a glutton for punishment. I don't know why you don't write off both your parents."

"You just spent the last five minutes telling me I have no life, and now you want me to cut off my parents too? I'd be the first to admit they aren't—"

"The type to appreciate that they were blessed with a beautiful, talented, and intelligent daughter like you?"

"James, they're all I have."

"No, they're not. You deserve better, and I think you may have just found him."

He picked up Toni's lunch trash and went to check on the others as she dug Hunter's satellite phone out of her bag and dialed. "Hi, Clarissa, it's me—Toni."

"Darling, how are you?"

"I'm fine. You?" Toni heard spritzing. Mother must be spraying her orchids.

"Are you in Iowa?"

"Idaho, and yes, I'm sitting at the base of a ten-thousand-foot mountain."

"Oh, it sounds lovely. So, have you read the book I sent you?"

"No. I haven't had a chance. I've been busy."

"With a man?"

"Clarissa—" She strung out her mother's name. "I'm surrounded by men all the time."

"I know, darling. I only wish you'd do more than just look. You *are* interested in men, aren't you, dear?"

"Oh my God, are you asking if I'm gay?"

"Well, the thought has crossed my mind."

Toni closed her eyes. "Mother, I'm not gay—not that there's anything wrong with that."

"Antonia Marie Russo! You know how I feel about you calling me Mother."

"Fine. Is this better? Clarissa, I'm not gay."

"Thank God for small favors. You know your Aunt Lucy on your father's side is gay, and they say it's genetic."

"Good to know, but I'm not. Can we talk about something else please?"

"Sure. It wouldn't kill you to take a man out for a spin every once in a while."

"I've had my share of test-drives. I can't believe I'm telling you this, but I'm seeing someone."

"Really? Is he one of your models?"

"No, he's a guide."

"Oh…"

"Oh? What's that supposed to mean? I thought you'd be ecstatic."

"Darling, it's fine to play with men from a different social strata, but good looks don't pay the bills. One must be smart about these things. One must always marry up."

"Why do I bother? He's not from a different social stratum. He owns the guide company and a few other businesses in Boise as well."

"In that case, read the damn book, and figure out how to keep him."

"Mom—" She stopped herself. "Clarissa, I've been here since Sunday. It's a little early to begin reeling him in, don't you think?"

"It's never too early. I only knew your father a week before we moved in together."

"And we all know how well that worked out."

"Yes, well, I'd really love to talk more, but I'm going to be late for my tennis lesson. The new pro at the club is just fabulous."

"I'm sure he is. Have a great time."

"Call me when you get back to civilization, darling. Bye."

Toni hit the end button and tried to lie back on the rock, but something or someone stopped her—someone as silent as a ghost. She looked over her shoulder. "Hunter, how long have you been sitting there?"

That crooked Dennis-the-Menace smile covered his face. He looked very pleased with himself. "You call your mother Clarissa?"

"After I hit about fifteen she said I looked too old to call her mom. I have a habit of conveniently forgetting when I want to tick her off."

He leaned into her, his arm resting on the rock next to her hip. "I thought you weren't going to talk to your mom about me."

"I threw mommy dearest a bone when she bugged me about reading that book on landing a man." Toni scooted around to face him, hugging her knees to her chest. "You want to tell me just what you were doing climbing that high? You could have killed yourself."

"I've done that climb since I was a kid. I know it like the back of my hand, but I'm sorry if I scared you."

Toni looked up the mountain and then back to him. "Your mother let you climb that? What was she thinking?"

"I don't know that we even told her, but she knew we were all good climbers. It's what we've always done—although truth be told, I think the first time we climbed it was because Karma had taken off on her own. I swear that girl is part monkey. She can still out-climb us all." He tipped the lid of Toni's baseball cap. "How old were you when you took your first subway ride alone?"

"I don't know, five or six."

"I wouldn't let any kid of mine ride the subway alone at that age. Don't you see? It all has to do with perspective. Kids here start climbing early—not climbs like that one." He pointed to the mountain he'd just scaled. "But they learn their limits, and they learn by experience what to look for. Just like you did on the subway."

She shrugged. "I don't know. Maybe you're right."

Hunter stretched out on the rock beside her, and Toni had the urge to join him and use his shoulder as a pillow. She wished she could spend the afternoon staring at the sky through the trees and listening to his heartbeat.

"Do you have plans tonight?"

She slid her legs down onto the sun-heated rock. "Plans? What do you mean?"

"I mean, do you have plans for dinner?" He rolled onto his side to face her. "I'm trying to ask you out."

"Like on a date?"

"Exactly. I thought if you wanted to we could head down to Ketchum, have dinner, maybe do a little shopping, and spend some time together away from here."

"How far away is Ketchum, and what kind of town is it?" She stopped and squinted at him. "It is a town, right?"

Hunter put his backpack under his head and used it as a pillow. "Ketchum is a resort town about an hour and fifteen minutes south of here. Sun Valley is next to Ketchum. It has great restaurants, shops, movie stars, the whole nine yards. We can stop at The Elephant's Perch and pick up a pair of decent hiking boots for you too."

"We're only an hour and fifteen minutes away from a real town, and we're staying at the inn?"

"Yeah, that's a real hardship."

"It is if you're a coffee drinker."

"Not if you bring your own." He waggled his eyebrows and handed her a thermos. "You just need to learn the ropes. So, do you want to go out or not?"

Toni opened the top and took a long drink. "God, that's good."

"I know. Now answer the question."

Toni looked down at her T-shirt and jeans. "I didn't bring anything dressy to wear."

Hunter grabbed the thermos and took a drink. "We're pretty casual here, even in Ketchum. If you want to dress up, you'd fit in just fine too. It has a real eclectic mix of residents."

"Okay then, sure. Just, you know, keep it under your hat."

"Why? Like it or not, Toni, everyone here knows about us." Hunter puffed up his chest and looked as if he wanted to have another disagreement.

Right. As tempting as the thought was, she wasn't biting—at least not yet. She rolled her eyes. "I know that. I just don't want to say anything because if the models find out there's a resort within driving distance, do you really think we're going to be there alone?"

"Good point. I guess we can tell them later. Karma and the guys can take them out there soon."

"Right, but then how would we get them to come back?"

"Okay, maybe on our last night here. That way, either they make it back, or they miss the van to Boise."

"That might just work."

He rubbed her thigh. "See. I told you we make a good team."

Chapter 14

HUNTER PARKED HIS LAND CRUISER IN FRONT OF THE Elephant's Perch and went around to get Toni's door only to find her hopping out on her own. How she did that in the short skirt she wore was a mystery. For someone who didn't bring dressy clothes, she sure looked well put together to him and to the three guys walking down the street. They probably needed a trip to the chiropractor to treat the whiplash they suffered when they got a load of her.

"You park in the middle of the street here?" She looked up and down; two rows of cars ran parallel the length of the street.

Hunter put his arm around her and crossed. "We get a lot of snow. It makes it easier to plow. Then the drivers and passengers don't have to open their door into snowbanks."

"Oh, I guess that makes sense."

They walked arm in arm over the wood plank sidewalk to the door of the white, A-frame building. Hunter held the door, and when Toni entered she looked a little gob smacked. Bikes were lined up in front of the wall of footwear. Backpacks, tents, and sleeping bags covered just about every surface. "How's it going, Mike?"

"Hunter. I haven't seen you in a while. What do you need?"

He put his arm around Toni. "Mike, this is Toni. She

needs a pair of lightweight hiking boots. I was thinking a pair of Merrell Moab Ventilators or maybe the Sirens."

Mike nodded. "Sure, what size?"

Toni shook her head. "Can't I just get a pair of Doc Martens?"

Mike bit back a laugh, and Hunter didn't bother to try. "Babe. Doc Martens won't cut it here. Trust me on this."

"I don't know why. I mean, you said they need tread, and Doc Martens have a hell of a tread."

"Yeah, but you also need flexibility and breathability. What size are you?"

"A seven, but I don't want to buy something I'm never going to wear again."

Hunter pulled her in closer. "Believe me. You'll get a lot of use out of these."

Toni just rolled her eyes as Mike walked back to the storeroom.

Grabbing a pair of light wool socks, Hunter helped her into a chair before dragging a stool over to sit. He took her foot in his hand and slid the high-heeled boot off before gliding his thumb down the length of her foot and pressing it into her arch.

A groan escaped her parted lips. "You did that on purpose."

"It's just payback for wearing that skirt and those boots out in public. Besides, I'll be damned if I'm gonna let Mike sit here. Not with the view I'm getting."

Toni pressed her thighs together, spoiling his fun. Shit, he knew he shouldn't have said anything.

By the time Mike had the boots out and laced, Hunter had her other foot massaged and socked. "Here, try these." He slid the lightweight hiking boot on and tightened the laces before tying them.

Toni moved to stand, and Hunter shook his head. "No, you need both of them on so you can walk around awhile."

"I'm sure they're fine."

"You say that now, but believe me, you don't want to be ten miles away from base camp and figure out they're too small. Blisters can be a bitch."

"So can guides."

Mike let out a chuckle and dropped the other boots he'd brought out on the chair beside her. "I'll just leave you two alone to fight it out."

Hunter turned to Mike. "Yeah, she loves me. She just doesn't know it yet."

Toni smacked Hunter's arm as he slid his hand up her calf.

Mike turned and winked. "It looks to me like you better keep giving her foot massages, Kincaid. That might help."

"Can't hurt," Hunter said, as he slid his fingers over the arch of her other foot.

"Just put the boot on, and leave my feet alone."

"What? You don't have a secret Cinderella fantasy?"

"Yeah, but with Jimmy Choo, not—"

"Who the hell is Jimmy Choo?"

Toni laughed. "Jimmy Choo is a shoe designer. I was talking about a pair of boots I would kill for, and they're certainly nothing like these."

"Oh." Okay, he felt like an idiot, but how the hell was he supposed to know she wasn't talking about a guy? "So buy them."

"They cost fifteen hundred dollars. I don't think

so. Jimmy Choo is way out of my price range—unfortunately. But a girl can dream."

"Damn, my Tecnica Dragons were crazy expensive, and they only cost about eight hundred bucks retail. But then, I always get them for cost—one of the perks of owning a ski shop. Fifteen hundred dollars for a pair of boots?" He whistled through his teeth. "Are they alpine or racing?"

"They're five-inch stilettos."

"Babe, you'd spend fifteen hundred dollars on a pair of boots you can't even ski in?"

"No, but if I could get them on the sale rack at Saks for fifty percent off I sure would. Besides, I don't ski."

He helped her up and then pulled her toward him for a kiss. "That's going to change."

She shook her head. "I don't like the cold."

"Me either." He took her hand and led her around the store.

"Then why do you ski?"

"I don't ski where it's cold. I ski here in Sun Valley, Castle Rock, sometimes I head down to Utah or over to Jackson Hole. I wear a sweater and a powder jacket, and I'm fine."

She looked at him like he was nuts. "Really?"

"Would I lie to you?"

She shook her head. "No, I don't think you would."

Hunter had never heard anything more gratifying. Finally, he was getting through to her. He wrapped his arm around her for a sideways hug. "I promise I'll never lie to you."

She gave him the sweetest look just before she kissed his lips. "You better not."

"So, how do they feel?" When she gave him a confused look, he kissed her again. "The boots, how are they?"

"Oh." She looked down at her feet. "They're really not very stylish. Do they have them in black? This tan doesn't go with anything I own."

"Toni, these are hiking boots. You don't buy them for the color. You buy them for the fit."

"You're kidding, right?"

"No, I'm not. How do they feel?"

"I don't know. They don't hurt if that's what you're asking."

"Does your heel slip up and down?"

"No."

"Do your feet slide forward if you stop short?"

She kicked her boot against the carpeted floor. "No."

"Do you like them?"

"No. But they're fine."

"Do you want to try on the others?"

"Not especially. Shoe shopping really loses its appeal when your only choices are Ugg and uglier."

Hunter stifled a sigh. "You can lead a horse to water—"

"Am I the horse in this scenario?"

Hunter led her back to her chair and started unlacing the boots. "I'm not going to touch that with a ten-foot pole." He tossed the first boot into the box. "Mike, I think we're going with these. Do you want to put them and a couple pair of these socks on my tab?"

"Sure thing, Hunter."

Toni stopped him. "I can pay for my own boots."

"Yeah, so can I."

"Hunter. Really, I—"

He kissed her. "Stop it, okay? I'm forcing you to buy the boots, so I'm paying for them. It's not a big deal."

"It is to me. It's really nice of you, but it's not necessary, even if they are fugly."

"Toni, just humor me. I want you to be safe. I want you to have good equipment. It's important to me. You're important to me."

She stared him down—or tried too. He obviously had a lot more practice. She looked as if she wanted to say something but chickened out and averted her eyes. He would have gladly lost this round if only she'd said what her eyes told him. He knew she needed more time and figured he'd pushed enough for one shopping trip.

"Thank you."

"You're welcome. Come on. Let's go for a walk. I'll show you around town." He looked down at her stiletto boots; they looked sexy as hell but probably weren't the most comfortable pair of shoes. "Are you sure you don't want to wear your new boots? They're better for walking."

"With this skirt? I don't think so."

Toni watched Hunter run across the street and put her boots in the truck. She'd probably drop the things in the incinerator when she got home, but then, if she kept seeing Hunter, he'd expect her to wear them again. God, her closet was too small for ugly shoes.

Maybe she could leave them at Hunter's place. It's not as if she'd ever need them in New York. She'd heard that when you're in a relationship most people leave clothing at the other person's place. She imagined other people leaving a change of underwear and a few tops. Well, she'd always been a little different, so she'd leave ugly boots. For some weird reason the thought of her ugly boots next to his in his closet made her smile.

Hunter ran back across the street. "What's that smile for?"

"I was just thinking of seeing you again. You know, after this trip."

"Really? What about it?"

"I just decided I'd leave my ugly boots here with you."

"Oh Toni, that's so romantic. Be still my heart."

"Hey, if you're not happy, you have no one to blame but yourself. You're the one who fell for me first, remember? You dragged me kicking and screaming behind you."

"Babe, the only time you were screaming was in bed." His green eyes seemed to go darker. "But then there was that time in the hot spring."

"I screamed your name *after* you jumped into the river, so that doesn't count."

"Oh no, I distinctly remember you screaming my name a few times before I swam for my shorts too."

She shrugged. "Maybe. But don't let it go to your head."

Hunter kissed her. "No chance of that with you around. But since you just admitted you fell for me, I think I can live with it."

"I did no such thing."

He laughed. "Oh yeah, you did." He kissed her right there on the sidewalk. It wasn't a friendly kiss either. It was a carnal, I-want-to-rip-your-clothes-off-and-tie-you-up-with-them kind of kiss.

"Hunter—" Damn, she couldn't even think straight.

"Shhh." He placed two fingers over her swollen lips. "Just give me a second to enjoy the moment, would you?"

Oh yeah, she'd let him enjoy it. As a matter of fact, she'd help him. She licked his fingers and slid them into her mouth before sucking on them.

He swallowed hard and pulled her close. "You keep that up, and I'm not gonna be fit to walk around in public."

He slowly slid his fingers from between her lips and groaned when she bit down and raked her teeth against the tips, not wanting to let them go. His stormy-eyed look had her wishing they were back at the cabin, or his house, or just about anywhere other than the middle of a sidewalk in front of his buddy's store.

She crossed her arms. "What did I say?"

"You told me you loved me."

"Oh no, I didn't."

"In Toni speak you did, and that's good enough for me. Are you ready to go?"

She walked down the sidewalk, and Hunter came around the outside, walking on the grass between her and the street until she moved over. Why the heck did he have to walk on that side? She listed to the right when she walked. She was going to spend the entire date walking into him.

"What? You're not gonna argue with me?"

Shaking her head to answer his question, she tried desperately to remember what she'd said and wondered if Hunter was right. Was it some sort of Freudian slip? And if it was, were they always true? She didn't think she'd subconsciously lie. Lying was definitely a conscious decision. And she never lied. Well, not since she was a kid.

She bumped into him and self-corrected. "You're walking on the wrong side."

"Guys are supposed to walk closest to the road. It's good manners. If a car goes out of control, I can push you out of harm's way. Or if the street is wet and a truck goes through a puddle, I get splashed, and you don't."

"Seriously? I've never heard that." He didn't look like he was making it up. Toni thought back to the whole love conversation and remembered telling him she was leaving the ugly boots at his place. That couldn't possibly be construed as an I-Love-You, could it? No way. Okay, since that wasn't it, she had to have said something else. She remembered he'd said something sarcastic about her not being very romantic. She stopped dead in her tracks.

"Toni, are you okay?"

"Oh shit! I told you you'd fallen in love with me first. After all, you're the Quick Draw McGraw of love. You picked me out."

"I resent the Quick Draw McGraw thing. I'm not quick, well, not in bed anyway."

"You're the one who fell for me, the Anti-Cupid, and then dragged me kicking and screaming along behind you."

"I was just teasing about the lack of romance. It was a joke."

"Oh God." She swallowed hard.

"Toni, what's going on?"

"It's like jumping from the high dive all over again. I see myself falling in slow motion, flailing around in relationship limbo, not knowing what the hell I'm supposed to do and doing everything wrong, until I hit the water in what will certainly be the most painful relationship belly flop imaginable. What was I thinking falling in love with you?"

"I don't think it's something you consciously decide."

"Are you telling me I have no control over my own mind? Like loving you is one big Freudian slip?"

He smiled. "You can control your mind, but not your heart. And there will be no relationship belly flops—not if I can help it." He steered her to a bench. "Maybe you should sit down. You don't look so good."

"Oh, you're a regular Rudolph Valentino, Hunter. I tell you I love you, and all you can say is, 'You don't look so good.' What's up with that?"

"It might have been different if you weren't fighting a panic attack when you said it." He squatted down in front of her so they were face to face. "Breathe, okay?"

"I'm breathing, dammit. The thing is, I don't do love. I'm the Anti-Cupid, remember? Love is against my genetic code."

"Obviously not. Face it, babe. You're human just like the rest of us. Give it some time to sink in, and then it won't seem so scary. Don't worry. It's not as if you're in this alone. I love you too." He gave her a gentle kiss and toyed with her hair. "We'll figure it out together."

———

Hunter woke up to his phone ringing. He let go of Toni's breast and grabbed the phone off the nightstand, hoping it was Emilio. Nope. "This had better be good."

"Houston, we have a problem." Trapper's voice sounded as if he was holding back a laugh. "You better get your ass over to Fisher's cabin on the double. I'll meet you there."

Hunter cursed under his breath and rolled out of bed. He was gonna fillet Fisher when he got his hands on him. It was almost 1:00 a.m. for the love of God. He'd fallen asleep less than a half hour before still unable to believe Toni admitted she loved him—not only on their date, but several times in the throes of passion. Damn, that was something he could definitely get used to.

Not wanting to wake Toni, he felt around in the dark for his clothes, pulled them on, stepped into unlaced hiking boots, and grabbed his phone and key card before leaving the cabin.

Cold air slapped his face, chasing away the last remnants of sleep and fueling his irritation at being ripped from his bed and the woman he loved. He stomped toward the far cabin, the lights glaring through the windows. Trapper fell into step beside him. "This better be damn good, Trapper."

Hunter rapped on the door before throwing it open. There was Bianca sitting on the bed. Fisher held up his hands as his unfastened jeans slid dangerously low. "I didn't touch her, I swear. Okay, I touched her, but I was asleep, so it doesn't count, does it? I don't even know her. I went to bed alone, and when I woke up she was there. I thought I was having a really great dream."

"Or nightmare." Trapper stepped inside and tipped his hat. "Ma'am."

Hunter wanted to punch someone or something. "Fisher, pull your damn pants up for God's sake." Bianca, the client, Toni's boss, was supposed to be in New York, not in the cabin he was assigned to. "Bianca, this would be a really good time for you to get out of my brother's cabin."

"But Hunter…" Her breathless croon made him wince, and both his brothers glared as if they were ready to scalp him.

"We'll wait for you outside." Trapper said, as he and Fisher exchanged looks before monkey-lifting Hunter out the door. They turned on him with matching sneers. Trapper stomped into his personal space, puffing up his chest, his hand clenched in a tight fist. "First Bianca and now Toni?"

Fisher followed. "She thought I was you. Her saying your name is what woke me in the first place. Shit, Hunter, when did you turn into such a horn dog?"

"I never touched her."

Trapper crossed his arms and did that judge thing that made him so damn good at his job. "So Bianca just waltzed into your cabin uninvited and started messin' with what she thought was your tackle? Talk about the old bait and switch. I thought you two outgrew that in high school."

Hunter couldn't believe he was being forced to explain himself. He'd done nothing wrong. "That's the only way she'd ever be in my bed. I don't sleep with clients—it's bad for business."

Trapper laughed, but there was no humor in it. "Yeah, this doesn't bode well either."

Bianca opened the door. Her booted feet were shoulder width apart, and she placed one hand on her hip. She pointed at Fisher with the other. "Who are you? And what were you doing in Hunter's bed?"

Hunter crossed his arms and stepped in front of his

twin. "I think the question is—what were you doing in my bed? My brother, Fisher, and I traded cabins. You're the intruder."

"Hunter." She moved toward him. His brothers both stepped forward, blocking her. "I was only trying to surprise you."

Trapper tipped his hat. "Ma'am, I don't know what it's like in New York City, but in these parts, that's breaking, entering, and a possible sexual assault. Fisher, if you want to press charges, all you have to do is call the Blaine County Sheriff's office."

Bianca blanched.

Fisher ran his hand through his blond hair. "No, it was just a case of mistaken identity. No harm done. It's happened before." Fisher smiled.

"Son of a bitch." Hunter would have given just about anything to pound the shit out of Fisher. The boy was really asking for it. "When?"

Trapper looked from Fisher to Hunter. "You two can reminisce later. Right now, I think I'd better escort Ms. Ferrari to the front desk and get her a cabin of her own. We'll see you in the morning."

"What about my bags?"

"I'll bring them to you myself after we get you settled."

Hunter held out his hand to Bianca. "Why don't you give me back the key so we can avoid any further confusion?"

She pulled a key out of the back pocket of her painted-on jeans and slapped it onto his palm. "I thought he was you. I didn't notice the blond hair in the dark. I was just trying to wake you. We have a lot to talk about. It's business mostly."

Hunter wanted to tell her she was damn lucky it had

been Fisher in the bed, because his brother was much more forgiving, but he held his tongue. As much as it pained him, it wouldn't help to make an enemy of his client. "We have a meeting at the lodge every morning at 9 a.m. We can talk business there. Trapper will make sure you get settled in the right cabin. Good night."

Hunter didn't bother to wait for Bianca's response. He only wished he could wait a lifetime before having to tell Toni her boss had arrived and was up to no good.

He stalked back to the cabin and tiptoed in, shedding his clothes before slipping back into bed. Toni rolled over and threw her arm and leg over him. He lay still, praying she was asleep.

"Where'd you run off to?"

"Just a little problem I had to take care of. Go back to sleep, babe. I'll tell you about it in the morning."

"Okay." She kissed him before resting her head on his shoulder. Her warm hand slid across his stomach, and within a minute she was asleep.

The rest of the night Hunter held Toni and worried. He spent an inordinate amount of time attempting the impossible—trying to figure out what Bianca was doing there—besides the obvious. Thank God they'd crashed in Toni's cabin. If they'd stayed in his, this minor disaster would have reached epic proportions—not that it still didn't have the potential to do just that. Bianca ending up in Fisher's cabin was going to be difficult enough to explain. If his brothers had a hard time believing there was nothing between him and Bianca, Toni certainly wouldn't believe him.

Chapter 15

TONI AWOKE TO THE SCENT OF FRESHLY BREWED coffee and a showered Hunter. When she pried her eyes open she was surprised to see him already dressed.

"Good morning, sleepyhead." He bent down to kiss her and sat on the bed before handing her a steaming mug of coffee.

She knew better than to say anything before caffeine, so she drank enough of the scalding liquid to hot-wire the nice side of her brain. She stretched, surprised she'd overslept, only to check the clock and see she hadn't. Toni snuggled closer to him and slid her free arm around his waist, nuzzling his neck. "It's not even seven yet. We don't have anywhere to be until nine." She trailed her fingers down the button band of his shirt to his belt. "Why aren't you naked and in bed?"

He took a good long sip of his coffee, and after taking hers, set them both out of reach. She smiled, wondering what he'd planned to do with her that would make him need to protect their coffee from spilling. Athletic sex? She nibbled his ear and ran her hand down his thigh.

He caught it and gave her hand a squeeze.

"Hunter?" She stopped to look at him, really look at him, and noticed his eyes were bloodshot as if he hadn't slept. His jaw was clenched, and a vein popped out in his forehead and throbbed. His back and shoulders were so tight and straight, it looked as if they might crack if he bent them.

She remembered waking last night to find him sneaking back into the cabin. "What happened last night that dragged you out of our bed at weird o'clock in the morning and is dragging you out of it again?"

Hunter turned her hand palm up and traced the lines, before kissing it and closing her fingers over the kiss. He made eye contact and looked so utterly miserable, Toni held her breath. Maybe he'd changed his mind about loving her? She felt the sting of tears and blinked them away. She'd known it was too fast. He was dumping her. Taking a deep breath, she braced for it.

"Bianca showed up last night in Fisher's cabin."

Huh? He hadn't changed his mind? "Bianca is here? What's she doing here? I just spoke to her twenty-four hours ago. I told her everything was fine. She didn't mention coming out."

Hunter wasn't moving, not saying anything, and he certainly didn't look as if his stress was decreasing. If anything, it looked like it was getting worse. What could have him so upset? "Oh God, did she find out about us?" Then it hit her. "Hold on. Did you just say she was in Fisher's cabin?"

He nodded. Hunter's look darkened. He looked dangerous. His glower wasn't directed at her, thank God, but she had to admit this hard, angry, rebel-without-a-cause thing Hunter had going was a complete turn-on.

"If Fisher and Bianca have something going on then we're off the hook." Toni shrugged and scooted closer. "I guess she figured if she couldn't have you, your twin is the next best thing. And really, personality-wise, I think Fisher is a much better match for her. He's easy-going, definitely not like you. I assume Bianca figured that out. Anyone who knows Fisher—"

"She certainly knows him now. Intimately. Or at least well enough to pick him out in a naked line-up."

"What's that supposed to mean?" Was he jealous? "Are you telling me they didn't meet each other the last time she was out?"

Hunter nodded.

"What? Did she pick him up at the bar last night?"

"No. He was asleep before she arrived."

"Then what was she doing in his cabin?"

Hunter remained mute.

"Oh God, Fisher's cabin was supposed to be yours. Bianca wasn't expecting Fisher. She was expecting you."

"She must have gotten an extra key to my room from the front desk. She couldn't tell us apart in the dark, and I don't think I ever talked to her about my family or anything personal. Fisher woke up when she called him by my name."

"What made Bianca so sure she'd be welcome in your cabin in the middle of the night?" Sure, the woman's ego knew no bounds, but this was over the top even for her.

"I know what this looks like, Toni, but I really need you to trust me on this."

"This is like a freakin' nightmare. What exactly happened?"

"Trapper called me at about 1:00 a.m. Said there was a problem at Fisher's cabin, and he'd meet me there."

"Had Fisher called Trapper?"

"I don't know. I don't know that he had time. When I walked in, Bianca was there, and Fisher was still climbing into his jeans. Fisher's a heavy sleeper. He didn't wake up until he heard her calling my name. Fisher—he just thought he was having one hell of a good dream."

"Oh God, she thought he was you."

"If it had been me, she'd never have gotten past the door. I'm nothing like Fisher. He just laughed it off as an accident and a case of mistaken identity."

Toni shook her head and scooted closer, hugging him sideways and wrapping her legs around his waist. "What are we going to do?"

"Nothing. She's your boss and my client, and as far as I'm concerned, anything that doesn't have to do with the job is off-limits."

"Well, good luck with that. But it's unrealistic as hell. She's a pissed off, humiliated, ex-supermodel—talk about an ugly combination. James and I are going to be right in her line of fire. This is a disaster. Would you do me a favor?"

"Whatever you need."

"Go get James for me while I jump in the shower. He's been with Bianca since their modeling days. He knows her like the back of his hand." Toni slid around on Hunter's lap so she faced him and kissed him, feeling the tension disappear. Too bad she had fires to put out, or she'd spend the morning fanning the flame that sparked between them every time they were in the same room. She ended the kiss and hugged his neck. "Thanks."

"For what?"

"For being straight with me. You could have candy-coated it, but you didn't. I appreciate that."

"I love you, and I promised I'd never lie to you. That includes candy coating."

"I thought it would be bad when I went back to New York, and Bianca found out about us. But with her here—things could get ugly."

Hunter reached for her face and forced her to look at him. "The only way Bianca can come between us is if we allow her to, Toni. I'm not going to let her do that."

Hunter looked so sure of it. What he didn't think of was that Bianca obviously cared for him—she must have if she felt it was okay to just walk into his cabin in the middle of the night and risk being turned down. Even if Bianca was a saint, that would smart. The fact that she had three eyewitnesses only made it worse.

Toni had just finished tying her new hiking boots when James knocked on the door and pushed it open without waiting for a response. He raised an eyebrow. "Is this a new fashion trend, Toni?" He took in her shorts, relatively plain T-shirt, and lack of accessories.

"No." She looked at her new boots and cringed. "I hate them, but Hunter insisted on buying the ugliest boots known to man."

"Well, aside from the unfashionable shoes he foisted on you, you look marvelous, darling. I think love agrees with you."

She blew her bangs out of her eyes. The boots definitely didn't match anything in her closet, but she wasn't about to rock the raft with Hunter by wearing her Vans again. Maybe she could dye the boots later.

"Word all over the inn is that Bianca showed up and had a busy night last night."

Toni looked up from braiding her hair and pasted on a wary smile. "That's an interesting way to put it. She thought she was in Hunter's cabin and got Fisher instead."

"Oh, to have been a fly on the wall."

"Hunter wasn't too happy about it. The poor guy looked about ready to blow a gasket when he told me this morning. He said he and Trapper walked in on Fisher pulling up his pants and Bianca sitting on the bed. Trapper ended up escorting her back to the front desk to get her own cabin."

"I take it she wasn't happy to hear the news about your reincarnated love life."

"Hunter didn't say, but it's not too much of a stretch of the imagination to think Bianca's not going to be happy a guy like Hunter passed her over for the likes of me."

James put his arm around her. "It's not like you're chopped liver, darling. You might have questionable fashion sense, especially in those boots, but you're beautiful and vibrant, and you have a hell of a head on your shoulders."

"But James, she's a supermodel. How can I compete with that?"

"There's no need to compete. You've already won. Just relax."

"Easier said than done. But let's not go there now. What we need is a plan."

"Toni, we have a plan. You have every shoot sched-uled to the nth degree, oh anal one. All we need to do is stick to it. There's no need to change the way we do anything—it's working, girlfriend. Bianca will see you have everything well in hand and realize she's not needed. Maybe once that becomes as obvious as the fact that Hunter has the word *taken* written all over him in black and red lipstick, she'll give up and hop the next flight to New York or LA."

"You and Hunter don't seem to get it. Bianca must have had a specific reason to drop everything and fly out here. You of all people should know that. You've worked with her for how long?"

"Almost twenty years, but she'll never admit it. She's still telling everyone who asks that she's in her twenties. She'll be thirty-four next April, not that you heard it from me."

"Like I'm going to mention it. I would really like to survive this trip and not be thrown off a cliff."

"Hunter would never allow that. He keeps such a close eye on you, I'm surprised he left you alone for this long." He smiled. "Look at you. You're blushing."

"I am not."

"Look in the mirror. You're blushing like a schoolgirl."

Toni's cheeks burned, and she covered them with her hands. "Leave me alone."

"So… have you told him yet?"

"Told him what?"

"Have you told Hunter that you're in love with him?"

"Yeah, okay. I told him. Are you happy now?"

James fanned his face and sniffed. "My little girl is growin' up. I'm so proud."

— ∿ —

Hunter walked the path that led past the cabins and

found Trapper on his porch sipping a cup of coffee. "Did you bring your own coffee?"

Trapper tipped back his hat. "To the inn? What the hell do you think?"

"Good." Hunter sat on the porch chair and passed him his travel mug. "Then pour me another cup, would you? I'm beat."

Trapper reappeared a minute later.

Hunter took a sip. "Ooh, Kona. You've been holdin' out on me, Bro."

Trapper shrugged, and they watched the models come and go while Hunter arranged his thoughts into words. "Something's been bothering me since last night."

"Besides the fact you have two beautiful women after your sorry ass, and one looks as mean as a mountain lion with PMS?"

"Yeah, besides that." He turned and studied Trapper. "How did you know there was gonna be trouble before Fisher did?"

"I saw the limo, the lady, and the luggage. There's no way in hell Fisher is capable of handling a woman like that, and since she had her own key, I knew she had to have bribed that kid at the front desk. You know... the one who's always following Karma around."

"Alan Meeks?"

"That would be him." Trapper sipped his coffee.

"If you knew what was going down, why didn't you stop Bianca?"

"Just because Fisher isn't capable of handling the woman doesn't mean he shouldn't have the opportunity to try. Besides, have you looked at Bianca Ferrari? There isn't a man alive who would mind waking up with her."

"Except me."

Trapper groaned. "Spoken by a true casualty of love. We all can't be so lucky. So how's Toni taking the news of her boss's recent adventure?"

"Better than expected, which makes me nervous. We've already fought about Bianca after Toni called her to check in. Bianca insinuated there was a hell of a lot more between us than a working relationship."

"Did you tell her the truth?"

"Yes. Both times." Hunter winced. "What choice did I have? I was up all night trying to figure out what to say, or a way to avoid it. I had to be straight with her."

"So you told Toni that Bianca, without invitation, snuck into what she thought was your cabin and Toni bought it?"

"I think so. She thanked me for being straight with her."

"I can see why you're nervous. Most women I know wouldn't take that kind of news well. Since you obviously didn't get kicked out of Toni's cabin, what are you doing here bugging me?"

"James is over at our place. He and Toni are putting their heads together trying to figure out how to deal with Bianca."

Trapper looked up from his coffee and shook his head. "Man, I don't envy you. Talk about an uncomfortable situation. You're right in the middle of a nightmare triangle—Bianca, Toni, and the job."

"Is stating the obvious a judge thing, or is it just one of your many annoying gifts?" Hunter took off his hat and wiped his tired eyes. "Hell, I'd take a few days off if I could, but as the owner I'm under contract to be one of the guides. Bianca's got me by the short hairs." He took a deep breath and smelled Bianca's perfume. One look at Trapper's sardonic smile confirmed her presence.

She propped a fist full of red lacquered fingernails on her hip. "I don't remember you complaining last month, but you weren't sleeping with my manager then either. You've been a busy boy, haven't you, Hunter? I must say, I'm surprised."

He didn't want to know why Bianca was surprised by his relationship with Toni. "I guess opposites attract." He took a long look at Bianca—all six feet of her, taking in the straight blond hair, which was long enough to play peek-a-boo with her breasts as it shimmered in the early light, khaki shorts highlighting the very tan length of her legs, and the black pushup bra that left nothing to the imagination under the almost see-through T-shirt she wore over it. Her green eyes sparkled with nefarious plans only a woman like Bianca could conceive. He didn't want to talk to her about anything but the job. "We have a team meeting at 9 a.m. then we're taking the rafts down to Mormon Bend and Rough Creek."

"I would have thought you'd have already done that shoot. After all, most of it is at your cabin."

"Toni and James put together the schedule. I didn't have much to do with it. The crew has been trained on the rafts. We took a float trip down to my cabin on their first day here. Since my sister, Karma, joined the team, James and Toni thought it would be a good idea to get some pictures of her shooting the Shotgun and Sunbeam Dam Class IV rapids."

"That wasn't on my list of scheduled shoots."

"True, but since Karma is an experienced River Runners guide, they thought we could do what you had planned and add more white-water shots. Karma's up for it, and from what James said she's a natural model."

Bianca turned up her perfect patrician nose. "We'll just see about that."

She didn't look enthused, but after last night, Hunter had a feeling there wasn't much anyone could do to improve her mood.

Trapper had been silent through the whole exchange, which was unusual for him. He watched her unnoticed from under the brim of his hat. "I don't know about you, but I'm going to get some breakfast. Bianca, would you join me?"

Bianca aimed that cover girl smile she always used on him, and Hunter thanked God Trapper willingly put himself in her line of fire. Hunter wasn't sure if Trap was taking one for the team, or if His Honor was looking for Bianca to fill one of his seventy-two-hour relationship slots. Hunter didn't really care to know Trapper's motivation, but he didn't hold back a relieved smile. If there was one man who could give Bianca a run for her millions, it was Trapper. He hoped.

"I do have something to discuss with Hunter, but I suppose it can wait." She slid her sunglasses on and ran both hands through her hair, starting at the base of her scalp and tossing it over one shoulder, posing before pumping up the wattage on her smile. "Breakfast sounds good. I'd love to." She slid her hand through Trapper's offered arm.

Trapper nodded at Hunter as he walked her toward the lodge.

Waving her fingers, Bianca shot a grin over her shoulder. "I'll see you later."

Damn, he sure hoped his big brother wouldn't get them all in a heap of trouble.

—◦◦◦—

Trapper walked Bianca to the restaurant at the inn and held the chair for her. She hadn't said a word on the walk over, and he wasn't about to start the conversation. He learned a long time ago that the less you say, the more you learn. Right now, Trapper was on a mission to learn as much about Bianca Ferrari as humanly possible.

She sat in the chair he held, crossed her uncommonly long, gorgeous legs, and sat so straight he wondered if she'd gone to a finishing school or had studied ballet.

He removed his hat and laid it on the seat next to his as Bianca examined him with the same intensity he'd directed toward her.

Jamie, the server, approached the table. "Coffee?"

Trapper shook his head, holding up his travel mug. Bianca, not knowing any better, turned her cup over. "Thanks."

Trapper waited until the server poured Bianca's coffee and left them to their menus. "You might not want to drink that."

"Why?"

"The inn's a pretty nice place as long as you bring your own coffee or don't mind drinking dishwater."

She bravely took a sip, and from the looks of it, fought the urge to spit it back into her cup. He had to smile at the face she made. He'd bet there were no photos of her wearing that expression on any magazine ads or posters.

"You bring your own coffee?"

He held up his cup. "I sure do. I'd be happy to share if you're interested."

"In coffee?"

"That's what I'm talking about. What were you talking about?"

"We can start with coffee I suppose, and see where we go from there."

Her face was blank. He'd always been great at reading people, but for the life of him he couldn't figure out what was going on in that mind of hers. She let nothing show. He looked over the menu and set it aside.

"Any other warnings you want to issue?"

"About what?"

"I don't know—the food, the people? I've already heard about Hunter and Toni. From the sound of it, they've been going hot and heavy since she met him. I have to tell you. I never would have thought those two would be at all compatible."

"Why's that?"

"Toni is afraid of the wild, and Wild Thing is Hunter's middle name."

"People grow. Toni's obviously conquered her fear. And there is a lot you don't know about Hunter. He doesn't open up to many people, especially not clients."

"We spent a week together less than a month ago, and no matter what you might think, I'm hardly a typical client."

"Your personal fantasies aside, Hunter never mixes business with pleasure. You're the client—that puts you in the 'do not touch' category in his book."

"And Toni's not?"

He just smiled. "She's not the client. She works for

the client, so she falls into the 'tread carefully' category. Obviously, Hunter thought Toni was worth the risk."

"I guess time will tell."

"So, are you going to tell me why you felt the need to fly all the way out here to check on a shoot that, for all intents and purposes, is going like clockwork?"

"Action Models is my business. This shoot is for one of my largest clients, and in this position, Toni is untried. Sure she's done a few shoots in the city, but when it comes to her personal handicaps, I felt it would be better for me to take over."

"I might have bought it if you hadn't snuck into what you thought was Hunter's cabin. Since you did, you're gonna have to come up with a better one than that, sweetheart."

"I'm not your sweetheart, and I don't have to explain anything to you."

"I don't suppose you do. But as Hunter's brother and legal advisor, I think it only fair to warn you that nowhere in your contract with River Runners does it give you the right to anything other than a guide service."

"What are you? A fishing guide and a lawyer?"

Trapper sat back and smiled. "Yes, ma'am, and a judge too."

Bianca laughed, and for the first time he saw the woman behind the mask. "Sure you are. On what planet?"

"The planet earth. The State of Idaho specifically." He pulled out his wallet, removed his card, and handed it to her.

"Judge Trapper Kincaid, Fourth Judicial District Court of the State of Idaho." She looked at the card and then scratched at the embossed state seal before returning her gaze to him. "If you're a judge then what are you doing working as a River Runner?"

"Just taking a vacation and helping out my little brother."

"Some vacation."

"I think so. It's been a lot of fun escorting a bunch of beautiful women around the wilderness. You can't beat the scenery—not to mention the beauty of the Sawtooth National Recreation Area."

"Do you do this often?"

"Take beautiful women out to breakfast? As often as I can. Between my courtroom gig, helping out River Runners on special occasions, and taking time off to ski, my docket's pretty full. What about you?"

Storm clouds brewed in her eyes.

"Oh, that's right. You like the less traditional approach. I think you would have had Fisher if you hadn't called him by his twin's name. They're a little sensitive when it comes to that. The two of them were almost indistinguishable when they were younger. They hated when people confused one for the other, well, except when they'd switched places, which they did often. But back to you. I assume you're usually more successful than you were last night. Was this just a one off or something you do regularly?"

Bianca took the coffee cup in front of her and tossed the contents right in his face, wiped her hands on the napkin, and left.

Good thing the coffee there was not only bad, but lukewarm.

Chapter 16

"YOUR BROTHER'S A PIG."

Hunter tossed aside a life vest and looked into Bianca's angry eyes. "I take it breakfast with Trapper didn't go well." He smiled when he saw Trapper walk by, his once white T-shirt stained light brown and plastered to his chest.

"What makes you think that?"

"Just a feeling. I'm told his brand of charm grows on you."

"That's doubtful, but I didn't come all this way to talk to Judge Trapper Kincaid. I have a proposition for you."

Hunter leaned against the back of his Land Cruiser. "If it's anything like the one you had for me or Fisher last night, I'm afraid I'm going to have to decline."

Bianca looked away, and if he wasn't mistaken, she blushed. "It's not." She squared her shoulders and continued. "This is business, and although I had hoped we could mix business with pleasure, it's certainly not a condition of the deal."

"What kind of deal?" Hunter locked the truck before grabbing his gear and throwing it over his shoulder.

"The kind that will take your plans to expand that little camp of yours and make them a reality."

"River Runners Camp?"

"Yes. You mentioned it when we scheduled this

shoot. Remember you sandwiched our shoot between the weeks you had the camp operating? I researched what you've done with the camp, and I contacted your friend Pat in LA—the rest is history. Come on." She took his arm and led him toward the cabins.

Hunter was more than a little skeptical. He didn't think Bianca was a bad person, just egocentric and maybe a little on the narcissistic side, which was probably typical among supermodels... or ex-supermodels in Bianca's case.

"I merely saw an opportunity for both of us to profit. Why do you think I skipped the first half of this shoot? I wanted to see if there was any corporate interest before I approached you."

"Interest in what?"

"A way to make us both fabulously wealthy and still satisfy your more altruistic tendencies. Come. I have the plans in my cabin." When Hunter hesitated she stopped. "Problem?"

"No." Bianca was his client, and they had business to discuss. The fact that it happened in her cabin shouldn't make any difference. He hoped.

She unlocked the door and tossed her bag on the couch. "Make yourself at home."

That was something Hunter was not going to do. He left the door open, only closing the screen door behind him, and stood in front of it as she dug through what looked like the world's largest designer purse. When she pulled out a laptop, he figured it must be a briefcase.

Bianca slid a file folder out of the bag and shuffled through papers. "When I flew back to New York last month, I started thinking about all the amazing work you do with those kids at your camp. I knew there had to be a way you and I could work together to our benefit as well as the camp."

"Bianca, the only ones who should benefit are the kids. That's what River Runners Camp is all about."

"That's where you're wrong. Sure, it will help the kids, but there's no reason we shouldn't profit from it too. And by going in on it with KidSports, the company I've contacted, we'll all come out ahead. You see, KidSports wants to proudly sponsor River Runners Camp, generously fund it, and supply all the clothes and any equipment you'll need. Action Models will work on the marketing campaign that will feature the kids and all the good work you do at the camp, giving it fabulous, free exposure. It's a win-win situation for all those involved. You, me, the camp, and KidSports."

"And the kids. Bianca, this is all about the kids." Still, he got more than a little queasy at the thought of the kids having to cute it up as models.

"Sure, sure." She waved her bejeweled hand. "That's a given. KidSports is very interested. They do have some conditions though, and I'm sure you will too. I've drawn up a deal memo with everything we've discussed so far. Nothing is set in stone. I just wanted to make sure there was a high degree of interest on their part before I approached you with the idea."

She handed him a pile of papers. He paged through information about KidSports—a company he had done business with for several years since he carried their merchandise in his store.

He looked from the sheaf of papers to Bianca, who bounced in front of him with her perfect C-cup breasts jiggling.

Turning to the next section titled "Deal Memo," he scanned the page. The initial investment amount made him almost swallow his tongue. With that kind of money, he'd be able to complete all three phases of his River Runners ten-year plan.

He'd have the money to build the cabins, a dining hall, and a kitchen. He'd be able to hire several child psychologists and social workers instead of using volunteers the way he had in the past. He could house kids year-round, whenever they were out of school, which would give River Runners more time with each camper. A week or two once or twice a year wasn't enough to make a lasting impact on the kids. With KidSports funding, that wouldn't be a problem.

Hunters mind spun. He swallowed hard and tried not to get his hopes up too high. "I'm going to need to take some time and look at this more closely, but I have to tell you, Bianca, I really like what I see so far. Thank you."

She threw herself against him, wrapped her arms around his neck, and kissed him. He stepped back, almost hitting the screen door behind him. "Bianca."

She loosened her grip but didn't let him go. "Oh Hunter. This is going to be just perfect—you and I working together. You'll have the camp you always dreamed of. I'll have the contract for the KidSports catalogue. All those kids will get what they need, and we'll all be paid very well."

He wasn't sure how to disengage himself from her without looking like an ungrateful ass. So she kissed him on the lips, but it was just a kiss, and it wasn't like he kissed her back.

"Bianca," He stepped back, thankful the screen door was on a spring and not a latch. "This is a lot to take in. Let me go and read this. Do me a favor. Don't say anything about this to anyone until we talk again, okay?"

She looked a little disappointed, not to mention confused. "Okay, but we'll talk soon, right?"

Hunter backed away. "Yes. I just need a little time to look this over." He turned and walked toward his and Toni's cabin.

When he unlocked the door, he was glad Toni wasn't there. He had to figure out what to tell her. He dug out the dating book he'd been reading while he scanned the deal memo. Maybe the book would have some advice on how women handle situations such as this.

The KidSports contract would be for five years, which meant he'd be dealing not only with KidSports, but with Bianca for the duration. And if it went well, it could be renewed. They'd like to use the kids from the camp for part of the catalogue, but that was only if the parents or guardians agreed.

His biggest concern was how Toni would handle it, and how he'd handle working with Bianca. Not that he'd have a problem, but if Bianca did, it could make the next five years of his life a living hell. Shit. He sat on the bed, thumbing through the book, looking for answers, and just coming up with more questions. He tossed the book aside and picked up the memo, making notes in the margin. There was liability associated with using child models if the camp kids weren't the models and paying the camp kids if they were. He wracked his brain trying to come up with a way to make it all work.

He saw the time and cursed again. He was late for the

damn meeting. He tossed the book and the memo into his duffel bag, kicked it under the bed, grabbed his gear, and ran for the lodge.

———m———

Toni felt much better after having spoken to James. Everything he said was true. Her relationship with Hunter was a nonissue. She had done a great job—in spite of her fear. The shoot had gone smoothly. Toni had a detailed plan for the rest of the shoots and knew she could handle whatever Bianca threw her way.

She grabbed her schedule and walked to Bianca's cabin, thinking she'd take a few minutes before the meeting to bring Bianca up to speed on the few changes she'd made to the day's shoot.

Toni turned the corner and recognized Hunter's back through the screened door. All those warm, mushy feelings enveloped her, and she realized that maybe Hunter was right. If she gave it a little time, she might just get used to this whole love thing.

The warm, mushy feelings turned into cold, wet concrete in her stomach the moment Bianca threw herself at Hunter. Toni watched in disbelief as Bianca wrapped her tentacles around Hunter's neck. He did nothing to avoid it. Toni expected Bianca to make a play for Hunter. What shocked her was the way he caught Bianca and kissed her for Toni and all the world to see.

Toni had heard people say that their lovers had cut their hearts out; she thought they were speaking metaphorically. When Hunter kissed Bianca, Toni felt physical pain. It was as if someone had stabbed her. She stumbled around the side of the cabin, leaned against the wall to keep from falling, and waited for the pain to abate—it didn't. Before he left she'd heard Hunter ask Bianca not to say anything until after they'd met again.

She wasn't sure how long she stood there trying to come to grips with what she saw and heard. No matter how many times she went over it in her head, nothing made sense. Why would Hunter tell her he loved her if he wanted Bianca? Why had he bothered with her at all?

There had to be a reasonable explanation for what had happened. Maybe Bianca kissed Hunter, and he didn't know how to get out of it. Maybe Toni had misinterpreted the whole thing—she didn't think so, but it wasn't out of the realm of possibility. Heck, Bianca wanted Hunter. After last night that was obvious, but Hunter claimed it was one-sided. At the very least, he deserved the chance to explain. He'd asked her to give him the benefit of the doubt, and she would. She took a deep breath, trying to calm down and not overreact. It still didn't make sense, but maybe if she just trusted in him, he'd tell her what was going on.

Numbly, Toni crossed what she liked to think of as the courtyard and went into the lodge. The screen door slammed shut behind her on its spring. She carried her clipboard to the meeting room and sat in the same chair she'd always used before she pulled out the day's schedule, taking out a copy for James.

"There you are."

Toni looked up and saw Bianca walking toward her. She stood, and that familiar feeling of fading away filled her. She looked down at her shorts, wool socks, and hiking boots, reached for the D-ring on her collar, and remembered that she hadn't worn it. Bianca, in her khaki shorts and see-through top, seemed to glow.

"I've been looking all over for you." She set her purse down and sat in James's chair. "Since I'm back now and ready to take over, you need to get back to the office. I'm sure you'll be happy to get back to the city. I know how hard this shoot has been for you, but James said you've done an incredible job."

Toni tried to erase the vision that repeated on the mental screen in her mind of Bianca kissing Hunter. She took a deep breath. She had to be professional. "Thanks, but it really was a team effort."

Bianca waved her response away. "I appreciate you pinch-hitting for me, Toni. I have scheduled meetings for you next week and have a new project I need you to work on." She handed Toni a file. "You can get a flight out of Hailey to Salt Lake with connections to Kennedy. Just put it on the corporate account. Your work here is done."

"But I still have a few shoots to do. I've planned them all—" She pulled out her folder with the information about the remaining shoots. She'd been looking forward to them.

Bianca smiled. "Good. Then I'll just need your notes."

"My notes?"

Bianca nudged her and took the file, paging through it. "Your notes have made you invaluable. I don't know what I'd do without them. You've always got a plan."

Toni nodded. "Yeah, that's me, the one with the plan." She just wished she knew what to do now. She couldn't believe it herself, but she wasn't ready to leave. She nodded as she mentally cursed that stupid poster she'd had hanging on her bedroom door growing up, the one with the seagull that said: "If you love something, set it free; if it comes back it's yours, if it doesn't, it never was." Her mother had bought it for her after husband number three pulled a disappearing act. It seemed she and her mother had one thing in common; no one was ever theirs—not the job, and maybe not Hunter. She put the rest of her things together and got up. "Okay. I need to say good-bye to a few people. If I don't get out today, I'll catch the first flight in the morning."

Bianca pulled her long blond hair into a ponytail and threw it over her shoulder. "That's fine. If I don't see you before you leave, have a nice trip. And Toni, you really did a great job out here. I'm impressed."

"Thank you." Toni looked at Bianca who practically shimmered, casting Toni and everything around her in a big shadow. Toni hadn't been out of that shadow long, but she missed the light that Bianca seemed to steal from anyone in her presence. It wasn't as if Toni thought Bianca stole it on purpose—men maybe, but not the light. Some people just naturally attract it. Bianca was one of those people, and Toni wasn't.

Hunter slipped into the back of the meeting room and leaned against the wall next to Trapper and Fisher. "Where's Toni?"

Fisher shrugged. "She didn't look so good when we saw her walking up to the lodge while we were checking equipment. We just got here too. Where have you been?"

"I got held up. Maybe I should go check on her."

Bianca chose that moment to look his way. "Oh

fabulous, Hunter. Why don't you come up and take everyone through your plans for the day."

Hunter stuffed his hands in his pockets and rocked back on his heels. "Toni has the plans. She's the one keeping everyone and everything on schedule."

"Yes, but she's not here. James, I'm sure you can fill us in."

James went to the front of the room and looked over the notes lying on the table and then summarized the day's schedule for the group.

The tortured look on James's face only added to the bad feeling Hunter had. As soon as an opportunity presented itself, he slipped out of the meeting.

"Hunter, we're about to leave. Where are you going?"

Son of a bitch. Bianca had followed. "I forgot something in my cabin. I'll meet you at the river. James and everyone know how to get there. Just give me a few minutes."

Bianca walked toward him and grasped his wrist. "Hunter, Toni is packing. She has a lot of work to catch up on in the city. She's fine. You know she's not a fan of the river, and since I'm here, there's really no reason she should spend the day on the edge of a panic attack, is there?"

He stepped out of her grasp. "Packing? Toni wouldn't just leave without saying anything. I'll be there in a minute." He left, feeling Bianca's eyes on him the whole way out the door.

Something was very wrong, and he knew it. Toni had come a long way in conquering her fear, and she was a trooper. She wouldn't let them go down the river without her. This was her shoot, and she'd never let Bianca

take over without a fight. He hightailed it to the cabin.
Relief crashed over him when he opened the door and
found Toni packing. He rushed up to her and pulled her
into a hug. "What happened?"

Toni pulled away and continued to empty the contents of her underwear drawer into the suitcase open
on the bed. "Bianca has work for me back at the office.
I have to leave sooner than expected. What happened
to you?"

What could he say? *Bianca kissed me, she offered me
the deal of a lifetime, and I'm scared to death of losing
you?* All in the two minutes he had before Bianca herself
came calling? He didn't think so.

Toni stared into Hunter's beautiful green eyes and
braced herself for the truth—the whole noncandy-
coated, ugly truth he'd promised.

"Nothing."

"Nothing?" She might not be sure what had happened
between him and Bianca, but she knew something had.
"Nothing happened?"

"No. I just went to the meeting and was concerned
when you weren't there. Fisher and Trapper thought you
weren't feeling well, so I wanted to check on you."

"Nothing happened?" He didn't try to candy coat
it. He just lied. Something happened—something he
wouldn't talk to her about.

"Listen babe, you don't have to leave now, do you?
Just stay here, and we'll talk when I come back. We'll
decide what to do then, okay? I'll be back by two
o'clock or so."

"I know the schedule. I wrote it." The terrible pain
she'd been holding off slammed into her and then was

gone. It was replaced by a somehow familiar numbness. Hunter held her tight in his arms, and still she felt nothing. Maybe she had learned the cure for magnetic attraction after all.

"I'll see you when I get back. Don't worry. We'll work everything out. I love you."

Toni nodded and collapsed on the bed when she heard the screen slam shut behind him. He loved her. Sure he did. How many times would she give him the benefit of the doubt? Would she wait years, like her mother had, making excuses for her second husband's incessant cheating? No. But Toni would hear Hunter out—if for nothing else than for her own piece of mind. She'd promised. And unlike some, she didn't renege on her promises.

When she could take a normal breath, Toni continued to pack and absentmindedly tossed the book her mother had sent her into her backpack.

She'd told Bianca she might not leave until the morning, so she could stay and hear Hunter out. Then maybe it was time to go home, take a good look at her life, and figure out how to make it less anemic.

Toni kicked off her boots and slipped on her Vans. There was little chance of leaving her boots in Hunter's closet, so she'd do the next best thing. She grabbed his duffel bag from under the bed to deposit her boots, unzipped it, and found the book her mother had given her with a bunch of papers stuck in it like an oversized bookmark.

"Wait a minute." She glanced at her backpack. This wasn't her book. Removing the sheaf of papers, she laid them on the nightstand and thumbed through the book. Handwritten notes were scrawled in the margins throughout—some with her name underlined twice. Hunter's notes.

Toni felt as if she hovered above herself, reading his comments and realizing her entire relationship with the only person who ever claimed to love her was nothing but a joke. Hunter had read the book and played her like Jimi Hendrix played his Fender Strat.

Why Hunter had done it was a mystery, but she'd known enough men to know sometimes there was no rhyme or reason for the hurtful things they did. To see how far they could go or what they could get away with was usually sufficient incentive. In Hunter's case, he'd gotten away with her heart.

Toni looked around their joke of a love nest as the walls closed in on her. She tried her cell, remembered its uselessness, and tossed it into her backpack before grabbing the landline to call for reservations.

Toni listened to the Muzak playing and the recording thanking her for her patience. The only thing holding Toni together was the need to be far away from Hunter before he returned. No explanations necessary—she'd read the writing in the margins.

She didn't know how he'd gotten a copy of the book. Sure, there were bookstores in Sun Valley and Ketchum, but she didn't remember him leaving the inn without her. It had to have been Karma—she must have brought it to him, which meant his brothers probably knew too. God, she was the joke of the entire family. Hunter had played her from the first day, and everyone was in on it. He'd done it with forethought, malice, and help.

"May I help you?" The Muzak had stopped, and a real human voice drew Toni back to earth.

Toni cleared her dry throat. "Yes. I need a ticket from Friedman Memorial Airport in Hailey, Idaho, to JFK. What's your next available flight?"

When she had come back from the meeting, she'd dropped her clipboard on the table by the door. Too bad the old-fashioned phone cord wouldn't reach that far. She grabbed the first piece of paper she saw, something from KidSports, and scribbled her itinerary on the back along with the number for Sun Valley Limo.

She disconnected the call and dialed the limo service. "Hello, this is Toni Russo, and I need a limo from The Sawtooth Inn to the Hailey airport as soon as possible. When can you get here?" Checking her watch, she nearly groaned. "Noon would be fine, but earlier would be better. If something opens up, I'm in cabin seven." She gave them all the necessary information and paid with her corporate credit card. At least she had a plan. Apparently, that was all she was good for.

Toni finished packing and tried to decide what to do about Hunter. She'd never broken up with someone before and wasn't sure how. She would rather just leave, never to be heard from again, since the thought of having to see Hunter was too painful to imagine. Maybe she'd leave the book opened to that interesting section he'd highlighted about insecurities and baggage. That would suit her just fine.

Dragging her luggage behind her, Toni gathered Hunter's papers and his copy of the book. The words *Deal Memo* caught her eye. She did a double take and wondered how documents from her office got here.

The memo was written on the template Toni had designed. It was copied to Hunter Kincaid, River Runners

Camp; Bianca Ferrari, Action Models; and Kevin Shultz, KidSports. "So that was the hush-hush deal Bianca had been busy negotiating." A deal with Hunter, a man Bianca wanted, and working together would put them in very close proximity. Knowing Bianca, that was exactly what she had planned. Now the kiss was beginning to make more sense.

Toni scanned the memo and nodded. It was everything necessary to obtain Hunter's goal, maybe more than he needed. Of course it contained more strings than the inside of a regulation baseball. Toni knew how much Hunter wanted that camp, and Bianca had just handed it to him on a silver platter. How could he refuse Bianca and not the deal? Why would he?

Toni waited for another slash of pain, but it didn't come. She figured by this time there was nothing left of her heart to break. Her eyes burned, and she blinked a few times. Feeling like a ghost looking down at herself going through the motions, she wondered when the numbness would wear off. She set the book and the memo on the table for Hunter to see when he returned. He was a bright guy. He'd figure it out eventually.

Toni removed her copy of the book from her bag. Lord knew she didn't need it now. The last thing in the world she ever wanted to do was put herself in the position to feel this way again.

Glancing around the cabin once more, Toni made sure she'd remembered everything and wished she'd never stepped foot in Idaho. She tossed her key card on the table, grabbed the boots she'd planned to leave at Hunter's, and tossed them and her book where they belonged—in the trash.

Rolling her bags out the door, Toni decided she'd rather wait alone in the middle of the freakin' forest than in the cabin she'd shared with Hunter.

Chapter 17

HUNTER JUMPED OUT OF THE VAN AND HEADED TO THE cabin. Without Toni being there to keep the shoot moving, the day had taken much longer than they'd planned. Bianca had been unprepared, even with Toni's notes. She should have known that and let Toni do her job.

He'd negotiated the waters and the people with a sense of impending doom. He'd lied to Toni. Sure he told himself he hadn't had the time to tell her the truth, but when it came right down to it, he'd been afraid to. He'd been afraid of the look he knew he'd see in her eyes. Afraid of letting her down. Afraid of losing her.

He'd spent the entire day worried about Toni, Emilio, the camp, and the deal with Bianca. He dropped his gear on the porch, slid the key card in the lock, and stepped into the cabin.

"Toni?"

The second he saw her boots and the book in the trash can, all the air left his lungs. She was gone. The memo and his well-read copy of that same book stared up at him as he crumpled onto a chair beside the table. Toni'd found out and left. He sat staring at the evidence of his stupidity. Sure, he'd just gotten the book as a joke at first, but then he used it to try to win her over. Toni would only see the negative.

The ringing of his phone cut through the fog of shock and self-recrimination. "River Runners." Hunter didn't recognize his own voice. It sounded as if it came from far away.

"Hunter, it's Pat."

"Can I call you back? It's a really bad time."

"It's not going to get any better. Listen, there's no easy way to say this. Emilio got busted last night."

"For what?" Hunter tried to draw a breath, but seemed incapable.

"Drugs. He's not talking. He must be protecting his buddies. The police are holding him. It's not looking good. I'm sorry, Hunter."

"When's the bond hearing?"

"We're not sure. The day after tomorrow maybe."

The image of Emilio behind bars danced before his eyes.

"Let me know. I'll be there."

"Hunter, that's not necessary."

"If Emilio was here, if I'd spent more time with him, he wouldn't be in jail now. My presence at the bond hearing is necessary. Just let me know the details. And Pat, tell his mother... Milana... tell her I'm sorry." Hunter barely choked that out. His throat felt as if someone had him in a headlock. He'd promised Emilio's mother he'd look after him. He'd screwed that up too.

"You did the best you could. Milana knows that. You have nothing to be sorry for."

The hell he didn't. He was too controlling, too stubborn, and too damn proud to ask for help, and Emilio paid the price. "Just tell her, okay."

"Sure. I'll call you when I have more information. And Hunter?"

"What?"

"Take care of yourself. There's only so much you can give before it starts taking you down. You did all the right things. Sometimes no matter how hard you try, you can't save them."

"I should have kept Emilio with me. I should have made it happen. If he were here, he'd be safe."

"Emilio should have been at the shelter with his mother and little brother. You didn't put the drugs in his pocket, nor are you responsible for him being out on the streets after curfew. He's going to pay the price, Hunter. You can't."

"I gotta go, Pat. Bye." Hunter ended the call, tossing his phone on the table as if it were a poisonous snake, and stared into space. Emilio was in jail, Toni was gone, and Hunter was responsible for both.

Hunter packed his things and was just about to leave when Trapper, Fisher, and Karma walked in without knocking.

Trapper picked Toni's boots out of the trash. "Problem, little Brother?"

Karma slugged Trapper then put her arm around Hunter. "What happened? God, you look like you've just lost your best friend."

"I did. Toni's gone and Emilio—"

She pulled away to look at him. "What about Emilio?"

"He's in jail. He got picked up for drugs last night."

"I'm so sorry." Karma pulled him in tight.

Jail for a kid like Emilio could very well be a death sentence, and they all knew it. Hunter didn't know who was comforting who. Karma fought a losing battle with her tears. He looked to his brothers to help him out, but they seemed almost as upset as Karma. Fisher, the doctor, the guy who stared death in the eye every day during his residency in Chicago, looked glassy-eyed, and Trapper, well, Hunter couldn't tell. His hat hid his eyes from view.

"Look, I've got to go. I need to talk to James—find out where Toni lives—"

Karma shoved him. "You don't know where Toni lives?"

"Manhattan's a big-ass island, Karma. I don't have her address. I didn't think I'd need it yet, and her cell was out of service the whole time she was here, so I never bothered to get her number. So yeah, I don't know where she lives. I just know I have to find her, and then I have to get to LA and see what I can do for Emilio. Maybe I can talk some sense into him. Can you guys finish the shoot for me?"

Trapper cleared his throat. "I thought you had to be here."

"An owner has to be here, and since we never got around to changing the LLC, the three of you are still technically owners, so we're golden. I just need to tell Bianca."

Hunter did a double take when Fisher sneered at the mention of Bianca's name. Fisher, his happy-go-lucky brother, looked about ready to open a can of whoop-ass on Bianca.

"What's your problem?

"Bianca's the problem. She's sent Toni home before finishing the job. That's just not right. She handled every shoot so well. Bianca didn't need to come out here and screw everything up."

Hunter, Trapper, and Karma all turned and stared at Fisher.

"Hey, just because I like to have a good time doesn't mean I didn't notice how hard Toni worked. I'm not an idiot. I'm a real MD."

Trapper patted Fisher on the back. "We know you're not an idiot. Nope, you get paid to play with X-ray machines, stethoscopes, and have women take their clothes off in front of you."

Karma shook her head. "Who's the idiot now?"

Both Trapper and Fisher gave him the evil eye. "Hunter." They said in stereo.

Fisher shrugged. "You let Toni get away."

"This doesn't make any sense." Karma crossed her arms. "Why would Toni just leave like that? Bianca said she was catching the first flight tomorrow. She didn't even say good-bye to us or you."

Hunter shook his head and couldn't meet her eyes.

"What did you do?"

"I fucked up. Okay? Toni found the book I was reading and a deal memo Bianca put together for the camp." He tossed the memo at Trapper. "I never agreed to it, but I'm sure Toni took one look at that memo and the book and thought the worst."

Karma rolled her eyes. "Well, you were using the book. Only you would take notes in the margins." She paged through. "God, I didn't take this many notes in college."

"I was just using it to figure out how to get in Toni's—"

Karma looked up. "Pants?"

Hunter sat back down, completely defeated. "I love her, Karma. I think I have since the first moment I set eyes on her. I saw something special in her eyes, and when she let me in, I discovered a treasure. I just wanted to make sure she felt the same about me."

Trapper grabbed the book out of Karma's hands and flipped through the copy.

Fisher dug the other out of the trash. "Damn, I guess it works as long as you don't get caught."

Hunter rose, feeling like an old man, and packed his things. He was just stuffing the coffeemaker into its small bag when James came to the door. Hunter tossed his duffel to Trapper along with his keys. "Would you guys make yourself useful and pack my truck while I talk to James?" Karma took the bag with the coffee and coffeemaker—probably to her own cabin knowing her. Fisher grabbed his other bags and gear and headed out.

James looked around the empty cabin. "Where's Toni?"

"I thought you'd know. When I left for the shoot, she said she'd be here when I got back. She wasn't."

"I know Bianca wants her back in New York, but I thought she wasn't leaving until tomorrow."

"I guess we were both wrong."

"She wouldn't leave without saying good-bye. Did something happen between the two of you?"

Hunter really wasn't up for going into that—besides, he'd lied. As nice as James was, he was very protective of Toni.

"James, you gotta help me out. I have to find her. I need to make sure she's okay. Where does she live?"

James crossed his arms and glared at Hunter. Gone was the nice easygoing guy he'd gotten to like. "You didn't answer the question."

"What happened is between me and Toni. I love her. I just need to find her and explain."

Hunter stared back at James, who seemed to be taking his measure. Finally the man relaxed, and Hunter breathed a sigh of relief. He been waiting for James to slug him—not that he didn't deserve it. After seeing the disappointed look on James's face, Hunter would have preferred a punch.

"I can't give you her address without her permission. I'm sorry, but that's rule number two in best friend etiquette. I'd be happy to contact her and ask if I can. But that's about all I can do other than put in a good word with her—not that you deserve it."

Hunter nodded and rubbed his eyes. He had a mountain of a headache and had a feeling it was only going to get worse. He ripped a piece of paper off the deal memo and wrote down all his contact information. "Would you call me when you talk to her? I'm worried sick. I know I fucked up, but she promised she'd hear me out."

James folded the paper and put it in his wallet. "I know she loves you. I don't pretend to know what the problem is, but I'll fill you in on one very important thing."

"What's that?"

"If you hurt her again, I'll do my best to kick your ass from here to New York and back. I like you, but Toni's like a daughter to me. I love her."

"You and me both, but I can't fix it if I can't find her."

"I'll see what I can do. Just remember what I said."

"I will. Trapper, Fisher, and Karma are taking over for me on the job. It's been good knowing you."

James clasped his hand and gave him a guy hug. "Good luck."

Hunter grabbed his phone and dialed as he walked toward the truck.

"Joe Walsh."

"Gramps, it's Hunter. I need help."

"What's going on, boy?"

"Toni's gone. I need to borrow a jet, and I need it in two hours."

"Now, slow down, son. Where's Toni?"

Hunter grabbed the keys from Trapper, jumped in the Land Cruiser, and started the engine. "I don't know, probably on a plane to New York by now. I screwed up, Gramps. I gotta find her."

"What in the hell did you do?"

"It's a long story. I promise to tell you the whole thing if you send me your fastest jet. I'm worried about her." He swallowed the lump in his throat. "And Gramps, Emilio's in jail. The bond hearing is in a day or two, so I've got to go out to LA and see if I can talk to him. I have to do something, but the fact is I've lost him. I can't lose Toni too."

"Aw hell. I'm sorry about Emilio, but you can't count the kid out yet. You just need to stand behind him and make things right with Toni. I'll have my pilots meet you at Friedman Memorial. And Hunter…"

"Yeah, Gramps?"

"I love ya, son."

"Love you too. I don't suppose you know anyone who would be able to tell you what flight Antonia Russo took out of Hailey, would you?"

"I just might. I'll call you back."

Toni watched the clock tick, wishing she could turn back time and avoid the last week of her life. She was numb, empty, humiliated, and alone. She snapped her collar and cuffs back on before pulling her hoodie around her, shivering in the air-conditioned terminal. Every time she reached for her collar she thought of Hunter—the lies, Bianca and Hunter kissing, and the way she'd faded to near invisibility. "That Time of Year" blared from her cell phone. She jumped and reached for it. "Hello?"

"Toni, thank God I caught you."

"James." Tears welled up in her eyes, like someone turned on a faucet. They ran down her face as pain slapped her and cut through the sea of numbness she'd floated in. It was as if someone dropped a live wire in the water, shocking, painful. It stole her breath. She sobbed and covered her mouth, trying desperately to keep another sound from escaping.

"Hunter's worried sick. He's coming after you."

"Oh, God. Did he leave the inn? When?"

"No, not yet. Toni, he looks like hell. He thinks you're long gone." A boarding announcement filled the air, and she clasped her hand over the phone. "Don't worry. I won't tell him you're still at the airport, doll, unless you want me to. When's your flight?"

She let out a shaky breath, trying not to cry. "3:09 p.m."

"He's asked me for your address and number."

"No, don't give it to him. I don't want to see him. Please, promise me?"

"Honey, what happened?"

"I can't—" She drew in a stuttered breath. "I've got to go, James. Just please, don't give anyone my address or number."

"Toni, honey, why not? I thought you loved him. Why are you running away?"

"James." God, she was losing it. "I can't do this. I gotta go." She closed her phone and turned the damn thing off. If it were up to her, she'd never talk to another human being again. Maybe when she got home she'd get a pet. No cats—they'd just ignore her, and she'd been ignored enough for one lifetime. A dog? No, she'd have to take it out and pick up poop. Gross. Maybe she'd get a turtle—a creature with as anemic a life as her own.

Hunter drove like a madman. Parking in front of the airport, he bought a ticket to somewhere, anywhere, praying he'd be able to find Toni on the other side of security. A woman fitting her description had taken off less than an hour before, to Salt Lake, which meant she'd probably be getting into Kennedy around 11:30 p.m.

Hunter left to cool his heels in the hangar waiting for Gramps's Gulfstream to arrive. He drank bad coffee, cracked his knuckles, and cursed his own stupidity. His only hope was beating Toni to New York and meeting her at the airport. If that didn't transpire, he could watch her office. At least he knew where that was. Of course, that didn't mean she'd actually see him.

When the plane arrived, he grabbed his duffel and ran for the tarmac. He'd have to buy clothes tomorrow. After all, he couldn't walk around New York looking like a mountain man. He climbed up the steps of the Gulfstream, handed his bag to the flight attendant, and cursed when he saw Grampa Joe talking to the pilot.

The old man smiled. "I thought since I was payin' for the ride, I might as well enjoy it. Sit down, and tell me what the hell happened."

Hunter took the shot of whiskey Gramps offered and downed it, passing it back for a refill. "I love her, Gramps."

"Ah hell, I knew that the minute I saw the way you looked at her. What did you do that got her knickers in a twist?"

"What's it matter? She's gone, and her friend James wouldn't give me her address or number. She thinks I lied to her."

"Did you?"

"Yeah, but—"

"No buts about it son, never lie to a woman. They always find out the truth eventually. Didn't I teach you anything?"

"I'm a slow learner, remember?"

"The hell you are. You're just stubborn and ornery— same as your mama. Everyone always said you're like your daddy, but I never saw it. You're your mama's boy through and through."

"No, I'm not. My father was the one who was always too busy to be there when Mom needed him. I just did the same thing with Toni. I was too busy to tell her the truth. It wasn't something I could explain in under two minutes, so I lied. Just like my dad."

"Your daddy didn't lie. He just never grew up. He never realized that when a man has a family his responsibility to his wife and kids comes before going huntin' and fishin' with his friends. You don't have that problem. You're the most responsible person I know. Just look at what you do with those kids you bring out."

"Yeah, I'm just great. That's why Emilio is cooling his heels in the county jail."

"Son, you're not God. You can't control everything,

and certainly not a troubled teenage boy. The only things you can control are your own actions."

Gramps poured them each another shot of whiskey as they taxied to the runway. "Buckle up, boy. I have a feeling it's gonna be a bumpy ride, and I'm not just talking about the flight."

Hunter downed the shot and then buckled his seat belt, wishing he could relive the day and do everything differently. He should have told Toni about Bianca's offer, the kiss, everything.

Gramps patted his shoulder. "Don't worry about Emilio. We'll see what we can do for him. Hell, I'll have someone out there first thing in the morning to pay his bond if that's what you want. Trapper can make a few phone calls and get one of his friends to represent him, and you can fly back to LA after you've straightened things out with Toni."

If he could straighten things out with Toni. If he could find her. If she gave him another chance.

The jet took off, the G-force pushing Hunter back in his seat as it climbed rapidly over the mountains surrounding the Wood River Valley. After a few minutes of climbing, the pilot announced they could move around the cabin.

Gramps took the opportunity to pour more shots. "I nearly fell out of my chair when you called. I think that's the first time you asked me for help since you learned how to tie your shoes. Now come on. Let's put our heads together and come up with a way to lasso that little filly of yours."

Toni's plane was rerouted to avoid nasty summer thunderstorms. She pulled her seat belt tighter and bounced around in the tin can with two hundred other souls wondering if she'd ever had a worse day. There was that time in the Pine Barrens when she was lost and alone, but the sense of disorientation and complete and utter isolation she experienced now was eerily similar.

The plane finally landed at JFK, four hours later than scheduled due to an emergency stop at Chicago O'Hare. She grabbed her luggage, hailed a cab, and crossed the Triborough Bridge, praying for some semblance of the sangfroid that had eluded her since her conversation with James.

As the east side of Manhattan came into view, the familiar streets, the scents and sounds of her home, did nothing but make her feel like the same ant on a larger anthill. Nothing had changed. She was alone, lost, and not sure of what direction to take. She sat still in the back of the cab and listened to her iPod as Robert Downey Jr. sang "Smile." The energy of the city washed over, around, and through her, but failed to take with it the despair that engulfed her soul.

When the cabbie stopped in front of her building, she paid the man, and followed Robert Downey's orders to smile. Humming "Lonely in New York," Toni dug for her keys and let herself in. The wet stink of rain followed her in to mingle with the scent of pizza and fried food from the shop on the first floor. She shivered at the coffin-like feel of the elevator as the doors closed mechanically. Ascending to the eleventh floor felt as if it took a lifetime.

Dragging her suitcase behind her, she unlocked the

three locks, and wondered if they were more to keep people out or to keep her in. Toni kicked open the door and took in a breath of stale apartment air. Exhaustion weighed heavy, but the need to see the sky surpassed it as she dropped her things, went out to the terrace, and sat on the still-damp metal chair until the sun rose over Manhattan.

She sat alone atop an anthill watching life go on. Morning delivery trucks tossed bundles of the *New York Times* and the *Post* at corner newsstands on Lexington, bread and liquor delivery trucks crowded the side streets, and lights in the apartments around hers flickered on. As John Lennon so famously said, "Life is what happens to you when you're busy making other plans."

What happens when life as you know it comes crashing to a halt? When there are no other plans? When the life you once lived isn't there for you to go back to, and the life you thought you'd live disappears in the blink of an eye? What do you do then?

Toni cried alone. There was no one other than James to call, and he was out of reach. There was no other shoulder to lean on, no one who cared. She sat on her terrace in the hazy, morning light, watching the other ants work on the hill and wished she could still smell the scent of fresh coffee mixed with pine and Hunter.

~~~

Hunter paced his cousin Ben's house in Brooklyn wishing Ben and Gina were there instead of back in Idaho. If they were, they'd help corral Gramps at the very least. Maybe Sam and Tina, Ben's live-in brother and sister-in-law would help with that. After spending half the night walking their baby Lea last night so Tina could get some sleep, she'd been awful grateful. Not that Hunter had minded. He liked babies. They were good listeners. And three-month-old Lea was just as pretty as her momma. He looked at his watch. Sam would be home from working the night shift in a few hours. Maybe Hunter would talk to him then.

Gramps meant well, but when he tried to help Ben and Gina's relationship, he almost destroyed it. Hunter did a good enough job at that all on his own. He sipped coffee and tried to figure out how to find Toni, since he didn't want to have this conversation at her office. With his luck, she wouldn't let him in the doors.

Last night on the phone Trapper had agreed to look into Emilio's case and get him decent representation, which was a load off Hunter's mind. Trapper also said he'd try to work on James, but Hunter didn't hold out much hope on that front.

Gramps, always an early riser, came into the kitchen wearing a bathrobe. "I figured I'd find you here. Did you even try to sleep?"

"No sense messing up a bed when I'm too wired to sleep." He leaned against the granite countertop and took a sip of his coffee.

"Maybe if you didn't drink so much of that damn stuff, you wouldn't be as jumpy as a long-tailed cat in a room full of rocking chairs."

Hunter shrugged and poured a cup for Gramps. He thought Gramps would be happy that Hunter's mom wasn't there to insist the old goat drink decaf. At least Hunter didn't have to listen to them fighting about it. He figured if the eighty-two-year-old wanted a real cup of coffee, he should have it. "I've been replaying every conversation I've had with Toni, and the only thing I remember her saying about where she lived was that she was on the eleventh floor. She didn't say what building, what street, or even if it was on the east or west side."

"I don't suppose you tried anything as old-fashioned as a phone book?"

"There was no listing for an Antonia Russo, but since she sublet her mother's place, the phone is probably under her name. With five husbands under her belt, God only knows Clarissa's last name."

Gramps took a sip of his coffee and slicked what was left of his hair back. "It's gonna be like trying to find a needle in a haystack."

"Clarissa. That's it!" Hunter grabbed his phone and scrolled through his calls. "Toni used my phone to call her mom the other day, which means somewhere in my phone is her mother's number."

"Good. Then just call her momma, and get her address. Send her flowers, buy her a gift, and knock on her door."

"Found it." Hunter checked his watch. "It's too early to call her, especially since I've never spoken to her before. I better wait until nine." He looked out into the small back yard of the massive brownstone. "I feel like a caged animal all cooped up like this. I'm going for a run."

Gramps opened up the morning paper. "I was wondering how long you'd last in here. Go ahead and take a run. It'll clear your head. Don't be too long. We have a lot left to do."

Hunter rubbed his unshaven cheeks. "I thought you were just coming along for the ride."

"And leave something as important as this to an amateur? Not a chance. No, I like Toni too much to let you screw it up any more than you already have."

The park was just a stone's throw away from the house, so after stretching on the sidewalk, Hunter made a beeline for the trees. Even as he ran through the wooded area, the air so thick he felt as if he could drink it, he still didn't feel free. Man, did he miss the sights and sounds of home. If he and Toni were back in Idaho, they'd be snuggled up in bed together sleeping peacefully with nothing but the rustle of trees, the hoot of an owl, or the howl of a wolf to disturb them. Not the sounds of garbage trucks, police cars, and ambulances. How anyone could live with all this noise was a mystery.

The hair on the back of his neck stood up as his instincts kicked in. He wasn't sure why, but he could swear he was being followed. He turned off the paved running path onto the dirt one he knew headed toward a little pond and slowed his pace. Sure enough, two men wearing knee socks, tennis shoes, and shorts that must have been circa 1970, turned in behind him. Hunter poured on the speed and once out of sight, stepped off the path, and doubled back through the woods, thankful for the dense foliage.

The two men, huffing like freight trains, passed within feet of him without even a look around. Hunter got a picture of them on his cell phone. The city must have dulled their senses. Hunter waited a few seconds and then followed the two guys. It was obvious neither of them were runners. They were too big and bulky.

They both looked like linebackers without the agility as they lumbered down the path. These guys were meant to look intimidating, but Hunter didn't think they could live up to the image. Not with him at least. He closed in on them. Neither noticed until he was about six feet away. One slowed the other and looked over his shoulder.

"Hi." Hunter stopped, keeping his distance.

"Hey, how did you get behind us? We were following you."

"I know. And just why is that?"

The bigger guy put his hands on his thighs, leaned over, and tried to catch his breath. "We want you to call your dogs off. That private dick, Dick Sommers, is sticking his nose into something that's best left alone. You get my drift?"

The other guy stuck his hands in his jacket, and for the first time Hunter wondered if confronting them was a smart move. It occurred to him that the only reason to wear a jacket while running in New York in July was if you were packing. He stepped closer to the edge of the trail. "Do you want to be more specific?"

"Look Mr. Walsh. We know where you live, where you work, and all about your cute little wife. You're a smart guy. Take this as a friendly warning, and call Dick Sommers off."

Oh God, they thought he was Ben, and they knew about Gina too. "How about this for a friendly warning? If you so much as look at anyone in my family, I'll hunt you down just like I did a few minutes ago, and you'll never see me coming. You get my drift?"

Both guys nodded. "Look. We don't want no trouble. We're just doing our job."

Hunter was disgusted. "Who do you work for?"

The bigger guy held out his hands. "We were just paid to deliver a message, and that's it."

The guys looked around nervously. Hunter didn't want to push his luck. "Tell your boss I'll call off Dick Sommers. Just leave my family alone."

The two guys nodded and backed away from him before turning and running away.

Finally the search for Rafael had taken a turn in the right direction. At least the kid was alive. That was a welcome piece of information. Hunter waited a few minutes before running toward Ben's brownstone. He pulled his phone out of his pocket and hit speed-dial. First things first, he needed to talk to Ben, email him the pictures, and tell him they were on to him and Dick Sommers. It looked as if Fisher had gotten his wish. The family had to take over the investigation now. He just hoped they'd do a better job of flying under the radar than Dick Sommers had.

Chapter 18

TONI ROSE STIFFLY FROM THE WROUGHT IRON CHAIR she'd sat on for hours and went back into the apartment. She had yet to go grocery shopping, so there was no food worth eating, not that she even had an appetite, but coffee always sounded good. She fixed herself a pot and after tasting it realized her mistake—compared to Hunter's, her coffee sucked.

Taking a sip and grimacing, she made her way to the bathroom, pulling her suitcase behind her while trying not to spill her terrible coffee. Maybe she'd break down and buy Starbucks. Even then, she doubted it would be half as good as his. There was something wonderful about a guy bringing her coffee in bed and kissing her awake, or better yet, loving her awake.

With another gulp of the bitter sludge, she reminded herself that it hadn't been love at all. It had been nothing but a game. He'd faked her out, led her on, and she followed like a needy puppy. God, how embarrassing was that? Worse, she missed him like she'd miss an amputated limb—the phantom pain making her believe it was still there, until she opened her eyes and found it gone. She was alone.

Toni opened her shower door and turned the water on to scorching, remembering how Hunter hated hot showers, but then, he had a way of warming her up even in the coldest water. Crap, she couldn't even take a shower without thinking of him. He had infused himself into her life so completely, she wasn't sure how to extract him without losing what little was left of herself.

Her phone rang, and she ignored it. There was no one she wanted to talk to. There was nothing left to say.

She finished her shower and went through her closet, finding nothing she was interested in wearing. She put on her favorite black plaid kilt and black T-shirt to match her mood with thigh-highs and the clunkiest pair of kick-ass boots she owned. Mechanically, she clipped on her collar and wristbands and took the subway downtown to her office. The whole way Toni kept fingering her collar. Nothing felt right. The boots were even heavier than the hiking boots Hunter had bought her and a whole lot less comfortable, her wristbands snagged on her skirt, and when she got pushed up against some big guy in the subway, they almost punctured her chest. Sheesh, she looked at the people walking by her and felt like a clown. She'd never felt that way before, but now... yup, definitely clownish. She pulled off her wristbands in the revolving door to her office building and shoved them in her bleeding heart backpack. Maybe she needed to change that too.

When she stepped off the elevator, Terri, the receptionist, met her at the door. "Toni, what are you doing here? You're supposed to be in Idaho."

Toni brushed her bangs out of her eyes. "Bianca took over the shoot and said I was needed here."

"Was it a disaster? Is that why Bianca ran to Idaho?"

"I guess that depends on your definition of disaster. The shoot went fine." She walked past Terri to her office, went in, and closed the door. Sitting at her desk was a red folder that hadn't been there when she left. It contained a list of projects from Bianca. Toni dug through her backpack and found the file Bianca had sent home with her. Pushing aside the green River Runners folder, she opened Bianca's file for the first time and booted up her computer.

It took Toni all of four hours to see she didn't belong there anymore. She felt like an impostor. She wasn't sure if she'd changed or if she'd just woken up—maybe a little of both. She knew if she stayed at Action Models she could have a very secure future doing the exact same thing she'd always done. It wasn't bad, but it wasn't good either. The few days she had with Hunter taught her more than what a broken heart feels like. It taught her what great felt like. Suddenly, not bad wasn't nearly enough—not anymore.

She no longer fit into her old life. She had to make a change.

Toni typed up her letter of resignation, walked it over to Bianca's office, and laid it on her desk. On the way back, she stopped at the copy room and grabbed an empty box. When she looked up, Terri was at the door watching.

"What are you doing?"

"I just tendered my resignation." She strode back to her office, Terri following in her wake. The walls of the hallway were covered with photos of shoots Toni had worked on, but when it came down to it, there was no part of her in them. She'd been as invisible in them as she'd been to Bianca, and that's one thing that would never change. As Clarissa always said, there's only room for one in the mirror, and that one was Bianca Ferrari.

Terri followed her into her office and closed the door. "Toni, please don't leave. Bianca will be back Monday. I'm sure you two will straighten everything out then."

Toni shook her head. "There's really nothing to straighten out. I've outgrown the job, and I need to find something more." Besides, the last thing Toni needed was to hear about, or God forbid, see Hunter. With he and Bianca working a deal together, there'd be no way to avoid him, and that was more than she could deal with. "No. I'll start looking for a new job on Monday."

"Bianca's not going to be happy about this."

"I wouldn't be too sure of that." Toni pulled out a thumb drive and copied her contact list—all the photographers, magazine editors, and everyone she'd ever worked with in the three years she'd been at Action Models—all the while praying she'd be able to find a job soon.

"She's hardly here anymore. You've practically run the place over the last year."

"Don't worry. I won't be hard to replace, and Bianca will be back Monday."

Terri sniffed. "Yeah, thanks for that."

"You and Bianca will be fine without me." She set the box on her desk and packed what little was hers. Looking around her office, she realized that she didn't have much there—nothing personal, no sign of her in any way. She'd been invisible. She took the wilted plant someone had given her last Christmas, not because she wanted it, but because she didn't want to be responsible for its death. She put it in beside a box of tampons and thigh-highs she kept in her drawer for emergencies, a black jacket she had on the back of her door for when the air conditioner went from comfortable to frigid, and a stained coffee cup that said, "No matter where you go, there you are." The quote was painfully true.

Toni lifted the box, nodded to Terri, and left. She'd become visible the moment Hunter had set eyes on her. It wasn't a comfortable transformation, but now she had somehow fallen back into her old self, back into the cocoon of invisibility, only to find it no longer fit.

She just needed to keep moving, putting one foot in front of the other, and maybe she'd get back to normal. Maybe she wouldn't feel as if she were someplace she didn't belong. Maybe she wouldn't miss the silence of the mountains and remember what she loved about the noise and scents of the city. Maybe she wouldn't think about Hunter every waking moment and feel she was missing a part of her soul.

~~~

Hunter waited until 9:00 a.m. and called the number he'd prayed was Clarissa's.

"Hello?" It was apparent where Toni got that husky voice of hers.

"Is this Clarissa?"

"Yes."

"Hi. I'm Hunter Kincaid, Toni's…" Shit, what was he? Her boyfriend? Her ex? "Look. I've spent the last week in Idaho with your daughter, and I love her. Something happened. She left, and I need to find her. I was hoping you could give me her address."

"How do I know she wants to be found?"

"Ma'am, you don't. If you spoke to her she'd probably say she never wants to see me again. I made a mistake, and she left before I even had a chance to explain. I have to see her. I flew to New York last night, and I really don't want to grovel in her office. I don't know what else to do."

"Young man, I hope you don't think me rude, but I'm going to need more information. You could be some kind of mad stalker for all I know. Why don't you tell me what happened?"

Hunter couldn't really blame her; his mother would do the same thing if someone called looking for Karma. "When we first met, I saw that book on dating you sent her." He couldn't believe he was telling her this. "*He Comes First: How to Find Your Perfect Man and Marry Him.* I called my sister and asked her to pick up a copy of the book for me. I just wanted Toni to feel the same way about me that I felt about her, and well, I used it."

"You read that book?"

"Yes, ma'am. I even made notes in the margins." He shook his head. Dumb mistake. "She found my copy and left on the first plane out. I don't know what Toni thought. I can only imagine."

"Yes, so can I."

"I have to talk to her. I love your daughter, ma'am. Whatever happens, I need to make sure she knows that, and it wasn't a game to me."

There was silence on the line. "Ma'am? Are you still there?"

"Of course, I'm still here. What do you need from me?"

"Her address and phone number."

"I can do better than that. I'll call my old neighbor; she'll let you in. Just go on up and wait for Toni to come home. Lilly said she saw Toni leave this morning. She got home at an ungodly hour and spent most of the night on the terrace. Lilly was worried and called me."

"Thank you, ma'am. You're a real lifesaver." Hunter wrote down the address and Toni's phone number. He gave his to Clarissa and got Lilly's number too.

"Lilly has known Toni all her life and has always kept an eye on her, not that Toni would appreciate that. She's so independent."

"I can imagine."

"So, Hunter. What are your intentions with my daughter?"

Yeah, what were his intentions? "I'm going to do my best to change her opinion of the institution of marriage, ma'am."

"Are you asking my permission to marry Toni?"

"No, ma'am. But your blessing would be appreciated."

"Young man, if you can change Toni's mind about marriage, you'll have more than my blessing. You'll have my eternal gratitude. Did you really read that book?"

"Cover to cover."

"And what did you learn?"

"You mean besides the obvious—never keep anything from Toni?"

"Yes."

Hunter smiled. "You know that saying, 'Love means never having to say you're sorry'?"

"I'm familiar with it."

"That's a bunch of bunk. I've spent more time apologizing to Toni than just about anything else."

The woman laughed the same husky laugh her daughter had. "I think you'll do, Hunter. I think you'll do."

"Thank you, ma'am. There's one more thing I was wondering, if you wouldn't mind?"

"Anything."

"Do you have any idea what kind of engagement ring Toni would like?"

"Not a clue. I don't suppose they have any with skulls and crossbones."

Hunter laughed. "No ma'am, I don't suppose they do, but I'll keep it in mind."

"You do that, but remember, if Toni loves you, you must be a very special young man. I'm sure anything you choose will be perfect. I wish you all the luck in the world."

"Thanks. I have a feeling I'm going to need it."

She laughed again. "You're smart too. I love that in a man. Obviously, so does Toni."

"Thank you for all your help. Good-bye, ma'am."

Hunter looked up from his scribbled notes to see Grampa Joe beaming. "I guess you better get your ass over to the diamond district and buy that little filly a ring. Do you need money?"

"No, I'm good. I just wish I knew what to buy her. Her sense of style is a little original."

"That's one way to put it. Well, come on, boy. I'll set you up with my buddy, Scott. He'll have the perfect ring for Toni, and he'll give you a good deal. I'll see to it. But first, go get a shower, and then grab the bag of clothes your mom sent for you. It's up in my room."

"What? Mom sent me clothes? From where?"

"She went to your house and packed what she thought you'd need. Why do you think it took me so long to get to Hailey?"

Hunter grabbed a cab to the city and dialed his phone. "Pat, it's Hunter. How's it going?" Hunter tried not to think of Emilio behind bars and hoped that the only effect this experience had on his life was the realization that jail was one hell of a scary place—a place he never wanted to visit again.

"I was just getting ready to call you. Emilio's bond hearing is set for Monday. Trapper's friend showed up and summarily dismissed the court-appointed attorney. She seems to be getting through to Emilio. I'm not sure if it was her no-nonsense legal attitude that impressed him or her legs. For me, it was the legs."

"Leave it to Trapper to know every long-legged legal beauty in the state of California."

"And she's smart too. She wasn't going to put up with any of Emilio's crap. He's talking to her, so it's all good."

"Well, that's a load off. Call me if you need anything."

"I'm off to buy Emilio a suit—Pamela's orders."

"Pamela Stacks?"

"You know her?"

"I know *of* her. She's one of Trapper's seventy-two-hour flings."

"Let's hope it ended well."

"It must have. She's there, isn't she? I have to go, Pat. Keep me in the loop."

"Will do."

Hunter ended the call just as the cab came to a halt in front of Scott's store. Hunter paid the cabbie, walked up to the door, and rang the bell.

"Yes?"

"I'm Hunter Kincaid. I have an appointment with Scott Masters. My grandfather, Joe Walsh, called."

A buzzer sounded, and when the door clicked Hunter entered the long, narrow shop lined on both sides with display cases.

"I'm Scott Masters."

"Nice to meet you." Hunter shook the short, balding man's hand.

"You're in the market for an engagement ring?"

"My grandfather said you're the man to see."

"I'll go get my diamonds."

Hunter swallowed hard. "That would be good. I'll just look around."

"Sure. Maybe you'll see something else you want."

Scott disappeared through a back door as Hunter browsed the estate jewelry, not sure of what he was looking for, but knowing he couldn't afford to screw this up. He glanced over the case, and a bloodred stone caught his eye. He found it—the perfect ring. If it was a ruby, it was the most beautiful he'd ever seen—surrounded by diamonds, it looked lit from within. It was unique and beautiful, just like Toni. Since Toni was different from every other woman he'd ever known, he doubted she had a vision of her ideal engagement ring. He knew in that instant this was the one, and buying Toni a ring was a way to prove he knew her inside and out.

Scott returned with a case of settings and loose diamonds, a jeweler's loupe, and a smile that peeked out from beneath his overgrown mustache.

Hunter pointed through the glass. "What can you tell me about this ring?"

"This one?" Scott said as he unlocked the cabinet and

bent to pluck the ring from within. "Ah, this is a beauty. I bought this during my last trip to Portugal." He laid it on the black velvet cushion. "It is circa 1930—an Art Deco engagement ring. The red diamond is the rarest of all the colored diamonds. It's received a grade of *fancy red*, which is rarer still."

Hunter nodded. Okay, it was going to cost him a mint.

Scott examined it through his jeweler's loupe. "The round, red diamond is 3.88 carats. It is a cushion-modified brilliant cut, surrounded by another 3.65 carats of white diamonds in a platinum setting."

When Hunter heard the price, he called Gramps. "I need a loan. I'll get the money back to you soon. I just need to move a few investments around."

"How much do you need, son?"

When Hunter told Gramps the price, Gramps barked out a laugh. "Let me speak to Scott, boy. We'll work out the details. You just go and get your girl."

Scott took the phone and cringed. "Joe, no, my cost—" He listened for a while. "Fifteen percent over cost. That's the lowest I can go."

Scott squirmed. Hunter felt sorry for the poor guy. More than a few times, Hunter had been on the wrong side of negotiations with Joe Walsh—the wrong side being any side Gramps wasn't on—and he knew just how difficult it was. "Okay, seven percent over cost. I'll show you my invoice, and you pay cash." Scott smiled a gap-toothed smile. "You better come before closing. I'll be here until 8:00 p.m. I'll see you later."

Scott handed the phone back to Hunter. Gramps laughed. "Take the ring. I'll take care of the money. We'll talk later."

"Thanks, Gramps. How much did I just spend?"

"A lot less than you were willing to, boy. Still, that must be one hell of a ring. It will all be worth it though if it ends up on Toni's finger and puts a smile on that girl's face. I have a feeling she's never had much to smile about before you."

"I think so too. I'm gonna do my best to make her happy or die trying."

"You'd better, or you'll be answering to me. Tell Scott I'm leaving Brooklyn now."

Hunter took the black velvet box Scott handed him and signed the receipt. No wonder Gramps was one of the richest people in America—he'd saved Hunter more than five grand.

Hunter took the ring, stuck it in his pants pocket, and walked up 6th Avenue, past Rockefeller Center and Radio City Music Hall. He headed east on 54th, past Park Avenue and the limos that lined the streets.

Damn. This area was well-moneyed. He cut in front of a mail truck and jaywalked, stopping to pick up flowers—red roses to match Toni's ring, lilies for Lilly to thank her for her help.

He passed the liquor store and considered buying a little Dutch courage but decided against it. It wouldn't help to be intoxicated while groveling, begging, and doing anything he'd have to do to get Toni back.

Hunter walked around feeling the effects of no sleep, too much drinking last night, and a hollowness he'd carried with him since he'd entered into the cabin yesterday. He'd been running on straight adrenaline for the better part of twenty-four hours, and he was flagging. He stopped for a quad shot of caffeine. The coffee burned his stomach; he hadn't eaten either and wondered if Toni felt half as shitty as he did.

He slowed approaching her building. God, the thought that he might fail and have to walk away without Toni had Hunter praying for divine intervention. Lilly said to go to the entrance next to the pizza place. She buzzed him in, and he took the elevator to the eleventh floor.

A tiny woman somewhere between the age of sixty and eighty, with dark brown hair and full makeup, waited for him by the elevator. She stood ramrod straight and looked as though she weighed all of eighty pounds. She wore a skirt, stockings, sensible shoes, and a sweater that looked more appropriate for December than August. "Lilly?"

Her lips curved into a smile. "My, my. So you're the man who stole my Toni's heart."

He shook her bony hand. "Hunter Kincaid, ma'am. I'm pleased to meet you. I picked up flowers for Toni and got you these as a thank you for helping me."

Lilly took the flowers and sighed. "Clarissa will be so happy to hear you have such fine manners." She wove her arm through his and led him down a hall. "She told me to let you in. Toni's not home yet. I think she went to work this morning, though I don't know how. She didn't get home until 3:35 a.m. and then sat out on the terrace for hours. Poor thing. She looked so despondent."

"Did you talk to her?"

Lilly shook her head. "I'm not supposed to spy. When Toni found out I was checking up on her for Clarissa, she threatened to move away if I didn't stop. This is the first time I've interfered in several years."

"Ma'am, if you'd feel more comfortable, I'll wait for Toni in the lobby or outside."

"Nonsense." Lilly unlocked a door with a key that hung off a skull-and-crossbones keychain. "Make yourself at home. I have no idea what Toni's up to, but she'll be home eventually." Lilly left the key on the hall table.

Hunter paced the living room and watched the door until he couldn't stand being inside any longer. He moved to the terrace and paced out there, not that there was enough space. His stomach growled, so he went to the world's smallest galley kitchen and opened the refrigerator. It was empty save for some spoiled milk and condiments. "She wasn't kidding when she said she didn't cook." He called Lilly. "Is there a market close by that delivers?"

"Yes, it's just around the corner. Let me give you their number."

"Thanks. I just thought I'd get some food. Do you need anything?"

"No, thanks. You just worry about you and Toni. Here it is."

Hunter smiled as he wrote the number. "Okay, thanks again."

"Sure thing—and Hunter?"

"Yes?"

"You know Toni doesn't cook, don't you?"

"Don't worry. I've got everything under control. Bye."

Hunter had never bought groceries over the phone before. He figured he'd better keep it simple. He looked for spices, but other than salt and pepper, he found none. There were cans of soup, and that was about it. He didn't even see any olive oil, and if he had, he probably wouldn't use it. There'd be no telling how long it could have been there.

There were plenty of pots and pans—some nice stuff too. He put together a list for linguine and clam sauce. If they didn't have fresh clams, he could always use canned. It didn't look as nice, but tasted almost as good, and right now, beggars couldn't be choosers. He looked for white wine or vermouth. Either would do. Bingo, Toni had both. He took a bottle of Chablis and put it in the empty refrigerator before calling the market. He had one hell of a list, buying a few staples while he was at it. Just in case he'd find himself in the position to cook her breakfast in the morning, he checked her coffee stash, turned his nose up at her selection, and added a couple of pounds of decent coffee.

He'd just ended the call when he heard the key going into the first lock. Damn, he probably should have thought this out a little more. The last thing he wanted to do was scare the shit out of her—the first time he'd done that, she'd slugged him.

Hunter leaned against the wall in the kitchen and folded his arms over his chest to keep from reaching for her.

The door swung open. Toni braced her foot on it as she pulled out the key, balancing a box containing what looked like a half-dead plant and clothes. She was drawn, paler than usual, and looked just plain beat down. He wanted to kick himself.

Hunter let out a breath when she set the box on the table. It was then she noticed the extra key; she picked it up, spun around, and saw him.

She didn't look happy. Son of a bitch. She looked as if she wanted to slug him again.

He smiled, hoping she'd go easy on him. "Hi honey, I'm home."

Chapter 19

She didn't ever hurry out of a beach. She backed as
if she was try to slam him again.   "I
He smiled, but it didn't quit reach his him. "I'll back.
I'm home."

TONI COULDN'T BELIEVE HER EYES. "HUNTER?"

He tried to pull off that sexy-as-hell grin of his, but it fell short. The smile didn't meet his eyes. He looked horrible and wonderful at the same time. He wore a pair of well-loved jeans that fit him better than any 501s had the right to, with a light green button-down shirt, and sleeves rolled up to show off his tan forearms. His watch was the only adornment he wore except for the tassels on his loafers. Loafers? Really? She couldn't believe she had actually slept with a guy who owned a pair of loafers. Which just proved what she knew—there was absolutely no future for them, no matter how great he looked leaning in the doorway of her kitchen.

"How did you find me?"

Hunter's artificial smile faltered. He looked as if he hadn't slept in days. Well good. Neither had she. He took a step toward her, and she backed into the door, which did nothing but piss her off. This was her home.

"How did you get in here? What did you do, bribe the super to let you in? I'll have his ass fired."

Hunter deflated. That was the only word to describe it. "What's it matter? Did you think you could leave without so much as a good-bye, and that would be it? Did you think if James shut me down, I'd just give up? That I wouldn't look for you? I got to New York before you did, babe. I planned to wait for your plane, but I had Gramps with me. Ever since his bypass surgery, he hasn't had the stamina he once had. He needed to get some sleep."

"You brought your grandfather to New York?" Toni pushed herself off the door and headed away from Hunter.

"No, actually, he brought me. We took one of his corporate jets. I called him and asked for help."

Hunter trailed behind her, keeping his distance. Maybe he was afraid she'd slug him again. Of course, that didn't stop him from following her. Toni slid open the door to the terrace and took a deep breath of humid air. It didn't help. She turned and glared. "You asked for help? Sure, okay. So tell me, have you taken any blows to the head lately? Are you feeling all right?"

He dropped down on the leather couch, as if his legs would no longer hold him. "No, actually, I feel like someone ripped my heart out and stomped all over it in size seven Doc Martens."

"I was being sarcastic."

"I wasn't." He leaned forward. "Toni, you said you would wait for me. You said we'd talk."

"Yeah, well things change. Get over it."

"That's not going to happen. I came to apologize."

"For what? Tricking me into falling in love with you? Cheating on me with my boss? Or working out a deal for the camp behind my back? God, I'm such a fool. So go ahead Hunter, absolve your conscience, say you're sorry, and get out of my life." She turned and looked out over the city, tears blurring her vision. She didn't bother wiping them away.

"I didn't trick you." He'd moved closer. She felt his

breath on her ear just before his arms wrapped around her middle, pulling her against his chest. "I just had help. I needed it. I never used that book against you, babe. Maybe at first I was messing with you, but I never meant to hurt you. I read it and took the advice offered. Call it research."

"Oh, it was research all right." She turned in his arms and pushed against his chest—hard. He didn't move. "I loved your notes on the chapter about baggage and insecurities. Fascinating stuff. If I were Bianca, you could have sold it to the tabloids."

"I didn't know about the deal Bianca had cooked up with KidSports until just before the morning meeting. I didn't cheat on you. I love you."

Toni rolled her eyes and gave him another shove. "Oh right, you love me so much that you were in Bianca's cabin examining her tonsils. Let go of me." She pushed against him again. He released her and took a step back, looking as if he'd been slapped.

"She kissed me. I didn't kiss her back, and I certainly didn't examine any part of her body. The only body I want to examine is yours."

"Oh, and I believe that. Come on, Bianca's a supermodel. And I saw you, Hunter. I saw you with her."

"I know what you saw, but I didn't instigate it. I want nothing to do with Bianca. No matter what you think, I love you. The idea of not having you by my side for the rest of my life just leaves me hollow and aching."

"Don't worry. You'll get used to it. Go—just go."

The intercom buzzed.

Toni went to the door and pressed the intercom. "What?"

"Delivery for Toni Russo."

"Fine. Come on up." She pressed the button and turned to Hunter. "I didn't order anything."

"I did. You don't have any food in the house, and I'm hungry."

"Well, isn't that just great? You're leaving, and I'm gonna be stuck with the bill, which sucks since I just quit my job."

Hunter seemingly grew another layer of guilt. His shoulders sagged even more than they had before under the weight of it. "You quit?"

"Don't flatter yourself. It wasn't because of you and Bianca. It was because of me."

"Oh."

Someone knocked on the door, and he shook his head. "That must be the delivery. Don't worry. I've already paid for it."

"That makes two of us."

He ignored her comment and answered the door. "I hope you like linguine and clam sauce, because that's what I'm making."

"You can put it in a to-go box and be on your way."

Hunter opened the door.

"What part of 'get out' don't you understand?"

"Nothing. I'm just ignoring it."

The delivery boy looked at Toni, shifting nervously from foot to foot, and handed Hunter a clipboard to sign.

"Keep sparring, dear."

"You can ignore me all you want. You're still leaving."

"Not until I've eaten, I'm not. Aren't you hungry?"

"No, you've made me lose any appetite—for all eternity."

Hunter tipped the boy and signed for the groceries.

He took the box, kicked the door closed, and carried the food to the kitchen with Toni close behind.

"You are not staying long enough to eat."

Hunter rattled a pan out of the cabinet and filled it with water. "Here, make yourself useful. Where's the strainer?"

"How should I know? You know I don't cook."

"Yet. You're about to get a lesson."

"How did we get from 'get out' to Cooking 101?"

"Everyone has to start somewhere, and pasta's easy." He handed her a mesh bag filled with little neck clams. "Wash these." Taking the pot he'd filled with water, he dumped a ton of salt in it and put it on to boil.

"How do you wash clams?"

"Just fill the sink with cold water and swish them around. Like you would when you wash your delicates."

"Like you know how to wash delicates. Hell, like I know how to wash delicates. I just throw them in the machine with everything else and hope for the best."

"I had to do all the laundry for the whole family, including my mom and sister. Damn straight I know how to wash delicates." Hunter shot her a cocky grin. "Woolite is my friend. I'll show you how later."

"Great, just great. There's not going to be a later." She swished the clams around the sink.

He grabbed a cutting board she'd never seen, dug through the box, and came up with garlic and spices.

Toni picked up the scent of roses. Looking over, she saw a bouquet on the bar. "What are those over there?"

"Oh, I brought you flowers. You should put them in water. Do you have a vase?"

"I don't know."

"Check over the refrigerator. Everyone I know keeps vases in the cabinet over the fridge."

She looked up and realized for the first time that there was a cabinet there. Who knew? She opened it. There were two vases. Leave it to Hunter to know where everything was in her kitchen. When she reached for one, he came from behind and plucked it out of the cabinet.

"Here you go." He handed it to her and went back to chopping green stuff.

She filled the vase and wondered how much water to put in. No one had ever given her flowers before. She took the bouquet and couldn't help but bury her nose in them for a second—hoping Hunter didn't notice. She shouldn't be feeling so pleased. It annoyed her that she did. It didn't help that when she looked up, she found Hunter grinning like a fool. "Don't get your hopes up."

He turned back to his chopping, and she tried her best not to notice how good he looked cooking in her kitchen. "What's that?"

"Basil. The parsley is next." He made little piles on the cutting board of each herb before he ripped open a head of garlic. When he slammed his hand down on the knife, she jumped.

"What are you trying to do? Kill it?"

"This is how you get the skins off, and it releases the flavor. I hope you like a lot of garlic."

"Sure, why not? It's not as if I'm going to kiss you."

"We'll see."

Toni took the roses out of the wrapper and stuck them in the vase.

"No, no. You have to cut the stems at an angle. They'll last longer that way."

"What makes you the rose expert? What do you do, buy them for all the women you've cheated on?"

"I've never cheated on anyone, not even you. My mother likes roses. I buy them for her birthday. Karma too."

Well, wasn't that just the berries.

Hunter dug through a lower cabinet as she ogled his butt. He sure had a nice one.

He grabbed a pot, poured olive oil into it, and raised his eyebrows when the doorbell rang. "Expecting company?"

"No, but then I wasn't expecting you either. It looks like this is the day for unwanted guests."

Toni left him in the kitchen doing whatever it was that he was doing and went to the door. She looked through the peephole, blinked, and took a second look. "Hunter, did you call my mother?"

"How'd you know?"

"Because she's standing outside my door."

Hunter wiped his hands on a towel she didn't know she owned and threw it over his shoulder. "Aren't you going to answer it?"

"No."

She plopped herself down on the couch and ignored the incessant doorbell.

"Fine. I'll get it."

"Don't you dare." Too late. Hunter opened the door.

"Hunter?"

"Clarissa?"

A knowing smile passed between them. Toni knew she'd been hoodwinked.

"Mom, what are you doing here?"

"I just thought I'd come and see my only child. After I spoke to Hunter this morning, I was worried."

"More like curious."

"I wanted to make sure you were okay."

"Well, now you've seen me. You can leave."

Her mother ignored her, batting her fake lashes at Hunter. "Something sure smells good. I'm famished. Do you know what they feed you on planes these days? Peanuts, nothing but peanuts. Hunter, do you have any wine open?"

"No, but I have some chilling."

Toni turned to him. "You do?"

"I found it in the liquor cabinet. I needed to make sure you had Chablis or vermouth for the sauce. You had both."

"Lucky me."

Clarissa went to the bar. "Great. I'll get the wine glasses. I didn't know my daughter knew how to cook."

Toni got off the couch. "I don't."

"She doesn't." Hunter opened the wine. "I'm teaching her."

Clarissa laughed. "This should be interesting."

"Hey, I'm not stupid. I washed the clams."

As usual, her mother looked like she just stepped out of Neiman Marcus in her perfectly tailored linen suit, which didn't even show a wrinkle. What did she do? Fly standing up? No, wait. Did brooms have seat belts?

The doorbell rang as Hunter poured the wine. He looked at Toni, and she shrugged. "Everyone I know is already here."

Clarissa breezed to the door and opened it with her usual flourish. "Well, hello there."

"Howdy, ma'am."

Hunter heard his grandfather's voice. "Son of a bitch."

Toni stomped into the kitchen. "If anyone else comes through that door, they're going to have to bring their own chair. Tell me. Did you invite him too?"

"No." He grimaced. "Gramps, what the hell are you doing here?"

"I'm just makin' sure you don't screw things up, boy."

Gramps walked in and gave Toni a hug. "There's my girl. How are you, darlin'? You sure looked better when you were in Idaho. I think the clean air agreed with you."

Toni didn't look too happy to have everyone there, but maybe it wasn't a bad thing. She hadn't asked him to leave since Clarissa had arrived. That was something.

Gramps set two bottles of champagne on the counter. "I brought fortification. You better put these in the icebox. Do we have anything to celebrate yet?"

Toni looked from Hunter to Gramps. "What does he mean by that?"

Hunter smashed some more garlic, picturing his grandfather's head. Leave it to the old man to jump the gun.

"I know you're avoiding my question." Toni hissed by his side.

"I'm not avoiding it. I just don't know the answer yet."

She rolled her eyes. "When you figure it out, let me know."

Hunter turned and pulled her into his arms. "Believe me, babe. You'll be the first to know." He gave her a quick kiss on the lips, released her, and tossed the garlic into the saucepan.

"Toni, do me a favor and get the baguettes out for garlic bread. Gramps, make yourself at home while Toni and I finish up dinner." He leered at his grandfather and mumbled. "You usually do anyway."

Toni held the bread like light sabers. "What am I supposed to do with these?"

"Take a bread knife and cut them in half lengthwise."

"What's a bread knife look like?"

"It's the long one with a serrated edge."

"Like that means anything to me. Speak English, please."

Hunter reached around her and pulled one out of the knife block. "Here. There's another cutting board in that cabinet next to the stove."

He glanced into the living room. Gramps and Clarissa had their heads together as if they were conspiring. He wasn't sure if he should be thankful or nervous. With Gramps, he never knew.

Toni sawed at the bread with a heavy hand. "What else needs to be done so we can get these people out of here?"

Hunter poured the wine and clam juice into the sautéing garlic and tossed the herbs in behind it. The water boiled, so he threw in the pasta and thanked God she hadn't included him as one of *these people*. "Set the table. I'll do the bread. Dinner should be ready in ten minutes."

"Can't we just nuke it? I know how to use the microwave." She pulled plates out of the cabinet. At least he didn't have to tell her where those were.

"Just leave the plates here, put out the silverware, and see if you can scrounge up some napkins. Look in the cabinet next to the dining room table. Your mom's probably got some in there."

"It's my apartment."

"Yes, but do you know what's in that cabinet?"

"Good point." Toni left to look for napkins. "Maybe there's silverware in there too."

It was Hunter's turn to roll his eyes. He put the finishing touches on the bread, popped it under the broiler, threw together a quick salad, and dropped the clams into the sauce.

Toni came back in. "You have thirty minutes before things start getting ugly."

"Why's that?"

"You don't know my mother. She's already on glass number three, and we're going to have to get a crowbar to separate her from your grandfather. By the way, she's in-between husbands."

"Don't worry. Gramps can take care of himself. He's met a lot of Clarissas in his day."

─── ~~~~ ───

By the time dinner was on the table, Gramps had poured Clarissa a fourth glass of wine. He smiled like a Cheshire cat at Hunter. "This sure looks good, boy. Just don't tell your mama what you fixed me for dinner."

"I didn't fix you dinner. I fixed Toni dinner. You just horned in."

"No boy, I just came to make sure you didn't screw this up."

Clarissa took a sip of her wine. "My, this is awkward."

Toni looked from Gramps to Hunter. "Screw what up?"

Grampa Joe shoved a piece of bread in his mouth as Hunter glared at him and spun his linguine around the fork. "We'll talk about it later, Toni. When we're alone. Okay?"

Clarissa dabbed the corner of her mouth with her napkin. "Well, I can't remember when I've had a more beautiful meal. You sure know how to cook."

"My grandson worked as a chef for years before he bought the ski lodge and started his River Runners Camp for kids. He likes to take care of everyone. No one goes hungry when he's cookin', that's for damn sure.

"That reminds me. Trapper called to say he got a lawyer for Emilio. He's all set for the bond hearing on Monday. The lawyer thinks she can get him off. The drugs they found on him were his mother's, and he didn't know if she had a prescription for them, so he kept his mouth shut. He was just trying to protect his mama. Can't fault him for that."

Toni dropped her fork. "Who's Emilio?"

Hunter swallowed. "He's one of the kids from my camp. He lives with his mother and brother in a shelter in LA. I found out he'd been picked up by the police for drugs just after you left. Trapper stepped in and found him a lawyer, since I couldn't be in two places at once. I promised I'd be there for the bond hearing on Monday."

Toni's face fell. "Why did you come here?"

Hunter placed his hand over hers. "Because you're more important. Everything that could be done for Emilio is being done, but you were all alone."

Toni opened her mouth and closed it. Her eyes got suspiciously glassy, and her hand shook as she picked up her wine.

Clarissa nodded. "What you're doing for that young man is commendable, but I don't see why you have to be there for his hearing. It sounds as if he's in good hands."

Hunter cleared his throat. "I promised. And I always keep my promises." He looked at Toni, who stared at her mother as if she'd just sprouted horns.

"Mother, nothing is as important to Hunter as his kids."

Clarissa's eyes snapped to Toni. "That's not true. He's here with you, isn't he?"

Grampa Joe smiled. "I think that's our cue to leave. Clarissa, what do you say we go find us some coffee and something sweet? That way, my boy can't rat me out to his mama about what I'm fixin' to eat for dessert."

Hunter watched as Clarissa giggled. "That sounds like an offer I can't refuse."

"My limo is waiting right downstairs."

Toni rolled her eyes as she rose and gave Gramps a hug. "You better watch Clarissa, Grampa Warbucks, she's on the prowl."

He smiled. "Don't you worry about me, girly. I know how to keep the she-wolves at bay."

Toni gathered her mother's purse. "Are you staying here or with Lilly?"

"With Lilly, of course. I wouldn't think to intrude on your privacy."

"Right. Just behave yourself, Clarissa."

"I could say the same thing, but I'd really prefer you didn't."

Gramps went around the table to where Hunter stood. "You need any advice before I leave?"

"No, I think you've done enough damage for one night. Thanks anyway."

"Just get 'er done, boy. Make me proud."

"Yes sir. Don't wait up."

Gramps laughed. "I was gonna tell you the same thing."

———

Hunter saw that Toni was dead on her feet. "Why don't you go sit and relax? I'll take care of the dishes."

"No, I can help."

Taking her hand, he walked her to the couch. "Please. You look like you're about to fall over."

"Fine." She sat and curled her feet under her. "I probably shouldn't have had the wine. Wine always makes me sleepy."

Hunter cleared the table and kept one eye on Toni. She was asleep in under five minutes. Good. That took some of the pressure off. He cleaned and tried to figure out a way to make things right. At least she'd stopped insisting that he leave. It wasn't much, but it was a start. He still had no idea how she'd feel when she woke up.

By the time he'd put the food away and done the dishes, he was dog tired too. He and Toni still had to talk, but it would have to wait until morning. There was no way he was going to propose to her with her half asleep.

He watched Toni sleep, wondering if he should wake her. She'd probably sleep better in her own bed. That decided, he went in search of her room. When he found it, he was surprised by how feminine it was. He didn't know what he'd expected, but not the soft pastels and frilly pillows. He took the pillows off the bed and pulled down the old-fashioned chenille bedspread before returning to her and picking her up. She startled. "Shhh. I got you. I'm just putting you to bed, babe. It's okay."

She mumbled something, but relaxed against his chest as he carried her to the bedroom and laid her gently on the bed before giving her pouty lips a kiss.

Pulling off her stockings and boots, he covered her with the sheet and a light blanket.

Toni curled up on her side, tucking her hand beneath her pillow, and sighed. Hunter unbuttoned his shirt, debating whether to sleep with her or on the couch. He knew he'd sleep a whole hell of a lot better with her. The thought of sleeping without her was what kept him up the night before. It wasn't as if they'd never slept together. He tugged his shirt out of his pants and took it off, tossing it on a nearby chair. He toed off his shoes, pulled his wallet and the ring out of his pocket, and put them on the bedside table. He couldn't resist looking at Toni's ring again. It seemed to gather all the light in the room, and even in the dim light, was the most beautiful engagement ring he'd ever seen, the only one he could picture Toni wearing.

Hunter tucked the ring back in its box and stuck it in his pocket before laying his jeans on the chair. He slid into bed beside her and couldn't resist pulling her close. She rolled over, rested her head on his chest, and Hunter relaxed for the first time in two days. "I love you, Toni." He kissed the top of her head and slept.

Chapter 20

THE OBNOXIOUS RINGING OF A PHONE WOKE TONI. SHE reached over to grab it and realized she was sleeping on top of Hunter. How'd that happen? "Hello?" she whispered as she slid off his still sleeping body and left her bedroom, looking back once, amazed to see how well Hunter fit in her bed, her room, even her life.

Her life didn't seem the least bit anemic with him in it. Without him—she knew what that looked like—she'd grow old and become the crazy turtle lady.

"Toni, it's Bianca. Terri called and told me about your resignation. I'm afraid I can't accept it."

"I'm sorry, Bianca. But you don't have much of a choice."

There was dead silence. Toni wondered if they'd been disconnected until she heard what sounded like a sob.

"You have to. Since James found out you resigned yesterday, everyone is threatening to leave. James hasn't spoken to me. The models have all gone to Ketchum and are hungover. I had to bail Yvette out of jail for indecent exposure—she was doing a striptease at some bar called The Mint. I think Karma is trying to kill me, Fisher does nothing but scowl, and I have to deal with that pig, Trapper, all the time." Bianca wailed. This was no fake cry; this was a snotty, wet, uncontrolled breathing, scream for help.

Toni felt sorry for the woman. "Calm down, Bianca. It'll be okay. Most of the shoots were finished before I left. There was one mountain biking shoot on Sun Valley's Bald Mountain, but I'm sure you could do it at Killington if you had to. It will put you over budget, but that's the least of your worries right now."

"Toni, please. I'm begging you to reconsider. If this is about Hunter..."

"Bianca, my resignation isn't about Hunter." Now that Toni thought about it, she realized it really had nothing to do with him. He'd just shined a blinding light on the problem until she could no longer ignore it. "I worked in your shadow for so long. I forgot what it was like to stand in the light on my own. I got a taste of it in Stanley, and I can't go back. I'm sorry."

Bianca sniffed and then blew her nose. "There's nothing I can do to change your mind?"

"Thanks, but I don't think so."

"Okay, fine. Just promise me two things."

Toni groaned as she straightened, waiting for Bianca to stage her attack. "What?"

"Promise me that we can have lunch together after I return. You have to at least give me the chance to woo you back to Action Models. I heard what you said, and I have an idea."

Toni relaxed. She could handle a difficult lunch meeting, especially if it would mean a good recommendation from her past employer. "Fine, but agreeing to a lunch meeting is not to be construed as anything but that."

"Point taken."

"What's the other thing?"

"This is personal."

"Bianca, I'm not trying to be rude, but we don't have a personal relationship."

"Please. Just hear me out. When I flew out here to Idaho, I had plans for Hunter. I knew you were seeing him, but I had no idea it was anything serious. I didn't figure that out until too late. I'm sorry. I hope you can forgive me, because I really don't need any more guilt. Promise me you won't give up on whatever you and Hunter have because of me or something I did. Hunter is one in a million. If you love him, don't let anything get in the way of that—especially not me."

Toni always knew Bianca had a soft side few had ever seen. She remembered the way Bianca said good night in Italian to the janitor, and when she found out his granddaughter needed surgery, the girl's hospital bill was paid anonymously. The man claimed it was a miracle—maybe not so much. "I'll think about it. Why don't you have James give me a call when he wakes up? I'll talk to him and see if I can smooth things over for you. Maybe Hunter will talk to the River Runners staff."

"I can have James call you, but Hunter isn't answering any of my calls—I'm persona non grata where he's concerned. Is there anything else you think I can do?"

"Give everyone the morning off. You need to rebuild the team spirit we had going, and you're not going to do that by making them work with hangovers. You can do the last shoot this afternoon. There will be plenty of light left."

"Done."

"Try talking to James and a few of the models and photographers. Ask them to stay an extra day. Pay them double time—it'll be less expensive than planning another shoot at Killington. James can handle it on his own. He's more than capable."

"You're right. I suppose it wouldn't hurt to ask."

"Oh, and Bianca? You really should rethink having Karma shoot the rapids. You've missed an incredible opportunity there, and she might just change her attitude if you tell her you were wrong and ask for her help."

Bianca groaned. "Do I have to?"

Toni shook her head. "No, but you should. Think of the shots you could get. Karma is the epitome of everything Action Models stands for—gorgeous, athletic, and strong. Karma is beautiful, fearless, and fantastic on the rafts."

"Fine. I'll swallow my pride if I must. I'm getting a lot of practice lately. So, Toni—you'll think about what I said?"

"I promised lunch, that's all."

"No, I meant about Hunter. He's yours if you want him. All you have to do is let him find you."

"He already has."

"And?"

"And I'm thinking about it."

"Good. Thanks for your help, Toni. I'll call you to schedule our lunch."

"I look forward to it." When Toni hung up the phone, she realized that she did. Something had changed to put her and Bianca on more equal footing. She wasn't sure what it was. Maybe Bianca had been taken down a peg, maybe Toni jumped up a few. But whatever it was, it felt pretty damn good.

Toni tiptoed to the bedroom, pulled off the rest of her clothes, and slid back into bed to watch Hunter sleep. If someone had told her two weeks ago that she'd fall in love with a man who lived in the woods of Idaho and looked at her as if she was the best thing since fishnet stockings, she would have called the nice men in the white coats for a pickup.

When she'd been in Idaho, all she had known was that she still wanted to keep him looking at her that way. Every time he did, she felt special, treasured, and loved. With one look Hunter filled a great yawning hole inside her soul, and when he put his arms around her, for the first time in her life she belonged. Too bad she'd been too stupid and scared to trust it.

Toni had decided well before her conversation with Bianca that she didn't want to lose what she'd found with Hunter—not because of Bianca, geography, a job, or her own sheer intractability.

The thing that had held her back from day one was that she hadn't believed in love. Maybe she hadn't believed she was worthy of love—not really. When she learned Hunter had come after her instead of going to LA to help one of his kids, it was a two-by-four to the head. She believed him when he said she was more important. He'd meant it, and he'd proven it every day they'd been together.

When she finally acknowledged it instead of trying to find a catch, the significance took her breath away. Hunter Kincaid truly loved her. She might not deserve it or him, but she was just selfish enough to overlook that. Besides, if they were going to do this relationship thing, she'd have plenty of time to earn the love he so freely gave and show him that same love in return.

Toni rested her head on Hunter's chest as his arm came around her. She listened to the beating of his heart wishing he'd awaken, but at the same time, wanting to stay just like they were.

Hunter had gone to bed with a fully clothed Toni. Sure, he'd taken off her shoes and stockings, but he'd left the rest of her clothes on because he didn't want to wake her and didn't want her to think he was a perv. He slid his hand down her back, then lower. Sure enough, she wasn't wearing a stitch of clothing. He wasn't certain what it meant. Hell, he wasn't sure there was any meaning at all. Toni always slept naked—well, at least since they made love that first time. So maybe she just woke up and took her clothes off because she was uncomfortable, or maybe she wanted to make love.

She kissed his chest and slid her hand down his stomach. "Your heart is racing. You're either awake, or you're having one hell of a dream."

He rolled over her. "I think it's a dream come true."

"Good answer." Her arms snaked around his neck, pulling him into a kiss that had all his cylinders firing.

Damn, they needed to talk, not make love, even though he really wanted to. God, this was going to kill him. He pulled away. "Toni, babe, we need to talk."

"Can't we talk later? We've only got a little while before calls start rolling in."

"Who's going to call?"

"Bianca called earlier. She got my resignation and tried to talk me out of it. I told her I'd have lunch with her when she returns."

Now he was really confused. Bianca spoke to Toni, and Toni was still in bed with him?

"Things got a little crazy after word of my resignation got to James and the models. The models are out of control—Yvette got arrested. It's a mess. They're all hungover and threatening to leave. James hasn't spoken to Bianca since he found out. Fisher, Karma, and Trapper aren't taking her under their wings, and Bianca had a meltdown. Besides begging me to retract my resignation, she was apologetic about what happened between the two of you. She was nice."

"Are you going back to Action Models?"

"No. I feel bad for her, but not that bad. I told her I'd talk to James and gave her some hints to get back on the models' good side, but I'm not going to retract my resignation. Why? Do you want me to?"

"Babe, I want you to be happy. If that means going back to work for Action Models, we can figure it out. If not, that's fine too."

"I told her you might talk to Karma and the guys—maybe ask them to give her a break—if you want."

"The only thing I want right now is to talk to you about us. I'm sorry I didn't tell you the truth about Bianca and the deal. I knew you'd be upset, and I only had a few minutes to explain before Bianca came after me. I was going to tell you, I swear. I fucked up. I'm sorry, babe."

"We did this last night. Can't we just move on? I'm sorry, you're sorry, we both made mistakes, and we both felt like crap. The thing is, no matter how mad or hurt I was, I still loved you. I still missed you so bad I felt like I was missing part of me. I felt sick, I ached, and I didn't think it was going to change anytime soon. It sucked, and I'd really rather not relive the whole thing. I spent enough time picturing myself as the crazy turtle lady to last a lifetime. I mean, can't we just have make up sex and figure out what we're going to do next? If you still want to give this whole relationship thing a try? You do, don't you? I know I can be a real pain, and then there's my mother. Although you seemed to be just fine with her, which is too weird to even think about, I still can't believe you—"

Hunter kissed her. He understood it all but the crazy turtle lady thing. He made a mental note to ask her about that sometime—just not now.

When he broke the kiss, he put his finger over her lips. "My turn."

"Remember what happened last time you did that?"

Hunter smiled and pulled his finger away. He couldn't afford any distractions. "I love you. I want us to be together, to live together. And if you want, we can even work together. But if you don't want to work, that's cool too."

"I guess I can work on fund-raising and with the camp."

"Toni, did you catch the first part?"

"Yeah, I got that. But what did you mean if I wanted to work? I have bills to pay, you know, health insurance, food, my share of the rent, though I don't know if I really want to give up my apartment—"

He was just about to kiss her again when the phone rang. Toni reached for it and sat up. "Hello?" Toni listened for a moment. "James, I talked to Bianca."

"No, he's right here. I'm going to put you on speaker." She pushed a button. "Can you hear us?"

"Hi Hunter. I guess you two worked things out?"

Hunter pulled Toni into his arms. "We're in the middle of negotiations."

"I'm sorry I interrupted. Toni, I found out you quit, doll. Everyone did. I've always loved you. It seems the models do too. They blame your quitting on Bianca sending you home, and it's not pretty, dollface. I guess someone saw you watching her come on to Hunter. Then when Hunter took off, Bianca was as welcome as Cruella de Vil at the Westminster Kennel Club."

"Yeah, she mentioned that."

"I quit, but not because of Hunter. I think I've outgrown the job. It just doesn't fit anymore, you know?"

James laughed. "Bianca said she's planning on hiring you back."

"I only promised to have lunch with her and listen to her idea. Look James, I just wanted to talk to you and ask you to give Bianca a break, okay? She apologized for making a play for Hunter. She swears she didn't know we were serious, and really, can you blame her? I guess she's had a thing for him since they met."

"Who are you and where is Toni?"

Hunter laughed, and Toni elbowed him. "Ow."

She stuck out her tongue. "Everyone's entitled to a screw up every now and then. She apologized, and I'm in a forgiving mood today."

"Bianca Ferrari apologized?"

"She did. She's having a hard time. Could you just try to be nice? For me?"

"Yeah, she can act like the bosszilla and send you away..."

"She didn't. She just played the game the way we

always have. I'm the one who changed the rules, not her. Give her a break. She's willing to let you pick a team and do the Sun Valley mountain bike shoot on your own. I told her she'd have to pay double."

"Did she agree?"

"If anything, she was afraid to ask you."

"Fine. I'll talk to her—"

"Nicely?"

"Yes. I'll be nice. Take care, Hunter. Toni, call me when you're finished with negotiations. I love you, doll."

"Thanks, James. I love you too."

The call ended, and Toni handed Hunter the phone. "You might want to call Karma and the guys."

"Can't I just text: B nice 2 Bianca or else?"

"No."

"Fine. Then I'm getting dressed." He got out of bed and grabbed his shorts.

"Why?" She didn't move.

"I can't talk to my family naked." He stepped into his jeans. "It was weird enough talking to James."

Toni rolled her eyes at him. "They don't have to know we're naked. It's not like they can see us."

"No, but they'll know."

"How?"

He handed her his shirt. "Just put this on. I don't want them talking to you naked either."

She slipped his shirt on. "Has anyone ever told you you're strange?"

Hunter grabbed his phone and called Trapper.

"You have any good news for me?" Trapper's voice came over the phone.

"Hello to you too. I'm in negotiations with Toni."

"Why isn't she naked?"

"'Cause I'm calling you. Do me a favor. Threaten Karma and Fisher's lives if they're not nice to Bianca. And you be nice too—just not too nice. Consider it a personal favor to Toni."

"Aw man, you really know what buttons to push. So, has she said yes yet?"

"No."

"If you don't mind, wait for another half hour before you get down on bended knee, okay? I got a hundred bucks riding on it."

"Just be nice to Bianca."

"Tell Toni she can take off your shirt now."

Hunter ended the call. "There. Are you happy? Trapper said you can take off my shirt if you want."

"How did he know I'm wearing your shirt?" She climbed out of bed and followed him to the kitchen. He needed coffee. He'd found a French press last night and put a kettle of water on.

Toni leaned against the counter staring at him. "Is something wrong?"

What the hell was he supposed to say? *Yeah, I want to marry you, but I'm afraid if I ask you'll run screaming for the hills?* "No." Damn, he was doing it again. He shook his head. "Yeah, I'm a little nervous."

"Why?"

"These negotiations are important."

"Hunter, I think we've gotten through the hardest part, right?"

"I don't know, babe."

Toni didn't understand what Hunter was so nervous about. Sure, there was a lot to decide, but at least they weren't fighting. Maybe he didn't think it could last. She watched him fix coffee. He poured the hot but not quite boiling water over the grounds and whipped up an omelet that looked like it came off the cover of *Bon Appetit*. If he kept cooking like this, she'd have to go on a diet. She took a bite of the spinach and feta cheese omelet and nearly groaned. "Do you cook like this all the time?"

He toyed with his food. "I cook when I'm nervous."

"Yeah, about that, I don't get why you're nervous. What's the worst thing that could happen?"

"Other than you freaking out, running away again, and breaking my heart?"

"Eww… that bad, huh?"

"Yeah." He pushed away his plate.

"What if I promise not to freak out?"

"You can't."

True. She really wasn't prone to losing it unless it was around Hunter. "Okay, how about I promise not to leave?"

He raised his eyes to hers. "For how long?"

"Twenty-four hours."

He nodded and stuck out his hand to shake.

Toni would have rolled her eyes if he didn't look so damn serious. It was starting to give her the willies. "Fine." She shook his hand. "What is it already?"

Hunter looked at her plate. "You're not done with your breakfast yet."

"So what? Are you afraid I'm gonna get sick or something?"

His eyes just about bugged out.

"Kidding. I might hyperventilate, but I've never thrown up."

Hunter scowled and pushed her plate closer. "Finish eating."

"Now you want me to eat? You can't be serious. I'm nervous too."

"This is just great." Hunter stood, grabbed both their plates, and tossed the contents in the trash. He grumbled something about a JumboTron and a Yankees game, and then proceeded to clean the kitchen. Fine, if he was going to be that way, she was going to force him to tell her.

Toni watched him as he bent over the sink, scrubbing the pan with a lot more force than she thought necessary. Truthfully, it had been years since she had done any real dishes—most of her food went from can or takeout container to plate with a quick stop in the microwave before she ate it, and a dishwasher after.

Wearing only Hunter's shirt, Toni unfastened one more button and rerolled the sleeves before jumping up to sit on the counter. She was right in his way, although the look on his face was anything but disturbed. Yeah, those years at Action Models gave her more than just a decent paycheck. Just because she rarely posed didn't mean she didn't know how.

Toni took the towel hanging over Hunter's shoulder, grabbed it on both ends, and tossed it around his neck, then pulled him in for a kiss.

Hunter vibrated with nervous energy. His wet hands roamed her body as his tongue tangled with hers. God, she'd forgotten how fast he could take her from lukewarm teasing to scorching need.

Toni shimmied to the edge of the counter and slid off mid-kiss, sucking his tongue into her mouth and slipping her leg between his. Her eyes shot open when she felt a bulge where there shouldn't be one.

He stepped away too quickly.

"What's wrong?" A slight red stain covered his cheekbones.

"Nothing."

Toni threw up her hands. "If it's nothing, then just say it for God's sake."

Hunter rubbed his eyes. "Okay. I bought you something."

"A present?" Another first. No guy had ever bought her a present.

"Not exactly."

"Well, what is it?"

He pulled a little black velvet box from his pocket. She'd seen her share of those before—every time her mother got another diamond to add to her collection and another husband to add to that collection as well—they came in pairs.

When Hunter opened the box, she'd expected to see a diamond solitaire—after all, that's what guys bought when they proposed, right? This wasn't one—it was a big red stone surrounded by little diamonds, but definitely not an engagement ring. She couldn't believe she was actually disappointed, which was weird. She'd never wanted to get married. She'd always sworn she wasn't going to be like her mother. She didn't want to change husbands more frequently than most women changed handbags, but then her mother had never found a guy like Hunter either.

With Hunter everything was different. So yeah, she was disappointed.

"It's beautiful." It was huge, not Easter-egg huge, but on the right side of the line between gorgeous and ostentatious. "Is it a ruby?"

"No, it's a diamond."

She tried to smile. After all, it was perfect, just her style—if she had a style—but that feeling of disappointment just got bigger and bigger like a balloon about to pop. God, she really wished she could figure herself out. "I know the stones surrounding it are diamonds. What's the red stone?"

"A red diamond."

She touched it. "Is it real?"

"Hell yeah, it's real, or at least it better be."

Her breath caught. She'd heard about red diamonds. She'd never seen one. Right now though, she'd trade it for a ring from the bottom of a Cracker Jack box if he'd just get down on one knee. She looked at the ring and then at the floor, doing her best not to cry when she really wanted to weep. Maybe she was PMSing, or maybe she was just a spoiled brat pissed that he didn't read her mind when she had no clue how to read it either. Still, she was hurt and crying, damn it. "It's beautiful. Thanks, but you really didn't have to buy me anything."

Hunter tipped her chin up. "Yes, I did. A man can't ask the woman he loves to marry him without a ring."

"What did you say?"

"Toni, I don't want to be your roommate. I want to be your husband. I love you more than I thought I could ever love anyone—enough to last a lifetime. I want us to say the 'I dos' and have everything that comes along with them. I want to have children of our own to love and love the ones who come into our lives. I want to spend the rest of my life waking up with you, to grow old holding your hand, and to share my world with you forever."

"This is an engagement ring?"

"What did you think it was? I'm trying to propose."

"Then why aren't you on one knee? I have to tell you Hunter—the red ring really threw me. I mean, if you'd done it right and gotten down on one knee, I could have followed along. But no, you just gave me a ring. How was I supposed to know it wasn't an I-screwed-up-and-I'm-sorry gift? Didn't they go over this in that book you read cover to cover?"

"No, the book was written for women. It said that you're just supposed to act surprised and say 'yes.' It never talked about the proposal per se. I'm making it up as I go along, and now you're mad because I didn't do it right."

"Not mad—just, you know, a tiny bit disappointed."

"Fine." He got down on one knee right there in the kitchen and didn't look too happy about it either. He removed the ring, tossed the box over his shoulder, and winced when he heard the splash when it landed in the sink. Holding the ring out toward her, he took her hand in his. "Toni, will you marry me?"

She wanted to remember this moment for the rest of her life. After all, she'd have to tell her kids and grandkids about it someday. She smiled through tears as she stared into the slightly disgruntled eyes of the man she loved.

Hunter was down on one knee, with Toni sitting on his other, waiting for her response to his proposal. He was sweatin' it, big time. "Babe..." He wished she'd just hurry up and give him an answer already. Was she trying to kill him?

"Wait a minute. What was it I'm supposed to say?"

"'Yes' would work for me."

"Shouldn't I tell you I love you?"

"Right after you say 'yes.'"

"Yes, on one condition. Let's get married in Vegas. I don't want the whole big wedding thing. We can leave tomorrow morning and hit Vegas on the way to LA. That will give my mother less than twenty-four hours to plan the wedding of the century. Grampa and Clarissa can fly out with us. Vegas isn't too far from Idaho, so Trapper, Fisher, Karma, and your mom can catch a quick flight. Hell, James, Bianca, and the models can come too if they want. Okay?"

"Deal." Hunter slipped the ring on her finger and picked her up.

"Where are we going?"

"To bed." He stepped out of the kitchen and headed toward the bedroom.

"We can't. We have to call everyone."

"No, we don't. Everyone already knows. One thing you'll find out about this family is they always know everything—usually before you do. You better start getting used to it."

"They don't know you're taking me to bed, do they?"

He sat on the bed, holding her on his lap. "Most likely, but I try not to think about it."

She pushed him down on the bed and straddled

him. "That's probably a good idea. Talk about a high *ick* factor."

He laughed as he pulled her down, rolling her beneath him, and kissing the disgusted look off her face.

He slid into the kiss, and all the fear, uncertainty, and pain of the last few days flowed out of him to be replaced by happiness, contentment, and a need so strong it blinded him.

Toni pulled the shirt over her head, baring herself to him.

"I could stare at you for hours, and I will, after we get married."

"Hunter, stop talking and lose the pants will you?"

"God, you're demanding." He stood and unbuttoned the rest of his fly. "I love it."

Toni kneeled on the bed watching. "Good, because you're going to be stuck with me for the rest of your life, buddy."

He climbed on the bed and kissed her. He was going for the slow, gentle slide of mouths, but got nothing but scorching heat in return. Fine, scorching it was. He lay down, pulled her on top of him, and reached for her breasts, only to have her slip from his arms.

Her hand squeezed his erection, her mouth hot and wet on the head. He grabbed her hair and groaned as she sucked him in, her tongue and teeth tormenting, her hands gliding up and down the length of him as her mouth followed. He tried to stay still, tried to keep from jerking his hips, but in a few minutes she had him at the limit of his control.

He groaned, reached for her, and pulled her up as he sucked a breast into his mouth and slid into her moist heat. Her muscles grabbed him, pulling him deep as she ground her pelvis into his with every thrust.

She rode him, her hands braced against his chest, her hair flowing black as ink against her shoulders, her breast bouncing.

He slid his hand between them, tormenting her until she pushed off his chest and arched her back as her hands slid to her breasts. She threw her head back and screamed his name.

Toni was the most beautiful thing he'd ever seen. Intense, wet, heat slid over him, as her muscles massaged and drew him deeper, closer as she rode him through her climax.

When she collapsed on his chest, he rolled them over, driving her up again, her legs wrapped around his waist, her heels stabbing his lower back, urging him on as he slid both hands beneath her, lifting her, changing the angle.

Toni's eyes shot open, and all the breath was sucked out of her as she came with a silent scream. God, she saw stars, and then one orgasm rolled into another. She wasn't sure how much more she could take, but she never wanted it to end. She felt more than saw him stiffen and groan, holding her tight, and almost whimpering into her shoulder, until he stilled and relaxed on her. Mini-orgasms ricocheted through her, curling her toes, and making her shiver. Every time she did, Hunter tensed and groaned as if they passed through him too.

"Did I hurt you?"

She shook her head, but tears leaked from the corners of her eyes, trickled down the side of her face. She took a stuttered breath and sobbed.

"I'm sorry, babe." He looked terrified. "Toni?"

"I'm fine." She sniffed and wiped her eyes. "I don't know what it is with the waterworks. I can't help it."

"It's okay. It's been an emotional few days."

He tried to move off her, but she tightened her legs around him. "Don't go yet, okay?"

"Babe, I'm not going anywhere." He kissed away her tears. She closed her eyes and held him, praying that this feeling of perfection would last forever.

Chapter 21

HUNTER WATCHED TONI SLEEP, HER LEFT HAND thrown over him, her ring shining like fire in the morning light. As much as he wanted to, he couldn't spend the day watching his fiancée sleep—plans needed to be made for their wedding. Hunter realized that he didn't even have a suit with him, but his mom could probably pick one up at his house and bring it to Vegas with her.

He slipped out of bed and jumped into the shower, wishing he'd brought a change of clothes and a razor. After looking through Toni's medicine cabinet and tossing a trash can full of expired cold and flu medicines, Hunter found an unused toothbrush.

Pulling on his jeans, he scrounged around Toni's drawers until he found an extra large T-shirt. Hunter hoped to hell it wasn't one of her old boyfriend's, but he figured he didn't have much choice. As he dialed Gramps, he gathered his underwear, shirt, and Toni's clothes and started a load of laundry.

"Joe Walsh."

"Gramps, it's—"

"About time you got your fool-self out of bed and called your grandfather. So when's the weddin'?"

"Tomorrow in Vegas."

"Damn, boy, you certainly don't waste any time."

"It was Toni's idea. She didn't want to give Clarissa time to plan a big wedding, and as far as I'm concerned, the sooner the better. We have to be out in LA Monday anyway, so we thought we could stop in Vegas and get everyone together. Fisher, Trapper, Karma, Toni's best friend, James, her old boss, and the models she worked with are all in Stanley. I thought if you wouldn't mind, you could fly Mom, Ben, and Gina to Hailey and pick up anyone who wants to come.

"I'll take care of it and the hotel and limo arrangements."

"You mean your secretary will do it."

"Of course. You want it done right, don't you? You'd better call your mama. She'll tan your hide if she finds out she wasn't the first to hear. I'll talk with Clarissa. She's right here."

"Where's that?"

"In the vicinity of none of your damn business, boy."

"Nice place, Gramps. Just be careful. That's my future mother-in-law you're talking about."

"Ah hell, son. I'm eighty-two years old with two hip replacements and a bum ticker. How much trouble can I get into?"

"More than me, that's for sure. Gramps, you call Shamus, and I'll call Mom. Let me know when Toni and I should meet you and Clarissa at the airport in the morning. And thanks for everything."

"My pleasure. You just take care of my newest granddaughter."

Hunter called his mother, and Kate picked up the phone on the second ring. "Hunter? Are you okay, sweetheart? I've been so worried."

"I'm fine, Mom. I've got great news. Toni and I are getting married."

"Well, that is a surprise."

"Mom, the wedding is tomorrow in Vegas. I know it's quick, but practically everyone we know is out in Stanley. So you, Ben, and Gina can just jump on a plane in Boise, fly to Hailey, pick the rest of the crew up, and then meet us in Vegas."

"Hunter, are you certain about this?"

"Sure, Toni and I have to be in LA on Monday for Emilio's hearing anyway, and Toni doesn't want her mother, Clarissa, going off half-cocked and planning a big wedding. Shamus is working on transportation and the hotel reservations for everyone. All you have to do is run by all our houses and get dress clothes for us."

"I'm not talking about convenience, Hunter. I'm talking about the rest of your life. Are you sure you're ready to marry Toni? She's a lovely girl, but you've only known each other a week. Don't you think that's a little fast, even for you?"

"No, Mom. I don't. I've never been so sure of anything in my life."

"Hunter, I can't help but be concerned. I love you, and I just want you and Toni to be happy."

"We are. We might be rushing the wedding a little bit, but we're not rushing anything else. Mom? Do you think you and Karma could do that something old, something new deal for Toni? I don't want her to miss out on anything important."

"I'd be happy to."

"Thanks, Mom. I love you. See you tomorrow."

"Wake up, sleepyhead. Time to shop."

Toni rolled over to find Hunter standing next to the

bed holding coffee. Smart man. "I hate shopping except for shoes."

"Good to know, but we're getting married tomorrow, and you'll need something to wear. I don't suppose you have a wedding dress lying around?"

"No." She took a sip of coffee. He looked like he was serious. "Maybe I can have James call his friend in the Garment District. He might be able to help me find something…" *that wouldn't make her want to run screaming from the room* "…appropriate."

"Good. You can buy shoes too, so it won't be a total loss."

He made her smile even before her first cup of coffee. He was pretty perfect.

Hunter sat and kissed her before resting his hand by her hip. "Scott's is closed on Saturdays, but I guess we can go to Tiffany's and get wedding bands."

"Tiffany's?" He gave her that look again. She drank more coffee and decided to pick her battles. If he wanted to go to Tiffany's, that was just fine with her. The sooner they finished shopping, the sooner they could be together.

"I did some laundry, hung up your clothes, and made a pile for the dry cleaners. You're going to need to pack enough for a few weeks."

"I am?"

"I'm not sure when we'll be able to get back. We have a lot of decisions to make. We haven't even talked about where you want to go on our honeymoon. River Runners is booked through the second week in September. Then I'm free through the second week in November, unless we get some killer snow. Castle

Rock usually opens on Thanksgiving Day. So where do you want to go?"

Toni's mind was still fuzzy, and he was bombarding her with questions and information. "For what?"

"Our honeymoon."

She leaned into him, resting her head on his shoulder. "Can we just stay at home and get settled in?"

Hunter rubbed her back. "Sure. We can always take a trip in the spring."

"Where is home, by the way?"

"Home? Boise, Stanley, and here, I guess. Where do you want it to be?"

Toni put her coffee down on the table and breathed in the scent of Hunter. "Anywhere you are."

He pulled away and looked into her eyes as if he could read her mind. "Are you doing okay, babe? Are we moving too fast for you?"

She kissed him and held on to him for a minute more before shaking her head. "I'm a little overwhelmed, a little scared—after all, I'm going to be moving. It's a lot to think about and even more to plan. I'm excited about our wedding, but I'm more excited about marrying you. I love you."

"I love you too, babe, but if you change your mind about tomorrow, we can always get married in September."

God, she really loved him. "You're not trying to get out of it, are you?"

"Not a chance. I don't want you to feel as if I dragged you down the aisle either."

"Hunter, this was my idea, remember? It will be fine—better than fine. It's going to be perfect." She

hoped. She gave him another sloppy kiss, ending in a fit
of laughter. She guessed the book worked after all. She
was getting married!

Toni jumped out of bed and took a shower, wishing
Hunter had come in with her. He made showers much
more fun. After she finished, she toweled off. When she
stepped into her room, she heard voices. God... Clarissa
and Gramps were there. Fabulous.

Toni dressed quickly in a skirt and a T-shirt knotted
in the back. She was careful to wear decent undergar-
ments since she'd have to try on dresses. She did take a
last desperate look through her closet to see if she had
anything she could get away with. Since Clarissa would
have a fit if she wore black, she was out of luck.

"Hunter, you and Joe should go buy the rings, and
Toni and I will buy the wedding dress," Clarissa said
as she stepped into the living room from the kitchen.
Clarissa wore her usual disapproving look as soon as
she spotted Toni.

Toni tugged on the T-shirt's collar. "Mom, I want to
make sure my wedding band will work with my engagement ring. And since I'm not taking my ring off, I'm
going with Hunter."

Hunter strolled over to Toni wearing an apologetic
look. He'd eventually learn never to open the door to
her mother. There was a reason doors in New York had
peepholes. Unfortunately, Toni was going to be the one
to suffer the consequences until he did.

Clarissa wore yet another perfect linen suit with
matching Chanel spectator pumps and quilted purse.
"Toni, that's just silly." She took Toni's left hand to
inspect the ring. "It's lovely, but do be serious and stop

acting like a child. Give the ring to Hunter, and he'll make sure it works. Where is the box, Hunter?"

"In the trash—it got a little wet, but Toni's right. Shopping for rings won't take long, and since she's going to wear it for the rest of her life, I think she should pick it out." He pulled Toni against his chest and kissed the top of her head.

Clarissa walked by the mirror to check her 'do. "Toni, if you insist on buying the rings, then you'd better hurry and get dressed so we can leave. We don't have all day."

"What am I wearing, the emperor's new clothes?"

Her mother shook her head. "How do you expect to get into the best stores if you're dressed like a hoodlum?"

"I'm not going to the best stores. I'm going to the Garment District. Mom, if you want to hit the shops don't let me stop you. Go right ahead. I'm sure Marcello, James's friend, will have a wedding dress that will be just perfect."

Her mother's nose twitched as if she'd smelled something rancid. "Darling, I simply can't let you pick out a wedding dress by yourself. God only knows what you'll come up with."

Hunter's arm tightened around Toni. "Clarissa, Toni will find a dress that's perfect for her. When it comes down to it, that's all that matters, isn't it? After all, it's our wedding."

Clarissa opened her mouth and then closed it.

Toni had never seen her mother shut down like that. Of course, if Toni had told her the same thing, Clarissa would have scoffed. She didn't scoff at Hunter. Interesting.

Gramps took Clarissa's arm and shot a wink at Toni.

"Clarissa, I know you wanted to go shoppin' for your mother-of-the-bride dress. Why don't I give you the limo for the day, so you'll have no problem gettin' around town weighed down with all your packages? We'll pick you up here by seven and head to Teterboro. Takeoff's at 8 a.m."

Hunter paced the suite at The Bellagio as he, his cousin Ben, and his brothers waited for the sun to hurry its way across the sky. A sunset wedding sounded nice, that was, until he got out of the limo at the hotel after obtaining their marriage license, and Toni was whisked away.

Clarissa had said something ridiculous about not seeing the bride before the wedding. At least Toni had his mom, Karma, Gina, and James with her—whether to protect Toni from Clarissa or the other way around, he wasn't sure.

He'd heard Gramps had put James, Bianca, and all the models up for the wedding and even supplied the trip to Vegas. Having James here had meant the world to Toni. Gramps certainly put a smile on her face.

Trapper stepped right in front of him, forcing him to stop his pacing. "We can get out of here and do a mini-bachelor party, since we didn't get to last night."

"No. Thanks anyway." Hunter turned and paced toward the window, wondering what the hell was going on with Toni. He'd been texting her, and she hadn't responded in the last hour. He stuck his finger into the too tight collar of his tux and yanked. He'd asked his mom to bring his suit. Of course, she didn't listen and brought them all their tuxes.

"Are you getting cold feet?"

"Hell, no. I'm just worried about Toni. She's not answering her texts."

Ben tossed his keys in the air, caught them, and dropped them into his pocket before throwing his arm around Hunter. "She's probably having her hair and nails done. Wet nails and texting don't mix. This I know."

The three of them stared at Ben who shrugged. "My wife told me, okay? You learn all sorts of things you really don't want to know when you're married. Believe me."

Fisher shook his head. "We can go hit the craps tables. Maybe you'll win enough to pay for that honkin' ring you bribed Toni with."

"It wasn't a bribe."

"Sure. Whatever you say. Still, it looked like it set you back ten year's poker money. Since this is your lucky day and all, maybe you can win it back."

"You guys go on ahead. I'll just meet you at the limo at six forty-five."

Trapper laughed. "Like we'd leave you in your time of need. Personally, I find watching you sweat more entertaining than that time I dressed Fisher up and played Pin the Tail on the Jackass."

"Yeah, and you wonder why I didn't make you my best man."

"Hey, I hooked Fisher up with the wedding chapel. My old friend, Judge Winston, retired out here and set up shop. He always said weddings were the best part of the job, so now he does them all the time."

Fisher looked very pleased with himself. "I planned the whole thing. He's giving us a great deal—the deluxe package for the price of the standard. It has video, live music, a wedding organizer, and all the flower arrangements—the works."

Hunter was beginning to get nervous. Fisher was good at planning keg parties and weekends with wild women, but weddings were uncharted territory. "What's this place called?"

"Lasting Impressions Wedding Chapel—Memories to Last a Lifetime." Fisher handed several cards around.

At least it wasn't written on a napkin. "Thank God it's nothing hokey like The Elvis Hound Dog Package or The Naked Wedding—Bow Ties Optional."

Trapper laughed. "No worries. From what I recall, Judge Winston is very conservative. I don't think we'll see anyone running around with rhinestones and muttonchops."

Fisher winked and grinned. "Or naked. Unless of course, Yvette shows up, and then all bets are off."

———— ∾ ————

Toni sat on a chair in her underwear and a robe while some lady, whose name she'd forgotten the moment they'd been introduced, added the rhinestone-and-seed-pearl-encrusted tiara to the complicated up-do she'd created with hair bands, bobby pins, and an entire bottle of hair spray, most of which Toni had inhaled. Who knew her hair could look so good? Her makeup was done, a little too heavy-handed if you were to ask her, but then she'd been overridden by Clarissa, who thought there was no such thing as too much money, makeup, or jewelry.

Looking in the mirror, Toni caught Kate's eye. Hunter's mother was a godsend. Calm and collected,

Kate had corralled everyone without much fuss and had taken charge—even managing the impossible. She sent Clarissa on an errand to make sure Hunter and the guys had received their boutonnieres.

The hair lady spun Toni's chair around and held up a mirror to show her the back, where seed pearls had somehow been woven throughout. She looked almost as good from the back as she did from the front. "Thank you. It's perfect."

The woman gathered her implements of torture, and Gina, a five-foot stick of dynamite, showed her out.

Kate smiled that calming smile of hers, and Toni felt her anxiety decrease. Toni knew where Hunter got both his smile and his calming presence.

Kate took a velvet roll out of her bag and set it on the table before untying it. "Now I don't want to step on your mother's toes, but since she hadn't expected to attend your wedding, Hunter asked me to make sure you didn't miss out on any important bridal customs. Feel free to use them or not. It's up to you."

She pulled a black satin ribbon from the roll and held something in her hand. "For something old, this cameo was my grandmother's. I thought we could slide the ribbon through the back, and you could wear it as a choker. The seed pearls surrounding it go beautifully with your tiara. It's yours if you want it."

"Kate, thanks, but I can't—"

"Of course you can. You're part of the family now. This is something you'll be able to pass down to your children someday. I want you to have it and wear it in good health." Kate tied the ribbon around Toni's neck. The ivory cameo was heavier than she expected. Toni's fingers ran over the relief of the woman's face carved there, feeling the smoothness of the pearls. She'd been reaching for her collar ever since she'd taken it off to do the makeup. Now she had something to worry if she needed it. She looked in the mirror and hardly recognized herself.

Toni turned and hugged Kate. "Thank you so much. I'll treasure it."

Kate kissed her cheek. "You're welcome. Your dress is new, so we have that covered."

Gina pulled a light blue lace handkerchief out of the bag and pressed it into Toni's clammy hand. "Here's your something blue. If you start crying, it's going to have smears of black mascara all over it, and then we're going to have to redo your makeup. So suck it up, and don't cry." She patted her shoulder awkwardly, sniffed, and turned away.

"Thanks, Gina. I'll be fine."

Karma held both hands behind her back. "I have the something borrowed. You have your choice of my absolute favorite vintage, peace sign mood ring." She held out her open hand, and sure enough, there was a large brass ring with a peace sign over the translucent stone. "Or..." She held out an opened blue velvet jewelry box. "The diamond earrings and bracelet that Gramps gave me when I graduated from college. So... which will it be?"

Kate shook her head. "Karma."

"Mom wants you to go with the diamonds, but personally, I think the mood ring would be a whole lot more fun." She waggled her eyebrows. "You can always borrow both."

Kate took the box. "Pay no attention to Karma. The bracelet and earrings will look lovely with your engagement ring. James has a sixpence for your shoe, but he's not going to join us until we get you into that beautiful wedding dress of yours."

Toni took a deep breath. "I guess it's about time, huh?" She looked out the window and wondered where in this huge hotel Hunter was. She'd only seen him a few hours ago, but she missed him. They'd been texting each other before her mother took her phone away, claiming it was bad luck. What was she, in high school? He was probably worried about her.

Gina and Karma brought the dress out, and Toni couldn't help but smile. Hunter was going to swallow his tongue when he saw it. It was the most beautiful dress she'd ever seen. She stepped into the strapless satin gown and pulled up the bodice, being careful not to wrinkle the black-trimmed, tailored box pleat. She smoothed down the fitted bodice and admired the simple, straight lines, while Kate zipped the back, which fell just under her shoulder blades. The back was adorned with a thin, black satin bow that hung right over the matching accent stripe running from the box pleat to hem. It was classy, elegant, understated, yet still, her.

A hush fell over the entire room, which was saying something, because when Karma, Gina, and Kate got going, there was never a dull moment. Kate dabbed at her eyes. "You look so beautiful."

A knock at the door disturbed the quiet, and Karma ran over to open it. James stepped in and gasped. Of course, he didn't come alone. He brought two of the photographers Bianca had sent to take pictures for the wedding album.

James smiled and pulled Toni in for a hug. "You look simply stunning, my love. I see my friend Marcello took good care of you."

Toni spun around. "He did. Thanks for calling him for me. The dress is perfect."

"Yes, it is. Hunter is a very lucky man."

"No, I think I got the best part of the bargain, this time at least."

James directed the photographers to do the bride and bridesmaids shots.

Toni was antsy. She just wanted to see Hunter, and she was beginning to worry about her mother. She'd been gone awhile. "Does anyone know where Clarissa is?"

James smiled. "Hunter's grandfather dragged her out of the guys' suite. Last I heard he was taking her to the bar."

"Oh God."

"I almost forgot. Sit down." James pulled a chair around and held it for her before he got down on his knee and unzipped Toni's wedding sandal. "Jimmy Choo? Very nice."

Toni admired the other shoe. "Aren't they gorgeous? They match the dress and were forty percent off—I couldn't pass them up."

"I got you a little something else—just in case you don't have one."

"What's that?"

James pulled a black lace, skull-and-crossbones garter from his pocket.

Toni threw her head back and laughed. "Where in the world did you find that?"

James slid it onto her leg, hamming it up for the cameras. "Ketchum, who'd of thunk? You know, that place is really growing on me."

"Yeah, I love it there too." She stood up and walked a few steps. "That coin is going to hurt."

"Doll, you're wearing five-inch heels. Your feet are going to kill you regardless. Are you ready to go?" James held out his arm, and Toni slid hers through.

Toni worried the cameo, before Karma handed her the bouquet of calla lilies. "Yes, I'm as ready as I'll ever be."

―――***―――

Hunter sat in the limo with Ben and his brothers, tugging on his collar. "Fisher, do you have the rings?"

Fisher patted his pockets. "Damn, I knew I was forgetting something."

Trapper reached over and smacked the back of Fisher's head. "Give it a break, Fisher. Hunter's about ready to stroke out."

Ben pulled the ring box out of his pocket. "Don't worry, cousin. I've got your back. And remember, first weddings are always nerve-wracking."

The guys all turned to look at him.

"What? I was married twice…"

Trapper sat forward. "Yeah, to the same woman."

"The second time is the charm, and the wedding night's an added bonus."

The limo slowed and stopped at the curb. Hunter caught sight of the marquee: *Toni and Hunter Forever*. "Nice touch."

Fisher reached for the door. "It was part of the package. It's deluxe."

As soon as the driver opened the door, a woman shoved her face in with a big microphone. "Joan Rivers here. Which one of you gorgeous men is the groom?"

Hunter blinked at the flash of lights in his eyes. "Son of a bitch. Fisher, if I live through this wedding, you won't."

Trapper turned to Fisher. "What the hell have you done?"

"Relax. It's the videographer. It's part of the package."

"Does it include cement shoes?" Planting his feet on the red carpet, Hunter looked up at the marquee once more. Lasting Impressions. "I'm gonna kill him." Hunter turned and picked Fisher up by the lapels. "How could you?"

"What? Trapper gave me the number. He said he was a stand-up guy."

Hunter looked around for Trapper, only to find him further up the red carpet with one arm around a Cher impersonator having his picture taken.

Ben stood beside Hunter, tossing his keys. "Just go with the flow. It's Vegas, baby."

Hunter released Fisher and straightened his jacket.

"Watch the threads, Bro." Fisher smoothed his lapels.

Hunter made a beeline for the door. He needed to check out the rest of this nightmare before Toni arrived. "Who's in charge here?"

Rodney Dangerfield stepped up to him. "That would be me." He adjusted his tie and rolled his neck. "I don't get no respect. What do I look like? A funeral director? No wait. That's my other gig. Here's my card. From the look of things, you might be needing it later."

Hunter turned to find Trapper extending his hand to old Rodney.

"Larry, good to see you. This is my brother, Hunter—the groom."

"He doesn't look too happy. I charge extra for shotgun weddings—bullets are complimentary."

Fisher walked up to them. "Did you get a load of Marilyn? All she's missing is the grate. With any luck the wind will pick up." Fisher spun around. "Hey, is that Chaka Khan?"

Hunter couldn't believe that this is where he was getting married. He just prayed Toni wouldn't call the whole thing off and catch the first flight back to New York. He felt sick. What else could happen?

A pink Cadillac convertible came to a screeching halt in front of the red carpet, and his heart sank as Elvis jumped out to get the passenger door. He watched as Gramps and Clarissa were accosted by Joan and Melissa Rivers.

Teetering on her heels, Clarissa pointed to the marquee. "Look Joe, their names are in lights!"

"This must be the right place then." Grampa smiled at the Rivers impersonators and looked over at Fisher. "You set this up boy? On your own?"

"Um, yeah."

"Good job. You make me proud."

Hunter wondered how many bourbons Gramps put away.

Gramps took one look at Hunter and smiled. "I had nothing to do with it, but that don't mean I won't enjoy it. Nice touch with the Rat Pack."

Hunter looked behind him to find Frank, Dean, and Sammy, acting as ushers. Dean extended his arm to Clarissa, humming, "Everybody Loves Somebody Sometime." Then he asked, "Bride or groom?"

"I'm the mother of the bride," Clarissa said with a hiccup.

Hunter rubbed his forehead when he heard Dean crooning his way down the aisle.

Ben slapped Hunter on the shoulder. "Let's get you inside before your bride arrives."

Hunter groaned and wondered if his best man was going to survive to see the wedding.

Fisher walked up to him and stuffed his hands in his pockets. "Don't worry. Trapper and I will wait out on the red carpet and smooth things over with the ladies."

Ben laughed. "Gina's gonna love this."

Hunter handed Ben Mr. Dangerfield's card. "Here. You can save this for wedding number three. I won't be needing it again."

~~~

When Karma caught a glimpse of Joan Rivers, she started to laugh. "Mom, brace yourself."

Kate looked out the window. "Oh, my."

Trapper and Fisher stood on the red carpet looking very pleased with themselves. Karma opened the door, took in the scene, and zeroed in on her brothers. "You are in so much trouble. It's a shame I didn't have anything to do with it." She tossed them a wicked smile and headed straight for George Clooney. "Thanks. I owe you one."

Gina got out of the car. "Ay! Carmamba!" She turned to Kate. "I don't think this is quite what you expected."

Kate shook her head. "Fisher Michael Kincaid, if I didn't know you better, I'd swear Trapper wasn't involved."

Trapper rocked back on his heels. "It's all in who you

know." He turned to Fisher. "Step up, baby Brother. It's your time to shine."

Gina interrupted. "Mom, you take it from here. I see Fabio."

Fisher shook his head. "I always wondered about that girl's taste, marrying Ben and all. He's gonna be pissed once he sees the film of his wife and that Fabio guy. Look, she's running her hand down his chest."

Karma stood back with George, who was just too sweet for words, as Trapper escorted their mom to Frank Sinatra. "You take it from here."

Frank winked. "My pleasure."

As the door to the chapel opened, Karma could swear she heard "Danke Schöen." She tried not to gag.

She turned to Fisher. "You better get inside and calm Hunter down. I'll stay out here and try to explain this to Toni. You owe me sooo big."

—⁓—

Toni sat in the back of the limo holding James's hand. "Do you even know where this place is?"

"No. Fisher made all the arrangements. He said he wanted to surprise you."

When the limo stopped she saw her name in lights. "He succeeded."

The car door was yanked open, and a microphone was shoved in her face. "You've gotta be the bride. Should you be wearing white?"

Toni laughed at the Joan Rivers look-alike. "Probably not, but what the heck, you only get married once, right?"

Joan Rivers laughed. "Toni, I like you all ready."

James handed Toni out of the limo as Melissa Rivers described Toni's dress in detail for the camera. He walked her toward the chapel. "Toni, you're the daughter I never had. Be happy."

"I am."

"Are you ready?"

"As ready as I'll ever be. These shoes are killing me."

"Then let's get this show on the road."

Karma waited at the door for them. "Toni, I had nothing to do with this. I'm so sorry."

"Why? I think it's great. Where is Hunter?"

"He's in the chapel praying you don't change your mind. Can we wait out here for a few more minutes? It's fun watching him squirm."

Toni chuckled. "You should have seen him when he proposed."

James cleared his throat. "Come on. Let's put the poor guy out of his misery."

Karma snuck in through the doors and cued the music. Toni expected the wedding march. When the doors flew open she saw Diana Ross in a gold sequin gown.

Soft music began to play, and Diana pointed at her and said, "I don't know how much you know about Toni and Hunter, so I want to tell you a thing or two…" Then she belted out the first lines of "Ain't No Mountain High Enough." Toni laughed the whole way down the aisle. There was never a more perfect song for them. The whole wedding was perfect.

Hunter stepped forward, relief etched all over his face. He broke into that crooked grin she loved so much and shrugged.

She and James reached the altar, and James gave her a

kiss on the cheek before he handed her to Hunter. She got caught in Hunter's gaze again and saw so much love staring back at her. It was all she could do not to kiss him. She looked away from Hunter to the man who was going to marry them. Rodney Dangerfield stood in front of her and straightened his tie. "You sure you want to marry this guy? You're lookin' pretty good. I got a few laps left in me yet."

Hunter scowled and pulled her against him as Toni tried not to laugh. "Oh yeah, I'm sure."

Rodney smiled and pulled a book out of his suit pocket. "I don't get no respect."

Fisher reached around Hunter and tapped her on the shoulder. "Psst... so what do you think?"

"I love it! It's perfect."

Trapper shook his head, took out his wallet, and handed Fisher a Benjamin.

Hunter glared at his brothers.

Fisher snapped the bill and held it up to the light before stuffing it in his pocket. "What? Just tying up loose ends."

Hunter shook his head. "Are you finished? I'd really like to get married now." He took Toni's hands in his, and when she looked up to him, he smiled. "Are you ready for another first?"

"Yes. I think I like living on the wild side."

———

Toni danced with Fisher while she scanned the crowd for Bianca. Toni still needed to thank her for coming and for supplying the photographers.

Clarissa was dancing with Grampa Joe, who had insisted he could handle Clarissa, even after she drank more champagne than any one-hundred-twenty-pound woman should consume.

Hunter had taken Kate for a spin around the dance floor, as Ben and Gina snuggled together, barely moving.

No matter where Hunter had been or who he'd been talking to, for the last couple hours, every time Toni looked for him, she'd found him watching her—just as she did now. She pointed to her wrist where her watch would be if she had one, and he nodded.

Toni didn't know about Hunter, but she wanted to take this party to a more private place—like the honeymoon suite. She'd already said most of her good-byes but didn't want to leave without saying good-bye to Bianca. The song ended, and Fisher returned Toni to Hunter.

She slid into his arms. "Have you seen Bianca? I wanted to thank her for coming and providing the wedding photos."

"She was dancing with Trapper earlier. Maybe he knows."

"I can't find him either."

Hunter shook his head and groaned. "Son of a bitch. I told him to be nice, but not too nice."

Toni patted his cheek. "Don't worry. Trapper's a big boy. He can take care of himself."

"Sure. Trapper can, but what about Bianca? Trapper's the seventy-two-hour relationship king."

"Come on. This is Bianca we're talking about."

"Hey, she's got a tough shell, but take it from me, she has a marshmallow center."

"And you know this how?"

"I'm observant. That's all, I swear. So, Mrs. Kincaid, are you ready to blow this pop stand?"

"Definitely. My feet are killing me."

Hunter picked her up, and Toni let out a scream. Everyone turned and clapped as they headed to the elevators.

Hunter kissed her as the doors closed and let her slide down his body.

She'd left her makeup case in the other suite, which wouldn't have been a big deal, but her case was where she kept her birth control. "Hunter, would you mind if we stopped back at the room I used before we go to our suite? I just want to pick up a few things I left there."

Hunter swung his arm around her. "No problem. Besides, it's closer than the honeymoon suite."

By the time they reached their floor, Toni was breathless. She fumbled with the electronic key as Hunter tormented her, nipping her ear, and telling her in excruciatingly vivid detail exactly how he planned to make love to her. By the time he had the door to the suite open Hunter had the zipper of her dress halfway down and her temperature past the boiling point. They slammed into the room, and Hunter kicked the door closed, backing her against the wall as he pulled her dress down.

Toni's eyes went wide. She could swear she'd heard something. Her vision adjusted to the darkness, and it took her a moment to realize someone else was using her room. Well, not so much the room, just the bed. "Um... Hunter." She tugged up her dress. "On second thought, let's just go to our suite."

"Toni, we're here now—"

Yeah, he'd heard it.

"Son of a bitch. Looks like Trapper and Bianca are going for a little walk on the wild side too."

The End

Acknowledgments

Writing is a solitary endeavor, but a writer's life isn't. I'm lucky to have the love and support of my incredible family. My husband, Stephen, who after twenty-one years of marriage, is still the man of my dreams. My children, Tony, Anna, and Isabelle, who in spite of being teenagers, are my favorite people to hang out with. They make me laugh, amaze me with their intelligence and generosity, and make me proud every day. My parents, Richard Williams and Ann Feiler, and my stepfather George Feiler, who always encouraged me and continue to do so.

And of course, there are my wonderful critique partners Deborah Villegas, Laura Becraft, Grace Burrowes, Hope Ramsay, and April Line. They shortened my sentences, corrected my grammar, and put commas where they needed to be. They listened to me whine when my muse took a vacation, gave me great ideas when I was stuck, and answered that all-important question: Does this suck? They help me plot, love my characters almost as much as I do, and push-challenge me to be a better writer. They are wonderful friends, talented writers, and the sisters of my heart.

I wrote most of this book in the Carlisle Crossing Starbucks, and I have to thank all my baristas for keeping me in laughter and coffee while my computer and I camped out in their store. They were always there for me when I was searching for the right word or falling asleep at my computer. I don't think I could have written this book without them. I also need to thank a few of the customers who have become wonderful friends: Dana and Steven Gossert, and Alan Monahan for giving me an excuse not to write.

As always, I have to thank my wonderful agent Kevan Lyon for all she does, and my team at Sourcebooks, my editor Deb Werksman, and my publicist Danielle Jackson.

About the Author

Robin Kaye was born in Brooklyn, New York, and grew up in the shadow of the Brooklyn Bridge next door to her Sicilian grandparents. Living with an extended family that's a cross between *Gilligan's Island* and *The Sopranos*, minus the desert isle and illegal activities, explains both her comedic timing and the cast of quirky characters in her books.

She's lived in half a dozen states, from Idaho to Florida, but the romance of Boise has never left her heart. She currently resides in Maryland with her husband, three children, two dogs, and a three-legged cat with attitude.

Robin would love to hear from you. Visit her website at www.robinkayewrites.com. Or email her at robin@robinkayewrites.com.

Romeo, Romeo

~ BY ROBIN KAYE ~

Rosalie Ronaldi doesn't have a domestic bone in her body...

All she cares about is her career, so she survives on take-out and dirty martinis, keeps her shoes under the dining room table, her bras on the shower curtain rod, and her clothes on the couch.

Nick Romeo is every woman's fantasy— tall, dark, handsome, rich, really good in bed, AND he loves to cook and clean...

He says he wants an independent woman, but when he meets Rosalie, all he wants to do is take care of her. Before long, he's cleaned up her apartment, stocked her refrigerator, and adopted her dog.

So what's the problem? Just a little matter of mistaken identity, corporate theft, a hidden past in juvenile detention, and one big nosy Italian family too close for comfort...

"Kaye's debut is a delightfully fun, witty romance, making her a writer to watch." —*Booklist*

978-1-4022-1339-7 • $6.99 U.S. / £3.99 UK

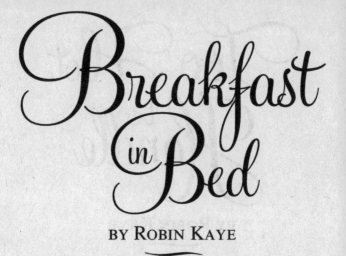

Breakfast in Bed

BY ROBIN KAYE

HE'D BE MR. PERFECT, IF HE WASN'T A PERFECT MESS...

Rich Ronaldi is *almost* the complete package—smart, sexy, great job—but his girlfriend dumps him for being such a slob, and Rich swears he'll learn to cook and clean to win her back. Becca Larson is more than willing to help him master the domestic arts, but she'll be damned if she'll do it so he can start cooking in another woman's kitchen—or bedroom...

PRAISE FOR ROBIN KAYE:

"Robin Kaye has proved herself a master of romantic comedy." —*Armchair Interviews*

"Ms. Kaye has style—it's easy, it's fun, and it has every–thing that you need to get caught up in a wonderful romance." —*Erotic Horizon*

"A fresh and fun voice in romantic comedy." —*All About Romance*

978-1-4022-1895-8 • $7.99 U.S. / £4.99 UK

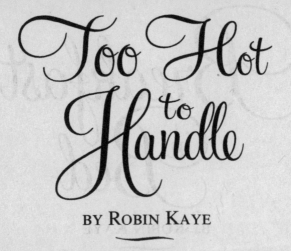

Too Hot to Handle

by Robin Kaye

HE SURE WOULD LOVE TO HAVE A WOMAN TO TAKE CARE OF...

To Dr. Mike Flynn, there's nothing like housework to help a guy relax, while artist Annabelle Ronaldi doesn't have a domestic bone in her body.

When they meet at her sister's wedding, Mike is sure this is the woman he wants to take care of forever. While Mike sets to work wooing Annabelle, she becomes determined to sniff out the truth of the convoluted family secret that's threatening to turn both their lives upside down.

PRAISE FOR *TOO HOT TO HANDLE*:

"Entertaining, funny, and steaming hot." —*Book Loons*

"A sensational story that sizzles with sex appeal."
   —*The Long and Short of It*

"Witty and enchanting." —*Love Romance Passion*

"From the brilliant first chapter until the heartwarming finale, I was hooked!" —*Crave More Romance*

978-1-4022-1766-1 • $6.99 U.S. / £3.99 UK

Love at
FIRST FLIGHT
BY MARIE FORCE

What if the guy
in the airplane seat next to you turned out
to be the love of your life?

JULIANA, HAPPY IN HER CAREER AS A HAIR STYLIST, IS ON HER
way to Florida to visit her boyfriend. When he tells her
he's wondering what it might be like to make love to other
women she is devastated. Even though he tries to take it
back, she doesn't want him to be wondering all his life. So
they agree to take a break, and heartbroken, she goes back
to Baltimore.

Michael is going to his fiancee's parents' home for an
engagement party he doesn't want. A state's prosecutor,
he's about to try the biggest case of his career, and he's
having doubts about the relationship. When Paige pulls a
manipulative stunt at the party, he becomes so enraged that
he breaks off the engagement.

Juliana and Michael sat together on the plane ride
from Baltimore to Florida, and discover they're on the
same flight coming back. With the weekend a disaster for
each of them, they bond in a "two-person pity party" on
the plane ride home. Their friendship begins to blossom
and love, too, but life is full of complications, and when
Michael's trial turns dangerous, the two must confront
what they value most in life...

978-1-4022-2006-7 • $6.99 U.S. / £3.99 UK

SEALed with a Kiss

with a Kiss

BY MARY MARGRET DAUGHTRIDGE

THERE'S ONLY ONE THING HE CAN'T HANDLE, AND ONE WOMAN WHO CAN HELP HIM...

Jax Graham is a rough, tough Navy SEAL, but when it comes to taking care of his four-year-old son after his ex-wife dies, he's completely clueless. Family therapist Pickett Sessoms can help, but only if he'll let her.

When Jax and his little boy get trapped by a hurricane, Pickett takes them in against her better judgment. When the situation turns deadly, Pickett discovers what it means to be a SEAL, and Jax discovers that even a hero needs help sometimes.

"A heart-touching story that will keep you smiling and cheering for the characters clear through to the happy ending." —Romantic Times

"A well-written romance... simultaneously tender and sensuous." —Booklist

978-1-4022-1118-8 • $7.99 U.S. / £4.99 UK

SEALED
with a
Promise

BY MARY MARGRET DAUGHTRIDGE

NAVY SEAL CALEB DELAUDE IS AS DEADLY AS HE IS CHARMING.

Professor Emmie Caddington's quiet intelligence and quirky personality intrigue him. When he discovers that her personal connections can get him close to the man he's vowed to kill, will their budding relationship be nothing more than a means to revenge…or is she the key to his salvation?

Praise for *SEALed with a Kiss*:

"This story delivers in a huge way." —Romantic Times

"A wonderful story that will have readers experiencing a whirlwind of emotions and culminating with an awesome scene that will have your pulse pounding." —Romance Junkies

"What an incredibly powerful book! I laughed and sniffled, was turned on and turned inside out." —Queue My Review

978-1-4022-1763-0 • $6.99 U.S. / £3.99 UK

SEALed
with a *Ring*

BY MARY MARGRET DAUGHTRIDGE

SHE'S GOT IT ALL…EXCEPT THE ONE THING SHE NEEDS MOST

Smart, successful businesswoman JJ Caruthers has a year to land a husband or lose the empire she's worked so hard to build. With time running out, romance is not an option, and a military husband who is always on the road begins to look like the perfect solution…

HE'S A WOUNDED HERO WITH AN AGENDA OF HIS OWN

Even with the scars of battle, Navy SEAL medic Davy Graziano is gorgeous enough to land any woman he wants, and he's never wanted to be tied down. Now Davy has ulterior motives for accepting JJ's outrageous proposal of marriage, but he only has so long to figure out what JJ doesn't want him to know…

Praise for *SEALed with a Ring*:

"With a surprising amount of heart, Daughtridge makes a familiar story read like new as the icy JJ melts under Davy's charm during a forced marriage. The supporting cast, including one really unattractive dog, makes Daughtridge's latest one for the keeper shelves." — Romantic Times, 4 stars

978-1-4022-3698-3 • $7.99 U.S. / £4.99 UK